THE MIDWIVES OF
RAGLAN ROAD

Summer, 1936. Newly trained midwife Hazel Price returns to the Yorkshire streets of her childhood, only to find that her modern methods and 'stuck-up' ways bring her into conflict with her family and other formidable residents of Raglan Road. Determined Hazel battles on, assisting with home deliveries and supporting the local GP. The days are long and hard but Hazel brings knowledge and compassion to the work she loves. Then tragedy strikes and accusations fly on Raglan Road. Will Hazel's reputation survive? And what of John, the man she is beginning to fall for – whose side will he take in the war between the old ways and the new?

THE MIDWIVES OF
RAGLAN ROAD

THE MIDWIVES OF RAGLAN ROAD

by

Jenny Holmes

Magna Large Print Books
Long Preston, North Yorkshire,
BD23 4ND, England.

British Library Cataloguing in Publication Data.

A catalogue record of this book is
available from the British Library

ISBN   978-0-7505-4519-8

First published in Great Britain in 2016 by Corgi Books
an imprint of Transworld Publishers

Published in Large Print 2018 by arrangement with
Transworld Publishers

Magna Large Print is an imprint of Library Magna Books Ltd.

Printed and bound in Great Britain by
T.J. (International) Ltd., Cornwall, PL28 8RW

*This is for Jenny Symons and Shirley Emptage.
Thanks for the endless measuring out of our lives
with coffee spoons (trace the quote, Jenny!)*

CHAPTER ONE

'Wakey-wakey!' A voice in the street roused Hazel Price from a deep sleep. It was followed by an urgent knocking and a cry of, 'It's Leonard Hollings here. Come quick – baby's on its way.'

Hazel jumped out of bed and slipped into the set of clothes laid out on her bedside chair – her underthings followed by a crisp white blouse and dark blue skirt.

Down on the first-floor landing, Hazel's mother Jinny appeared, keen to make sure that her daughter had heard the call. 'Get a move on before Leonard wakes the whole street,' she grumbled.

It was six o'clock in the morning, and Raglan Road was silent except for the raucous caller at number 18. Slipping on her shoes and jacket, Hazel picked up her bag and flung open her attic door to see her bemused father in shirtsleeves, with braces dangling from his waist, standing alongside her mother in their bedroom doorway.

'Do you want me to go down and tell him you're on your way?' Robert's voice was still thick with sleep.

'No, ta. I'm all set.' Rushing downstairs two at a time, Hazel brushed past her mother and father then down again to open the front door just as the scrawny man waiting there raised his fist to knock a second time. His hair was prematurely grey and his figure small and permanently stooped, as if in recognition of the fact that the life he'd been born into was hard and getting harder by the day.

'About time too,' Leonard grumbled, backing down the stone steps and wheezing his way up Raglan Road until he reached one of the alleyways leading into Nelson Yard. Following close on his heels, Hazel almost bumped into him as he paused for breath. 'At this rate Betty will have gone ahead and done the job herself,' he complained.

'Let's hope not.' Hazel gave a shake of her head. She knew every crack of these stone pavements, the worn steps, the rusty iron railings and the lion-head knocker on each front door. Even the dank smell of the alley and beyond that the washing lines strung across the yard, with weeds pushing up between the cobbles, were familiar to her. All the details seemed just as they had always been – except for her, of course. She was the one who had changed.

Leonard fumbled in his jacket pocket for his cigarettes, then thought better of it and shuffled on across the yard that consisted of four rows of inward-facing dwellings, each row made up of eight terraced houses. Even in their heyday, these dwellings had never offered local mill workers more than basic accommodation. Most were owned by absentee landlords who shirked their responsibility to keep the houses in good order so it was no wonder that when roof tiles slipped and fell, they were left in the gutter and when a windowpane was shattered by boys at play, a wooden board was haphazardly nailed to the frame, never to be replaced.

Hazel and Leonard passed a row of dustbins lined up against the wall of an outside privy and then a lean-to shelter that housed a dented pram with a broken hood and a bicycle frame without wheels. Beyond that, tucked away in the corner, was an open door.

'Home sweet home,' Leonard muttered sarcastically, standing aside to let Hazel cross the threshold into a cramped kitchen with a chipped pot sink piled high with dishes. Hazel saw the heel of a stale loaf of bread on a bare table and from under the table two grubby faces stared up at her. They belonged to Leonard and Betty Hollings' half-naked offspring – a boy of three or four and a girl under two – sitting cross-legged, still and silent as little Buddhas amidst the chaos around them.

'The midwife is here!' Leonard yelled up the stairs.

'Take the kiddies to Doreen next door,' his wife called back before a fresh wave of contractions must have gripped her – the sentence ended in a series of groans.

'I'll need hot water,' Hazel instructed the down-at-heel father. 'Plenty of it. Plus towels and some sheets of brown paper if you have them.' She hurried upstairs, following the sounds of a woman in labour into the bedroom where she found her patient prone on the bed. The grate in the small fireplace was empty and the only objects in the room besides the old-fashioned iron bedstead were a washstand with an enamel basin and a rack with a scrap of striped towel hanging over it.

15

'Hello, Betty. It seems Leonard called for me in the nick of time,' Hazel remarked as she put her bag on the washstand then picked up the frayed cloth. 'I take it this is the only towel you have?' It was straight down to business and no mistake.

Betty turned her head away and gripped the sides of the thin mattress. She was propped up on two pillows, their covers stained a nasty brown. A torn yellow eiderdown had slipped from the bed onto the bare floorboards.

Once the latest contractions had passed, Betty looked wearily at Hazel. 'Do me a favour – make sure Len gets off to work, there's a love.'

Hazel tilted her head to one side. 'Are you sure? Won't he want to stay until after the baby's born?' Quickly taking everything in, she grew concerned about the lack of hygiene and heat in the room. Still, she'd better lay out her instruments on the washstand – scissors, cord clamps, foetal stethoscope – and not act in any way that would cause alarm.

'Not Len; he's not interested in this end of the business,' Betty told her matter-of-factly. 'Don't get me wrong – he'll be happy enough after baby puts in an appearance. But for the time being, he's better off putting in his shift at Kingsley's.'

Hazel took out cotton swabs and forceps. Betty was as scrawny as her husband and her hips were narrow so it was best to be prepared. By the look of things, there would be no brown paper available to slide under her to absorb some of the mess. Hazel could manage without this, but not the hot water. Approaching the bed, she put her stethoscope against Betty's swollen abdomen.

16

'I'm sorry – this will feel cold,' she murmured, counting carefully until she was satisfied that baby's heartbeat was normal. She finished just in time, because Betty drew up her knees sharply and clenched her teeth at the start of yet another contraction. 'I'm afraid we've left it a bit late to give you something for the pain,' Hazel admitted.

'Not to worry. I never had anything for the last two either. They say it slows things down.'

Hazel patted Betty's hand and smiled. How was it that the ability to endure labour pains without chloral hydrate was still seen as a badge of courage in these parts?

'I never went to the infirmary either – not once. You wouldn't catch me in one of those places, not even for a check-up. I stayed at home both times and I've got two healthy kiddies to show for it.'

Though ill-informed, Betty's pride in her own achievement drew a warm smile from Hazel. Then, hearing movement outside the room, she went out to find Doreen, the elderly next-door neighbour, struggling up the narrow stairs with a large pan of steaming water. 'Champion!' she exclaimed, hurrying to relieve the stout woman of her burden. 'We'll need more of this. And towels, too, if you have any to spare.'

Doreen nodded then bustled away while Hazel took the water into the room. The maternity pads that she carried in her bag would have to do the mopping-up job of the more usual brown paper, she decided. 'Would you like Doreen to send for your mother?' she asked as she prepared Betty for a further examination.

'No ta,' came the resigned reply. 'Mam and Len fell out soon after little Poll was born. Mam's gone to live with my sister over in Welby.'

'Is there anybody else – someone closer to hand?'

'There's no one.' Raising her head from the pillows, Betty attempted to peer beyond the clean sheet that Hazel had draped over her crooked knees. 'How are things looking down there? Please tell me baby's ready to make his entrance.'

'I think so, Betty.' Gentle palpation of the lower abdomen and a rapid vaginal examination had confirmed that the cervix was nicely dilated. 'Now, I want you to turn onto your left side and draw your right leg up towards your chin. That's good. Breathe deeply – in, out, now in again as deep as you can. Try not to push until I tell you to.'

There were more contractions and this time Betty did cry out – so loudly that Doreen came scuttling in from next door.

'Why have you got her on her side, trussed up like a Christmas turkey?' she demanded as she burst into the room. 'What are you trying to do – finish the poor blighter off?'

'This is what's recommended,' Hazel calmly explained. 'We need to go nice and slowly now, Betty, so the head isn't forced out. Steady as we go.'

'Recommended?' Doreen echoed, her face aghast. 'By who?'

'By the Royal College, that's who.'

As Hazel and Doreen debated the pros and cons of the new method, Betty's free hand clutched at the rails of the bedstead. She cried out again and pushed hard, despite Hazel's warning.

'They never did this in my day,' Doreen muttered.

'No, well, this is 1936. And we need more hot water, please.' Casting a firm glance in the old woman's direction until she backed out of the room, Hazel used her trumpet-shaped pinard stethoscope to listen again to the foetal heartbeat. Still regular, still normal, which meant there were no complications with the cord, thank heavens, and really the only difficulty would be the size of the head compared with the mother's narrow hips. 'Betty, you have to keep your knee up to your chin as high as you can,' she advised. 'More deep breaths – that's good. And now – now you can take short ones. That's right – pant as fast as you like. But don't push yet.'

Hazel saw the dark crown of the baby's head. The contractions were stronger than ever and now she must let Betty push down as hard as she could until the face appeared, bluish in colour, its mouth puckered. 'Push now. That's good, Betty – that's grand.'

Sooner than expected, Hazel saw a shoulder emerge and then part of a tiny torso covered in mucus and blood, then a second shoulder. After another moment or two she was able to clamp the cord in two places and make a clean cut then take the baby by the ankles and hold her upside down until she sucked the first vital breath of air into her lungs.

'It's a little girl,' she said gently as an exhausted Betty rolled onto her back and held out imploring hands.

Quickly Hazel wiped the baby's head and face, swaddled her in a square of soft cotton fabric from her bag, then gave her to Betty.

The mother's job was done, the pain already put behind her, and she was holding perfection in her arms, but Hazel had to work on. She must follow the textbook and see to it that the placenta was delivered whole and that haemorrhaging did not occur.

As Betty cuddled and cooed over her infant, Doreen reappeared with more water and towels, together with further old wives' advice and grumbles about what it cost these days to have a baby, what with doctors' visits and medicines to stop morning sickness, not to mention the money that Hazel would charge.

'Believe me, you won't get much change out of a pound note,' the garrulous neighbour warned Betty. 'Not like in the good old days when you knocked on your fire-back with the end of a poker and someone like Rhoda Briggs, God rest her, or Mabel Jackson from down the road came running and you paid her fifteen bob for her trouble. That was all it took back then. Not college girls with certificates like Hazel Price here. Just nice and natural did it – flat on your back and with no one breathing down your neck telling you what to do.'

For a second or two Betty managed to tear her attention away from her newborn baby. She looked at Hazel with the sleeves of her white blouse rolled up waiting patiently at the bottom of the bed, then at Doreen standing hands on hips by the washstand. 'Pipe down,' she said sternly to the old woman. 'Do you think Len and me are wet behind the ears? No – everyone knows Hazel is fresh out of college so my Daisy here is her first since she got herself qualified.'

Listening with half an ear as she dealt with the afterbirth, Hazel allowed herself a smile. She liked the name Daisy, and especially enjoyed the disgruntled frown that had appeared on Doreen's face.

'As soon as we heard she was back, Len went straight round to Raglan Road and haggled until she brought the price down to what we can manage,' Betty announced with a triumphant smile, followed by a sly wink at Hazel. 'A pound note, my backside! We're paying her ten shillings and sixpence for my lying-in, not a penny more. So tell Mabel Jackson to stick that in her pipe and smoke it.'

At home in the kitchen later that day, Hazel took off her tan-coloured brogues and rested her feet on a padded footstool. She undid the top button of her blouse then loosened her thick, shoulder-length fair hair from its tortoiseshell comb. There was no fire in the hearth on this warm September day. A trapped wasp buzzed against the window-pane.

That didn't go too badly, she told herself as she reflected on her first solo delivery. Her London college had set her up nicely with a mixture of theory and hands-on experience, but walking out after a year through those wrought-iron gates into the big wide world didn't quite prepare you for the real thing – the taking charge and being responsible for the life of both mother and baby.

21

There had been a few anxious moments on Nelson Yard and the state of the Hollings' house was far from ideal, but on the whole everything had gone smoothly, thank heavens.

Leaning her head against the antimacassar draped over the back of the chair and looking around the neat, orderly room (everything familiar, everything just so), Hazel felt a glow of satisfaction. True, compared with what Betty Hollings had just been through, her role had been the easy one. All she'd had to do was to follow her training step by step in what had turned out to be a straightforward delivery. The less palatable fact was that Hazel was yet to be paid, but the money was promised for a week's time when Leonard would have put in the overtime.

'Ta very much for everything,' Betty had said in her pragmatic way as she'd pushed her lank hair behind her ears and accepted a cup of tea. Holding her baby close to her chest, the new mother had watched Hazel pack her bag. 'Doreen's happy to look after Keith and Polly for the rest of the day, love. That means I can have time all to myself with Daisy here. It'll be the only chance I get.'

The words echoed in Hazel's ears as she relaxed in the quiet kitchen at the end of a busy day on Raglan Road. Betty had two kiddies under four and now an infant to look after in a house that hadn't seen a good spring clean in Lord knows how long. Not that it was any different from most on Nelson Yard, which was notorious for putting a temporary roof over the heads of families who failed to keep up with the

22

rent and were regularly moved, on to even less salubrious quarters on the far side of the canal. Unlike Leonard, the men in such families were often on the dole, their wives worn down, their children underfed.

I don't envy Betty, Hazel thought, padding to the window in her stockinged feet to waft the wasp out into the open. *She'll be up and about tomorrow morning, I shouldn't wonder, slaving over the cooking, washing and ironing as usual. And Leonard will be no help. He'll leave it all to her...*

But then again Hazel remembered with a sigh of satisfaction the look of joy in Betty's eyes as she'd held her baby for the first time and her lips had touched Daisy's soft cheek. It was a feeling Hazel could only imagine – that bond between mother and newborn child.

The dazed wasp refused to leave. It buzzed back into the room and spiralled to the floor where it settled on the hearthrug. 'Dozy thing,' Hazel murmured as she tried to persuade it to crawl onto a sheet of newspaper.

The sound of mill buzzers in the distance signalled the end of the working day – soon the peace would be broken by the tramp of feet on cobbles, the chatter of voices and the rumble and rattle of trams on nearby Ghyll Road.

Succeeding with the wasp at last, Hazel quickly released it into the open air then closed the window. Then she lit the gas ring under the kettle to make tea for her father. She put two rich tea biscuits on a saucer and two scoops from the tea caddy into the pot. *I can't wait for Dad to get here,* she thought. *He'll be pleased as Punch when I tell*

23

him about Betty and the baby.

The kettle had boiled itself almost dry before Hazel gave up on her father and turned off the gas.

'Where's Dad got to?' she asked her mother without preliminaries when Jinny returned home from a long afternoon spent behind Ken Bishop's fruit and veg stall at Clifton Market.

Jinny sighed as she deposited a big bag of potatoes, onions and carrots at the cellar head. 'Hello, Hazel. Lovely to see you too,' she mocked.

Hazel grinned sheepishly. 'Sorry, Mum. Here, let me take them down for you.' No sooner said than done – the heavy bag was safely stored in the keeping cellar and Hazel was back in the kitchen refilling the kettle before Jinny had removed her coat.

'Where is your dad, anyway? Why isn't he back?' Jinny looked in the mirror over the mantelpiece to pat her hair back into place. She caught sight of Hazel's reflection behind her own – so like her but minus twenty years of wear and tear. Both had small, delicate features, blue eyes and finely arched eyebrows, and both were fair skinned. What's more, they were alike in making the most of their slender figures and wearing clothes and make-up that were up-to-the-minute. 'Two peas in a pod,' people would often say. 'More like sisters than mother and daughter.'

'Maybe he stopped behind for a bit of over-time,' Hazel suggested, holding back the news about Betty's baby until her mother's mood improved.

Jinny tutted. 'There's been no overtime at Oldroyd's mill since January. Nor at Kingsley's or Calvert's, for that matter.'

So much for Leonard Hollings' promise. Hazel was struck by the thought that she might not get her money as soon as expected.

'As a matter of fact, your dad mentioned earlier this week that they're thinking of cutting back hours in the spinning shed.'

Hazel had the good grace to blush and apologize once more. 'I didn't realize. But you know Dad – he doesn't talk to me about his work.'

'Yes, though he'd have come clean if you'd bothered to ask.' Since Hazel's return from college, Jinny had made it her business to bring her daughter back down to earth. 'I don't want her flouncing around all over the place,' she'd told her own mother Ada and her sister Rose on her last visit to them in Nelson Yard. 'What use is a certificate in midwifery if you stick your nose so high in the air that you don't notice what's going on around you?'

Ada had nodded but kind-hearted Rose had disagreed.

'Don't be too hard on the girl,' she'd advised her sister. 'Hazel's thin skinned. She'll take your criticism to heart and so will Robert. It'll lead to arguments if you're not careful.'

At home on Raglan Road, Hazel now took the latest rebuke from Jinny in subdued silence and retreated to the corner of the kitchen to pour the tea. 'Dad's been overseer at Oldroyd's longer than anyone,' she reasoned. 'His job's safe, surely.'

Jinny's reply came in the form of pursed lips

25

and a sour look, interrupted by the opening of the door and Robert's belated entrance. He was all smiles and he carried a slim, neatly wrapped parcel under his arm.

'I know – before you say it, I'm late and I'm sorry!' He laughed, spilling good humour into the frosty silence. Ten years older than his wife, he was a tall, strong-looking man whose dark hair was streaked with grey and whose clear brown eyes could be read like an open book.

'What are you looking so pleased about?' Jinny challenged, but she softened when Robert slipped his free arm around her waist and kissed her cheek.

'This!' he announced, holding up the parcel before offering it to Hazel. 'I had to drop in at Redman's to collect it after work. That's why I'm late.'

'What is it?' Hazel asked.

'Open it and see.'

Quickly she untied the string and folded back the stiff brown paper. She lifted out her recently awarded midwifery certificate, complete with college coat of arms and her name written out in beautiful copperplate, all encased in a frame that had been specially made at the picture-framer's on Westgate Road. 'Oh!' she said, her face flushed with unspoken gratitude.

'Stand aside, you two – this gets pride of place, here on the mantelpiece.' Robert took the frame and got Jinny to move a heavy marble clock out of the way.

'This clock was a wedding present from my mother,' Jinny grumbled as she looked in vain for a different place to put it.

'I was telling Sidney Redman all about our Hazel,' Robert went on as he stood back to admire the effect. 'What a clever girl she is and how hard she's worked to qualify. Sidney promised to pass the word around, since he and his missis don't have any more call for the services of a midwife, if you know what I mean.'

A prim glance from Jinny did nothing to dent his garrulous high spirits.

'What?' he said with a grin. 'I'm only stating the obvious. Anyway, I expect there'll be plenty of young couples from Westgate Road knocking on our door before too long, and all up and down Raglan Road and in Nelson Yard...'

'I delivered Betty Hollings' baby this morning.' Hazel was unable to contain her excitement any longer. Her eyes shone and a dimple appeared in her left cheek – a characteristic that somehow made her seem younger than her twenty-one years. 'Mother and baby are both doing well!'

With a whoop Robert gathered her in his arms and gave her one of his strong hugs that squashed the breath out of her. 'You hear that, Jinny? Hazel doesn't let the grass grow. No, not her. She's only gone and started as she means to go on.'

'I know – I'm not deaf,' Jinny replied stiffly. 'Anyway, Hazel, I hope you made the Hollingses stump up the money before you left...? No, I can see from your face that you didn't.'

'Next week,' Hazel explained. 'That's when they've promised to pay me.'

Jinny didn't need to go on – her expression said it all.

'They will!' Hazel insisted. She felt her cheeks burn. Why did her mother always have to put a dampener on things? Why couldn't she be pleased with her for once? 'Leonard swore to me that he'd put in the overtime.'

'My, my – Thomas Kingsley's filled his empty order book, has he? He must have if he's handing out overtime to his loom tuners left, right and centre.' Taking her apron from the hook and tying it around her waist, Jinny turned her back on Hazel and Robert and took a loaf of bread and a wedge of cheese from the food safe above the sink. 'Ask anyone around here, the first rule of working for yourself is to make sure you get paid on the dot. Didn't they teach you that at college?'

Robert stepped in to ease the bad feeling in the room. 'Leonard will stump up the money, don't you worry,' he told Hazel. 'If not, his name will be mud.'

But Jinny wasn't so easily deflected as she sliced through the bread with a deft sawing motion. 'I ran into Mabel Jackson yesterday. She was asking after you, Hazel, then telling me how hard it is to get cash out of folk these days, even for someone like her who's been at it for years. She's lost count of the women she's helped, me included. Back then, when you put in your appearance, we were properly grateful for what Mabel did and she could rely on us to pay up. Not now, though, not when everyone is so hard pressed.'

'All right, Mum. There's no need to go on about it.' Hazel felt like one of those hot air balloons whose steering went awry so that it got snagged on a tree branch and punctured. Whoosh, the air had gone out of her, leaving her deflated.

Of course the money side of being self-employed was a worry, but Hazel had thought through the practical angles and reached the optimistic conclusion that setting up as a midwife was a bit like being a hairdresser – there would always be women having babies and needing her help, just as there were always women who needed a haircut.

'Set the table for us, there's a good girl.' Jinny ignored the fact that Hazel was upset. The cheese was sliced and laid on the bread. The gas was lit. 'Cheese on toast with a nice slice of cream cake to follow,' she announced. 'I called in at Sykes' bakery for the bread and Marjorie knows how partial you are to a Victoria sponge, Robert. This one came out of the oven lopsided so she let me have it cheap.'

CHAPTER TWO

One of the problems Hazel had come up against after her year away in London and her return to Raglan Road was the unshakeable feeling that she was fourteen years old again, a school leaver about to embark on the rocky road to adulthood.

For that was how her mother treated her – as a naive girl with ideas above her station and a tendency to answer back.

'I don't know where you get it from,' had been Jinny's incantation throughout Hazel's teenage years, up to the elbows in sudsy water as she scrubbed away at Robert's stiff shirt collars. It didn't matter what the argument was about – a request for privacy from Hazel as she heated her Friday-night bath water in the kitchen copper or a refusal to run an errand because she was getting ready to go out – the charge was always the same. 'You don't get it from me, for a start. You never caught me cheeking my elders when I was your age.'

'I'm not cheeking my elders,' Hazel would retort before her mother gave her the thin-lipped look that said, *That proves my point exactly!* Then Hazel would retreat to her attic room to sulk and dream of escape.

Her father, too, sometimes behaved as if she was a child, though in a different way – spoiling her as he had from the moment he'd married Jinny and they'd all three moved into the house on Raglan Road. He was Jinny's second husband – her first, Alec Sharpe, having been killed in the war.

Alec and Jinny had married late in 1913, during the slow build-up of hostilities between Britain and Germany. Hazel had been born in the autumn of the following year, just a week before Alec had gone off to the Front. The eager young private didn't see in the New Year, but met his bloody end alongside thousands of comrades slaughtered in a muddy Flanders field.

Five years later, Robert Price had cautiously courted and married the beautiful, sad-eyed young widow, stepping into the role of husband and stepfather without a moment's hesitation.

Even-tempered and hard-working, Robert had lavished attention on Hazel and it was he and not her mother who had eventually backed her over leaving home and going to college. The frame for the certificate was a case in point. It showed Robert's unswerving pride in his stepdaughter. He hadn't stopped to consider if it was something she or, more to the point, Jinny would wish to have in prime position on the mantelpiece.

'Hazel deserves a treat,' he would tell his wife in the early days, when Hazel won an essay-writing competition at Lowton Junior School. Then he would take her into town for Saturday-afternoon tea at the Kardomah refreshment rooms and he would boast about her to all and sundry. *Top of her class again – I don't know where she gets it from.*

His words echoed Jinny's refrain, though for different reasons, Hazel thought with a wry smile as she finished her tea then retreated to her attic bedroom. This, she reminded herself, was the day of her first delivery – signifying a new life for baby Daisy Hollings, joy soon followed by extra drudgery for Betty and a professional road opening up for Hazel. *And yet here I am,* she reminded herself, *listening to Mum's grumbles and stuck at home on a Friday night with nowhere to go.*

She hung her work skirt on a hanger and put it away in the wardrobe. Then she rolled up the pair of silk stockings that had been drying over the back of her chair and slid them into her top drawer. After that she went downstairs in jumper and slacks, took cleaning materials out of the shoe box and began to polish her brogues.

'Not going out tonight, love?' Her dad glanced

31

up from the newspaper he was reading.

'Not tonight,' Hazel replied. She'd already heard the click of the front door as Jinny went out, presumably to drop in on her mother and Rose. 'I thought I'd have a quiet night in.'

'That's a shame. You should be out enjoying yourself, getting back into the swing of things.'

'Maybe tomorrow.' She sighed as she noticed her certificate on the mantelpiece, the glass gleaming in the gaslight. She heard the faint, insistent hiss of gas and the intermittent, soft *pop-pop* of the mantel in the alcove that housed Jinny's treadle sewing machine. Everything was the same as in the old days, Hazel thought again – except for her mood, which was a mixture of mounting irritation and apprehension that she'd seldom felt before.

She brushed polish from her shoes then buffed them until they shone. *What's wrong with me?* she wondered, punishing the shoes with firm swipes of her yellow duster. *I have plenty to keep me busy. For a start, I've promised to call in on Betty tomorrow morning to see how she's getting on. On Monday I've arranged to go to the surgery on Westgate Road to see if there's any work coming up there. The more people know about me and my new venture, the better.*

'I'd have done that for you,' Robert said, folding his newspaper and noticing Hazel at work on her shoes.

'I don't mind. I got used to doing it myself while I was away.' The response sounded sharper than she'd intended and she was relieved when the door opened and her cousin Gladys breezed in without knocking.

'Put those away this minute and come with me!'

she cried, snatching the shoes from Hazel and pulling her to her feet – a whirlwind of blonde, bubbly energy that sucked in everything in its path. Tonight twenty-two-year-old Gladys was dressed in a red knitted bolero and high-waisted white slacks, with peep-toe sandals that showed her crimson-painted toenails. 'Hello, Uncle Robert. A little bird tells me Hazel is down in the dumps for no reason so here I am to sort her out!'

'Who says I'm down in the dumps?' Hazel protested feebly.

'Aunty Jinny did. I bumped into her at Nana's house. And look at you – it's true. Anyone would think you'd come back home with your tail between your legs instead of getting top marks in your year. And don't deny it – Uncle Robert's been spouting off about it to the whole family.'

'Dad!' Hazel's sigh of protest matched her glum expression.

Gladys wrinkled her nose in a sign of impatience. 'Come on, Hazel, shake a leg. You've got ten minutes to put your glad rags on. Don't go mad, though: change into your best pair of slacks and a nice, fitted blouse – that kind of thing.'

'Why? Where are we going?'

'To town – where else? To the new jazz club next to Merton and Groves. Don't worry, Uncle Robert, I'll look after her!'

Sitting beside Gladys on the tram into town, Hazel couldn't help feeling like the ugly duckling. Where Gladys sparkled (fingernails painted to match her toenails, silver earrings and locket necklace), Hazel gave off a quieter glow. Her

33

hands and nails were scrubbed clean, she wore hardly any make-up and her fair hair was less bold and brassy. True, she matched Gladys and perhaps outshone her in other details, such as the trimness of her figure and the violet depth of her heavily lashed eyes, but she lacked her cousin's breezy confidence, coming across as more thoughtful and reserved.

As the conductor took their coppers and gave them their tickets, it was Gladys he winked at and it was with her that he acted out the pretence that she had tendered the wrong fare.

'That's tuppence you owe me next time you take my tram,' he kidded, his cap tilted back, a dark forelock curling down. 'I've got a memory like an elephant so I won't forget.'

'Cheeky blighter!' Gladys laughed, springing from her seat as they approached the stop. 'I know your face – you work with my brother, Dan Drummond. I'll be sure to tell him how you tried to trick me.'

And at the entrance to the jazz club, Hazel was sure that it was Gladys who attracted the attention of the small gang of smokers hanging around on the pavement, puffing away at their cigarettes.

'Aye-aye!' they chanted with a rising intonation that showed their approval.

'Watch out, lads – things are looking up.'

'Fall in behind me – I'm first in line.'

'Behave yourselves!' Gladys tutted as she and Hazel avoided the scuffle at the door and made their way down some stone steps into a dingy, smoke-filled cellar with a bar and a small stage where musicians were tuning their instruments. 'Get a move on, Hazel. Dan and Eddie are here already – I asked them to save us a couple of seats.'

So Hazel followed meekly, threading between tables in the crowded room until they found the corner where Gladys's brothers sat. There was just time to say their hellos and take their seats before the band struck up the first tune – a smooth, fluid combination of clarinet and saxophone backed by the beat of drums and a tinkling waterfall of piano notes that launched the singer into a doleful, gravel-voiced plea for his unfaithful lover to return.

Hazel's eldest cousin, Dan, leaned in close and nudged her with his elbow. 'Well, Hazel, what do you reckon to this place?'

'It's grand,' she said with a nod. It was the type of music she'd heard in the cinema, watching suave men in white dinner jackets and dicky bows flirting with screen goddesses like Carole Lombard. The musicians onstage were not in the same league as that but they were good enough to make you tap your feet and pay attention.

Dan nodded back. 'By the way, congratulations on your college thingumajig. Though it's rather you than me any day of the week with that job.'

Hazel laughed. 'Thanks, Dan. Lucky for you, no woman in her right mind would ask you to bring a baby into this world. Anyway, how's life?'

'The same, ta. Still driving a corporation tram. Still hoping to pick a winner at the dog track.'

She started to tell him about the incident between Gladys and the cheeky conductor then thought better of it. The band had begun a new tune and a few people, Dan and Gladys among them, were standing up to trawl the room for partners to dance with. Soon couples held each other close and shuffled around the confined space as the lovelorn singer sang of fresh woes.

'Dance?' Eddie offered, diffidently holding out his hand to Hazel. Like his brother Dan, he had the handsome charm of the Drummonds – a clean-cut look with regular features and a side parting in his sandy hair. But his face retained an innocent air and lacked the brash sophistication of the others, allowing Hazel to see that he was only inviting her out of politeness.

'No thanks, Eddie. Where's Joan tonight, anyway?'

'She's not keen on jazz so she's stayed in to get her hair done.'

Eddie and Joan were childhood sweethearts. They'd been engaged at eighteen and after seven long years they were still saving hard from his job at the brass foundry and hers behind the counter at Pickard's butcher's until they could afford to be married. 'Steady Eddie' was what Gladys called him, whereas debonair Dan was dubbed the black sheep of the family – still single at twenty-eight and regularly drinking away his week's wages in the Green Cross or chucking his money down the drain at the greyhound track.

'I'm not too keen on this new type of music either,' Eddie confessed.

'No? I like it,' Hazel said, tapping her fingers on the table. The rhythms were earthy and carried you along, and there was a kind of underworld glamour to it that seemed to ride roughshod over the narrow rules she'd grown up with.

Two songs later, her view was blocked when someone came between her and the stage. 'Is anyone sitting here?' a man asked.

In the glare of the footlights, Hazel couldn't make out the tall figure hovering nearby but she recognized the voice of John Moxon, one of Dan's newer friends and a recent neighbour on Raglan Road. Guessing that Gladys would stay on the dance floor until the band stopped for a break, she pulled back the vacant chair. 'No, help yourself.'

John put down his beer and sat next to her. For a moment she was blinded by the glare. 'You're not dancing,' he commented.

'No. It's a tight squeeze out there.'

'You don't say.' Letting the conversation drift, he seemed happy to soak up the atmosphere.

Hazel was aware of him relaxing in his seat beside her. John carried himself quietly as if reluctant to draw attention despite having a past that was a little out of the ordinary. For a start, he hadn't lived in the town all his life. He'd been born in a small village in the north of the county and only came to Raglan Road when he'd married Myra Pennington from the fish and chip shop. They'd moved into a house two doors down from her parents and Myra was currently pregnant with their first child. Secondly – and this was what came to the forefront of Hazel's mind – John Moxon had played cricket for Yorkshire.

'He was a wizard with the bat,' Dan had boasted to everyone soon after he'd got talking with John at the Green Cross. 'It was a few years back, mind you – before he had his accident. His name came up in the *Yorkshire Post* every week, scoring a century against Worcestershire, playing in a winning innings against Surrey at Lord's. You wouldn't think to look at him now, but he was a leading light in the cricketing world, was John Moxon.'

Never having had the slightest interest in cricket, the name had meant nothing to Hazel, but now, when she called to mind that her old school friend Myra was soon due to give birth, she deftly took charge of the conversation. 'Say hello to your wife from me,' she began. 'I'm Hazel Price. Myra and I went around together a few years back.'

John nodded, glanced sideways at Hazel then back at the stage.

'You might not remember me, by the way. I've been in London, training as a midwife.'

This time John paid more attention. He leaned over to shake her hand. 'John Moxon. Pleased to meet you.'

'Hazel scored top marks in her class,' Eddie chipped in, giving her a small nudge of encouragement. 'And she only lives a few yards down the road from you at number 18 – nice and handy for Myra when the time comes.'

Hazel squirmed in her seat at the brazenness of their joint approach. But this was what you had to do to get on in life.

'Did she now?' John held Hazel's gaze with his light brown eyes. There was a slight curl to his lips and a timbre to his voice suggesting amusement.

At her expense? Hazel wondered. *Was he laughing*

38

at her?

Just then Dan broke away from his dancing partner and made a beeline towards the table. He clapped John on the back then launched into a loud conversation about the upcoming match at Headingley and Yorkshire's current position in the County Championship table. Before long he was inviting John to the bar for a refill of his pint glass.

'I'll make sure to let Myra know you're back,' John assured Hazel before Dan led him off. 'But don't get your hopes up over the question of a midwife. I think her mother's already made arrangements for that side of things.'

'Rightio, that's fair enough.' Hazel tried to conceal her disappointment by smiling and turning her head towards the stage.

'Good for you, anyway,' Eddie told her as the music changed to a faster, more upbeat number. 'It might not come easily but you have to learn to blow your own trumpet if you want to get ahead.'

'I know,' Hazel said with a sigh. Was it the music that had made her pulse race, or embarrassment at being turned down, or the way John Moxon's eyes had fixed on her? Something had quickened her heartbeat and brought a flush to her cheeks – that much was certain.

Two songs later, when the singer moved away from the microphone and the musicians put down their instruments, a breathless Gladys came back to the table. 'Fetch Hazel and me a drink, Eddie, there's a good lad,' she said as she sank into her seat. 'Dan's up there at the bar – he'll pay if you ask him nicely.'

'I can't make out why Eddie lets you boss him around,' Hazel observed as he went off meekly.

'Mum trained him well.' Gladys giggled. 'Dan was a tearaway from the start. She'd already given up on him when Eddie came along. Lord, I'm hot!'

'Here.' Hazel picked up the cardboard drinks list and suggested Gladys use it as a fan.

'Ta – that's better.' Still smiling, Gladys picked out John Moxon standing head and shoulders above Eddie and Dan at the bar. 'What do you make of our famous cricketer?' she asked in a voice laden with innuendo.

'He seemed decent enough,' Hazel answered defensively.

'Come on, Hazel – I saw you sweet-talking him and don't pretend you didn't.'

The colour rose again in Hazel's cheeks. 'I never did! We were discussing Myra, if you must know.'

'Trust you.' The disappointed grimace on Gladys's face was exaggerated. 'You bump into the best-looking fellow for miles around – in a jazz club, in a smoke-filled cellar room listening to the best music you'll ever hear – drums and saxophones and words that get under your skin without you realizing it – and all you find to talk about is his pregnant wife!'

'Best-looking, maybe,' Hazel agreed, 'but married.'

Gladys laughed then pointed to two new arrivals. 'Look out – here comes trouble.' And with that she turned to ask a stranger at the neighbouring table for a light for her cigarette.

Through the smoke Hazel made out Sylvia, the youngest Drummond sister, on the arm of a man she didn't recognize. Sylvia was seventeen – hardly old enough to be let loose, as Gladys put it. She was the only dark-haired member of the family – a throwback to her grandma Ada in her younger days, according to Jinny and Rose – with a pretty, heart-shaped face, rosebud lips and hair styled into a sharp bob that mimicked the look of Clara Bow. Tonight she was wearing a sleeveless, tightly belted dress made of silky cream material, decorated down the front with a contrasting band of gold trim, together with dainty, high-heeled shoes.

'Who's that chap with her?' Hazel asked Gladys, watching as Sylvia dragged her young man through the crowd towards the stage where she boldly engaged in conversation with the jazz band's singer.

'That's poor Norman,' Gladys replied with mock gravity.

'Why "poor" Norman?' Hazel couldn't help smiling. Sylvia's companion seemed ordinary enough in his blue blazer and fawn slacks, though he looked a little reticent and perhaps no match for vivacious Sylvia.

'His name's Norman Bellamy. He's a warehouse man at Calvert's, apparently. He and Sylvia have only been walking out for a month or two.'

'"Apparently?"' Hazel echoed. 'Does that mean you haven't found out every last thing about him?'

'No. Lord knows where Sylvia dredged him up from but she started as she meant to go on, mak-

41

ing him tag along and stump up for everything – a ticket to the flicks, a day trip to Scarborough, a new dress...You name it, poor Norman has to fork out for it.'

'Miaow!' Hazel commented then reacted as Gladys dug her in the ribs. 'Ouch!' She was still smiling when Eddie came back with their drinks, followed soon after by Sylvia and Norman. Introductions were made as the band went back onstage.

'Did you see me put in a request?' Sylvia cooed. 'I asked Earl to sing my favourite song.'

'Earl?' Hazel prompted. She'd been off the scene for longer than she realized. Long enough for Sylvia to transform from a skinny, sparrow-legged shop assistant into a svelte, sophisticated frequenter of clubs who was on first-name terms with members of the band.

'Earl Ray. This is Earl Ray's Dixie Jazz Band all the way from New Orleans – surely you've heard of them.'

Hazel shrugged and shook her head.

'"All the way from New Orleans" – my, my.' Gladys's flat, dry attempt at an American accent was meant to bring Sylvia down a peg or two but it had the opposite effect.

For five whole minutes Sylvia insisted on sharing her knowledge of the band – Earl this and Earl that – followed by a complete list of the songs in his repertoire. Hazel picked up a marked unease behind her young cousin's over-excited account, but she quickly dismissed it from her mind. Norman, meanwhile, drank his beer and made a show of listening intently to the music. It

42

was only when Sylvia stopped chattering and dragged her young man onto the floor to dance that Gladys drew her chair closer to Hazel's and grew more confidential.

'You won't tell anyone...' she began, her eyes narrowing as she followed Sylvia and Norman's twisting, turning progress across the room. A frown appeared on her delicate, powdered face and she allowed a dramatic pause to develop.

Hazel tilted her head towards Gladys. 'Tell anyone what?'

'Sylvia wanted to keep this a secret but it'll be out in the open soon enough.'

'Come on – spit it out.'

'She and Norman only went and got engaged!'

The news made Hazel sit back in her seat. 'You don't say. How old is he, for goodness' sake?'

'Eighteen – a year older than Sylvia. Not to put too fine a point on things, everyone thinks they're in a "rush" to get married. The date's set for a week tomorrow, as a matter of fact.' Gladys's emphasis on the word 'rush' was accompanied by raised eyebrows

'And what do Uncle Cyril and Aunty Ethel think about it?' Hazel didn't really need to ask. Sylvia was the baby of the family, spoiled rotten, flitting from job to job, by no means ready to settle down. Besides, as Gladys pointed out, the reason behind this rush to the altar must surely be obvious to everyone.

'Mum and Dad said no at first.' Flicking ash from her cigarette into the glass ashtray, Gladys let her real feelings show. 'Think about it – Norman's on short time at Calvert's and Sylvia's presently

43

without a job of any kind. There isn't even enough money for a ring.'

Hazel watched the sleek young couple dancing cheek to cheek. No one would think to look at them that they were about to put their heads into a tight noose – getting married on a shoestring, scrabbling together furniture from second-hand shops, begging and borrowing whatever they could. Never mind 'poor' Norman, what about poor Sylvia?

'I know what's going through your mind.' A sombre Gladys finished her cigarette then stubbed it out with three short, sharp dabs. 'It's what the world and his uncle will think.'

'But we don't know for sure?'

Hazel's worldly cousin brushed away the question but there was real concern beneath the flippancy when she spoke again. 'Put it this way, love, wedding or no wedding, come next spring, Sylvia will be calling on you for your services, you mark my words.'

CHAPTER THREE

Here was another case of the women of Nelson Yard failing to move with the times. The bothersome thought preoccupied Hazel as she mulled over Sylvia's situation on the morning after her visit to the jazz club.

Back in the bad old days, before anyone mentioned the word contraception, ignorance

44

had ruled and unwanted pregnancies had been ten a penny. But then Marie Stopes had come along and supposedly changed all that risky dependence on so-called 'safe' periods. Now there were clinics to go to and reliable methods to use if you only knew how to ask for them, unless, like Sylvia, you were flighty by nature and had the habit of burying your head in the sand when it came to sex.

Hazel's conclusion unnerved her as she went downstairs to put on her hat and coat, ready to call in on Betty Hollings as promised. *That's not very kind,* she told herself. *This is your cousin Sylvia you're talking about and 'flighty' is not a nice word to use. Besides, at this stage it's all guesswork. We don't even know if she's pregnant yet.*

Following her train of thought, Hazel failed to notice her mother sitting with her hair in curlers at the kitchen table until Jinny spoke.

Slowly and deliberately she started to unwind the curlers from the top of her head. 'We need more bread. Can you buy a loaf while you're out?'

'I'm working this morning but I will if I can. What sort would you like?'

'The usual.' Jinny eyed her daughter up and down – from her jaunty straw hat with its narrow brim, past her lightweight, summer coat and canvas midwife's bag down to her shiny tan brogues. 'Someone looks tip-top this morning,' she conceded.

'Ta.' The grudging compliment took Hazel by surprise and she gave a quick smile. 'I'm off to see Betty Hollings. What are you up to?'

45

'I've a pile of mending to get through before I catch the ten o'clock tram. I'm due behind the stall at half past.'

'So is there anything else you'd like me to get from the shops besides bread?'

'Something for your dad's tea from Hutchinson's – a slice of ham or a pork pie. Oh and you could call in at your nana's with a pint of milk.'

'Rightio. Now I have to go or I'll be late.' Briskly Hazel stepped out of the house into the Saturday-morning buzz of housewives chatting on their top steps or shaking dusters out of upstairs windows.

There were children playing hopscotch, a lad wheeling a barrow laden with wooden planks and two men with horse-drawn carts having a bad-tempered dispute about who had right of way up and down the narrow cobbled street. The impatient horses stamped and snorted as Hazel squeezed by then turned down the alley into Nelson Yard.

'Look who it isn't!' None other than Mabel Jackson greeted her with forced joviality from the far end of the ginnel. Her stocky outline blocked Hazel's way and, despite her face being in deep shadow, it was clear that Hazel's rival in the midwifery business was in no mood to stand aside.

Hazel felt her hackles rise. 'Good morning,' she said as cheerily as she could. 'How are you?'

'I'm doing nicely, thank you.' With feet planted apart and dressed in the faded, wrap-over apron she always wore, Mabel was as much a part of the neighbourhood as starched net curtains and scrubbed doorsteps. Her age was difficult to judge

– she'd always looked ancient to Hazel, though in fact she was probably in her mid-sixties, the same age as Hazel's grandmother. She was certainly not frail. 'How about you?' she prompted, arms folded.

'I'm well, ta.' Hazel attempted to sidestep the woman but was thwarted by Mabel's deliberate shift of weight.

'So you're our new broom sweeping clean, are you?' As an established handywoman of the old school, with long experience of bringing babies into the world and laying out the dead, Mabel made it plain with a sceptical glance at Hazel's canvas bag that she was not in favour of stethoscopes, sterilized kidney dishes and surgical forceps.

'I suppose so.' Hazel's attempt at a breezy smile was met by a blank look and a loud sniff. 'I'm on my way to see how Betty Hollings is getting along.'

'Betty and baby are both fine.' Mabel spoke forcibly as she fixed Hazel with a steady gaze.

'They are?' Hazel stalled for time as she worked out the implications of this last remark.

'Yes. As soon as Doreen tipped me the wink that Betty had had the bairn, I made it my business to pop my head around the door. I've just come from there now, as a matter of fact.'

'You don't say.' Hazel switched her heavy bag from her right hand to her left. Honestly, what was she to make of this open interference?

'I made myself useful while I was at it – tidied up and made them all porridge for breakfast, laid a fire and suchlike.' Though not hostile, Mabel's gaze didn't flinch. 'That was me being neigh-bourly. I hope you don't mind?'

'Not at all.' Acknowledging that the wind had been well and truly taken out of her sails, Hazel was by now desperate to get past. 'My job is to take temperatures, check for jaundice – that kind of thing.'

'Of course it is.' Slowly Mabel nodded and moved out of the way. 'Betty was singing your praises, by the way.'

Setting out across the untidy, weed-strewn yard, Hazel hesitated. This was certain to turn into a back-handed compliment, she was sure.

'You kept a cool head by all accounts,' Mabel went on. 'Even though it was your first time and Betty said you were shaking like a leaf...'

'Thank you,' Hazel said through gritted teeth. Here it came – *the coup de grâce.*

'And your tea-making wasn't up to much either, according to Betty.' Mabel's glee was evident as she watched Hazel hurry about her business. 'Weak as dish-water, she told me, and only two sugars instead of three.'

'Don't worry – everyone knows that Mabel's bark is worse than her bite.' Hazel's Aunty Rose was keen to reassure her niece as she sat down on the lumpy chaise longue in the kitchen of number 6 Nelson Yard. The room was otherwise laid out identically to the Hollings' kitchen – a fireplace with an iron range, a sink in the back corner, with just enough space in the middle for a table and chairs – though here there was not a speck of dust to be seen and everything was scrubbed, polished and starched to within an inch of its life.

Hazel's grandmother sat in an upright wooden chair, keeping a beady eye on proceedings out in the yard.

'I wouldn't bank on that if I were you,' Ada argued from her perch by the window. 'I've known Mabel Jackson for fifty years and I can't remember her backing down from an argument – not for anything or anyone. No; if you give that woman something to sink her teeth into, she's like a dog with a bone.'

'Ta for the warning.' Hazel shuddered and prepared herself for cross-examination.

'I caught you two having a chinwag earlier,' Ada went on. 'It looked to me like Mabel was giving you a good dressing-down. Why was that? Was it over Betty Hollings' new baby, by any chance?'

'It was,' Hazel confessed. *Here we go again,* she told herself. *I've barely sat myself down, and already I feel as if I'm being got at.*

'I hope you stuck up for yourself, our Hazel,' her grandmother said more kindly. 'You have to, or else Mabel will make mincemeat of you.'

'Don't worry, Nana. I won't let her.' Hazel meant it. Appearances were deceptive; beneath her youthful good looks there was plenty of grit and determination. 'In any case, it's not as if I'm setting out to argue with anyone,' she insisted. 'I only want to be allowed to get on with my work.'

Accepting tea from her Aunty Rose, Hazel was struck by how like a little bird her grandmother appeared, with her chest puffed out by creamy frills over the grey plumage of her fringed woollen shawl. And Rose in her loose crimson smock was a robin redbreast – hopping quickly from person to person for titbits of information.

Rose, the middle-aged, stay-at-home daughter, had never been expected to marry due to an accident she'd had as a child. This had happened when she'd been out playing with her brother, Cyril, and had fallen backwards from a high wall into a field below. Seven-year-old Cyril had carried her home in tears but at first Ada hadn't noticed the lump on Rose's spine and when she'd finally taken her to see a doctor the damage was done. Nothing could now remedy the resulting twist in her daughter's spine or her stunted growth.

'Let's not talk about Mabel any more,' Rose suggested with a hopeful pat of Hazel's hand. Her own hand seemed big and bony in comparison to her small stature. 'Tell us about you.'

This was more like it. Hazel settled into the familiarity of her surroundings, unchanged since she and her mother had moved in with her aunt and grandmother after Alec Sharpe had been killed in the war. Here was the old pot-bellied coal scuttle next to the range, the brass fender and red and blue rug, and on the walls a sampler worked in tiny cross stitch, next to an amateurish seascape painted by Hazel's long-dead grandfather. 'What would you like to know?'

Rose cocked her head to one side and studied Hazel with twinkling eyes. 'For a start, did you meet any nice young men on your college course – the type you could bring home?'

While Hazel blushed and smiled, Ada stepped

in with a timely reminder. 'For heaven's sake, Rose, since when did men study to be midwives? And even if they did, why would they traipse all the way up north to see the likes of us?'

'Anyhow, I was too busy studying,' Hazel explained. *And too like a fish out of water,* she might have added. She'd arrived in London to find herself the only Yorkshire girl in that year's intake. Her fellow students were from Dublin, London and Bristol and they'd seemed to Hazel a lot more worldly wise and at home in the bewildering maze of city streets surrounding the college. It had taken months for her to find her feet and convince herself that rigorous training in transverse presentations, pre-eclampsia and placenta previa would eventually turn her into a real, hands-on midwife. Meanwhile, she'd found no time for Rose's 'young men'.

'And were you homesick while you were away?' her aunt asked, ever the eager robin tugging for worms.

'I was,' Hazel declared. Much as she'd felt that she didn't belong at home and had dreamed of escape from her humdrum, downtrodden world, leaving Raglan Road had proved to be a wrench. 'I stood at the door of my digs and pestered the postman for letters from Yorkshire every single day, poor chap!'

The answer pleased a beaming Rose. 'You hear that, Mother? Hazel is glad to be back. Now she's ready to strike out and make a great success.'

Ada switched her gaze to two men in overalls who were emptying the ash pit outside the Hollings' house. 'I'm glad to hear it,' she said.

51

Success didn't come easily, Ada knew. Look at Dan for a start. As a doting grandmother she'd held high hopes for her first grandson – a sunny-natured young chap who'd won favour wherever he went. But it turned out he'd done little with his life so far. Truth be told, Dan was on a downward slide and would end up going to the bad if he didn't watch out. Then Eddie; he'd been stuck in a rut at the brass foundry for twelve years, glad to hang onto his job when men were being laid off left, right and centre. As for the girls, it was true Gladys held down an office position and could charm the birds out of the trees but Ada was afraid the girl thought too much about enjoying herself instead of settling down. And Sylvia – well, the less said about her youngest granddaughter's present predicament the better.

Now here was Hazel, back at home after a year of study and expecting everything to fall neatly into place for her. Well, Ada knew that wouldn't happen if the first thing she did was to put Mabel Jackson's nose out of joint.

'I wish you luck, love – you're going to need it,' Ada said, short and to the point as Hazel brought her brief visit to an end. She didn't move from her straight-backed chair and only relented at the last second by turning her head and softening her tone. 'Then again, you've always had something about you – I can't put my finger on what exactly. So maybe it's more than luck that will carry you through.'

On the following Monday Hazel arrived promptly at the imposing entrance to Dr Bell's surgery on

Westgate Road. The practice had been set up fifty years earlier by Dr Moss, then a young and ambitious general practitioner with a special interest in alleviating the painful symptoms of lung disease developed by workers in the Yorkshire woollen mills. He'd chosen a spacious terraced house from which to run his practice – approached by a wide flight of stone steps that led through a porch into a hallway decorated with an elaborate plaster cornice, complete with picture rail and several large oil paintings of Highland cattle and sheep set in mountain scenery.

Making a good first impression is important, Hazel reminded herself as she hesitated outside the panelled outer door. She'd chosen to wear her loose-fitting linen coat with wide lapels over a calf-length blue dress with crisp white collar and cuffs, all topped by her straw hat and finished off with white gloves and shoes.

'Yes?' A woman sat busily typing at a mahogany desk as Hazel opened the inner door and walked into the large reception area.

'I have an appointment to see Dr Bell at twelve,' Hazel began.

'Sit.' Instead of looking up from her typewriter, the woman pointed to a room off to the right – evidently the place where patients waited to be seen.

Hazel realized that the receptionist had made a mistake. 'No, I'm not–'

'Not what?' came the sharp rejoinder as the tap-tap-tapping of the keys continued unabated.

'My name is Hazel Price. I'm a midwife.'

'Why didn't you say so straight away?' The

53

prickly receptionist looked up at last, peering over the rim of her glasses. 'Dr Bell is running late. You're to wait in there.'

This time the direction was to go straight ahead, so Hazel thanked the woman and went into a small room furnished with a plain desk and two chairs, together with a doctor's examination table, weighing machine and folding screen. Dr Bell's framed certificate, not unlike Hazel's own, hung on the pale green wall behind the desk, accompanied by anatomical prints of various kinds. Hazel filled the time by poring over a detailed drawing of a uterus and female reproductive organs and was so absorbed in the study of Latin names that she didn't hear anyone come in until the door clicked shut and she turned to find a man of around forty standing with a smile on his face and his hand outstretched.

'Hello, I'm David Bell. You must be Hazel Price,' he began without ceremony.

'That's me.' The new doctor's handshake was predictably swift and firm, she noticed, though his appearance didn't match the picture she'd built up during their brief conversation on the telephone. Back then she'd imagined someone tall and dark with a confident manner and penetrating gaze, not the shortish, slight figure with a pale complexion, steel-rimmed glasses and receding mid-brown hair who greeted her now. 'Thank you for agreeing to see me,' she added.

'No, it's I who has to thank you for getting in touch,' he countered, gesturing for Hazel to take a seat. His voice was courteous, with a strong north-eastern burr, and he displayed spotlessly manicured nails as he spread his freckled hands palms down on the desk. 'As you know, I took over Dr Moss's practice in April this year so I'm still finding my way.'

She nodded eagerly. 'That makes two of us.'

David Bell studied Hazel closely and seemed to approve of what he saw. 'You look younger than I expected. However, from what you told me on the telephone, your qualification will stand you in good stead. In fact, I'm hoping that you can be of as much help to me as I am to you. Shall I go first?'

Hazel nodded again, aware that she'd taken to the doctor straight away. He was less stuffy than old Dr Moss and not at all condescending.

'Well then – speaking frankly, I'm interested to know which parts of your recent training you found most valuable and whether or not you'd be prepared to share some of that knowledge with me.'

Hazel felt wrong-footed by the directness of the appeal. 'Of course,' she said falteringly.

'Don't look so surprised. It's fifteen years since I qualified as a GP and I'm the first to admit that obstetrics has moved on a lot since then.'

'Yes, thank heavens,' Hazel agreed. She knew from her studies that mortality rates even in some of the worst areas had finally started to shift from the fifty per cent that they had reached at their mid-nineteenth-century peak – mostly from eclampsia, haemorrhage or mal-presentation.

Dr Bell drummed his fingers gently on the desk as he continued. 'It's hard to believe, but when I first started out, hospitals weren't even using rubber gloves and face masks to prevent infection. And checking urine for the first signs of pre-eclampsia was just being introduced.'

'It's routine now – but only if you can get expectant mothers to attend a clinic,' Hazel assured him.

'And that's a big "if",' he agreed. 'In fact, it's precisely the problem I want to discuss with you. I recently set up a Tuesday-afternoon antenatal clinic here at the surgery, but patients seem reluctant to attend. Most of the time I still have to go out to them and it's not everyone who can afford to pay for a doctor's visit, even with their thirty shillings maternity benefit from the government, which they don't all get, of course.'

As he warmed to his subject, Hazel had time to form a further opinion of the man. He was direct to the point of bluntness, she decided, and seemed committed to improving services for his patients. Better still, for the first time since she'd left college she felt hopeful that here was someone who would value her skills. 'I'll do my best to persuade the women in my neck of the woods to attend the clinic,' she promised. 'It helps that it's not at the lying-in infirmary for a start.'

'Yes; why do they hate the idea of that place so much?'

'I can easily explain that,' Hazel assured him. 'It's housed in the old workhouse building. Everyone, myself included, remembers tales of families shipped off there by the Board of Guardians. I was at school with the Tyler twins. The father had abandoned them so they went to the workhouse with their mother, who was set to work in the laundry. Henry Tyler got TB and died. It was diphtheria that did for Albert. They were both gone within the year.'

'I see – the place is full of ghosts.'

This was as good a way of putting it as any, Hazel thought, though it went against the practical, professional tone Dr Bell had used so far.

He gave the desk a smart tap then stood up to take a sheet of paper from one of the drawers in his filing cabinet. 'This is a carbon copy of my list of pregnant mothers who are registered with this practice – a total of fifty-three in all,' he told her. 'There's a tick beside the names of those I've managed to visit in person, which as you can see is around one in three. Can I suggest that you take this and call on the remaining two-thirds with the intention of inviting them to clinic?'

Hazel took a deep breath. She too stood up from her chair. 'That's an excellent idea,' she agreed, preparing to take the paper from him.

Dr Bell held it close to his tweed-suited chest. 'The important thing is to tell them that the clinic is free – they don't have to pay me any money to attend. The list covers the area between Westgate Road and Canal Road, including Ghyll Road, Chapel Street, Raglan Road and Albion Lane, plus all the courtyards of back-to-back houses in between.'

'Don't worry; I know the streets around here like the back of my hand.' Her eyes were fixed on the sheet of paper. This was better than anything she could have dreamed of – a ready-made list of women who might soon need her professional help.

'However, before you agree to follow up the names on this list, I'd like your assurance on one thing.'

'Anything!'

'This is it. I need to be sure that you won't simply poach my patients away from me in your capacity as a self-employed midwife. Your task is to get them here to Westgate Road for regular antenatal check-ups.'

'Oh, I see. Yes – I understand,' Hazel said, her forehead creasing into a frown as she decided to be as forthright as the doctor had been. 'But then, what's in it for me? I mean, I'm all in favour of women using the service you offer – that goes without saying–'

'Quite,' Dr Bell interrupted. 'And you're canny enough to tackle the financial side of things with me – which is what I suppose you're leading up to?'

Hazel met his eye and managed not to blush. 'It is,' she agreed.

'Then this is what I propose. For every new woman who attends clinic because of your efforts, I will pay you the princely sum of one shilling.'

Hazel grimaced at the small amount.

'And...' He raised a forefinger for her to hear him out. 'If, in the event of that patient subsequently choosing a home delivery that I'm not free to attend because of other commitments, then you, Hazel Price, will step in as a qualified midwife to answer all their needs. You will charge them a fee to be settled between you – I will have no involvement in that arrangement. Is that clear?'

'Completely. That seems fair.'

'Good. Then we're both happy.' Dr Bell passed the list to Hazel before glancing at his wristwatch and looking up again with a serious expression. 'I like both you and your qualifications, young lady, and I can see that this cooperation between us will work well. Nevertheless, I ought to issue a word of warning.'

Hazel frowned, not knowing what to expect – only that it probably wouldn't be good.

'I don't need to remind you that times are hard – I know, I know, it's what everyone says and you smart young people are sick of hearing it. You want to make your way in the world regardless.'

'No – I do know what it's like,' Hazel insisted. She thought back to Betty Hollings' bare, cold bedroom and the threadbare, dirty towel hanging from its rack.

'It was bad enough back in my home town of Durham when the coal mines shut down. But here, men and women are being laid off from the mills and foundries in their droves without the hope of any other job to go to. I've seen some bad cases of malnutrition in my surgeries, and if a family can't afford to put basic food on the table, what hope is there of paying for a doctor or a midwife to attend a birth?'

'And does that mean we give up on them? What do we do – turn our backs and walk away for the sake of a few shillings? Is that how you think we should act?'

Hazel's spirited reply had brought colour to her cheeks. He liked her idealism and the energy in her voice. 'Obviously not,' he argued. 'And I

59

don't want to dent your enthusiasm, believe me. But be aware that your bills may not always be paid – either on time or in full. And try not to blame or look down on those who can't pay their debts. Remember, if it's uncomfortable for you to be in that situation, it's likely to be a hundred times worse for them.'

In the ensuing pause, Hazel took a deep breath to regain control of her feelings but said nothing.

'And meanwhile,' Dr Bell said with another glance at his watch, 'perhaps you should think of a way to supplement your income.'

'Another job, you mean?' The casual suggestion appeared like a dark cloud on Hazel's horizon.

'Part time,' he explained as he held open the door. Hazel saw the narrow back and crimped dark hair of the receptionist and heard the clickety-clack of her typewriter then the ping of a tiny bell as she pushed a lever and the carriage shot sideways.

'You could try office work to fill in the gaps between delivering babies,' Dr Bell suggested helpfully as Hazel shook his hand and prepared to leave. 'There are many worse fates than typing letters and licking envelopes – ask Eleanor on your way out. She overhears stories from patients in the waiting room that would make your hair stand on end.'

CHAPTER FOUR

'Anyone would think I was persuading them to have all their teeth pulled out instead of inviting them to a free clinic,' Hazel said with a sigh as she shook raindrops from her umbrella then sat down opposite Gladys in Nixon's café on the corner of Ghyll Road and Albion Lane. As the only customers in the small tearoom late on Tuesday afternoon, they'd been free to choose a table by the window, looking out at the shuffling throng of mill workers making their way home, the men with their caps pulled down over their foreheads, the women with grey shawls around their heads and shoulders.

'What did you expect?' Gladys had readily agreed to meet up with her cousin straight after work. 'People don't like opening their doors to strangers, especially busybodies who try to boss them around.'

'I'm not a busybody,' Hazel objected. She was wet through and her feet ached from a full day of walking the streets and rapping on the doors of more than thirty houses on her new list. Sometimes the pregnant women who answered her knock would listen politely and promise to make a note of the time for Dr Bell's clinic, but more often they would open their door a fraction, take a quick, suspicious look at Hazel then close it again before she'd reached the end of her first sentence.

'But you are telling them what to do,' Gladys insisted. '"Go to a clinic, get yourself weighed, have your blood pressure taken..."'

'Which is common sense.'

'*We* know that, but they don't. Remember, women around here have been having babies without any of that rigmarole since the year dot.'

'And dying in the process,' Hazel pointed out crossly. 'And having babies that have been starved of oxygen because–'

'Don't!' Gladys put her hands over her ears. 'I hear enough of that sort of thing at work to last a lifetime, ta very much.' For the past year and a half Gladys had worked at the King Edward's Hospital, making appointments for children suspected of having poliomyelitis to be seen by a specialist. Though not often in contact with the patients themselves, she would overhear gloomy discussions about callipers and wheelchairs and would observe through the office window tearful parents receiving the diagnosis for the first time. 'It's enough to break your heart,' she confessed now.

'I'm sorry.' Hazel decided to change the subject as the waitress brought them a pot of tea and a scone apiece. 'Anyhow, on a more cheery note, what will you wear to Sylvia's wedding on Saturday?'

Gladys raised her eyebrows. 'It'll have to be my cream dress with the little rosebud design – if we get that far.'

'What do you mean "if"? Sylvia's not likely to back out at the last minute, is she?'

'Who knows what Sylvia's likely to do? Let's say this – I wouldn't put it past her to leave poor

62

Norman standing at the altar.'

'Imagine that.' Hazel sipped her tea. 'Of course, I realize it's all happened in a rush, but surely she loves him? She wouldn't let him down.'

Gladys shrugged then raised a finger to her lips. 'Speak of the devil,' she warned as Sylvia entered the café in a gust of wind and a flurry of raindrops.

'Look at you two sly things, sloping in here for a treat behind my back!' she proclaimed before ordering an extra cup and a scone from the waitress. 'Hazel, you've gone red. What are you up to?'

'Nothing. As a matter of fact, Gladys and I were just talking about your wedding.'

'Oh, I know – I have a thousand things still to do.' After an awkward pause, Sylvia took up the reins and galloped ahead. 'Mum says Marjorie Sykes has promised to bake and ice a cake in time for Saturday – only a single tier but never mind. The church is booked for two o'clock. We're having the reception afterwards in a back room at the Working Men's Club on Westgate Road – they're the only ones who could fit us in at such short notice. Norman is still looking for somewhere for us to live. Let's hope we won't have to start married life in a tin shack on Overcliffe Common allotments, eh, Gladys?'

'Whoa!' Hazel was relieved to find that her youngest cousin had every intention of going ahead with the wedding despite Gladys's doubts. Though windswept and bedraggled, she marvelled at how Sylvia still managed to look strikingly pretty, her large brown eyes alive with excitement and her cheeks aglow. 'You've forgotten to tell me the most important thing – what are you going to wear?'

'Oh Lord!' Leaving her scone untouched, Sylvia jumped up from her chair. 'What time is it?'

'Almost half five,' Gladys told her. 'Why?'

'I have to get to Chapel Street before Jubilee shuts for the day. Muriel Beanland has promised to lend me the wedding dress they have on display in their shop window. You know, the one in slipper satin with georgette sleeves.'

'Lucky you. You'd better run.' The words were scarcely out of Gladys's mouth before Sylvia fled from the café. 'You see what I mean,' she told Hazel darkly. 'It'll be a miracle if we get as far as Saturday without Sylvia going pop.'

'She's not a balloon,' Hazel laughed. But she did see the point of Gladys's remark – Sylvia's excitement appeared to have reached fever pitch, yet it seemed to have an artificial, worked-up quality to it. But maybe this was normal with brides-to-be. 'What does either of us know about pre-wedding jitters?' she ventured.

'Nothing, thank heavens,' Gladys acknowledged with a wink. 'We're both single and fancy free and planning to stay that way – unless you let me down by suddenly falling for this new man at Dr Moss's surgery.'

'Dr Bell? Fat chance of that!' Hazel declared. 'Oh, I like him, don't get me wrong...'

'But?'

'He's forty years old if he's a day, and wearing a wedding ring.'

'Hmm. Forty would bother me but the wedding

ring might not.'

'Gladys, you wouldn't!' Hazel's scandalized expression failed to silence her cousin.

'Why not? All the doctors at the hospital are married men but that doesn't stop them.'

'You ... you're not!' Hazel gasped.

Gladys laughed. 'No, as a matter of fact I'm not. I'm too busy going to evening classes and doing keep-fit twice a week to bother with them. Anyway, let's get back to the subject of you and Dr Bell.'

'As I said, I like him. We got on like a house on fire until...'

'Until what?' Gladys prompted again. 'Why are you frowning?'

'Well, he ended by telling me I should try for a part-time job in an office while I waited for mid-wifery work to come my way.'

'And?'

'And I don't want to do that.' Hazel had stayed awake the previous night thinking about Dr Bell's unwelcome suggestion. 'It's not what I'm trained to do. And anyway, that's a typical man for you.'

'What is?'

'To recommend office work. Don't you think it was big-headed of him to suppose that it's all right for a girl like me to type letters and lick envelopes?' Realizing that she'd put her foot in it, Hazel hurriedly backtracked. 'Not that it isn't all right. Working in an office is a big step up from mill work and suchlike.'

'Stop before you dig yourself a deeper hole.' Gladys rattled her teacup down into its saucer.

65

'What you mean is – it's good enough for someone like me without any qualifications, but not for you. You deserve better.'

'I'm not saying that.'

'Yes you are, and you might be right. Who knows? But tell me, oh cousin dear, how many women did you enrol for the clinic today?'

Hazel faltered over her reply. 'Three, I hope. Two said they would definitely come next week. One said she would if she could.'

Gladys's steady stare didn't waver. 'Out of how many?'

'Thirty-four. I know it's not a lot but it's better than nothing.'

'But will it keep the wolf from your door?' Gladys was determined not to let Hazel off the hook. 'And if not, mightn't you have to take up Dr Bell's suggestion?'

'I might,' Hazel conceded as the dark cloud on her horizon grew bigger. This was not what she'd planned when she'd come back to Raglan Road, brim-full of hope and ambition. Then, the way ahead had looked bright and sunny. But today she'd experienced more of the squally showers of disappointment and the way things were going, it was likely that heavy rain would soon be forecast. 'Let's face it, unless I line up more work over the next few days, I might jolly well have to.'

'Try the houses further along Overcliffe Road.'

'There's Margie Briggs-as-was on Ada Street – she's expecting her second.'

'And what about her sister, Evie? Didn't she get wed to Stan Tankard earlier this year?'

Helpful suggestions fell thick and fast from Ada and Rose's lips when Hazel called into their house on Nelson Yard.

On the Wednesday and again on the Thursday morning she followed them up, only to be disappointed time and again.

'Sorry, we've already got Mabel Jackson lined up for the lying-in.'

'No thank you. We'll stick with what we know.' Hazel's knock always drew the same response – courteous on the whole but nevertheless a firm 'no'.

Midway through the Thursday afternoon, Hazel steeled herself to call in at Dr Bell's surgery to report her lack of progress so far. The doctor was out on a house call and it was Eleanor who'd been left to hold the fort.

'No need to look so down in the mouth about it.' The receptionist's reprimand brought Hazel up short. 'Dr Bell never expected to have women falling over each other to attend the clinic.'

'They might at least give me a chance to explain the benefits,' Hazel grumbled.

Eleanor gave Hazel a long, hard stare over the rim of her glasses. 'Don't talk – just do,' was her curt advice.

'Do what, for heaven's sake?' Hazel was on the verge of tears, which she tried to hide by taking out her handkerchief and roughly blowing her nose. Once more she felt cowed by her surroundings – the high ceiling with plaster cornices depicting the Yorkshire rose and garlands of laurel leaves, the red and green stained glass of the porch door. 'I've been to every address on Dr Bell's list and

67

others besides.'

'Then think of something else besides knocking on doors. Have you tried making a poster and putting it on display in the town library for a start? Or in chemist's shops, or on parents' noticeboards in the local schools?'

'I haven't,' Hazel admitted, giving herself a shake. 'It's a good idea, though.'

'Then do it,' Eleanor told her. 'And look sharp about it. It'll be Tuesday again before you know it.'

After her talk with Dr Bell's receptionist, Hazel went home with renewed determination. That evening she enlisted her father's help with the posters. While her mother sat quietly knitting in the last of the daylight, the two of them cleared the kitchen table and got out a ruler, an alphabet stencil and some coloured crayons that Robert found tucked away at the back of the cutlery drawer. Then they measured out lengths of plain wallpaper and began the task of writing in bold letters some facts and figures about the new antenatal clinic on Westgate Road.

'I'll be the first to admit these posters are not going to look perfect,' Hazel conceded, tucking a red pencil behind her ear and standing back to assess their first amateurish effort. 'We could do with something extra to draw people's attention – photographs of nice, chubby babies for example?'

'Go upstairs and look on the tallboy for my copy of *Woman's Weekly*,' Jinny suggested from her corner of the room. 'There's a section in there showing knitting patterns for baby bonnets and bootees.'

Robert nodded at his wife and smiled as Hazel ran upstairs to fetch it. Then he fetched a pot of glue from a shelf in the cellar.

'Here – give me that.' Jinny put aside her knitting and took the magazine from Hazel as soon as she returned. 'You carry on stencilling your letters while I cut out some baby pictures for your dad to stick along the top. That way we'll get on twice as fast.'

Small favours such as this from Jinny meant a lot to Hazel. It had taken her a long time and much heartache to understand that her mother made few shows of affection and that her reserve was a deeply ingrained part of her character.

'Don't worry – it's not your fault,' Hazel's Aunty Rose would console her when Hazel was a small child going to Rose for comfort after Jinny had failed to praise her for coming home with a good end-of-year school report. 'Your mum is happy you're doing well even if she doesn't say so.' She'd always been the same, Rose said– 'Even before she lost Alec to the war and she had to soldier on alone.'

'The Lord knows how Robert managed to break down Jinny's defences,' Hazel's grandmother had remarked to Rose in an unguarded moment shortly before Jinny's second marriage. Hazel was five and Ada might have assumed she was too young to pick up on what was being said.

But Robert had proposed and Jinny had said yes as long as he promised to be kind to Hazel and treat her as his daughter.

'Which goes to prove she does care about the

child,' Ada had observed.

Robert had been as good as his word. Poorly schooled himself, he'd made up for his lack of education by bringing books into the house. In addition, when Saturday came around, he would take Hazel to the town library to borrow the latest *Just William* adventure or a much-thumbed copy of Johanna Spyri's *Heidi*.

On Sundays he would take her out on rambles and bike rides across Overcliffe Common to the moors beyond, leaving behind the sooty chimneys and high factory walls to explore hidden green glens that smelt of wet ferns and peat. They would return home to a dinner of roast beef served by Jinny in her best dress, her hair in soft waves, face freshly made up. To Hazel she looked like a beautiful, sad princess.

So her mother's offer to cut out baby pictures gave Hazel a warm glow of gratitude the next morning as she set out on her mission to display the posters in the town library, then closer to home in the chemist's shop window on Canal Road.

Yes, there was room for one on the General Information noticeboard, the lady in the Lending section told her. A clinic aimed at improving the health and well-being of pregnant women stood a good chance of success so long as it was free. The librarian would put Hazel's poster in a prominent position and recommend it whenever the opportunity arose.

From the library in the centre of town, Hazel took the tram out along Canal Road and got off at the stop opposite the streamlined, shiny entrance to the Victory Picture House. Carefully threading her way through the rumbling traffic, she crossed the street and headed for Barlow's chemist's, rehearsing her speech as she went: *Good morning. My name is Hazel Price. Is it possible to speak to the manager, please?*

'Hazel!' The dark-haired girl who emerged from behind a glass partition recognized her before she'd had the chance to open her mouth. 'It is you, isn't it?'

'Glenda?' For a moment Hazel was taken aback.

'Yes – Glenda Morris. Well, look what the cat dragged in!'

The two girls had been at school together, though Hazel had been a few years ahead. She remembered the younger girl mainly from sports days, when she regularly won prizes for the hundred-yard dash and the high jump. Now she was looking grown up and smart in a crisp white uniform, working as a dispenser, making up pills and potions to prescription. 'It's nice to see you too, Glenda,' Hazel joked, aware that she was under scrutiny.

'What are you doing here? I heard you'd left us for the bright lights.'

'I did, and now I'm back and asking for a favour.' Hazel took a rolled-up poster from her bag and put it on the glass counter.

Determined not to be impressed, Glenda took her time to unfurl it and lay it flat.

'Can I have a word with your manager?' Hazel asked. 'I'd like him to display this notice in your window.'

'"He" is a "she".' Glenda's fingernails were

71

painted a shade of coral pink that matched the colour of the blouse she wore beneath the white coat. Her thick hair was cut stylishly short and straight. 'Mrs Barlow has gone out. She left me in charge.'

Concentrating on her task, Hazel ignored the sound of a car pulling up outside the shop followed by the tinkle of the doorbell behind her. 'Well, how about it? Will you put the poster in your window?'

Glenda glanced up at her new customer, letting the paper roll back into a tight scroll. 'Yes, sir, how can I help you?' she asked in a pleasant tone.

Hazel turned to see that it was John Moxon. His dark hair had been ruffled by the wind and he'd lost his neat side parting. He was dressed in dark blue overalls, looking ill at ease amongst the feminine displays of perfume, talcum powder and shampoo, but he recognized Hazel and managed a polite hello.

'I've been sent to buy a pick-me-up for my wife,' he explained to Glenda. 'She's in the family way. Is there anything you can recommend?'

While Glenda turned to the shelves laden with proprietary medicines, Hazel gave John a pleasant smile. 'Don't worry – these last few weeks are often the worst.'

'So they say. But Myra's mother called in on her an hour ago and found her passed out on the floor. She sent a neighbour to fetch me home from work.'

'Myra fainted?' Hazel couldn't disguise her concern. 'Shouldn't you call the doctor and make sure everything is as it should be?'

John shook his head. 'Myra doesn't want a fuss. According to her mother, it's normal for her to be feeling a bit light-headed at this stage. She says a tonic should do the trick.'

'Something like this?' Glenda showed him a bottle containing a thick, clear syrup. 'It's cod liver oil with extra Vitamins A and D. My sister swore by it when she was expecting.'

John took the bottle and read the label. 'We'll give it a go,' he decided, feeling in his pocket for the money.

'Calling the doctor doesn't mean she's making a fuss,' Hazel persisted, picking up an edge of worry beneath John's casual manner. 'It might be wise for Myra to have a proper check-up, you know.'

The father-to-be bit his bottom lip. 'Ta, but Myra's the type who runs a mile if you so much as mention having her temperature taken. You don't know what she's like.'

'But I do,' Hazel reminded him. 'We've lived on the same street for years and we went to the same school.'

'That's a point.' John took the wrapped bottle of cod liver oil from Glenda then thought a while.

Hazel was the first to break the silence. 'I know it's a tough nut to crack. No one can force some-one to see a doctor if they don't want to. And the Penningtons are like a lot of people around here – they've never been ones to make a fuss, as you put it. But this is Myra's first pregnancy. She really ought to have proper advice in the build-up to the baby being born.'

John took her counsel with a grateful smile.

'This might seem a bit of a cheek after what I told you at the jazz club last Friday,' he ventured, 'but would you mind dropping in to say hello to Myra?'

'Of course I wouldn't mind,' Hazel replied. 'We don't have to mention her fainting. I could say I'd popped in for a good old chinwag for old times' sake.'

'But you'll take a look at her on the quiet?'

'Yes, by all means. When would you like me to visit?'

'Now, if you've got time,' John decided on the spur of the moment. 'My car's outside. Why don't I give you a lift?'

Hazel turned quickly to Glenda. 'Can I leave this with you?' she asked.

'Yes, give it here,' the dispenser agreed.

No sooner said than done, Hazel and John left Barlow's together. He strode ahead and held open the passenger door of his gleaming grey Ford then quickly took up position behind the steering wheel. He turned the key in the ignition and signalled to join the stream of lorries, buses and carts.

'This is nice.' Hazel admired the dials on the walnut dashboard and the soft comfort of the black leather seat.

'It's a Model A,' he told her with pride. 'Ford stopped making them a few years back but I hung onto this one and try to keep it in good nick.'

'Very nice,' she said again. She turned to look at the back seat and noticed two cricket bats, several red leather balls and some wicketkeeper's pads.

74

'I coach the youngsters at Headingley,' John explained before she had the chance to ask. Spotting a gap in the traffic, he lurched away from the kerb, narrowly missing a delivery boy on his bike.

'Bloody hell,' the lad yelled, 'watch where you're going!'

'You've got to have eyes in the back of your head these days,' John muttered, lifting one hand from the steering wheel then running it through his dark hair. Hazel noticed that there was black dirt under his fingernails and oil smears on the backs of his hands as well as down the front of his blue overalls. She realized again how preoccupied he was when he forgot to signal left onto Ghyll Road, this time incurring the wrath of Jim Napier driving his horse and cart loaded with scrap metal.

John gritted his teeth and drove on. 'Remember, don't let on to Myra that I've asked you to come,' he told Hazel as they careered up a steep hill then took another left turn onto Raglan Road.

'Cross my heart,' Hazel promised, gripping the door handle as the car swung round the corner then came to a sudden halt at the bottom of the street.

'I'll drop you off here,' John decided. 'I'll go on ahead.'

Relieved to get out of the car in one piece, Hazel agreed. *This is a lot of trouble to go to,* she thought, *just so Myra Moxon doesn't suspect that we've cooked up this visit between us.* But then again, who knew what games were played by husbands and wives behind closed doors, especially when the woman was eight months' pregnant and the man befuddled by the best-left-alone business of childbirth?

CHAPTER FIVE

Hazel walked steadily past her own house and on up the hill to reach number 80 just as John Moxon hurried back out, banging the door after him. He took the steps two at a time, pausing only to nod at her and mutter a quiet thank-you before jumping into his car.

The door opened again as Hazel prepared to go up the steps and she found herself face to face with Myra's mother, Dorothy Pennington.

'Now then, John – what's the big rush?' Dorothy called fractiously after her son-in-law.

'Sorry, Mum – my boss will tan my hide if I don't get back to the garage,' he called over the throttle of the car's engine. 'You know Baxter – he'll dock an hour off my pay as soon as look at me.'

The car was gone in a cloud of exhaust fumes and Dorothy was left in the doorway holding the bottle of cod liver oil that John had bought. She was a small woman with a loud voice and dyed red hair that framed a long, pinched face. 'If he thinks I can find time to stay here and mollycoddle Myra all afternoon, he's got another think coming,' she grumbled. 'What are you up to anyway?' she thought to ask Hazel, who hovered uncertainly at the bottom of the steps.

'I was passing so thought I'd knock on Myra's door for a good gossip,' she fibbed. 'Why? Is something the matter?'

Dorothy jerked her head backwards then rolled her eyes. 'She's a bit under the weather, that's all. But you can still go in if you like. Myra!' Dorothy called without more ado. 'Hazel Price is here. Go on in and give her a spoonful of this to buck her up,' she muttered to Hazel, handing her the cod liver oil as they passed on the steps.

'Myra?' Hazel went into the kitchen where the embers of a fire glowed in the hearth and flimsy under-things had been hung to dry on a wooden clothes-horse nearby. Silk stockings were draped over the back of a chair and a pair of women's shoes had been kicked off onto the worn hearth-rug.

'Here I am; over here.'

'Where? Oh, there you are.' Hazel stepped past the drying laundry to find Myra lying on a brown moquette sofa, one hand resting on her pregnant belly, her head propped on two green cushions. She seemed listless and made no attempt to sit up and greet her visitor. Instead, she turned her head away from Hazel and immediately started to sob.

'There, there,' Hazel soothed as she pulled up a chair. 'There's no need to talk if you don't want to. Why not have a good cry and let it all out?'

'What's up with me?' Myra whimpered. 'I try not to let things get me down, but I can't help it.'

'There, there,' Hazel murmured again. Her gaze flicked around the room, from the iron resting in

77

the hearth to some crumpled shirts on the table and on to a man's jacket and cap hanging on a hook beside the front door. It came to rest on the pitiful sight of her old friend mopping her puffy eyes with a sodden handkerchief.

In fact, Myra was scarcely recognizable as the vivacious girl Hazel knew from a year earlier. Then she'd been a real beauty, her startling red hair and pale complexion drawing attention wherever she went. Now the curly mane was unwashed and flat, the green eyes dull. More to the point, as far as Hazel was concerned, Myra's ankles and fingers were badly swollen.

That decided it. Having read the textbook theory that the innocuous-looking cod liver oil could worsen hypertension in pregnant women, Hazel hid the bottle in her bag. 'I'm here to cheer you up,' she said with a bright smile. 'Dry your eyes while I make us a nice cup of tea. Which cups shall we use? Where do you keep your milk?'

As Hazel chatted, Myra rallied. 'I'm a nuisance, aren't I? And I must look a right sight,' she said as she took the tea. Her voice was light, the tone pleading.

'Not at all,' Hazel said, like a mother soothing a child.

'Did you know Mum found me spark-out on the hearthrug? It turns out it was nothing to worry about, though.' Wincing, Myra passed both palms over her stomach then let out a groan. 'There I go again,' she sighed. 'I'm such a cry-baby.'

'No, you're not,' Hazel assured her, her worries increasing the more closely she observed the pitted appearance of Myra's swollen limbs. 'You must be due any time now. You're bound to have aches and pains.'

Myra smiled weakly. 'I've got a blinding headache so I definitely won't be burning the candle at both ends like we did in the good old days, worse luck. You remember that, Hazel?'

'How could I forget?'

'That's where I met John – at the Assembly Rooms where we all used to go. He turned up there one night with your cousin Dan.' A dreamy look came into Myra's eyes as she remembered the moment.

'Your eyes met across the dance floor?'

'It was love at first sight,' Myra said fondly. 'They say it doesn't happen in real life, but it did with me. We danced the night away and I didn't have eyes for anyone else. Two months later we were married. That says it all, doesn't it?'

'You're lucky,' Hazel admitted.

'Don't I know it? John was a good catch, even if I say so myself.' Colour came back into Myra's cheeks but then a frown appeared. 'Too good for the likes of me, a lot of people said.'

'Hmm – they were jealous, I bet,' Hazel said quickly, as more tears appeared in Myra's eyes.

'Honestly?' The childlike appeal was genuine and it was swiftly followed by another whispered confession. 'Don't tell anyone, Hazel, but I'm not a very good wife. Look around you. I can't remember the last time I dusted or polished.'

'You mustn't expect to – not in your condition.'

'It's too much for me – all the mending and ironing.'

'Of course it is.' Hazel noticed that the flush on

Myra's cheeks had intensified into two hectic spots. Fresh tears began to trickle down her cheeks towards the corners of her mouth.

'And how will I ever cope with a baby, that's what I'd like to know! How will I feed him or keep him clean or stop him from crying when I'm in such a state?'

'You will. Mothers do.' Hazel took Myra's hand and squeezed it, then deliberately broke the promise she'd made to John. 'Listen to me, Myra. I know you don't like to make a fuss, but I really think it would be better if you let Dr Bell take a quick look at you.'

Myra pulled her hand away. 'No,' she said weakly. 'Anyway, what for?'

Not wanting to alarm her, Hazel prevaricated. 'I'm only saying, where would be the harm? Let the doctor come to the house and give you the all-clear.'

'No.' Myra's answer was louder and more insistent than before. 'I've got this far without him, haven't I?'

'Well then, come to the clinic on Tuesday.' Hazel suggested what she hoped might be an acceptable alternative. 'Get John to take an hour off work and bring you along in that smart car of his.'

The frown didn't clear from Myra's face as she looked at Hazel with suspicious eyes. 'What kind of clinic?'

'It's an antenatal clinic where mothers get weighed and have their blood pressure taken – that kind of thing. It's nothing to be worried about.'

'When do you say it is?'

'Tuesday at half past two. Let me add you to

the list, then you can come and give it a try,' Hazel pleaded.

Slowly Myra agreed to consider it. 'I'll have to see what Mum has to say first, though.'

'Champion – you do that.' Pleased that they were inching forward at last but still deeply concerned, Hazel took the teacups to the sink. 'Talk to John, too.'

'I will. But don't put my name down just yet,' Myra objected. 'There's Mabel to consider as well, don't forget. The last thing I want to do is step on her toes.'

'The lilac or the royal blue?'

Knowing that she'd done all she could at Myra and John Moxon's house, Hazel had gone home and turned her attention to Sylvia's wedding the following day. She couldn't decide what to wear and flitted between two choices.

Now she held up the two dresses for her mother's inspection. The lilac dress had short sleeves and a flared, panelled skirt with a row of pearl buttons down the front; the blue one was more tailored, with a pleated skirt and contrasting white piping around the collar and cuffs.

'The blue.' Jinny looked up from her task of ironing Robert's best shirt. 'It picks up the colour of your eyes.'

'What about a hat to go with it? I couldn't borrow that smart little Empress Eugenie you bought from the market, could I?'

'Help yourself.' Jinny had already decided on her own outfit – a bolero jacket and calf-length dress in green and pink floral print that would go best with her summery straw hat. 'You're leaving it a bit last minute, aren't you?'

'I'm nothing compared to Sylvia.' Hazel went up to the mirror to study her reflection. The blue dress definitely suited her and her mother's hat would add an up-to-date touch. 'Gladys says the wedding dress from Jubilee needs alterations – it was too big across the bust for Sylvia, apparently. Muriel has volunteered to stay behind and do it for her tonight, after the shop closes.'

'It's decent of Muriel to lend it in the first place.' Jinny pressed hard with the iron, making sure to get all the creases out of the shirt front.

Hazel agreed. 'Sylvia will look lovely in it so I suppose Muriel will think of it as a good advertisement for Jubilee. It could bring in extra business.'

'Anyway, let's hope Sylvia realizes how lucky she is.' Slam went the iron on the starched cotton as Jinny began on the shirt tail. 'Talking of luck, your dad went out to fetch you something that might come in handy.'

'For the wedding?'

'No, not for the wedding, silly. He heard of a Raleigh bike going spare from the office manageress at Oldroyd's. She said she only wanted a couple of bob for it so your dad leaped at the chance. That's where he is now – collecting it from her house on Ada Street.'

'A bike for me?' Hazel waltzed her blue dress around the kitchen table, her face wreathed in smiles. She pictured herself, once she'd got established, loading her midwife's bag into the front basket and cycling out on her rounds.

'It's an old one, mind you,' Jinny cautioned. 'But your dad will do it up and make sure everything is in working order.'

Hazel was still quietly celebrating the prospect of owning a bike to help her in her work when Gladys and tomorrow's bride-to-be opened the door and blew into the kitchen like a whirlwind.

'Calamity – my dress will never be ready in time!' Sylvia wailed as she slumped into the fireside chair.

'Muriel says it will,' Gladys countered steadily. 'We've just come from a fitting. She's taking in the bust-darts as we speak.'

'It won't. I know it won't!'

Gladys winked at Jinny and Hazel behind Sylvia's back. 'Mum says you can borrow hers if you're stuck. She's kept it wrapped in tissue paper in a drawer all these years.'

'Ugh – it'll stink of moth balls. Anyway, I wouldn't be seen dead in that old thing! *And* it turns out that the satin shoes I bought from the market are too small. I'll be hobbling up the aisle at this rate.'

Rolling her eyes, Gladys worked towards a solution. 'What size are your feet, Hazel?'

'I'm a size five – why? Oh, I see what you're getting at – Sylvia can wear my white shoes and they can be the "something borrowed".'

'Except that I'm a size six.' Sylvia thumped the arms of the chair in frustration. 'Drat!'

'So, no dress and no shoes.' Jinny didn't hide her amusement. 'At this rate you'll be walking down the aisle in your birthday suit.'

'It's not funny, Aunty Jinny!' Sylvia sprang up

83

from the chair then stormed around the kitchen. 'All eyes will be on me and I'll have sewing pins sticking in me everywhere and blisters on my feet. I'll look a right sight.'

'You'll look lovely, love – you always do,' Jinny assured her, ignoring Gladys's sceptical look. 'Forget about the shoes and the dress for a moment; I have something nice for you if you wait here a second.'

While Jinny went upstairs, Gladys and Hazel tried to calm Sylvia down by talking of more practical things.

'Have you found a house yet?' Hazel asked.

'Number 15 Nelson Yard is empty,' Sylvia replied airily. 'Dad went to see the landlord about renting it to us earlier today.'

'Without telling poor Norman,' Gladys added quietly.

'And what about furniture?'

'Not a stick!' Sylvia said with a high laugh. 'It's ridiculous, isn't it?'

'Norman doesn't know that either,' Gladys pointed out. 'He's probably thinking the Drummonds can magic a bed and table and chairs out of the air. The poor lad doesn't have a clue.'

'Anyway, I don't care about what happens after we say "I do",' Sylvia declared, defiant sparks flying between her and her sister.

'Just get her to the church on time,' Gladys said sardonically.

'Here,' Jinny said as she came back downstairs with a small box in her hand. It was covered in red leather, lined with cream satin and contained a delicate silver brooch in the shape of a swallow in flight. The marcasite wings glittered and a sparkling blue stone formed the bird's eye. 'I'll lend this to you for your wedding if you like.'

'Something borrowed.' Sylvia seized the brooch with delight. 'Ta, Aunty Jinny, it's lovely.'

'Look after it, mind you,' Jinny said quietly.

'I will, I promise. Now, come on, Gladys, we have to pick up my flowers from Blamey's – they're staying open specially for us.'

'Yes, sir!' Gladys sprang to attention and gave a mock salute. 'Quick march!' she barked as she led the way to the door and Sylvia followed. 'See you girls tomorrow.'

'Ding-dong, the bells are going to chime,' Hazel said in the silence that followed their departure. 'Does Norman know what he's letting himself in for?'

'I don't know,' Jinny murmured. 'Does any man?'

'Sylvia was pleased with the brooch, though. It's not one that I've seen you wear.'

Jinny picked up the iron and took up where she'd left off. 'I bought it a few years ago and kept it safe in a drawer, thinking you might be the one to wear it some day.'

'For *my* wedding?' Hazel grasped the implication and blushed.

'Yes, but it seems there's fat chance of that happening,' Jinny went on, casting firm strokes of the iron across the crisp white cotton. 'Between you, Gladys and Sylvia, who'd have thought that the youngest would be the first to trip down the aisle?'

The second Saturday in September – Sylvia's wedding day – was a raw, rainy day with a blustery wind that gusted down from Brimstone Rocks and across Overcliffe Common to annoy the guests gathering in the porch of St Luke's church. The women had to hold onto their hats while the men thrust their hands in their pockets and stamped their feet.

'It's nippy out here,' Mabel Jackson, who was amongst the early birds, remarked to Sylvia's mother, Ethel. Sylvia's brothers, Dan and Eddie, stood sentinel at the church gates. 'I'll carry straight on inside if you don't mind.'

Ethel didn't mind at all. 'It's best to keep out of the wind. Rose is already in there with Mother,' she informed their neighbour before going on to greet Eddie's fiancée, Joan, followed by other family members, including Hazel, Jinny and Robert who were battling their way up the path.

Mabel, meanwhile, trundled on inside the church and found a seat between Dorothy Pennington and Marjorie Sykes in the pew directly behind Ada and Rose.

'Ethel Drummond is looking her age,' Mabel opined in a voice loud enough for people to hear.

'Hush!' Marjorie raised a warning finger, which Mabel ignored.

'Let's face it, she looks closer to sixty than fifty.' Ethel might have had a new perm and got dressed up for the occasion of her daughter's wedding, but you couldn't make a silk purse out of a sow's ear, Mabel decided.

'She has put on a bit of weight,' Dorothy conceded.

On the pew in front, Ada bridled. She turned her head sharply and gave a curt greeting. 'Hello, Mabel.'

'How-do, Ada.' Mabel was unabashed – after all, she only spoke the truth about Ada's daughter-in-law.

'*Someone* might have made a bit more effort.' Staring straight ahead again, Ada exacted her revenge.

'Mother!' This time it was Rose who did the hushing.

But it was true – Mabel hadn't even bothered to change out of her everyday dark brown coat and old cloche hat. She sat with a typically disgruntled air, crossing work-worn hands on her broad lap and casting a critical eye over the absence of church flowers and other sure signs that Sylvia's marriage had been arranged in haste and would be repented at leisure.

'Where are the groom's family and friends, for a start?' Mabel nudged Dorothy with her left elbow and rolled her eyes to indicate the empty pews on the other side of the church. 'No guests on the groom's side, and I hear there's no organist and only one bridesmaid tripping down the aisle after the blushing bride,' she muttered, this time to Marjorie on her right.

'Luckily for them, Berta White was on hand to step in at the last minute to play the piano,' Marjorie replied.

Fearing that her mother would turn round with another rejoinder, Rose glanced over her shoulder and was glad to spot Hazel come in out of the cold with her mother and father. She stood up and signalled for all three to join her and Ada in the front pew. 'You're a sight for sore eyes!' she murmured to Hazel, who looked fresh as the morning dew in her blue outfit.

Hazel squeezed her hand. 'You too, Aunty Rose.'

Rose smiled and blushed. She'd dressed with care in a long cream skirt and loose-fitting cream jacket over a snow-white blouse fastened at the throat with a cameo brooch. Her hat's wide brim was adorned with peach-coloured silk flowers.

'Make sure there's enough room for Ethel on the end there,' Ada instructed. She sat upright as always, resplendent in a crimson velvet jacket and a straw hat bedecked with ostrich feathers. The hat had come out of its round box for weddings and christenings, funerals and Easter parades for as long as anyone in the family could remember.

'Here she comes!' Rose was the first to spot her sister-in-law plodding flat-footed down the aisle in her Sunday best of low-waisted green dress and jacket, topped off with a red felt hat with a narrow brim. Unflustered as ever, Ethel stopped to say hello to Mabel, Dorothy and Marjorie before sliding into the pew next to Robert.

All the guests had arrived, but as yet there was no sign of either the groom or the bride. Eventually, though, Berta took up her position at the upright piano and the vicar emerged from his vestry.

'Now what's the hold-up?' Ada tapped her wristwatch.

'Hush, Mum!'

Rose's admonishment was drowned out by throat clearing and scuffling in the doorway, followed by the entrance of Eddie and Dan, one on either side of Norman as they frog-marched him down the aisle.

'Like a condemned man on his way to the gallows,' said Mabel, drawing another dark look from Ada.

The groom and groomsmen occupied the front pew across the aisle from the Prices and the Drummonds. Norman's face was peaky under his slickly Brylcreemed hair. However, he looked smart enough in his pinstriped suit and striped tie.

'I'll tell you what, Dorothy, this is different to when your Myra tied the knot with John Moxon last year.' Mabel's commentary was still clearly audible. 'They had all the trimmings – a big reception, three tiers to the wedding cake, a honeymoon in Blackpool...'

Seated directly in front of her rival for work, Hazel gave a small, irritated shake of her head. Surely for once in her life Mabel could keep her opinions to herself.

'Take no notice,' Rose advised quietly.

'That's right,' Jinny agreed. 'If Mabel knows she's riled us, she's won.'

So the family set their minds to waiting patiently amidst the coughs and rustling of hymn books and the increasingly nervous exchange of glances between Norman and his groomsmen until at last Berta looked out from behind her sheet music and at a signal from the vicar struck up the first loud chords of the Wedding March.

Here comes the bride, short, fat and wide – the mocking words from a childhood song ran unaccountably inside Hazel's head. What was it that undermined the solemnity of the occasion for her? Was it Sylvia's last-minute dramas of the night before or Hazel's awareness of the rumour mill grinding out suggestions that Norman had been pressganged into the marriage? In any case, she had to fight for control by focusing on the slow progress down the aisle of Sylvia, Uncle Cyril and Gladys.

The sight transformed Hazel's mood. The young bride was so beautiful in her borrowed gown that she took the onlookers' breath away. The white satin of the bodice and long train gleamed in the subdued light that suffused the church and a gauzy, shoulder-length veil gave only a vague impression of Sylvia's serious features beneath. Her hand trembled as she carried her bouquet of white carnations.

There was a low buzz of appreciation as, leaning on her father's arm, Sylvia approached the altar and the Wedding March drew to a close. Gladys stood by, making no attempt to upstage the bride in her calf-length rosebud dress. She took the bouquet on cue then stepped onto the sidelines while Norman, still beset by jitters, took Cyril's place in front of the vicar.

The words were spoken, the rings exchanged. Sylvia lifted her veil and the groom kissed his bride.

Hazel's heart was full. She saw Aunty Rose pull out a handkerchief from her small velvet bag and dab her cheeks. On her other side, Jinny turned to Robert with a fond smile. The deed was done – Sylvia was married to Norman, for better or worse, and let no man put them asunder.

CHAPTER SIX

'Hazel, are you awake?' Robert called up the stairs on his way out to work on the following Monday morning. 'The postman's brought you a letter.'

'Ta, Dad.' It was seven o'clock and she was still in bed, mulling over what she would do that day to drum up more custom. When nothing new came to mind, she fixed on paying Betty Hollings another visit before knocking on Myra's door with a reminder about getting herself to tomorrow's clinic.

'I've left it on the mantelpiece,' he told her.

'Rightio.' She heard the door close and then there was silence for a while until the familiar sounds of her mother making her way along the landing and down the stairs prompted Hazel to get up too. She dressed quickly in navy blue slacks and a primrose-yellow jumper, ran a comb through her hair then joined Jinny in the kitchen.

'About time too, lazy bones.' Jinny scooped porridge from the pan into two bowls and set them down on the table. 'Fetch the milk while you're still on your feet.'

Hazel opened the door to bright sunshine and the sight of her neighbours setting off for work.

Despite the drudgery that lay ahead, most exchanged cheery greetings then chatted as they walked in groups of five or six. The talk was of Saturday's football match or of the latest flick showing at the Victory, or else of recent family matters such as ailments and fallings out.

'Your Sylvia looked a picture on Saturday,' Dorothy Pennington remarked as Hazel stooped to pick up the milk bottle from the top step. Dorothy, dressed in a faded overall and carpet slippers, was on her way to Newby's to pick up a copy of the *Daily Express*. 'And it was a good do at the Working Men's Club afterwards.'

'Yes, it all went very well,' Hazel said with a smile. 'By the way, how's Myra getting along?'

'Oh, you know...' Dorothy's sentence trailed away and ended in a shrug. 'Myra makes mountains out of molehills.'

There was no time for anything else as Myra's mother rejoined the flow of people moving down the hill onto Ghyll Road. Hazel took the milk inside and sat down for breakfast, only remembering about the letter when she was washing up and Jinny was putting on her hat and coat. Hurriedly she dried her hands then took the envelope from the mantelpiece, opening it to find a scrawled note with an illegible signature.

She squinted at the untidy handwriting. 'I can hardly read it. Wait a minute – this must be from Dr Bell!'

'What's it say?' Jinny's tone suggested she was expecting bad news. 'He hasn't given you your marching orders, has he?'

'No, Mum, it's the opposite. He says here that

92

there's been a good response to the posters I put on display and a fair few women have signed up to be seen.'

'Is that right?'

Hazel's eyes were bright with excitement. 'Yes. So he's moved on from asking me to drum up custom for him – now he wants me to run the actual clinic. I'll be on duty every Tuesday and Dr Bell will pay me for the privilege.'

The unexpected invitation filled Hazel with fresh hope and energy. This was more like it, she thought, a fixed point in the week where she could put her training to good use and be in touch with the very women she needed to meet.

'How much?' Jinny was on her way out of the house, thinking as usual that Hazel shouldn't count her chickens before they were hatched.

'Three shillings per clinic,' Hazel said proudly.

Jinny nodded. 'It's a start,' she conceded. And without any further word of encouragement she set off to catch the tram to Clifton Market.

Still in high spirits, Hazel altered her plans for the morning. First she would write an acceptance letter to Dr Bell, and then she could cycle to his practice on Westgate Road to drop the letter off. After that she would check in on Myra and, if there was still time before dinner, she would visit Betty in Nelson Yard.

Her very first port of call after writing her letter, however, was to pick up the newly refurbished bike from Baxter's garage on the corner of Ghyll Road and Ada Street.

'Philip Baxter let me use a corner of his

workshop to take the bike to bits and bring it up to scratch,' Hazel's dad had explained. He'd been gone all day Sunday, fitting new brake pads and tyres, then replacing the old dynamo light and polishing the chrome spokes with wire-wool until they shone. 'It's as good as new,' he'd reported to Hazel when he got home. 'Ready for you to pick up whenever you like.'

So just before nine o'clock Hazel breezed down the hill, letter in pocket, hurrying to the workshop, hoping as she went that she hadn't lost the skill of riding a bike. It was years since she'd tried, she realized, and she kept in mind her dad's warnings about the busy traffic on the main roads into town.

'Keep your eyes peeled, especially when you're turning right,' he'd advised. 'Those bus drivers don't care – they'd as soon run you over as look at you.'

Hazel practised in her imagination how she would signal to make a right turn then pull out into the centre of the road and it was only when she spotted the grey Ford parked a short way along from the bright yellow and red petrol pump that she remembered that Baxter's was where John Moxon worked.

Should she mention Myra and get an up-to-date report on how his wife was doing? she wondered. *Better play it by ear,* she decided, before striding on.

The man himself emerged onto the pavement to serve petrol as Hazel arrived. Without noticing her, he wiped his hands on a piece of rag which he stuffed into his back pocket then unscrewed

94

the petrol cap of the customer's car.

He had his back to her, blocking her way. 'Excuse me, please,' Hazel said quietly. She had to repeat her request a second time before he heard her.

'Sorry – I didn't see you there,' he apologized as he stood to one side.

Hazel inhaled petrol fumes from the car's tank. She noticed a man in a trilby hat and tweed jacket leaning against the side of his car, taking in her appearance with undisguised relish. 'I came to pick up my bike,' she explained to John.

'Oh, it's yours, is it?' Seemingly as embarrassed as Hazel, he waited for her to step past. 'I saw it back there and wondered whose it was.'

'Dad bought it second hand and did it up for me.' Entering the workshop, Hazel saw Philip Baxter holed up in a small office to one side. Glancing up from his paperwork, the military-looking, moustachioed garage owner recognized Hazel then jerked his thumb towards the far corner.

Hazel hesitated. She was out of her element surrounded by car parts and stacks of tyres and was working out how to avoid the patches of black oil that had dripped from broken engines onto the concrete floor when she was overtaken by John, who had finished with his customer and obligingly fetched the bike for her, lifting it clear of the dirty floor and carrying it across.

'Ta very much.' Emboldened by the gesture, Hazel met his gaze and ploughed on. 'I hope you don't mind – I'm thinking of dropping in on Myra again.'

Setting the bike down on the pavement, John's eyes narrowed. 'When?' he asked.

'Later this morning, if that's all right.'

'She was still in bed when I left home; she said she wanted to take it easy.'

'Bed is probably the best place for her,' Hazel agreed. 'But did she mention you taking an hour off work to bring her to the clinic tomorrow, by any chance?'

John shook his head. 'Not a dicky bird. Do you think I should?'

'I do,' Hazel said firmly. 'Don't worry – it doesn't mean Dr Bell and I will be jockeying to take Mabel's place when the time comes. But it does mean we can keep an eye on her blood pressure and such like.'

'What's wrong with her blood pressure?' Alarm registered on John's even features as he compressed his lips and furrowed his brow.

'It might be a bit higher than it ought to be.' Not wanting to say too much before she'd examined Myra, Hazel underplayed the possible problem.

'I knew it,' he said abruptly. 'I'm no expert but you just have to take one look at her to know.'

'Know what?'

'Something's not right. She goes dizzy at the drop of a hat and she gets bad headaches. Her mother says she has to take it in her stride, it's to be expected. The trouble is – Myra has never been able to stand up to Dorothy and she's not about to start now.'

'Bring Myra to the clinic,' Hazel told him even more firmly than before.

'I will,' he decided, glancing over his shoulder at his boss sitting hunched over his desk in his office. 'Even if I lose an hour's pay, it'll be worth it for the peace of mind.'

An hour and a half later, after an unsteady bike ride along the cobbled streets to deliver her letter to Dr Bell on Westgate Road, Hazel cycled back to Raglan Road. She stopped outside number 80, leaned her bike against a lamp-post then knocked on Myra's door. Getting no answer, she decided to call in at Pennington's instead. So she entered the green-tiled fish and chip shop and waited at the back of the short queue until her turn came.

'Next please!' It was Henry Pennington who looked up at Hazel from behind the stainless-steel range. He was a skinny, small-featured man with thin grey hair and a dark, bushy moustache, dressed in a white cotton coat with a blue and white checked apron over the top. 'Now then, stranger. What can I do for you?'

'Cod and chips, please.' Hazel watched him lift a battered fish from the hot fat, drain it then place it on a sheet of greaseproof paper. 'I just knocked on Myra's door but I didn't get an answer,' she remarked as casually as she could.

'That's funny.' Henry put a portion of chips beside the fish then sprinkled salt and vinegar over the lot. 'Myra's taken to her bed but Dorothy decided to call in on her a few minutes ago. She's still there as far as I know.'

And not answering the door, Hazel thought uneasily. She'd suspected at the time that one corner of the net curtain in the bedroom window might have twitched then settled; in which case it meant that Myra's mother was standing guard and there was nothing she could do about it. 'Tell Myra I was asking after her and I hope to see her at clinic tomorrow,' she said as she paid her money, took her newspaper-wrapped parcel and departed.

Outside number 80, she put her fish and chip dinner in the basket of her bike then freewheeled down the hill. She would grab a bite to eat then pop into Nelson Yard to see Betty. After that she would come back home and read through some of her college textbooks to refresh her memory on the major symptoms to pick up on during each trimester of pregnancy. She wanted to be absolutely ready for her first clinic.

She followed this plan without incident, enjoying her time spent with a chatty Betty who, with infant Daisy at her breast, had resumed her chaotic daily routine. Dirty nappies soaked in a bucket just inside the door, within reach of Polly and Keith until Hazel found a new place for it up on the draining board. A smell of burnt toast mingled with soot and smoke from the unswept chimney, overpowering the more savoury smell of vegetables as the new mother fed her toddlers a meagre ration of bubble and squeak.

'Sit yourself down,' she told Hazel, who was relieved to see the slight, underfed woman tackling breastfeeding with her usual unruffled calm.

Hazel moved a pile of old newspapers from the only available chair. 'Are you drinking plenty and managing to rest?' she asked.

Betty laughed as if this was the best joke she'd

heard in weeks. 'Most of the drinking in this family is done by Len down at the Green Cross,' she crowed. 'As for rest – I don't know the meaning of the word!'

'Listen to me, Betty, you must try not to overdo it,' Hazel instructed, startled to hear the rattle of a poker against the fire-back.

'That's only Doreen sending me a message by Morse code,' Betty told her with a wink. 'She'll want to know if I need anything from Hutchinson's. Since you're here, can you nip next door and ask her to fetch me a packet of cream crackers – they're Keith's favourite.' Seeing Hazel hesitate by the door, she rattled on. 'I've no money to pay for them, if that's what you're wondering. Doreen will ask old man Hutchinson to put it on the slate till Friday. You never know, one of these days he might even say yes.'

Hazel scanned the eager faces of Keith and his little sister sitting at the table with their unappetizing dinner. 'Don't worry, I think I can scrape together a couple of pence,' she assured Betty, going outside. She had to dodge the wet laundry flapping in the breeze then took time to inhale a deep breath of fresh air as she mounted the steps next door and raised the iron knocker. She brought it down with a smart rap but was put off her stride by the appearance at the door not of Doreen but of Mabel Jackson, with Berta White close behind.

'Well, well – look who it isn't,' a steely-eyed Mabel said almost without moving her lips. 'Come in, young lady, welcome to the witches' coven.'

Hazel couldn't help but smile. Doreen, Mabel

and Berta made a fine triumvirate of wicked sisters, though doughty Doreen and po-faced Berta paled beside Mabel, whose deep voice carried authority and whose round, horn-rimmed glasses gave her an air of owlish wisdom. 'I won't stop, ta. I've just brought a message from Betty – she'd like a packet of cream crackers from the grocer's if anyone is going that way.'

That had torn it, she realized as soon as the words were out of her mouth. Now Mabel knew where she'd come from and naturally she didn't look any too pleased.

'You hear that, Doreen?' Mabel said over her shoulder. 'Betty's after more cream crackers. I only took her a packet yesterday. She must have gobbled them up already.'

'They're for Keith,' Hazel said, quaking in her shoes.

'Says who?' Mabel countered with a look of disbelief. 'Whoever heard of a little nipper asking for dry crackers instead of something sweet? No, it was Betty who got a taste for them when she was expecting. I've seen her dip them in her tea and down half a packet in one go.'

'It's all right, Hazel – leave it to me,' Doreen said from the recesses of her dark, stuffy kitchen.

'Right you are. I'll be off then.' Hazel had backed down the steps and was on her way towards the ginnel connecting Nelson Yard to Raglan Road when Mabel followed her.

'They tell me you'll be working at the surgery from now on,' she said with a confidential lowering of her voice followed by a pause that invited a reply.

100

'Once a week, in the new clinic,' Hazel confirmed, able to picture the scorn oozing through the pores of Mabel's skin at the very word 'clinic'.

But to her surprise, Mabel tipped her glasses further up her nose then gave a nod of approval. 'Good for you. Dr Bell is snowed under with new cases ever since those posters went up. He could do with a helping hand.'

Was there nothing this woman didn't know? Hazel wondered. And why on earth wasn't she having a go at her for poaching the local mothers-to-be?

'He's not everyone's cup of tea, though.' Mabel glanced at her companion for support. 'Is he, Berta?'

Berta, who was a small woman with a prim air, dressed from head to foot in church-mouse grey, spoke up for the first time. 'He's not,' she confirmed. 'A lot of people round here wish Dr Moss hadn't retired. And it's not just the likes of us who are long in the tooth. I've heard the younger ones say they're not sure about Dr Bell either.'

'Better the devil you know, I always say,' Doreen chipped in as she pushed past her visitor with an empty shopping basket. 'With Dr Moss you knew he wasn't going to write a prescription for something you couldn't pay for, for a start. And he didn't send you off to hospital at the drop of a hat either. Come on, Berta; step aside, you two.'

While Doreen locked her door and made off with Berta down the alley towards Chapel Street, Mabel kept Hazel talking a while longer. 'You hear that? It's hard for newcomers to make their mark, which could be the reason behind Dr Bell enlisting your help. At least you're a familiar face in the neighbourhood.'

Hazel felt the slight behind Mabel's last remark and, forgetting her mother and Aunty Rose's good advice, took the bait. 'Oh, and my employment at the clinic has nothing to do with my training, I don't suppose?'

Mabel tucked her chin to her chest and peered over the rim of her glasses. 'Training's all very well...'

'But experience is ten times better?'

'Exactly,' Mabel said with such finality that Hazel blinked and took a step backwards. 'That's what matters in this job – getting to know how people tick, not taking things at face value, being ready for anything. And definitely not a fancy certificate on the mantelpiece and a stack of text-books by your bed.'

There were eight women waiting at the door of Dr Bell's surgery next day when Hazel opened up the clinic at half past two on the dot. All were pregnant – some cheery and confident with toddlers in tow, while first-time mothers arrived alone and unsure about what might lie ahead.

'Come in, everyone. Please follow me.' Hazel led the way past Eleanor's reception desk up a flight of stairs to a large, first-floor room whose cream walls were lined with tubular-steel chairs. There was a tall screen in one corner and a wooden play-pen in the other. Scattered across a low table were toys to keep the children occupied – a wooden train, a set of farmyard animals, colouring books and a game of snakes and ladders.

'Josephine, you play nicely while Mum sees the nurse,' the first woman in the queue told her small daughter, taking off the toddler's green knitted bonnet and coat then depositing her inside the play pen with the farmyard animals. Then she gave her name and address to Hazel. 'Margie Daniels, 23 Ada Street.'

Clipboard in hand, Hazel entered her name at the top of her list then asked her to step behind the screen and strip down to her underthings. 'Thank you for coming,' she told everyone else with a bright smile. 'There'll be tea and biscuits along shortly.'

'It was worth coming, then.' A woman in a shabby coat and worn-down shoes shared a deadpan joke with her neighbour. Her chin-length hair was pinned back behind her ears and her face was marked by old chickenpox scars.

'Yes, that'll be two sugars,' someone piped up.

'Make that three for me,' a second woman said.

Hazel left them chatting or leafing through magazines and went behind the green screen. 'Your maiden name wouldn't be Briggs, by any chance?' she asked her first patient – a fresh-faced, dark-haired woman whom she thought she recognized.

'That's me,' Margie replied. 'And you're Hazel Price; I remember you from school.'

'You're looking well,' Hazel told her as she went about the business of weighing Margie and measuring her height.

'I'm tickety-boo,' Margie confirmed. 'Happily hitched to Roy Daniels for the last year and a half, in case you're wondering. I don't know what I'm doing here really, except that my sister Lily pestered me so here I am.'

'Lie down here, please. How is Lily?' A quick glance told Hazel that Margie was around twenty-five weeks' pregnant and a listen with her stethoscope confirmed a normal, regular heartbeat. After that, she palpated the abdomen and established that the baby was currently presenting as breech, although this was by no means unusual at this stage and it would probably change position several times in the coming weeks.

'Lily's fine, ta. She's thinking of going back to dress-making work with Sybil Dacre next spring. I said I'd be happy to look after her littl'un for her since I'm at home anyway with mine and then with this one, touch wood.' Margie patted her stomach.

'That sounds like a good arrangement.' Satisfied that all was well, Hazel noted down more details and asked Margie to get dressed. 'If you can remember to bring a sample of urine next week, we'll be able to do some more checks.'

'Oh, I'm coming again, am I?' Margie raised an eyebrow as she sat up and slipped her dress down over her head.

'Yes. Regular check-ups are important,' Hazel insisted, confident that Margie's minor rebellion was just for show. 'Everything looks straightforward at the moment but nearer to your due date I'd like to get Dr Bell involved.'

'So long as it's still free,' Margie agreed, doing up her buttons and slipping on her shoes, 'I'll be a good girl and do as I'm told.'

Hazel smiled and nodded as Margie made her exit. She called for the next in line – the poorly dressed woman with the scarred face, who came behind the screen with a worried expression.

'I hope you're not going to prod and poke me about,' she muttered, unsure of what to do until Hazel put her at her ease, asking her name and address – Irene Bradley, 14 Nelson Yard – and telling her to take off her outer clothes and stand on the weighing machine.

Irene's weight was low and her manner listless. Her face was pale, her scraped-back hair thin and her skin unwashed. 'How many pounds do you think you've gained since you found out you were pregnant?'

'How should I know?' Irene replied with a touch of resentment. 'I've never been on one of these weighing contraptions before.'

'And how far gone are you?'

'I don't know – you tell me.'

'We'd have to work it out from the date of your last period.'

The remark elicited a weary smile. 'That's a tricky one. I've not had one of them for going on two years.'

'Are you sure?' Putting down her clipboard and asking Irene to lie down on the examination table, Hazel was already starting to think Dr Bell might have to be called from his afternoon surgery. Irene Bradley was severely underweight and this could have led to her long-standing amenorrhoea. Of course, improved nutrition and a slight weight gain could have brought her back into fertility just at the point when the menstrual cycle had started

105

again – hence she'd become pregnant without realizing that such a thing was possible.

'That's freezing cold,' Irene complained as Hazel put her stethoscope to her abdomen.

'I'm sorry.' Hazel listened hard, trying to pick up a heartbeat. When she found one, it seemed faint and irregular. That decided it. 'All right, Irene, I want you to stay right where you are while I fetch Dr Bell.'

'You what? I'm only here in the first place because I mentioned to Betty Hollings I couldn't feel baby moving like he should and she said for me to come,' Irene complained peevishly.

'That was good advice.' Hazel placed a blanket over her patient then hurried downstairs to speak to Eleanor. 'Would you ask Dr Bell if he can leave off what he's doing and come upstairs for a few minutes?'

Eleanor reacted quickly, coming out from behind her desk and knocking on the door of the examination room where Hazel had first met David Bell. He came straight out and followed Hazel upstairs. By now, their sense of urgency had caught the attention of the women in the clinic still waiting to be seen.

'What's up, Doctor?' one of them asked as he and Hazel disappeared behind the screen. 'She's not going ahead and having it while we sit here and twiddle our thumbs, I hope?'

Dr Bell ignored the curious looks and got down to business. He too listened for the foetal heartbeat then palpated Irene's stomach. He stepped back and spoke kindly but firmly. 'Now, my dear, Hazel is going to go downstairs again and ask for an ambulance to come and take you to the infirmary.'

'Over my dead body!' Irene shook her head and made an effort to get up. 'I'm not going there.'

'Call the ambulance,' Dr Bell told Hazel regardless. 'Now, Irene, we want this baby to be born safe and well, don't we?'

Following orders, Hazel ran back downstairs. When she returned, she found Irene obediently sitting up with the blanket around her shoulders and Dr Bell quietly explaining what would happen next.

'The ambulance will come and whisk you there before you know it. The doctors and nurses will carry out all the tests that we can't do here in clinic.'

'I don't want to go. I've been there before. I know what it's like.'

Hazel sat down beside her and spoke softly. 'When were you at the infirmary, Irene?'

'When I was a little kid. I'm not going back.'

'Listen to me – it was different in those days. It wasn't a hospital.'

'No, it was a prison.' Irene shed bitter, angry tears. 'As good as. They took me away from my mum, stuck me in a room with a lot of other poor blighters then locked the door.'

'It's not like that any more.' Determined to get Irene's cooperation, Hazel took her hand. 'There's no need to be afraid. Everything's different now, you'll see. The people are kind. They'll look after you and your baby.'

Slowly growing calmer but still not loosening her grip on Hazel's hand, Irene waited for the ambulance to arrive then allowed herself to be walked out of the clinic and down the stairs.

The ambulance driver parked on the pavement. 'Right you are, love, we'll take it from here,' he told Hazel as he and his assistant jumped down from the cab.

Reluctantly Hazel wrested her hand free and watched as Irene was led into the back of the cream ambulance. It was a pitiful sight – the malnourished mother-to-be walking with head bent between two strong ambulance men into the back of the vehicle. Knowing that the baby was at risk of being stillborn only made it worse. 'Good luck!' she called as the door slammed.

Giving herself a good shake, Hazel hurried back to the clinic, passing Dr Bell on the stairs.

'Nicely done,' he told her in his lilting Geordie accent. He gave her an approving smile then went on his way.

'Next please!' Hazel's brisk announcement as she took up her clipboard meant that normal service was resumed. She was quietly pleased by how she'd succeeded in winning Irene's confidence and given her at least a chance of going to term and producing a healthy baby, but now there were half a dozen women still to be weighed and measured, forms to be filled in and lists ticked.

But no Myra Moxon, worse luck, she said to herself. It seemed that in spite all of her and John's efforts, Myra was still not willing to seek the medical help she so obviously needed.

CHAPTER SEVEN

'You can lead a horse to water, but you can't make him drink,' was Robert's opinion when he sat across the tea table from Hazel and Jinny that night.

'Or, in this case, "her",' Jinny added. She'd listened to Hazel's worries about Myra and agreed with Robert. 'It turns out Myra is as pig-headed as her mother over some things – like forking out for doctors' visits for a start.'

'But the clinic is free,' Hazel pointed out. 'I even persuaded John to take some time off work to fetch her, but to no avail.'

'"To no avail"?' Jinny echoed the highfalutin phrase with a quizzical look.

Robert took a sip of tea then shook his head. 'Leave the lass alone. What do you think, Hazel – is it Myra or her mother who's in charge?'

'Well, it's clearly not John. He admitted he was worried about her so he wanted her to come.'

'As I said: like mother, like daughter,' Jinny observed. 'I've heard on the grapevine that life is not always a bed of roses for John Moxon up at number 80.'

'Well, anyway,' Hazel said, shying away from the topic, 'on a more cheerful note, we did manage to get one poorly patient off to the infirmary.'

Jinny went to the kettle and refilled the teapot. 'So clinic wasn't a washout?'

109

'Definitely not. We had eight altogether. Five of them came because they read our posters, so that was five shillings I earned. Then Dr Bell paid me three shillings for doing the clinic, and it'll be the same again next week, all being well.'

'And what about Betty Hollings – has she paid you yet?'

'No,' Hazel admitted. Then, before Jinny could go any further down that particular road, she stood up and took her plate and cup and saucer to the sink. 'Dr Bell said clinic went better than he expected, which is a compliment, isn't it? And I didn't feel awkward or shy working there – in fact, I felt right at home.'

'Of course you did,' her father said.

'And was there any sign of Sylvia?' Not afraid to break the unspoken rule that such things shouldn't be mentioned until Sylvia herself came out into the open, Jinny forged ahead. 'Oh, for heaven's sake, Robert, there's no point beating about the bush, is there? We all know that there's only one reason why Sylvia and Norman were in a rush to get to the altar.'

'She wasn't at clinic,' Hazel interrupted. 'I expect she'll come in her own good time, though. I did pop in on Nana and Aunty Rose on my way home and picked up some news there. They said Sylvia and Norman are settled in at number 15. Sylvia's bright as a button and not letting marriage or anything else slow her down, according to Aunty Rose. She wants to come to the jazz club again on Friday night, along with me and Gladys. It's the same Dixie band as before and Earl Ray is Sylvia's all-time favourite.'

'Yes – Sylvia's not one to miss out,' Jinny said.

'You two should come along as well.' Hazel expected a resounding 'no' to this suggestion and she wasn't disappointed. 'What's the matter, Dad?' she laughed. 'Jazz is modern. Everyone's listening to it these days.'

'Not us,' Robert said on Jinny's behalf. 'We're behind the times, we are.'

'You speak for yourself.' Contrary as ever and finishing her tea of scrambled eggs on toast, Jinny rattled her knife and fork down onto the plate. 'So keep your eyes peeled, Hazel – I might surprise you by turning up there one of these nights.'

The rest of that week seemed to fly by for Hazel. On the Wednesday she followed up two enquiries from women who had attended the clinic. The first took her out on the tram past St Luke's church, almost to the edge of town, where she found Lydia Walker, her mother-to-be, ensconced in a house at the entrance to Herbert Oldroyd's moorland estate. The small stone lodge, like the mansion behind it, was built in the style of a castle, complete with Gothic arched windows and battlements, constructed at a time when the now-struggling mill owner's family had had pretensions of grandeur. The lodge house was well kept, both outside and in, with an oak sideboard and two comfy chairs in the living room, which was separate from the kitchen. The sideboard sported a silver trophy and two carnival-ware glass dishes, plus assorted china ornaments.

111

Sitting in one of the chairs, Hazel listened quietly to Lydia's first question.

'I've asked you to come here because I want to know, if you were me, would you want to have this baby in hospital or at home?'

'That's entirely up to you,' Hazel explained. 'Some women choose hospital for a first baby because for them it feels safer to have the doctor and midwives on the spot. Others prefer to be at home in familiar surroundings.'

'I'd be happier here with you,' Lydia said without much hesitation.

'Ah, but you've been on Dr Bell's list for a long time. He's probably the one who'll come out to you.'

'Why not you?' The blunt response came from a woman who was approaching her due date and not in a mood to be thwarted. Her broad, scrubbed features were set in determined lines.

Hazel smiled. 'Thank you, I'm flattered. But I've only just started with, Dr Bell and you've been his patient for all of your pregnancy, so it's only right that he attends the birth – unless of course he's caught up somewhere else when you go into labour.'

Lydia's stern expression broke into a knowing smile and a wink. 'Is that right? Then I'll have to see what I can arrange.'

Hazel laughed. 'No, no – we have to let nature take its course. Baby will only come when he's ready. But whether it's me or Dr Bell, I can promise that you'll be well looked after.'

There were more questions, which Hazel answered honestly and fully, then it was time to leave. Her second visit was closer to home and followed much the same lines, though this time the patient, Evelyn Jagger, was a nervous type who needed more reassurance. She was halfway through her second trimester and willing to keep on coming regularly to clinic.

'Good for you,' Hazel said enthusiastically as Evelyn showed her out. If she got a move on, she would just have time to go from there to Betty's house for another post-natal visit before dinner. In the afternoon she would cycle over to the infirmary to see Irene.

'Oh, it's you again,' Betty greeted her from the top step of her house. Ordering Keith and Polly to stay put, she carried a basket of wet laundry into the yard and began to peg it out on the line.

'Yes, it's me.' Putting her bag down, Hazel sat on the step to wait, happy at first to let Polly settle on her lap until she noticed that the little girl's hair was crawling with head lice. At this point she swiftly set her down on the step. 'I've come to weigh Daisy for you,' she explained to Betty. 'Do you have a pair of kitchen scales I could use?'

'Yes – help yourself,' Betty replied, midway through a haphazard pegging of shirts and blouses to the line. 'And have you got something for sore nipples while you're at it? I've tried the old cabbage-leaf trick but it's not done a ha'p'orth of good.'

'You should use a barrier cream. I'll see if I have some with me.' Knowing it was best to keep her amusement about the old remedy to herself, Hazel went inside and duly found the scales in a cupboard under the sink. She was midway through

113

weighing Daisy when Betty came in. 'By the way,' she asked, 'have you tried washing Polly's hair in a vinegar solution and using a fine comb on it? Or else there's a special shampoo you can buy from Barlow's.'

Cooing over Daisy, who lay naked on the scales, Betty seemed unconcerned. 'I did see Polly having a good scratch the other day, but no, I haven't got round to it yet.'

'Baby weighs in at six pounds ten ounces,' Hazel reported, thinking that she would bring the shampoo herself on her next visit. 'We need to keep her weight up. How sore are you, Betty?'

'Not too bad. You give me some cream and I'll soldier on.' Betty carried Daisy to the table and put a clean nappy on her.

'And how is your milk? You know, if you get too cracked and sore and you feel your milk supply is slowing down, we can always bring in bottle-feeding as a back-up.'

'You won't catch me doing that!' Betty gave Hazel a dark look. 'I've managed with these other two, haven't I?'

'Very well indeed,' Hazel admitted. At this rate both Keith and Polly might end up with shaved heads, but neither looked underfed or miserable – in fact, quite the opposite. They were calm, contented children, showing the right mixture of curiosity and caution towards her – a stranger in their house – and happily following their mother around to tug confidently at her skirt for attention. Handing over a jar of cream and refusing payment, Hazel packed her bag, promised to call again before the weekend, then left the house.

'Ta for coming,' Betty called from the top step as Hazel ducked under the damp laundry that threatened to flap against her face. 'By the way, Len says he can bring half the money to you on Friday after work. That'll be five shillings and three pence we still owe you. Is that all right?'

'That's more than all right,' Hazel assured her with a smile. 'Ta, Betty. I'm much obliged.'

After dinner and with her confidence still on the up, Hazel cycled out to the infirmary as planned. On the way there, an idea came to her. *It's high time I got myself a smart nurse's uniform for clinic,* she decided. *Maybe a pale blue one with a white apron – that would do nicely.* She freewheeled down the hill onto Ghyll Road then out of town past the Green Cross and on towards the old workhouse, the scene until recently of so much misery. Its change of use had done little to soften the harshness of its exterior, with its thick stone walls, high, narrow windows and central archway leading into a shadowy courtyard that had once been the exercise ground for inmates. It was here that Hazel left her bike and found her way inside the building to Matron's office where she stated her business and asked about Irene Bradley's condition.

'There's been no change since she was admitted.' Matron Fuller's facial expression was as stiff and starched as her white collar and cuffs, and her slender frame belied a steely will. During her fifteen years in charge of the infirmary she'd seen thousands of pregnant women in and out of its studded oak doors; in the end they became

115

names on a list and little more. However, she did break off from checking an invoice of bandages and dressings long enough to give Hazel a cursory glance. 'Dr Bell is with her. Perhaps he can tell you more.'

So Hazel followed directions and met the doctor coming out of Irene's ward into the long green corridor, head bowed to expose a bald patch on his crown and with his hands clasped behind his back as if lost in thought.

'Hello, Dr Bell. How's Irene?' Hazel asked anxiously.

'Hmm? Oh, Hazel, it's you.' Seeing her, he raised his head and smiled. 'We're colleagues now, so it's David, please. Irene's sleeping at the moment.'

'Then I won't wake her,' she decided.

'Best not. According to the nurse on duty, Irene seems to have accepted that this is the best place for her. What she and her baby need now is plenty of good food and rest.'

Hazel turned to accompany him back down the corridor. 'How is the baby – can they tell?'

'Alive, at least. There's a stronger heartbeat and now Irene says she can feel the occasional kick.'

'So we'll keep our fingers crossed.' Passing Matron's office and coming out onto the flagged courtyard together, Hazel prepared to say goodbye.

'My car is parked out on Ghyll Road if you would like a lift,' David offered. He smiled again, this time a little awkwardly.

The invitation flustered her. 'Oh no – I came on my bicycle.' She pointed across the yard.

'Ah well.'

'But thank you anyway.'

'You're welcome – any time.' Moving off towards the wide gateway, he cleared his throat then stopped and turned to call after her. 'I'll see you at clinic next Tuesday, Hazel, if not before.'

'Which was odd, when you think about it,' she confessed to Gladys when she recalled the incident on their way to the jazz club on the Friday evening. It was a warm, late-September night, and the two young women were dressed for dancing in summery dresses with floating skirts and nipped-in waists, topped with light jackets and finished off with dainty high-heeled shoes. Gladys had had her hair cut in a brand-new style, much shorter and shaped to her head, giving her a pixie look, while Hazel had carefully crimped hers into a cascade of waves that fell about her face. 'Why would David say, "Tuesday, if not before"? Why not just, "See you at clinic, Hazel"?'

'It's "David" now, is it?' Gleefully Gladys prepared to step off the tram as it rattled to a halt outside Merton and Groves. 'So what did you reply?'

'Nothing. The offer of a ride in his car took me by surprise.'

'He asked you to call him David and then he offered you a lift home?' Gladys hopped from the still-moving tram onto the pavement. 'Oh my, Hazel. You *are* going up in the world!'

But that was just Gladys being Gladys, Hazel thought as they bought their entrance tickets and left their jackets in the cellar cloakroom. Before she knew it they'd entered the same crowded, smoky room as before, with tables and chairs backed up against the walls and the brightly lit stage at the far end. Earl Ray's band was already in full swing and among the familiar faces she spotted Dan and Norman at the bar, and of course Sylvia, cigarette in hand and standing close to the stage, gazing up in apparent adoration.

'Long time, no see,' Dan told Hazel when Gladys dragged her to the bar to cadge a cigarette.

'Yes, I've been busy.' *This music really does get under your skin*, she thought. The beat of the drum in the background was like a tom-tom under the seductive sway of clarinet and saxophone. Not to mention the words, which were quite shocking if you paid attention. In this song, for a start, the singer was inviting a woman to his room and promising to make love to her all night long.

'Hazel?'

A dig in the ribs from Gladys made her aware that Dan was offering her his packet of cigarettes. 'Oh, I forgot – you don't smoke. Ta, I'll keep yours for later.' Jumping in to snatch a second cigarette and perch it behind her ear, Gladys then drifted away to chat with a group of friends from the King Edward's, leaving Hazel to exchange small talk with Norman.

'You've got over the excitement of the wedding, I expect?' she began pleasantly.

'Just about.'

'Sylvia looked a picture, didn't she?'

'She did.'

Winkling information out of the new husband was harder than Hazel had expected. Though taller than her and broad across the shoulders,

118

his shy air made him somehow small and insignificant – an impression not helped by his quiet, light voice and a persistent tic at the corner of his mouth. So Hazel was forced to go on taking the lead with talk about the high cost of rents even on Nelson Yard and reassurances that Sylvia's mother and father would be bound to help the young couple in any way they could.

'Sylvia's father wasn't keen on me marrying her,' Norman admitted in what was a breakthrough from his usual two-word offerings. 'He asked us what the rush was.'

Though tempted to follow this through, Hazel resisted. 'Don't worry – Uncle Cyril will soon come round. And once he has, you'll find he's a dab hand up a ladder with wallpaper and paste.'

As the band came to the end of one tune and took up another, Hazel seized the chance to break away from Norman, using the excuse of going to spend a penny. When she came back from the cloakroom, she spotted Gladys in amongst her friends from work – one woman and three men, none of whom Hazel recognized. They seemed a jovial lot – the men dressed in sports jackets and white shirts with dark ties, the auburn-haired woman in a low-cut, bottle-green dress with a pearl necklace and red lipstick.

Gladys invited Hazel to sit at their table then gestured towards Norman who had retreated to a corner of the room. 'He's a cheerful Charlie, isn't he?'

'Yes, he's like Eddie – he doesn't have a lot to say,' Hazel agreed before responding to Gladys's round of introductions with a smile.

'Mary, Bernard, Hugh, Gilbert – this is my cousin, Hazel Price. They're all doctors at the hospital, except Mary. She's a secretary like me.'

'Hello, Hazel. How has Gladys managed to keep you tucked out of sight for so long?' the man named Bernard asked with a bold, appreciative stare.

Gladys pouted at him then petulantly seized Hugh by the hand to lead him onto the dance floor while Mary went off with Gilbert, leaving Bernard to carry on flirting with Hazel.

'I mean it.' He smiled seductively as he leaned across the table. 'Gladys and Mary are certainly easy on the eye, don't get me wrong, but you, Hazel, are definitely a cut above.'

Hazel felt the colour rise to her cheeks. If Bernard, who was already slurring his words at this stage of the evening, expected her to thank him for the silly compliment, he was mistaken. Instead, she decided to turn the conversation towards areas that they might have in common. 'How long have you worked at the King Edward's?'

'For ever,' he quipped. 'Actually, I've had ten hard years of taking out appendixes and tonsils so it does feel like an eternity. After all, one set of tonsils is very like another. But never mind me. What do you do, Hazel?'

Her answer surprised him.

'Blow me down – I didn't have you down as a midwife! Where do you work?'

'I work for myself most of the time,' she explained, wishing now that she'd gone back to 'poor' Norman, even if he was hard going. 'And I've just started to help out at Dr Bell's antenatal clinic on Westgate Road.'

'Well, I never! Not *David* Bell!' Bernard rocked back in his chair.

For a moment Hazel was afraid he was mocking her. She picked up her bag, ready to make her excuses.

'No, don't go. I trained with David in Durham donkeys' years ago. I heard that he'd moved down here from the north-east and started afresh after he lost his wife, but I didn't know where exactly. You say he's on Westgate Road?'

'Yes. What happened to his wife?' Hazel asked, curiosity overriding her dislike.

'From what I hear, she died in childbirth – I know, it's ironic. There's a chap with all that knowledge and experience and yet when it comes to it, he can't save his own wife and baby son. Imagine that.'

Shocked into silence, Hazel was relieved when the music ended and the others rejoined them.

'Why weren't you two dancing?' Gladys demanded as she subsided breathlessly into the seat next to Hazel.

'Because, as you well know, I've got two left feet,' Bernard reminded her, standing and fumbling to button up his jacket. 'Anyway, I promised my better half that I'd be home before ten.'

'You're late,' Gilbert pointed out. 'It's already a quarter past.'

Bernard groaned then mumbled his goodbyes.

'That'll be the end of the silly so-and-so's night passes,' Hugh said with a grin. 'Vera will be sure to keep him on a tighter lead from now on.'

Hazel listened to the light-hearted exchanges

and watched as the music and dancing resumed. She saw Dan approach a showy, raven-haired girl in a red dress. He bent over her to work his charm then stubbed out his cigarette and offered her his hand as he led her onto the dance floor. Sylvia and Norman soon followed then Gilbert asked Hazel to dance with him, leaving Gladys and Mary to fight over Hugh. And so the night went on in a fug of cigarette smoke, dancing cheek to cheek with strangers. At half past eleven, as the lights dimmed and the clinches grew closer, Hazel decided it was time to leave.

'I'll catch the last tram,' she told Gladys, who was glued to Hugh in a tight hold on the dance floor. She slid past them and out of the club, collecting her jacket and running upstairs just in time to see the tram trundle into view. She was glad of the chance to catch her breath before stepping onto the platform then sitting close to the back, keeping herself to herself as raucous groups of young men and women got on and off. It was midnight by the time she alighted at the Green Cross then doubled back a hundred yards to the bottom of Raglan Road.

She'd had a good time, she decided – once she'd got over her affront at Bernard's louche behaviour. Their conversation about David Bell had stayed with her, however, and she was picturing what he must have been through and how he must still be grieving for his wife and child, when the sound of a door being slammed at the top of the street pulled her back into the present.

A figure burst from a house and sprinted towards her and she soon made out that it was

John Moxon. He wore only a shirt open at the neck and trousers without braces – no shoes or socks, so that his steps were soundless in the dark, silent street.

Hazel froze on the spot.

'Baby's on its way,' he gasped as he drew nearer and recognized her. 'But something's gone wrong. Dorothy sent me to fetch Mabel.'

The look of panic on John's face told Hazel that this was an emergency. 'Why – what's happening?'

'Myra passed out again, only this time I couldn't wake her. I rushed up the street for her mother and she saw signs that the baby was being born. Myra's still asleep – unconscious, I don't know...' His words broke up and fell away into silence as he looked pleadingly at Hazel.

'Wait here,' she decided on the instant. She ran into her house and up the stairs to fetch her bag and was out on the pavement again before John could gather his wits. 'We have to hurry,' she told him.

He ran up the street ahead of her and flung open his front door, standing aside to let Hazel pass. 'She's upstairs in bed.'

Hazel steadied herself and hurried up, to be confronted by an angry Dorothy blocking her way and demanding to know where Mabel was. Like many small, older women, Dorothy had a surprising amount of sinewy strength. She advanced on Hazel and thrust her back towards the landing, allowing only a glimpse of Myra lying on the bed.

Hazel gasped. Myra was not only unconscious

but writhing and flinging her arms this way and that. Her head was back, her eyes closed, her teeth clenched. Without a shadow of a doubt these were convulsions brought on by full-blown eclampsia.

'Fetch Dr Bell!' she told John, pushing Dorothy to one side. 'Now!' she urged. She heard him leave the room and take the stairs two at a time.

'Stay away from her,' Dorothy insisted as Hazel set down her bag on the dressing table and took out a blood pressure meter. Dorothy ran forward again and tried but failed to grab the equipment.

Hazel held her ground and waited for Myra's latest convulsion to ease before she proceeded. 'Please, Mrs Pennington, listen to me – this is very serious. You have to help me by holding Myra still while I take her blood pressure.' As she spoke, she was able to lift the sheet and determine that Myra's waters had broken and labour was indeed underway. Now that she was here and able to assess the situation, she overcame the shock she'd felt when she first saw John and then the flurry of nerves on her way to the house. She made her decisions calmly.

Myra's mother, in contrast, had taken leave of her senses. 'You're having me on – I'm not laying a finger on her.'

'It's frightening, I know.' Hazel continued with her work and found that Myra's blood pressure was extremely high. This meant that things had reached a critical point. Another fit quickly succeeded the last and Myra's features distorted, her jaw remaining tightly clenched. 'We need to get Myra's mouth open to stop her tongue from rolling backwards and blocking her oxygen supply,' she explained to Dorothy.

'Not me – I'm off to Nelson Yard to fetch Mabel!' With a look of horror, Dorothy backed out onto the landing. 'She'll know what to do.'

So Hazel was left alone in the battle to save both mother and baby, working quickly to take Myra's temperature, which had reached 104 degrees. She had no tongue wedge with her, so between fits, when Myra's jaw relaxed, Hazel managed to ease open her jaw and use a bandage from her bag to make a gag, which would hold down her tongue. Then, when she was sure that the airway was open, she moved on to see how labour was progressing.

There was hardly time to observe the crown of the baby's head, however, before the next convulsion sent fresh rigors through Myra's body. She threw back her head in agony, her red hair darkened with sweat, foam frothing at the corners of her mouth. Her spine was arched clear of the bed, her arms flung wide.

Hazel inhaled deeply. It was as bad as could be, but once David arrived and was able to sedate the patient, they might yet get through this. Meanwhile, the baby was being born. Here came the head and then, to Hazel's horror, a glimpse of the dark umbilical cord wound tightly around the infant's neck. She acted on instinct, using her, hands to twist the baby around to allow the shoulders to slide out but she knew from the limp feel of his body that the muscle tone was wrong. His face was blue. The child was stillborn.

Hazel's heart missed a beat and cold shock

coursed through her. But she must go on and deliver the infant – clamp and cut the cord then wrap him in a clean sheet and place him in the Moses basket to the side of the bed that Myra had lined with warm blankets and a small pillow ready for his arrival.

Again Myra was seized by a shuddering convulsion so that Hazel didn't notice John return with the doctor. She was only aware of a hand on her shoulder and David's quiet voice informing her that he was here to assist. Then she moved to one side to let him attend the patient, aware that John was torn between staring aghast at the sight of his dead infant son in the basket and his wife thrashing wildly on the bed.

With difficulty David felt Myra's pulse then sounded her chest. Sitting on the edge of the bed, he removed his stethoscope and laid it across his knees then watched as Myra's final fit eased and her head lolled to one side.

'Do something, Doctor.' John's voice was low and desperate.

Gently David removed the gag from Myra's mouth, felt for her pulse then stood up.

Hazel could hear more voices at the bottom of the stairs – Dorothy's and Mabel's.

'Do something.' John stood tall and helpless, seeming too big for the room. His eyes darted from Myra to the baby and back again.

David felt once more for a pulse. 'I'm sorry, John. We were too late – for both of them.' The room was thick with silence, the air suddenly unbreathable. 'Hazel and I will leave you with them for a few minutes to say your goodbyes.'

'Thank you, Doctor.' With a stricken look and a low, robotic response, John moved closer to the bed.

Hazel followed David out of the room and down the stairs where they came face to face with Dorothy and Mabel.

Mabel was the first to speak. 'Never!' she said in disbelief when she saw their closed, drained expressions.

'I'm afraid so,' David confirmed. 'There was nothing we could do.'

Hazel took another deep breath. Shock hollowed her out and rendered her speechless. She saw only Dorothy's look of horror. Upstairs the silence was unbroken.

CHAPTER EIGHT

'How was it your fault?' Robert would have none of it. Though it was the middle of the night, he sat Hazel down at the kitchen table, took out the bottle of brandy he kept at the back of the cupboard above the sink, poured her a glass and set it before her. Jinny stood in her blue dressing-gown by the window, listening quietly.

Hazel sat dry-eyed, but she was trembling all over. 'There was no one there except me to start with. Myra and the baby died – both of them, right there in front of me.'

'Drink,' her father insisted, pushing the glass towards her. He was in his pyjamas, his grey hair ruffled from sleep.

Hazel took a sip and felt the brandy hit the back of her throat. She brought her hand up to her mouth as she gagged then gasped.

'Better?'

She took a deep breath then nodded. 'You say I'm not to blame, but I am,' she went on. 'I knew Myra needed to see a doctor the minute I set eyes on her but I couldn't make her understand.'

Jinny came forward and sat next to her, taking a long time to come out with what she was thinking. When she spoke, her words were firm and to the point. 'And what were you meant to do – tie Myra's hands behind her back and drag her to the surgery?'

'No, but I should have told David – Dr Bell – about her symptoms.' *Yes, that was it – that was exactly where the fault lay,* Hazel realized. 'Then he would have gone to the house and examined her. Myra would have had no choice – the ambulance would have come and taken her to hospital.'

Hazel looked so sad and bereft, so young and lost, that Robert felt a lump in his throat. 'You did your best,' he said.

'Even if Dr Bell had knocked on the Moxons' door, who's to say he wouldn't have got the same treatment?' Jinny was the logical one, as usual. 'He'd have had Dorothy and Mabel to contend with, just like you did. And if he'd got past the old guard there would have been Myra herself. From what I remember, she wasn't the type to face up to anything that frightened her – she'd rather bury her head in the sand.'

'Drink,' Robert reminded Hazel. 'Go on –

swallow it.'

'I'm still to blame,' she said after a second sip of brandy had slid down her throat. Then she covered her face with her hands. 'Say what you like – when it came to it, I was the only one who could have saved them.'

'By what miracle?' Jinny wanted to know. 'Myra was already unconscious, wasn't she? And from what you've said, the bairn didn't stand a chance either.'

Hazel kept her face hidden. 'Oh, I wish we'd got there earlier! David could have sedated Myra with morphine. We could have tried to save the baby. It was a boy, poor thing.' She remembered the shock of seeing the thick purple cord around the child's throat and knowing in an instant that he had not survived.

'Your dad's right – you *did* try.' A glance at Robert's bowed head told Jinny that he was too upset to say more and so it would be left to her to talk Hazel round. 'I can't think of anyone who could have done any different to keep Myra and her little boy alive – definitely not Mabel, or even Dr Bell for that matter. It just wasn't meant to be.'

Her mother's calm voice prompted Hazel to take her hands from her face then slowly look up. 'It feels so sad,' she whispered as the first tears began to fall. 'Poor Myra – I've known her as far back as I can remember. And that poor, poor baby – he never even drew breath.'

'But it was bound to happen sooner or later,' Jinny said, taking her hand and letting her cry. 'They must have taught you at college to expect it.'

Hazel grasped her mother's hand tightly. 'I wish it had been later then.' Not now, during her first month as a midwife – before she'd really got into the swing of things. Yes, she'd learned in the lecture theatre about mortality rates and the complications of pregnancy, and she'd convinced herself that she would be able to deal with it. But back then it had been names and numbers on a list not pretty-as-a-picture Myra Moxon, who was a novice at dusting and ironing, who had fallen in love with her handsome husband at first sight but feared she wasn't good enough. Not her old friend Myra from Pennington's fish and chip shop at the top of Raglan Road.

After Hazel had at last taken herself off to bed, Jinny and Robert sat a long time in silence. They still faced each other across the kitchen table as the sun rose and a grey light filtered in through the curtains.

'That'll be Fred delivering the milk,' Robert murmured, at the sound of dray horses' hooves on the cobbles.

Bottles clinked onto their top step then the rhythmical clip-clopping receded, replaced by the sharp seven o'clock rattle of the knocker-up's pole against bedroom windows – the call for workers from Oldroyd's, Kingsley's and Calvert's in advance of their Saturday-morning shift.

'I'd better have a shave and get dressed,' Robert said without stirring.

'Try not to wake her when you go up,' Jinny reminded him.

Still he didn't move. 'What do you think will

130

happen now?'

'There'll be a funeral, of course.' Though it wasn't a prospect Jinny relished, she decided she would have to be there to pay her respects.

'No – I mean, what will happen to Hazel?'

'Nothing. She followed the rules. She didn't do anything wrong.' Staunch in her daughter's defence, Jinny was surprised that Robert should worry about this. She pulled her dressing-gown tighter across her chest.

'But how will she feel when she wakes up?' This was what troubled him and stopped him from getting ready to go to work. 'You know how much she minds what people think of her. And everyone's bound to talk about how it turned out, and who was to blame.'

'They are,' Jinny agreed.

'Do you think she'll be able to – you know – face the music?'

Outside in the street there were more sounds: doors opening and closing, feet shuffling down the hill and bicycle bells being rung. Jinny went to the window and opened the curtains. It was raining – the slate roofs of the houses opposite shone a greasy, leaden grey. Noticing the first passers-by nudge each other and cast their curious glances towards number 18, she gave the curtain a sharp tug then stood back. 'I don't know,' she muttered. 'We'll have to wait and see.'

For two days Hazel stayed at home, too shaken to venture out. The world around her went on – mill hooters sounded, children played skipping games on the street. Girls swung their rope and chanted

131

their song: 'Lord Nelson lost one eye. Lord Nelson lost the other!' On the Sunday Jinny cooked braised rabbit for dinner. Hazel took two mouthfuls then pushed her plate away.

'Never mind.' Robert consoled her with a gentle pat of her hand. 'You'll soon come round.'

Would she? Hazel felt dizzy and oddly detached from her surroundings, noticing the skill of her mother's embroidery on their best linen tablecloth – loop stitch, cross stitch and French knots to make pink and white daisies all along the border – as if she, Hazel, had no physical presence in the room.

On Sunday evening there was a knock on the door and her mother called her down from her room where she lay on the bed resting.

'Hazel, there's someone to see you.'

'Ta – I'll be down in a minute.' Pushing her feet into her slippers and smoothing her hair, she went down tentatively to find David Bell waiting hat in hand by the front door. Her mother and father had retreated to the far side of the kitchen and sat awkwardly at the table, trying to escape attention.

'Hello, Hazel. I hope you don't mind my calling,' David began, turning the brim of the hat and clearing his throat. His pale skin and fair hair, together with his starched white collar and dark tie, made him look clean and smart – too formal to be standing in the Prices' humble kitchen.

'No, I don't mind,' Hazel said softly. She was acutely aware of her father's threadbare work jacket and cap hanging on the door hook and of the dirty pots from teatime still sitting on the

132

draining board.

'I took a stroll on the Common after Evensong. It's a fine evening.'

'Yes.' She gave a cautious nod. What had brought him here? It was one thing for David to take the air on Overcliffe Common on his way home to Westgate Road, but he'd had to come well out of his way to make this visit.

Her wary expression pushed him into abandoning formalities. 'I ran into Mabel Jackson and her cronies outside church. Of course they were tittle-tattling about recent events.'

Hazel's heart skipped a beat. She glanced in alarm at her watchful mother and father.

'What were they saying?' Jinny wanted to know. Her voice rose above its usual low pitch. 'No, Dr Bell, there's no need to spell it out. I can guess for myself.'

David pursed his lips then continued. 'Marjorie Sykes was asking Mabel for her version of what had happened to Myra. They were all eager for scraps of information – you know how it is.'

Hazel pictured the scene at the church gate – Mabel in her brown hat and coat at the centre of a storm of questions, people crowding round her like iron filings drawn to a magnet. Her faltering heart thudded. She'd known this would happen – that she would be the butt of criticism, the person whom everyone blamed.

'To be fair to Mabel, she was careful in what she said,' David continued. 'It was a case of "These things happen". And she didn't pretend to know the ins and outs of what went on. It's more the others that I thought I should warn you about – they're out for our blood, I'm afraid.'

'Not Marjorie?' Jinny asked.

'No. I mean Berta and Doreen. But I'm here to tell you not to worry too much about what people in general think. There's a good deal of ignorance dating back to the Dark Ages where something like this is concerned.' Keeping his gaze on Hazel, David tried to interpret the emotions flickering across her face, showing mainly in her violet-tinted eyes – the frown followed by a flash of desperation then a sign of impending tears. 'The point is that Dorothy was at the service too. She caught the drift of the conversation – that we didn't do what we should have done, we should have stepped aside and let Mabel deal with things – she's an old hand and would have known what to do, et cetera.'

'When you say "we", you mean "me".' Hazel knew that he was trying to soften the blow. 'I'm young and inexperienced so I didn't do what I should have done. I should have stepped aside. That's what Dorothy believes too, isn't it?'

'I'm afraid it is,' he admitted, tapping his hat against his thigh with an exasperated sigh. 'It's to be expected – Myra's mother isn't thinking straight. It's natural for her to look around for someone to blame.'

'And did anyone stick up for Hazel?' Robert spoke for the first time.

'Rose Drummond did, in the face of a lot of opposition. She let everyone know that it was Myra and her mother's choice to stay away from our clinic and not to seek medical help. I know Rose quite well from surgery visits – she's to be admired.'

134

Again Hazel pictured the scene – Aunty Rose in her big church hat and smart smock coat, tiny and bent, striding down the church pathway with all guns blazing, sticking up for her niece. She cried grateful tears at the thought of it.

'It's just as well I wasn't there,' Jinny said darkly. 'I'd have had plenty of my own to say.'

Hazel managed to wipe away her tears and cling on to some shreds of dignity. 'Thank you for coming,' she told David now that he'd delivered the bad news and was turning for the door.

'Thank you, Doctor,' Jinny and Robert echoed.

Hazel saw him out onto the street, trying to overcome the flood of guilt that threatened to engulf her. The sun had gone down below the rooflines, leaving the pavement in shadow though the sky was tinged fiery red.

'I'll see you at clinic,' David said, his gaze steady and kind. 'I mean this, Hazel – you must take no notice of the gossips. And if Dorothy sets Mabel onto you, you'll let me know?'

She nodded. If she tried to thank him again, her voice would be sure to break down.

'It's a pet hate of mine – the way these old handy-women still lord it over everyone.' He launched into a speech that he hoped would ease Hazel's obvious pain. 'The sooner they're stopped, the better. They're untrained, self-taught medievalists who, as often as not, abandon or let down women in their hour of need. They permit and provoke the spread of infection, have nothing at hand to prevent haemorrhage and offer nothing by way of proper pain relief. There – I've said what I think. Now I can get down off my soapbox and leave you in peace.'

Taken aback, Hazel walked a little way up the street with him. 'I do know, deep down, that Myra's case on Friday night was hopeless. I think I realized it the moment I saw her.'

'Good. So you'll rise above the gossip.' Settling his hat on his head, David gave a reassuring smile. 'I speak out of experience. I've been subjected to all sorts of accusations in my time. And I've suffered my own losses.'

Hazel reached out a hand and lightly touched his arm. It wasn't the occasion to say more, but she wanted to let him know that she understood.

'I will see you on Tuesday,' he affirmed, striding away from her.

She watched him go – square-shouldered and brisk, his warm words filtering through the wall of ice-cold shock she'd felt for two days. They gave her little comfort as she lay awake all that night, reliving events and feeling the courage she needed to carry on doing her hard, risk-filled job drain away.

Next day, Jinny went upstairs to Hazel's room and announced that she'd taken the day off work.

Hazel sat fully dressed in the chair next to her bed, staring up through the skylight at the leaden sky. The sleepless night had taken its toll and her spirits were at rock bottom.

'Why did you do that?' she asked lethargically.

'To help you find homes for the rest of these – that's why.' A determined Jinny waved Hazel's roll of posters in front of her face. 'Shift! Get your coat on – we're going out.'

'No,' Hazel protested. She didn't have the energy, and besides, she dreaded people staring and pointing.

'Yes.' Her mother pulled her to her feet and bundled her down the stairs. In less than a minute, she'd helped her on with her coat and had her out on the street. 'You know what they say – when you fall off your horse you have to get straight back in the saddle.'

Hazel frowned at the flippant comparison. 'You make it sound simple.'

'And it's not,' Jinny agreed, waiting for Hazel to look up from the pavement and meet her gaze. 'You've taken a bad knock. That's why we're doing this together, you and me. We'll drop in on some chemist's shops in town and get them to put a poster in their windows. Then we'll take the bus out to Hadley and ask at the library there.'

'I don't know...' Hazel faltered.

'But I do!' Jinny's blue eyes gazed intently at her daughter's pale face, as if by merely looking she could put back together and heal her fractured heart. 'Shall we catch the tram into town or walk?'

'We'll walk,' Hazel whispered.

So they set out arm in arm, across Ghyll Road and down onto Canal Road, weaving between cars, bikes and buses – mother and daughter on a mission to put Myra's death behind them.

'Yes' was the answer at Hawkins' Chemists on Booth Street and 'yes' again at Lawson's in Market Square – they were more than willing to

137

advertise the Westgate Road clinic.

And another 'yes' at the small branch library after Hazel and Jinny's bus journey out to Hadley, up the steep hill out of town and along the moor top to the old pit village in the next valley. The narrow main street, with its church, village institute and pub, was dominated by disused mine workings and by grey, barren slag heaps that formed a backdrop to life here.

'If anyone's interested in coming along, remind them that the number 65 bus will drop them off right outside the surgery,' Jinny told the librarian behind the counter.

The young woman held her rubber stamp aloft over an open book. She looked from Jinny to Hazel and back again then spoke in a hushed, library voice. 'Who runs this clinic then – you or her?'

'I do.' Hazel forced herself to step forward, though she trembled inwardly.

'She has a certificate,' Jinny informed the sceptical librarian. 'From the Royal College.'

The girl nodded and smiled. 'In that case, you can count me in. I'll display your poster and pass the word around.'

'Ta – that's good.' Hazel managed a grateful smile.

'I'll tell my sister Cynthia, for a start. She's six months' gone with her first.'

Hazel thanked her again then she and Jinny left the library and walked back to the bus stop.

On the ride home she noticed patches of blue in the sky and a dappled pattern of light and shade across the open moorland.

'Feeling better?' Jinny asked.

'A bit.' Sheep grazed among the heather. There were rabbits wherever you looked, sitting at the roadside or hopping lazily along the verges.

'That's the ticket.' Jinny rested her hand on Hazel's. 'Rather him than me,' she said about a man beginning a hard slog up the steep hill.

A bit better, Hazel acknowledged to herself, feeling the warmth of her mother's hand.

They arrived home in a state of rare harmony, in time to meet the postman delivering a parcel for Hazel.

'My new uniform,' she guessed as they hurried inside. Placing it on the kitchen table, she untied the string then peeled back the brown paper to reveal a neatly folded, blue cotton dress, white hat and apron. 'I ordered it from the people who supply uniforms to nurses at the King Edward's. What do you think?'

Jinny held the dress up against Hazel's slim frame. 'It looks like the right size.'

Hazel felt a new resolve form inside her. She wouldn't shut out the memory of Myra and her stillborn baby, she decided, but from now on she would think of them more calmly and move forward in her career – slowly, one step at a time.

'Will you wear it tomorrow?' Jinny asked gently.

'I will,' she said with grateful tears in her eyes.

Her mother smiled then thrust the fresh new uniform towards her. 'Good – that's my girl. But this will need a good iron before you put it on.'

Before the end of the day, Hazel steeled herself to call in on Irene Bradley at the infirmary on Ghyll

Road. She approached the grim building with fingers firmly crossed, parking her bike in the shaded courtyard and doing her best to avoid formidable Matron Fuller by slipping in through a side entrance close to Irene's ward. Her luck was in and she found her patient sitting up in bed in a room shared with five other women. Irene's bed was by the window overlooking the yard.

'I thought I spotted you,' was Irene's opening remark. 'I told the others, "Hey-up, it's the girl from the clinic."'

Not knowing which way to take this, and still shaken by recent events, Hazel hovered in the doorway. 'I came to find out how you were,' she began nervously. All eyes were on her – six heavily pregnant women wearing nightdresses and crocheted bed jackets of various pastel hues, all tucked up under crisp white sheets and green bedspreads. They eyed the newcomer with open curiosity, one with curlers in her hair, one rubbing face cream into her cheeks, another knitting baby's bootees.

'I said, "That's the one who got me sent here in a blooming ambulance,"' Irene went on.

Neither her expression nor her voice gave anything away but Hazel was reassured to see that her lank hair was newly washed and her cheeks had a better colour than when she'd seen her at clinic, so she ventured towards the bed. 'You're looking better. How are you feeling?'

Ignoring Hazel's question, Irene went on addressing the other women in the ward. 'You wouldn't think it to look at her, being a little slip of a thing, but she wouldn't take no for an answer.

She takes one look at me and has a listen to the baby then she dashes off to fetch the doctor.'

'You don't say,' the woman in curlers said as the scrutiny continued.

'She doesn't look anyway near old enough to be a midwife.' Knit-one, pearl-one – the knitter in the next bed – voiced what they were all thinking.

Irene pointed to the chair beside her bed. 'Now, Nurse, take the weight off your feet, why don't you?'

'Ta, I will.' Hazel sat on the edge of the chair, glad of the invitation but still ready to make an exit if things took a turn for the worse.

'I don't hold with doctors and nurses as a rule.' Irene seemed to enjoy holding the floor for once in her hand-to-mouth life. 'I only turned up at the clinic because Betty said there'd be tea and biscuits. Then lo and behold, they take one look at me and whisk me in here! Now they're everywhere I look.'

'Talk of the devil,' a woman in the bed nearest to the door warned as Matron Fuller stalked in from the corridor, resplendent in dark blue uniform, with her white cap starched like the peaks of the Himalayas.

'This is not visiting time,' she informed Hazel with a frown, taking in her casual appearance and apparently failing to recognize her from her previous visit. 'I'm afraid I'll have to ask you to leave.'

Hazel had only just begun to frame an explanation when Irene broke in.

'This isn't a visitor,' she said with a nod of her head towards Hazel. 'This here is my midwife,

141

I'll have you know.'

'Indeed?' With an air of disbelief Matron Fuller studied the slight, fair-haired girl in the pink blouse and dark slacks sitting by the side of Irene's bed.

'Yes, h-indeed!' Irene didn't budge an inch as she held Matron's stern gaze, her arms crossed defiantly. 'Her name is Hazel Price and she's the one I've chosen to look after me when my baby's born.'

Buoyed up by her experience at the infirmary and by Jinny's precious support, Hazel got ready for clinic next day. She was up early, had washed and dressed and was eating breakfast when her father came down the stairs.

'Good luck for today.' Robert stooped to kiss the top of her head as he left for work.

'Luck won't come into it,' Jinny insisted from her position at the sink where she washed and dried the dishes. 'Hazel will prove herself by doing her job right and that'll be the end of it.'

Not quite, Hazel thought at the time, and later that day she was proved right.

It was two o'clock when she donned her new uniform and set off for clinic, cycling up Raglan Road. She felt her heart judder and miss a beat as she passed the drawn curtains of number 80 – and on around the corner onto Overcliffe Road. Unluckily for her, on the edge of the Common she found Dorothy Pennington gathered in a huddle with Berta, Doreen and Mabel – the witches' coven plus one, she thought wryly. Spotting them before they saw her, she tried to avoid

142

them by making a U-turn, intending to double-back down Albion Lane and take a different route onto Westgate Road.

That was her first mistake.

'Well, look who it isn't!' Mabel caught Hazel midway through her ill-thought-out manoeuvre.

Panicking, Hazel wobbled and tipped to one side. She put her foot out to save herself but her heart sank further to discover that the sudden back-pedalling had made the chain come off her bike. She dismounted then crouched to fix it without replying – her second mistake.

'Giving us the cold shoulder, are you?' Mabel taunted, muttering something under her breath before crossing the road to join Hazel.

The oily chain slipped through Hazel's fingers and she failed to loop it back around its cog. Brushing back stray strands of hair, she looked up at Mabel with a frustrated air.

The handywoman's expression was sourly judgemental. 'Ignoring poor Dorothy won't make things any better.'

'I know – I'm sorry.' At last Hazel fixed the chain and stood up, her face burning with embarrassment. 'I thought she would rather not have to talk to me.'

Mabel shook her head slowly. 'The funeral's on Friday. John's decided to bury them both in the same coffin – the baby and Myra together.'

The detail, delivered with an unsparing directness, demolished Hazel's still fragile confidence. Her mouth went dry and she was only able to mutter a barely audible 'Sorry'.

'Likewise – I'm sorry John didn't fetch me
143

sooner and that he wasted time taking you up to the house. Those few precious minutes might have made all the difference.'

Hazel frowned, stared down at her oily fingers then up at Mabel. 'I doubt it,' she said quietly but more steadily. 'Myra was already very poorly when I got there.'

'Aye, but she was used to me and my way of doing things. If I'd been there, I would have been able to quieten her down.'

Mabel's claim angered Hazel.

'No – she was already unconscious. At that stage she wasn't responding to anything anyone said.'

Aware of Dorothy, Berta and Doreen's stares, Mabel held her ground. 'I've seen it all a hundred times before. There are still ways of bringing people round when something like that happens.'

'Not without a strong sedative, there aren't,' Hazel argued. 'And even then, the mother's high blood pressure had probably put paid to the baby's chances of being delivered safely.' On sure ground over medical matters, she found that she was able to stand up to Mabel after all, though her heart was pounding. 'I am truly sorry for Myra's family, but that doesn't alter the facts of the case. And now, if you don't mind, I'd better be on my way to clinic.'

'Oh yes, don't keep them waiting.' Sarcasm was Mabel's last resort. Instead of making Hazel feel small, as she'd intended, she recognized that the tables were in danger of being turned. 'But remember – the word is out.'

'What word?' Hazel was about to remount her

144

bike and head off down Albion Lane, but the hidden threat made her pause.

'About you and your qualification,' Mabel scoffed. 'We all know it's not worth the paper it's written on. And if folks didn't realize before, they do now.'

'What do you mean? What have you been saying?'

'Me? I've not said a word. I don't have to.'

Mabel's gloating attack broke down the last of Hazel's defences, so she turned and cycled shakily towards Ghyll Road where she picked up speed, threading through cars and delivery vans until she turned left again, back up the hill onto Westgate Road. There she dismounted and pushed her bike down an alley into a small yard at the back of the surgery. Leaning it against a dustbin and taking her midwife's bag from the basket, she hurried onto the street, up the steps and into Reception.

'There were only two or three of your ladies waiting outside the door, so I let 'em in and made a list of names – there it is, right under your nose,' Eleanor told Hazel without preliminaries. Dressed as usual in a neat white blouse with pin-tucked panels and a Peter Pan collar and with her dark hair swept back from her forehead in a fashionable roll, Eleanor's fingers didn't cease flying across the typewriter keys. 'They're upstairs waiting for you. Oh, and I'd wash my hands before I went in if I were you,' she added.

'Thanks.' Hazel's reply was breathless as she took the receptionist's advice and rushed into the cloakroom, scrubbing her hands to remove the oil then dashing out again. She took the stairs two at

145

a time to find the clinic room almost empty. Hiding her disappointment, she said hello to Lydia and Evelyn, whose houses she'd visited. They gave cheery replies and quips about not being whipped off to the infirmary like poor Irene. Hazel responded with a thin smile then went behind the green screen to open her bag and lay out her instruments. Then she emerged and called the first name on her short list. 'Cynthia Houghton, please!'

'Here!' Cynthia looked the picture of health as she got up. Her face was rosy, her skin smooth and her bobbed hair formed a glossy, nut-brown cap. She chatted non-stop as Hazel weighed then examined her, telling her that her librarian sister in Hadley had sent her. 'She's a bossy boots, is Tilly – she takes books off the shelf and bones up about having babies, says we women have to take charge and not follow the old ways. That's why I'm here.'

Average weight gain; steady foetal heartbeat – strong and regular; no oedema. Hazel was quickly satisfied that all was well. She praised Cynthia for taking good care of herself and said she hoped to see her in two weeks' time.

As Cynthia departed, Hazel called out the next name on her list. 'Evelyn Jagger, please.'

Evelyn, the nervous *primigravida*. Here was someone who would need more careful handling, Hazel decided. She softened her voice as she invited Evelyn to lie down to be examined and did everything as gently as she could. 'Baby's in a good position and kicking nicely,' she reassured her. 'What are we – thirty-two weeks? Not too long to go now.'

Evelyn – a tall, ungainly woman with rounded shoulders and a permanently worried expression – was evidently not enjoying pregnancy. 'I haven't got any get-up-and-go,' she complained as she got dressed. 'It's not like me at all.'

'Which is why you should put your feet up whenever you get the chance,' Hazel told her. 'Don't do too much – and that's an order!'

Evelyn responded with a weak smile. 'Easy for you to say. Father's poorly with his chest and that means Mother needs a lot of help. I'm at their beck and call.'

'Well, it's time to put yourself first for a change,' Hazel insisted. 'Starting right now. I've just heard Eleanor bring in the trolley. It's a good strong cup of sweet tea for you before you leave. And I'll see you next week.'

Lydia came in next and luckily the examination presented no problems, though Hazel grew more and more aware of the silence in the waiting area.

'Not so busy today, I see.' Lydia's pointed comment drew an awkward response.

'More might come along later,' Hazel said without conviction.

'Or maybe that to-do with Myra Pennington has put 'em off.'

Hazel didn't reply as she brought Lydia's notes up to date.

'Not me, though,' plain-speaking Lydia assured her on her way out. 'I trust you, I do. You hear that, Dr Bell? I like Nurse Price and I'm keeping on with the clinic regardless.'

Rid of his last patient of the day, David had

147

come upstairs to find out how Hazel had coped. 'Not so good, eh?'

'No. Only three came.' She put away her stethoscope with a dejected sigh.

'Never mind. We expected people to gossip and sure enough, they did.' A kind smile softened his sharp features and his eyes followed Hazel around the room. 'As you know, the real job is not the science of delivering babies, it's convincing patients that they can rely on you, come what may.'

'I'm not doing a very good job of it then, am I?'

'But it takes time and there are bound to be hiccoughs along the way.'

'This feels like more than a hiccough,' Hazel confessed with a face full of woe.

David nodded then attempted to lighten the mood. 'Don't worry – you've got Eleanor on your side.'

'Have I?' She stopped tidying and shot him a surprised look. 'Or are you just teasing me?'

He smiled. 'No, I'm serious. Eleanor is like one of the sentries on guard outside Buckingham Palace: she treats everyone who comes through the door with maximum suspicion. You've been here for how long?'

'Three weeks all told.'

'See – and you've already got her eating out of your hand.'

'Honestly?' Hazel couldn't tell how serious he was. As far as she was aware, the receptionist still cast a cool eye over her and rarely said anything positive.

'Believe me.' Leaning against the door post in a

relaxed manner, his smile broadened. 'By the way, is there any point offering you a lift home, or are you on your old sit-up-and-beg bike?'

'Bike,' she confirmed. Recalling Gladys's glee over David's first offer of a lift, she blushed. 'But thank you anyway.'

'Well, when winter sets in and you stop wanting to brave the elements, the offer will still stand.' He stood aside to let her pass.

She dipped her head then hurried down the stairs, aware that he was following close behind. In Reception she nodded a farewell at Eleanor, who was still typing away. Then, through the stained-glass panel of the main door Hazel made out the outline of a man. She stepped back as the door knob turned and John Moxon came in. His left wrist was bound by a blood-soaked tourniquet and he nursed his left hand in the palm of his right. The hand bled profusely from a deep gash between forefinger and thumb.

'Doctor, can you put a stitch in this?' he asked David, ignoring Hazel. 'I had a mishap at work.'

This was Hazel's second piece of bad timing of the day – bumping into first Dorothy and now John. Her heart plummeted into her boots.

'Come with me.' David reacted quickly, directing him towards the examination room while Eleanor tutted at the splashes of blood on the tiled floor. 'I'll need to give you an injection to stop it getting infected as well as a local anaesthetic for the stitches.'

'*Go,*' Eleanor mouthed at Hazel who was half hidden behind the door.

But John sensed her presence and turned. For

a second he looked startled then rapidly brought himself under control. 'Wait a second,' he said to David.

Hazel bit her lip and prepared herself for the outburst that would surely follow.

John towered over her, his face etched with sorrow, his injured hand forgotten. 'Hello, Hazel. I was hoping I might run in to you at some point. I have something I wanted to say to you.'

'This way, please.' David's brisk tone warned John that he wouldn't stand for any nonsense.

But John ignored him. His eyes locked onto Hazel, leaving her unable to move away. 'Don't worry – I only want to thank you.'

'For what?' she murmured. She overcame the band of guilt and fear that had tightened around her chest. After all, what she had suffered since Myra's death was nothing compared to what John must be going through. She imagined the undiluted torment of losing those he loved in one fell swoop, the deep well of sorrow down which he stared.

'For doing your best.' His voice cracked and ended in a sigh.

'I'm so sorry.' There were no words, no way of raising him out of his grief. Though there were tears in her eyes, she didn't flinch under his gaze.

He stood with one hand cradled in the other, pale and bleeding but determined. 'Thank you,' he said again.

Eleanor came out from behind her desk and took him by the elbow. 'Doctor is ready for you,' she said as she led him away.

Hazel's lips quivered. She went out and closed

150

the door, paused on the top step and glanced back through the red and green leaded glass. In the midst of grief John Moxon had looked her in the eye and said the decent thing. It took courage. Another word came to mind as she hurried down the stone steps onto the busy street. 'Honour.' John was an honourable man, head and shoulders above others in more than the obvious sense. She admired him for rising above his own suffering to offer her a scrap of comfort. Not many men would have done that – of this she was certain.

CHAPTER NINE

September eased into October without Hazel realizing how fast the year was slipping away. Though Jinny went to Myra's funeral, she said nothing to Hazel afterwards about Dorothy's cold looks or Mabel's forthright criticism at the church gate.

'That girl of yours is still wet behind the ears, Jinny Price. That's how we've come to this.'

Jinny had told Mabel to keep her opinions to herself. 'If anyone's to blame, it's Myra's mother for not getting her the proper help in time.'

'We'll agree to differ,' Mabel had muttered stiffly, bowing her head as the cortège had pulled up.

There'd been no weeping and wailing from the thin-lipped chief mourners, just a sombre silence as the single coffin containing both mother and child had been carried inside.

Afterwards, life returned to normal for most of the residents on Raglan Road. Hazel continued her struggle to bring more women back to the clinic as strong winds brought down the rust-red leaves from the beech trees bordering the Common and morning mists crept down from the moors into the narrow streets and crowded courtyards. They combined with black smoke churned out by the mill chimneys to form a choking, foul-smelling smog that cut visibility to a few feet. On some days this was so bad that traffic came to a standstill, requiring a man to walk ahead of each vehicle carrying two bright lights. Hazel heard of several old people in the neighbourhood being taken to hospital with acute respiratory failure, while four of the women in her clinic developed bronchitis. Two others were laid low by influenza.

However, Margie Daniels did come back to the clinic and was one of the lucky ones who sailed through pregnancy and whose home birth under Hazel's care went without a hitch. At half past eleven at night on 24 October, after a four-hour labour, she delivered a baby boy, weighing in at a bouncing eight pounds two ounces. Mother and baby thrived from the off; Margie took to breast-feeding for the second time like a duck to water and little Bertie soon put on weight, so that Hazel's post-natal visits to the house on Ada Street quickly ceased.

With Evelyn Jagger, however, Hazel was presented with a more difficult situation to test her skills. Despite her worries during pregnancy, careworn Evelyn had insisted on giving birth to her first baby at home and went into labour in

152

the early hours of a Wednesday morning, having attended clinic the day before. Her husband Archie was away from home looking for work so Hazel got the call from Evelyn's mother who lived next door to her daughter and son-in-law.

Hazel's heart lurched at the sound of urgent knocking in the middle of the night and the usual call of 'Baby's on its way!', but she was up and dressed, running through the deserted streets ahead of the older woman, down slippery, moss-covered steps and through dark alleys until she arrived at the house on Canal Road to find Evelyn in great distress.

Within minutes she'd found out the cause – the baby's presentation was wrong and it needed strong manual manipulation on Hazel's part to bring the head into a position where it would engage and labour could progress, hopefully without the use of forceps, which usually required a doctor.

'Just my luck!' Evelyn moaned between bouts of agonizing pain. But she had more grit and determination than Hazel had expected and she delivered her daughter unaided. In the end there was no need for Hazel to call on David for assistance. Instead, she used ergometrine to ensure that the placenta was spontaneously pushed out and by this time a smiling Evelyn was cradling the baby in her arms.

'She's called her Sally, after the girl in the Gracie Fields song,' Hazel told David when she dropped in at the surgery to complete Evelyn's record card at midday. She smiled at his raised eyebrows. '"Pride of our alley". They're all naming them

153

after well-known songs and film stars these days.'

'It could have been worse,' he admitted. 'At least it's not Tallulah.'

'Sally's a pretty name; I like it.' The light-hearted banter sent her on her way with a smile. She was quietly pleased with how well she'd coped with the tricky situation. *I'm moving on,* she thought. *I'm remembering the reasons why I came into midwifery in the first place.* Yes, it was still a struggle to find enough work to make a good living and yes, there was every chance that there would be another case like Myra's waiting around the corner – a baby delivered too prematurely to survive, say, or more transverse presentations, and worst of all, other cases of full-blown eclampsia. But being the mainstay at David's antenatal clinic had helped Hazel get over the feeling of being an outsider that she'd suffered when she first came home. It was true that Dorothy Pennington still harboured bitter resentment – a feeling made doubly obvious by the cold shoulder offered by the women whom Hazel had fixed in her mind as 'the coven'.

'Her? She's clueless,' Mabel would say with a shake of her head whenever Hazel's name was mentioned.

'Book learning never got anyone anywhere,' Doreen or Berta would wholeheartedly agree.

Jinny's steady advice to Hazel was to take no notice.

'Easier said than done.' Hazel's weary response came at the end of another fruitless day trying to drum up custom. She carried upstairs her mother's parting advice to stick at it regardless

154

and crept miserably into bed.

At teatime on 4 November, shortly after Evelyn's home birth, there was a loud knock on the door of number 18.

'Leave it – it's probably kids,' Jinny remarked as Hazel went to answer the door. 'It's Mischief Night, remember.'

This was the night before Bonfire Night when there was a tradition of letting the boys and girls of the neighbourhood go wild with any number of practical jokes. They knocked on doors then ran away, posted jumping-jacks through your letter box or else tied a dustbin lid to your door handle and scarpered.

There was a second knock with no surprise fireworks and then a third more impatient one before Hazel decided she'd better see who it was.

'Five shillings and three pence!' Betty Hollings stood on the doorstep with a bright smile and an outstretched palm full of sixpences, three-penny bits and coppers. 'It's the rest of what we owe you. Sorry it's taken so long!'

Hazel returned the smile. 'Come in, Betty!'

'Quickly, before we freeze to death in here,' Jinny added

'No, ta. I'm not stopping.' Betty had braved the usual November pea-souper without hat or coat. 'Doreen's keeping an eye on the kids. I promised her I wouldn't be long.' She tipped the coins into Hazel's cupped palms. 'Never say we don't pay up, eh?' she said with a wink.

'Ta – I appreciate it. It'll come in handy in the run-up to Christmas. How's little Daisy getting

155

on, by the way? I haven't called in to see her for a while.'

'Fit as a fiddle,' Betty reported. 'I had Mabel having a go at me the other day, though.'

Hazel came out onto the step and held the door closed behind her. 'What for?'

'The usual. She'd overheard Len in the Green Cross saying he was having trouble scraping together what we still owed you then next day she ran into me at Hutchinson's, asking the grumpy old sod to put a few things on the slate for me until the end of the week – meat paste, a tin of sardines and suchlike. Well, that was Mabel's cue. "It serves you right for going to Hazel Price in the first place. If you'd stayed with me like you did for the first two, I'd have kept the price down and you wouldn't be in here begging for favours" – on and on like a stuck record.'

Hazel was by now used to the rivalry between herself and Mabel so she skipped over that part of what Betty was saying. She concentrated instead on a picture of the hard-up housewife wheedling her way into getting basic groceries from Ben Hutchinson on tick. 'Are you sure you can afford this?' she asked, jingling the coins between her hands.

'We'll manage, don't you worry,' Betty said, pulling her brown cardigan across her chest. 'We always do; one way or another.' With a cheerful goodbye she backed down onto the greasy pavement and was lost in the yellowish-grey fog. Further up the street there was the sound of fire crackers followed by children's running footsteps and laughter.

Hazel went into the kitchen and spread the coins across the table, making piles of sixpences, three-penny pieces and pennies that she pushed towards Jinny. 'That's for my keep this week,' she told her.

Her mother counted out three shillings then pushed the rest back. 'This is more than enough.'

Hazel calculated that she was left with two and three for herself, which she would deposit in the bank tomorrow. Over the years she'd been a careful saver and now the total in her bank book stood at ten pounds, seven and six – more than enough for her to pay the deposit on a flat or a house plus the first week's rent if she so chose.

'You'll soon be thinking of moving out into a place of your own at this rate.' Jinny seemed to read Hazel's mind. 'Don't look at me like that – it's bound to be the next step for a girl like you.'

Hazel sat down beside her mother and studied her with a worried frown. She had a close view of the wrinkles forming at the corners of Jinny's eyes and the lines just visible from her nose to the corners of her mouth – signs of ageing that rouge and face powder couldn't hide. 'What kind of girl is that?' she asked.

'One who sets about doing things without letting anyone get in her way,' Jinny said with a sigh.

'Am I like that?' Hazel's dismay showed in her face. The real her, hidden from view, certainly wasn't the out and out go-getter that Jinny described.

'It's how it comes across – yes. I've always said to Mother, ever since you were little: "Hazel will do what she wants to do – come what may."'

'But it doesn't feel like that to me. Often I'm quaking in my shoes – when I first left home and went to college, for a start. That was very hard.'

'You still went ahead, though,' Jinny pointed out. 'We may be alike in some ways, you and me, but we're opposites in that respect. I always followed what people expected of me – the same as Rose. In my case it was to get married to Alec and leave home. For Rose it was to stay and look after Mother. Neither of us would ever have been able to branch out on our own. But times change; I realize that.'

'So would you and Dad mind if I found a place of my own?' Hazel wondered aloud.

'Like I said, it wouldn't make any difference if we did.'

'But would you?' Hazel persisted. Part of her longed to hear her mother say that she wanted her to stay here on Raglan Road where she belonged, but a more urgent, forward-looking voice was telling her to spread her wings.

'Where are you thinking of?' Jinny asked. 'Would it be very far away?'

'No, not far. I've got my group of women from the clinic to think of. I thought I'd start looking for a flat on Ghyll Road. That would be handy.' Hazel was frustrated that Jinny still hadn't told her how she felt about the idea. Why couldn't she share her feelings, just this once?

'Your dad will miss you.' Jinny's reflective remark led to a short silence, broken by the boom and clang of a banger exploding under a metal dustbin lid. The racket echoed down the street. 'Don't breathe a word until you've found somewhere –

158

he'll only get in a state.'

'All right. Anyway, it might not be until after Christmas.'

'Yes, it would be nice if we could have Christmas together.'

'Mum, I'm not planning to emigrate to Australia.' Hazel's exasperation broke through. 'With a bit of luck I'll only be round the corner.'

'You'll need pots and pans.' Jinny's mind turned to the practical as usual. 'I've got a spare pair of curtains in a drawer upstairs that I can let you have.'

Best to put a lid on any hopes of Jinny expressing her feelings or even offering an opinion, Hazel realized. She looked sadly around the kitchen at the clock on the mantelpiece that had taken second place to her framed certificate and at the green and cream wallpaper with its up-to-date geometric pattern that her mother had carefully chosen from a heavy book of samples. Jinny was now pestering to get rid of the old black range and replace it with a tiled fireplace but the cost was against it, Robert said.

'I'll miss you too,' Jinny admitted out of the blue, going to answer a fresh knock on the door.

The confession startled Hazel more than any Catherine wheel whizzing and sparking in the dark. Now this was something out of the ordinary – it really was. She wished that their heart-to-heart hadn't been so rudely interrupted.

'It's Sylvia for you.' Jinny reached for her coat and disappeared down the steps. 'I'm just popping round to Nelson Yard,' she called back as Sylvia brought in the sour smell of fog, smoke

159

and exploding fireworks. 'I want to make sure those kids aren't pestering Mum and Rose with their bangers.'

'Well, if it isn't Mrs Bellamy – come in, come in!' In newly buoyant mood, Hazel sat her cousin down in the fireside chair. 'Wait while I fettle the fireguard for you – we don't want sparks burning holes in your lovely nylon stockings.'

'I won't stop long,' Sylvia insisted as she took a small box from her coat pocket and handed it to Hazel. 'I'm returning the brooch that I borrowed from Aunty Jinny.'

'Well, it's lovely to see you.' Hazel took a peek inside the box at the glittering bluebird then went on to make her visitor feel at home. 'Shall I put the kettle on?'

'Unless you've got something stronger,' Sylvia grunted.

'Only Dad's brandy, but that's strictly for medicinal purposes, I'm afraid.'

'Tea it is, then.' Ignoring Hazel's conspiratorial wink and leaning back listlessly, Sylvia made no effort to help. 'Norman went out to the Green Cross with Dan, leaving me all on my ownio.'

'I see. Is Dan leading him astray already?'

'Yes, and Norman doesn't have the backbone to say no.' The remark brought a resentful twist to Sylvia's pretty features. 'Dan only has to click his fingers for him to go running. Calvert has cut Norman's hours to three days a week at the start of this week, so it's not even as if he can afford to splash out.'

'That's bad luck so soon after you got married.' Seeing storm clouds gathering, Hazel handed her a cup of tea then hoped to open up a brighter topic of conversation. 'And how are you in yourself? Are you keeping well?'

'Why shouldn't I be?' Sylvia retorted, crossing her legs and tapping her foot impatiently. The action made her skirt ride up above her knee, giving a glimpse of stocking-top and suspender.

Quickly Hazel retreated from the obviously touchy subject of Sylvia's health. 'And how's life on Nelson Yard? Is Aunty Ethel lending you a hand to settle into your new house?'

'Don't ask!' Sylvia raised her eyebrows.

From which Hazel gathered there'd been a falling-out between mother and daughter. Yet another dead end. 'And how's Gladys? I haven't run into her lately.'

Sylvia didn't answer but went on rolling her eyes and tapping her foot. 'If you must know, I'm not keeping at all well,' she burst out. 'Married life doesn't suit me, if you know what I mean.'

'Oh.' Hazel pursed her lips while she searched for a response.

'You do know, don't you?'

Hazel filled the uncomfortable pause with a cautious reply. 'Yes, I think so.'

'Don't get married, Hazel – that's my advice.' Uncrossing her legs, Sylvia lapsed from anger into a sullen silence, broken at last by a heartfelt sigh. 'Unless you're lucky enough to fall head over heels, that is.'

Hazel nodded, thinking back to Gladys's account of Sylvia and Norman's rushed courtship. The phrase 'Act in haste, repent at leisure' sprang to mind. 'It's early days,' she said gently. 'Perhaps everything will settle down.'

'No. I know people are hoping it will – Nana and Aunty Rose, especially. I don't have the heart to tell them it won't.'

'You just have to give it a chance. Norman will do his best to find extra work, I'm sure. Things will be better again when there's more money coming in.'

'It's not that.' Tears appeared suddenly in Sylvia's eyes and she made no attempt to stop them from trickling down her cheeks. 'It's what I was trying to tell you about just now – the part of marriage that nobody talks about. That's what's wrong.'

Moved by the awkwardness of Sylvia's tearful confession, Hazel crouched by her side. 'You're very young, you know. They say it takes a while to get used to.'

'"Young and daft."' Sylvia's self-mockery introduced a new, more bitter tone. 'That's what you all thought – you and Gladys, even Nana and Aunty Rose. That's why Aunty Jinny lending me her brooch meant such a lot to me. She was the only one who was kind.'

Hazel settled onto her knees, her face flushed from the fire and from a sharp pang of guilt. 'What can I do to help?' she asked.

Sylvia sniffed and wiped her tears with the back of her hand. She seemed to take time to screw up her courage. 'As a matter of fact, there is something.'

'Anything.' Hazel's mind raced ahead. She imagined that Sylvia was building up to confessing that she was having a baby, which they'd suspected

162

all along, and that she'd come to her for advice and support.

'I would've gone to Mabel about this,' Sylvia went on, confirming Hazel's suspicions. 'Only then, the cat would be out of the bag.'

'No, not Mabel,' Hazel agreed, with information about antenatal care and the importance of attending the clinic on the tip of her tongue.

'I can't have people tittle-tattling. This has to be between you and me – no one else.'

Doubt darted into Hazel's mind. 'But surely, if this is about what I think it's about, the news will be out before too long anyway?'

'Oh, for heaven's sake, Hazel; do I have to spell it out?' Exasperated, Sylvia sprang from her chair and paced the room.

'No, I understand. You're expecting. You need my help.'

'But not to *have* the baby, silly!' Now that the flood gates were opened, the words poured out. 'The help I need is for the opposite. People like you can stop things from going any further, I know you can. I'm not too far gone so I just have to take some medicine and it'll all be over. If you do it right, there'll be nothing else for me to worry about.'

'I can't do that!' Hazel was shocked to her core. Yes, occasionally women had abortions that were official and above-board. But they were usually in their late thirties and forties with multiple births behind them, where a further pregnancy posed a risk to their own or their baby's health. What possible reason could a young newlywed like Sylvia have? 'Listen to me – it's your first

163

time and I know you must be frightened. But really, this is perfectly natural.'

Sylvia left off pacing and shot an angry glance at Hazel. 'If I'd wanted someone to get on their high horse and talk down to me, I'd have gone to Mum or Gladys. The question is – will you help me or not?'

'No,' Hazel said. The answer came from deep down and with a force that surprised both of them.

Sylvia tossed her head. 'Ta very much!'

'I mean it. This is all happening in a rush and it's frightened you. Take some time to think.'

'I've had nothing else on my mind for weeks on end, ta.' Clenching her jaw to stop her lip from trembling, Sylvia realized she would have to accept Hazel's answer. 'You're not to say anything to anyone – not even to Gladys,' she said with a final flare of defiance. 'You promise?'

'I promise,' Hazel echoed as calmly as she could, though she felt helpless and worried beyond belief.

'Cross your heart.'

'Cross my heart. But does Norman know yet? Have you talked to him about this?'

'No. You're the only one.' Chin up and with a fixed, defiant smile, Sylvia opened the door onto the street. 'I'm a real chump, aren't I?'

Two boys ran past the house, their feet slapping on the dark pavement. 'Why are you a chump?'

'For getting into this mess in the first place and for thinking you would help me,' came the bitter reply.

'Talk to Norman,' Hazel pleaded.

164

But Sylvia shook her head. 'If you won't do it, I'll find someone who will,' she said, slamming the door behind her.

On the next Tuesday, with Sylvia's situation frequently on her mind, Hazel got to the surgery early, half an hour before any of her women had arrived.

'Someone's keen!' Eleanor commented from behind her desk.

From up on the first-floor landing, David peered over the banister. His outline was lit from the domed skylight on the second floor so his head and shoulders appeared in silhouette. 'Ah, good – come up and join me, will you, Hazel? There's tea in the pot if you'd like a cup.'

'Yes, please.' Seizing her opportunity, she took off her coat and hat then ran up the stairs.

'Welcome to my lair.' David's voice was warm and genuine. He led the way up another, narrower flight of stairs to his living quarters – a small room with sloping ceilings, cosily but shabbily furnished with a dusty oak bureau and worn leather armchairs. There was a faded oriental rug on the floor and red chenille curtains across one corner, hiding what must be his kitchen. Offering Hazel a seat by the fire, he ducked behind the curtains then quickly emerged with two plain mugs of steaming, dark brown tea. 'I hope it's not too stewed for your liking,' he said, pointing to a sugar bowl resting on a small, low table close to the fire.

'I take it as it comes. Actually, I arrived early on purpose, hoping to catch you,' she explained. The room told her a lot about David – there was nothing here for show; no ornaments, no pictures on the wall and only a plain clock on the chimney breast. On top of the bureau sat a pile of un-opened letters and one small photograph of a dark-haired young woman. 'I'm worried about something and I wanted to pick your brains.'

The 'something' was Sylvia, of course. Since her youngest cousin's tearful visit a few days earlier, Hazel had thought of little else. Sylvia was rash and could easily have followed up on her threat to get 'help' already. Still, there would most likely be a week or so between seeking out an abortionist and the actual act, which gave Hazel time to ask for advice.

'Pick away,' David invited, studying Hazel with his usual thoughtful gaze and perhaps expecting a discussion about Hazel's ongoing struggle to boost clinic numbers.

'I can't mention any names,' she began, then paused and frowned

He nodded and sipped his tea.

'But say, as a general rule, if someone came to you as a doctor and asked you for help that you didn't feel you could give–'

'What would I do?' he interrupted, trying to help her out of her obvious difficulty in framing the right sentence. 'Let's suppose that in this case we're talking about an early termination of a pregnancy?'

Hazel nodded and gave him a grateful smile for his astuteness. 'And there were no medical reasons, only strong feelings of not wanting the baby. And you said no, hoping to talk that person out of it for the baby's sake, but that person won't

166

take no for an answer.'

'And is angry and says, "If you won't help me, I'll find someone who will."'

'Exactly!' Hazel was thankful that he'd been so quick on the uptake. 'Someone around here who knows what to do.'

'Still mentioning no names,' he acknowledged, 'you're right to be worried. There certainly are women in the neighbourhood ready to step in, even though it's against the law and has been for a good few years now. Oh, I could quote you chapter and verse of the Infant Life Preservation Act, but of course it goes on anyway – using anything from ancient herbal purgatives, through hot baths combined with gin to the abortifacients you still see openly advertised as being for "female ailments". Not to mention the use of any pointed implement you care to think of.'

Hazel drew a sharp breath.

'Unpalatable but true,' David insisted. 'Only last week I had to deal with a girl of seventeen who was well into her second trimester. Her circumstances were ... unfortunate, shall we say? So she took it into her head to visit one of these so-called handy-women in secret. The result? Severe haemorrhage, agony and humiliating exposure. She's in hospital and disowned by her family. Still pregnant, as it turns out.'

'I can't think of anything worse,' Hazel murmured, her fears for Sylvia increasing.

'My advice would be to talk to this person again,' he said, his gaze intensifying while his voice grew more determined. 'Present her with the facts. Winkle out her reasons, try to allay her fears.'

167

'I will.' Hazel decided there and then that she would get hold of Sylvia that very evening and talk to her again.

'But be fair with her. Let her know that taking the baby to full term is not without risks either.'

Hazel's eyes flickered involuntarily towards the silver-framed photograph of the smiling young woman.

'Her name was Sara,' David said quietly but plainly. 'It's been three years and I still think about my dear wife and our lost baby boy every day without fail.'

CHAPTER TEN

At half past seven that evening Hazel knocked on the door of 15 Nelson Yard, hoping to speak to Sylvia.

'She's not in.' Norman held the door open a fraction and peered out at Hazel. 'I'm sorry if you've come out of your way.'

'I only live around the corner,' she reminded him. Norman's response had been too pat and had aroused her suspicions. 'Do you mind if I step inside and wait?'

Casting a precautionary glance over his shoulder, Norman opened the door. 'I've no idea when she'll be back,' he warned.

'It doesn't matter – I'm in no hurry.' Once inside, Hazel took in the sorry state of Sylvia and Norman's kitchen. A meagre fire made of coal-slack and coke flickered miserably in the grate while yesterday's ashes lay unswept on the tiled hearth. A washing line laden with dripping shirts and socks was slung diagonally across the room, giving off a strong whiff of carbolic soap – surely the results of Norman's efforts at keeping up with the laundry rather than Sylvia's. There were no chairs to sit on, only upturned orange boxes, their bright blue and yellow Jaffa labels still in evidence. The table, such as it was, cockled on three firm legs, the fourth being fashioned from a rotting clothes-line prop that Norman had rescued from the yard.

'It's not much to write home about, is it?' Norman said before Hazel could comment. Standing in his stockinged feet and with tousled hair, he looked even younger than eighteen, despite his current attempts to grow a moustache. 'Chairs and suchlike will have to wait until we find our feet, worse luck.'

'Where did you call home before you came to Nelson Yard?' she asked, wondering what his life had been like before he met Sylvia and realizing she knew nothing at all about him.

'A cottage on the main street over in Hadley. Why?'

'And didn't you have any furniture to bring with you? I'm sorry – there's no need to answer that if you don't want to. It's just me being nosy.'

Norman's fair colouring meant that he blushed easily and the tic at the corner of his mouth seemed impossible to control. 'We flitted about a lot, my mum and seven of us kids. Four sisters and two brothers, plus me.'

169

'Where are you in the pecking order?'

'I'm the eldest by five whole years. We've had to go wherever there was work ever since I can remember. We only had what we wore on our backs and one tea chest of belongings between us.' Norman spoke matter-of-factly and Hazel noticed that his boyish features relaxed more readily into a smile than a frown. Despite her suspicion that he'd lied about Sylvia's whereabouts, she warmed to him.

'Here's me rabbiting on,' he apologized. 'Don't let me keep you from whatever else you've got to do.'

'You're not,' she said, ducking under the wet washing and trying to think of ways in which she could help the struggling newlyweds. 'I'm sure Mum mentioned to me she has curtains going spare. Do you think Sylvia could make use of them?'

'I'll ask her.'

'And Dad could take you down to Napier's – do you know it? It's a scrapyard on Canal Road. There might be bits and pieces there that would come in handy.'

'It's a thought,' he muttered distractedly.

Hazel wondered why he took the poker and rattled it hard against the grate, disturbing the remains of the fire, until she realized that it might be to hide creaking floorboards above their heads. Was Sylvia creeping about upstairs, she wondered, having left Norman with strict instructions not to let on? Irritated, she took the bull by the horns. 'That isn't Sylvia I can hear, is it?'

'No. It must be coming from next door.' His

170

face flushed bright red as he thrust the poker further into the fire.

'And how is she? Is she well?'

The question took him by surprise. 'Fit as a fiddle. Why?'

In that moment and from the puzzled look on Norman's innocent face, it struck Hazel that Sylvia still hadn't told her husband about her pregnancy, let alone the rest of the family. She took a deep breath, knowing that she ought not to be the one to break it to him. 'No reason,' she said, ready to beat a retreat and think again. 'I'd best be off. Tell Sylvia I called.'

'Will do.' Norman pushed the washing to one side, ready to show Hazel to the door. 'If it's about Friday night, she's already decided she won't be going to the jazz club – I know that much.'

Hazel breathed deeply again then nodded before she braced herself for the cold, blustering wind. 'Me neither. Gladys has arranged a day out to Blackpool on Saturday and she wants an early start.'

'Ta-ta, then,' Norman concluded sheepishly. He hadn't relished lying to Hazel and communicated this reluctance with a what-can-I-do shrug.

'Ta-ta for now,' Hazel responded. *Poor Norman,* she thought out of habit as she made her way across the yard then down the dank alley onto Raglan Road. *Gladys was right – he really doesn't know what he's let himself in for.*

'You've done all you can for now,' David told Hazel over the phone. She'd called from a public telephone box on Ghyll Road, hoping to catch

171

him before the start of surgery on Wednesday morning and bring him up to date on her failed mission to offer Sylvia more advice.

'Remember, she's a grown woman with a mind of her own.'

'Hardly,' Hazel pointed out. 'She's ever so young. That's part of the problem. She does have a husband, but I don't think he knows anything.'

David clicked his tongue against his teeth. 'Worse and worse,' he commiserated. 'I still say, if she won't talk to you there's little you can do except wait until she's ready.'

'But by then it might be too late.' Hazel stood poised with extra coins in case the warning pips sounded. She strained to hear his voice against the roar of early-morning traffic. By 'too late' she meant that Sylvia might have already got rid of the baby, with who knew what consequences. 'Perhaps she would listen to her sister or her mother if I put them in the picture. What do you think?'

'No, don't do that.' David's reply was immediate. 'The information is confidential.'

He was right, of course. 'Thank you. You're busy. I'd better let you get on.'

'Goodbye, then. Oh, and Hazel, before you go – this sort of thing happens in our line of work. You mustn't think you can always solve other people's problems. Sometimes you have to leave them to get on with it.'

'I know; thank you,' she said again before the pips sounded and the line went dead.

Right again. But David didn't realize it was her cousin Sylvia they were talking about. So Hazel

172

went on worrying and wondering for the rest of the week, while Sylvia kept out of her way in what turned into a chilling game of hide-and-seek with at least one life at stake and possibly two.

"'Oh I do like to be beside the seaside!'" Gladys sat in the front passenger seat of John Moxon's borrowed car. Her voice trilled gaily above the purr of the engine as she, Dan and Hazel caught their first glimpse of the ocean. "'Oh, I do like to be beside the sea!'"

"'I do like to walk along the prom, prom, prom...!'" Dan joined in with an out-of-tune contribution. He winked over his shoulder at Hazel.

"'Tiddley-om-pom-pom...'" she hummed from the back seat. The mass of water below was steel grey and heavy clouds swept along the horizon. 'Brr – there was definitely no need to bring our swimming costumes in this weather.'

In fact, she was wearing her heavy winter coat and felt hat for her day trip to Blackpool, having taken a quick look out of the kitchen window early that morning at the damp streets and the wind gusting litter along the pavements.

'I'd get well wrapped up if I were you,' her dad had advised as Dan had pulled up at the kerb and hooted the horn.

Hazel had compromised between fashion and warmth, leaving off the hand-knitted woollen scarf Robert had offered her and opting instead for a colourful silk one, but sticking with the less than glamorous brown coat. She'd left the house in high spirits and jumped into the grey Ford, shoving to one side John's cricket equipment that

173

still took up most of the back seat.

'Lucky us!' From the start, Gladys had played the lady of leisure, sitting back in her luxurious leather seat and giving a royal wave to Mabel Jackson who had come out onto her top step to shake out her doormat. 'It's not every day a girl gets chauffeured all the way to Blackpool.'

'Yes. How did you wangle it with John?' Hazel had asked.

'Let's just say he owed me a favour,' Dan had replied, cheerily enigmatic. 'And when Gladys mentioned a trip to the Illuminations, I thought, why not do it in style?'

'And lo and behold!' Gladys had said with a laugh.

Lo and behold, they'd been on the way well before eight o'clock, bowling along the Skipton Road and from there out towards Colne, over the Yorkshire county line, continuing along the main road towards Preston and then into Blackpool itself.

And now they could see the sea.

'What do you say to fish and chips for dinner?' Dan suggested as they dipped down towards the town and caught their first sight of the famous Tower. He too was dressed for cold weather in a light brown trench coat, checked scarf and trilby hat.

'Hark at Errol Flynn!' Gladys's taunt highlighted the new, trim, film-star moustache that decorated her brother's top lip. 'He certainly knows how to treat a lady.'

But workaday fish and chips wrapped in newspaper it was, followed by a stroll along the prom in

174

the grey dregs of daylight, glancing at solitary dog walkers on the wide, wet beach, breathing in the salt air before they were drawn to the stalls selling candyfloss and lollipops at the entrance to the Pleasure Beach. Then there was the terror of a ride on the Big Dipper ('Why did we put ourselves through that?' Gladys gasped afterwards. 'I nearly had a second viewing of my fish and chips,' was how green-at-the-gills Dan put it) before the hilarious Hall of Mirrors, which distorted their reflected faces into gurning clowns. The girls finished up by throwing themselves into the screams and thrills of the Ghost Train – an experience that Dan avoided with the feeble excuse of going to the bookmaker's to place a bet on a sure-fire favourite in the three o'clock at Aintree. He would see them later, he said.

Gladys and Hazel went ahead without him, emerging from the ghostly tunnel shaking and clinging to each other, half-convinced that the giant spiders and rattling skeletons had been real.

Then it was time to leave the Pleasure Beach and sit over a cuppa in the Copper Kettle café where they'd arranged to meet up again with Dan.

'I'll let you into a secret,' Hazel told Gladys when they were cosily settled at a corner table.

'About Sylvia?' Gladys's mind shot straight away to her sister's supposed predicament. 'What's she done now?' she asked with a sigh.

'No, it's not about Sylvia,' Hazel said a touch too hastily. 'It's about me. I'm thinking of leaving home.'

'Blow me!' Gladys was genuinely surprised. 'Where are you gadding off to this time?'

'Not far – and not just yet. But I'd like to have a shot at living in a place of my own as soon as I can afford it.'

'You and me both,' Gladys admitted. It set her thinking about how she and Hazel might find somewhere together. 'We could split the rent between us and put a few finishing touches to the place – new cushions and rugs and so on. It would be easier to scrape up the money if there were two of us.'

Hazel quickly saw the logic. 'It's not just a pipe dream,' she assured Gladys. 'This really is something we could do!'

They were excited, talking non-stop so that by the time Dan rejoined them they practically held the keys to their envisaged lodgings in their hands.

He, on the other hand, looked glum. He remained quiet after they left the café and joined a queue for the decorated tram that would take them from Starr Gate in the south to Bispham in the north – a six-mile stretch of miraculous illuminations. Three hundred thousand electric light bulbs had been used in this year's display of animated tableaux, according to the posters. They would see Aladdin with his magic lamp, fairies fluttering overhead, Cinderella's coach pulled by six white horses, countless jugglers and clowns all designed to take the visitor's breath away.

When the tram arrived, Hazel, Gladys and Dan went upstairs and found seats at the front.

'This gives us the best view,' Hazel commented, sitting between the others as the tram started its journey through festoons of multicoloured lights. She felt a child's glee at the glittering display, her

176

enthusiasm undimmed by the gradual onset of a cold drizzling rain. It lasted until the final stop where they got off the tram then shuffled, heads down, away from the thronged promenade, down back streets lined with cheap boarding houses to the place where they had parked the car.

'That was grand!' she said with a sigh, ensconced in the front seat of John's Ford for the return journey, with Gladys in the back this time. 'It does you good to throw away your cares and have a jolly day out once in a while.'

Gladys agreed but Dan stayed silent as he followed road signs out of town.

'Take no notice,' Gladys advised as they left behind the red rose county for the white of Yorkshire. The car's headlights raked across hedgerows and stone walls, over stark hillsides and black escarpments. 'He probably lost his shirt by backing the wrong gee-gee as usual, but we won't let that spoil our day.'

Dan scowled and pressed his foot down harder on the accelerator. When the road ahead curved suddenly, he slammed on the brake. Hazel and Gladys slid this way and that on the shiny leather seats.

'Steady on – we'd like to get home in one piece if you don't mind,' Gladys complained.

Dan gave a humourless laugh and gripped the wheel as he picked up speed again. 'John wants his car back by ten on the dot. Hang onto your hats, girls, here we go!'

In fact, Dan's daring driving meant that they were back home by half past nine. 'We made

177

good time,' he told John, who came out of his house to give his car a quick once-over.

John opened the doors for Hazel and Gladys. Collarless, and with his top shirt button undone, he didn't seem to notice the bitter cold.

'Such a gentleman!' Gladys teased, showing plenty of leg as she got out of the car.

Hazel said nothing but gave him a quiet smile.

'I'll fill her up before we go to the dog track on Monday night,' Dan promised as he tossed him the keys.

'No rush.' Satisfied that there were no new dents and scratches on the gleaming bodywork but seeming in no hurry, John asked Gladys if they'd had a good day out.

'Yes, ta – they don't call it the greatest free light show on earth for nothing,' she replied.

'And did it live up to its reputation as far as you were concerned?' he asked Hazel.

'It did.' Though she'd seen John in passing in recent weeks, she hadn't talked to him since he'd come to the surgery needing stitches in his injured hand. There'd been a lot of water under the bridge since then – Myra's funeral then back to work at Baxter's for him, weeks of clinic and home visits for her, shortening days and long, foggy nights for them both. Despite time passing, she still felt awkward answering his friendly enquiry and was reluctant to meet his gaze.

Ignoring Dan and Gladys who were loudly calculating the cost of splitting the petrol three ways, John kept his attention firmly on her. 'Good. I'm glad it was worth the effort.'

'Oh, definitely. And ta for lending us the car.'

'I didn't need it today, so it was no trouble.' Though his sentence tailed off and he found nothing else to say, he still regarded Hazel with keen interest. It was only when Gladys broke in to ask Hazel for her share of the petrol money that he turned to speak to Dan. 'There's still time for a swift pint if you fancy it?'

Dan readily agreed.

'What about you two girls?' John asked, looking from one to the other. 'Can we buy you a drink down at the Green Cross?'

Gladys smiled brightly. 'Now you're talking! Make mine a Cinzano.'

'No, ta.' Hazel suspected, wrongly as it turned out, that accepting the invitation would make things as awkward for John as they were for her. 'I've had enough excitement for one day.'

'You're sure?' He hid a flicker of disappointment by stooping to lock the car door.

'Quite sure.' While John went inside to fetch his jacket, Hazel said goodbye to Dan and Gladys and set off briskly down the street.

'Shall I start looking around for a nice flat for us both?' Gladys called after her, a little too loudly for Hazel's liking.

She stopped and retraced her steps. 'Yes, but let's keep it under our hats until we find somewhere. You know what Dad's like – he'll only fret.'

Just then John came back out of his house. The collar of his jacket was turned up and he was settling his cap on his head. 'Good, you changed your mind,' he said when he saw Hazel. 'Come on, everyone, hop in the car. It'll be quicker.'

179

Hazel had no time to argue. With a conspiratorial wink, Gladys pushed her towards the car then slid into the back seat beside her. Dan and John jumped in the front. Before Hazel knew it, they were heading down the hill for a convivial drink in the crowded lounge bar of the Green Cross.

'I wouldn't worry about John Moxon if I was you,' Rose said when Hazel called on her and her grandmother before she set off for clinic the following Tuesday.

The purpose of the visit was to tell them all about the Illuminations and show off her pale blue uniform, complete with starched hat and apron. A belted mackintosh and her tan brogues completed the outfit.

'Who says I'm worried?' Hazel replied. 'I was only saying it felt a bit awkward chatting in the pub with him after – well, you know – after what happened to Myra. I can't help thinking of how lonely he must be.'

'You're bound to run into him from time to time.' Hoping to smooth things over as usual, Rose went back to Hazel's lively account of the trip to Blackpool. 'Did Dan and Gladys have a nice time too?' she asked.

'Did they behave themselves, more like?' Ada's wry intervention made Hazel smile. Her nana sat poker-backed and alert in her hard chair overlooking the yard, hands crossed in her lap, unpicking every detail of the conversation. 'Or did they get up to no good?'

'We had a whale of a time,' Hazel insisted.

'There was no end of things to see and do. I'd go again at the drop of a hat.'

'What do you say, Mum – shall we catch the coach to Blackpool and see the Illuminations with Hazel?' Rose winked at her niece as they awaited Ada's reply.

'What for? You'd have to pay *me* to sit on a draughty coach for half a day there and half a day back again just to look at a few measly electric light bulbs.'

'But it's like magic, the way the lights flicker on and off to make it look as if the tableau is moving,' Hazel insisted. She saw that she'd lost her grandmother's interest, however.

'Who's that going into Sylvia's?' Ada pointed across the yard towards number 15.

Rose and Hazel hurried to the window in time to glimpse a figure stepping over the threshold before the door closed.

'It looked like Mabel Jackson,' Ada said with a puzzled frown.

'Why would Mabel visit Sylvia?' Rose wondered.

Hazel's heart lurched but she managed to hide her reaction. 'Does there have to be a reason?' she asked. 'Perhaps Mabel's just being neighbourly.'

'Maybe it wasn't her,' Ada said with a distracted air. 'It might have been somebody else.'

'Yes – we only saw the back view.' Placatory as ever, Rose returned to the fireside.

'No.' Ada changed her mind. 'I'd know that old brown coat and hat anywhere. It was definitely Mabel.'

'Oh dear,' Rose said. Her mind raced ahead and alarm showed in her face.

'Well, I'll say it if no one else will,' Ada broke a lengthy silence. 'Mabel's visiting Sylvia can only be because Sylvia's in the family way.'

'Surely not!' Rose's bony hands flew up to her mouth.

'"Surely not", nothing! She's married, isn't she? What could be more natural than her needing Mabel's help in the near future?'

'I didn't mean that.' Rose looked towards Hazel. 'It's just that it's so soon. Sylvia – she hasn't...? I mean to say, she and Norman haven't had chance to settle down yet.'

'Stop beating about the bush.' Ada's reprimand reduced Rose to silence. 'Hazel, what we both want to know is why would the silly girl choose Mabel over you?'

Hazel sighed and shook her head. 'My lips are sealed.'

Ada fixed her sharp, dark eyes on her granddaughter. 'This isn't the first you've heard about it, is it? No need for you to say anything – I can see it in your face.'

'I wasn't sure she would go to Mabel,' Hazel said weakly, her head spinning as she imagined the conversation going on right then and there in Sylvia's disorganized kitchen. Was the old handywoman even now explaining to Sylvia about pennyroyal and brewer's yeast – a toxic combination that had been tried and tested over centuries – or about juniper and black hellebore? Or perhaps she would bring the more modern Beecham's pills into it, describing how they might

182

work when combined with aloe, ginger and soap.

'What's the matter?' Ada wanted to know when she saw how pale and quiet Hazel had grown. 'Why have you clammed up all of a sudden?'

'I haven't. When it comes down to it, Sylvia can go to whoever she likes – it's nothing to do with me.'

'Rose, fetch me my coat.' Ada stood up, steadying herself against the shallow window ledge. 'Don't just stand there, Hazel. Don't you have a clinic to get to?'

'Yes, but where are you going?'

An anxious Rose held her mother's black, fur-collared coat while Ada slipped her thin arms into the sleeves. 'Never you mind,' she told Hazel. 'Hat!' she reminded Rose.

'Nana.' For a second Hazel stood in the doorway and barred her way. 'Don't get on the wrong side of Sylvia. It won't do any good.'

'Not to mention Mabel,' Rose added as she put on her own jacket and shawl.

But there was no stopping Ada. 'I can deal with Mabel Jackson, don't you worry.' She elbowed Hazel to one side and limped down the steps. 'Rose, go and knock on Ethel's door. Tell her she's needed at number 15 – right this minute. And don't take no for an answer.'

From there on, Hazel's day went from bad to worse. Much as she wanted to stay in Nelson Yard to help sort out the family storm that was brewing, she was due in clinic in less than an hour. This meant running home to fetch her bike from the back yard and setting out straight away for Westgate Road.

Spotting her from the window, Jinny held up a knife and fork and mouthed, *What about your dinner?*

'I'll heat it up later,' Hazel called back. Her name would be mud with Eleanor if she arrived late at the surgery.

Emerging from the alley, she set off up the hill, wobbling into the gutter as a car overtook her. *Drat!* Her front tyre scraped against the kerb and when she started to pedal again she heard the loud hiss of escaping air. She got off to find the tyre already flat as a pancake.

Ahead of her, the car came to a halt and a door slammed. John Moxon strode down the street towards her. 'Is everything all right?' he asked.

'No, it's not!' Her testy reply suggested that he was to blame for forcing her into the kerb. She gestured towards the tyre. 'Now what am I going to do?'

He quickly assessed the situation: Hazel dressed for work, the flat tyre, the ticking clock. 'I can see to that,' he offered as he crouched to examine the tyre. 'I'm on my dinner break and it'll only take two ticks.'

Somehow his unlooked-for kindness drove Hazel's irritation clean away. 'There's no need for you to give up your dinner time,' she protested as she tried to work out if she had time to simply abandon the bike and get to the clinic on foot.

'Or else I could give you a lift to wherever it is you're going,' he volunteered. He registered her confusion and took a step back to give her time to decide. 'Either way – it's up to you.'

Hazel came down on the side of mending the tyre.

'Would it really only take you a couple of minutes?'

'Really and truly.' Without more ado, John loosened the bike pump and screwed its narrow connecting tube in place. 'Where's your puncture kit, in case we need it?'

'Here, in the front basket.' Hazel lifted out her midwife's bag to find the small tin box containing a tyre lever, rubber patches, glue and everything else necessary. She watched anxiously as John prised the tyre from the metal wheel rim and quickly spotted the source of the problem – a tiny, sharp stone that had pierced the inner tube.

'Can it be mended?' she asked when he showed her the stone.

He nodded and worked on, sitting on the kerb while he cleaned the site of the damage then applied glue and a round patch. 'We have to let it dry,' he explained, 'but it won't take long.'

'It's very good of you to do this.' Hazel spoke hesitantly, still not sure of her ground with him, even after the visit to the Green Cross.

He glanced up at her. 'It's my pleasure,' he assured her with a smile she recalled from the first time they'd met. Behind it lay amusement with something she'd said or done that she couldn't work out. 'Tell me more about Saturday's jaunt while we're waiting. Did you visit the Pleasure Beach while you were there? The Big Dipper's still my favourite – I don't know about you.'

'I loved all of it,' she admitted, looking up the street to avoid his gaze. The smell of fish and

185

chips from Pennington's wafted towards them and brought her attention back onto more sober matters. 'You'd no need to do this, you know,' she murmured.

'I wanted to,' he insisted as he fed the mended inner tube back inside the tyre then went to work with the pump. 'And I might as well say now what I meant to mention in the pub on Saturday night: Dorothy might still have it in for you, but there's no reason for us to avoid each other – at least not as far as I'm concerned.'

'That's good to know – ta.'

'So we've cleared the air.' Testing the tyre with the flat of his thumb, John unscrewed the pump then clipped it back into place on the bike frame.

'We have,' she agreed. She took the bike from him.

'Shake hands on it?' He offered his hand and gave his characteristic smile.

'Agreed,' she said. Her hand was small in his but she made sure not to let it rest limply. Instead, she gave a vigorous shake and a firm nod. 'And now,' she said as she perched on the saddle and pushed away from the kerb, 'I'd best be on my way.'

CHAPTER ELEVEN

'Who says miracles don't happen?' David greeted Hazel in the entrance to the surgery. He smiled broadly from behind Eleanor's desk where he'd been signing referral letters and bringing his records up to date.

'What's this? Have I got a full waiting room for once?' Hazel's question revealed her ongoing worry about clinic numbers.

'No, sadly not,' he replied. 'But Irene Bradley has given birth to a healthy baby girl. She's named her Grace.'

'That's wonderful.' Hazel couldn't have been more pleased. She was on her way up the stairs when Eleanor called her back.

'That's not all,' the receptionist said, casting a significant glance over her shoulder at her busy employer. 'Shall I tell her the rest or will you?'

David screwed the top of his pen in place then came out from behind the desk. 'No time to tittle-tattle,' he said on his way out.

'House calls.' Eleanor explained the hasty departure. 'Yes, Irene and her baby are doing well, thanks to him,' she went on. 'Matron called him out at midnight. She could see Irene was having trouble and forceps would be necessary, and it turned out she was right. Baby was born at breakfast time but Dr Bell didn't get back here until the middle of the morning, what with tidying up

187

afterwards, et cetera.'

Though Eleanor didn't go into details, Hazel was easily able to picture the episiotomy procedure and the care that Irene would have needed after a difficult birth. 'I'm glad it ended well and that she was in the right place.'

'Thanks to you,' Eleanor insisted. 'But that's only half the story.'

Hazel glanced at her watch and saw that it was almost half past two. 'How many have we got waiting upstairs?'

'Four so far. But listen to this. Dr Bell has only gone and offered Irene the job of housekeeper.'

The news stopped Hazel in her tracks. 'Where?'

'Here! He was adamant he didn't want her and the baby going back to Nelson Yard and the conditions there. No heating, no hot water, and such like. There's a spare room here and he says he needs someone to clean and do for him. So the solution was obvious – Irene should move out of the Yard and come here.'

'And she said yes?' Hazel wondered about the baby's father and his place in the new scheme of things but she had no time to ask because Lydia Walker opened the main door and made a breezy entrance before heading upstairs.

'Come along, Nurse, chop-chop!' she said as she passed Hazel.

Hazel followed quickly and was soon engulfed by clinic business – measuring, weighing and examining amidst the desultory chat of the mothers-to-be and the clatter of instruments on metal trolleys. Behind the green screen one woman bearing her seventh child confided her resentment about her husband who blamed her for conceiving one child too many, as if she alone were responsible. Another talked of practicalities – from the enema administered during labour to the stitching-up afterwards, and everything in between. Hazel's answers were clear and calm and she gave each of her patients – a total of six in this session – her full attention. By the end of the afternoon she was tired out and ready for home.

'My stomach's rumbling,' she told Eleanor, who had come upstairs to help with washing up the tea things. 'I didn't have any dinner. And my feet ache something rotten.'

'But you love every minute,' Eleanor reminded her as she dried a stack of saucers.

'I do – especially now that numbers are creeping up,' Hazel said with a satisfied sigh. She shut her bag then put on her mackintosh. 'A couple of months back I didn't even know if I'd find any work.'

'And now look at you – rushed off your feet, thanks to Dr Bell and the risk he took when you landed on his doorstep.'

Hazel nodded. 'Yes, thanks to him.' It was true – she owed a lot to one man. A thought struck her and she blurted it out without stopping to think. 'Do you think he puts me in the same boat as Irene?'

'How do you mean?' Eleanor hung her tea towel over the radiator to dry.

'Am I someone he was sorry for and felt duty-bound to help?'

The receptionist raised her eyebrows and treated Hazel to one of her blunt home truths.

189

'Don't be daft. You're not the same thing at all. You only have to see the way Dr Bell looks at you to notice the difference.'

'You do?'

'Plain as the nose on your face,' Eleanor concluded with a hint of thinly disguised envy in her voice. 'But then there's none so blind as those that will not see.'

It was unusual to see Rose off her home turf in Nelson Yard so it was a surprise for Hazel to find her ensconced with her mother on Raglan Road.

'Your dinner's in the oven,' Jinny told her as she took off her coat. 'Good job it was a hot pot that can be reheated.'

Famished as she was, Hazel delayed setting out her knife and fork in order to listen to what Rose had to say about the day's events. 'Hello, Aunty Rose. What happened at Sylvia's house earlier?'

'What didn't happen?' her aunt replied with a sigh. 'We had tears, we had doors slamming – the lot.'

'Trust Sylvia to turn on the waterworks,' Jinny commented.

'But what did you find out? Was Mabel still there when you arrived? I take it Aunty Ethel went with you and Nana? Was Norman at work?'

'Hold your horses,' Jinny warned. 'Poor Rose has already been through it all for my benefit. She's worn out, poor thing.'

Hazel tried not to show her exasperation. 'All right, well, you can tell me later then. Shall I make you a cup of tea, Aunty Rose?'

'No, no, I don't mind telling you all about it.'

Rose sat by the fire, her face pale and her hands trembling slightly in her lap. 'By the time Mother, Ethel and I had got ourselves organized, Mabel had already made herself scarce, so it was just Sylvia in the house on her own. We spotted her at the upstairs window so we knew she was in, even though she refused to come to the door.'

'She's taken to doing that lately.' Hazel hated to see her aunt upset like this and had a mind to go round and tell Sylvia a few home truths as soon as she'd heard the full story.

'Mother wasn't having it,' Rose went on. 'She hammered on that door until Sylvia was forced to answer. Mother's first words, before she even stepped over the threshold, were, "When were you thinking of telling me that I'm going to be a great-grandmother?"'

'And what did Sylvia say?' Hazel pictured it – wizened old Ada face to face with firebrand Sylvia. She thought she knew who would back down first, but she was surprised.

'She flatly denied it,' Rose explained. 'It was three against one – Ethel, me and Mother – all demanding to know why Mabel had paid her a visit, telling her she couldn't go on pulling the wool over our eyes and anyway, what was the point?'

'Exactly,' Jinny agreed. 'What is the point?'

'Perhaps it's because she hasn't told Norman yet,' Hazel suggested without much hope that this would ease Rose's worry.

'So she doesn't want anyone discussing it until she's put her husband in the picture – is that it?' Jinny was sceptical.

'With anyone but Sylvia that might be true,'

191

Rose conceded. 'The thing is, we all knew she was lying by the look on her face and poor Ethel felt ashamed of her own daughter. It didn't help when Sylvia turned it all around and said nasty things about us that I won't repeat but you can imagine. In the end she told us to mind our own business, shouting at the top of her voice then weeping and wailing, saying it wasn't fair and we were to leave her alone.'

'Which they did,' Jinny concluded.

'Mother has washed her hands of the whole business,' Rose reported sadly. 'Ethel, too. They went away leaving Sylvia to stew in her own juice. It's hard when your own child or grandchild is untruthful about something so important – it must cut very deep.'

'And how did you feel?' Hazel expected a different reaction from Rose – softer and less judgemental – and she was right.

'I'm sorry deep down. I say we should be celebrating, not arguing. But Lord knows what Sylvia's up to – that's what worries me more than anything.'

In the end, Jinny's advice to her worried older sister had been to give Sylvia time to calm down and talk to Norman. It was the only way forward, she said.

But Hazel had brooded over the problem long into the night and come to a decision. She was up at dawn, dressing quietly and slipping out of the house before either Robert or Jinny was awake. Walking in the grey light on Overcliffe Common, she rehearsed in her own mind exactly what she would say.

I need a clear head, she told herself, relishing the cold gusts of wind blowing from the moors and looking down into the valley at the network of twinkling lamps that lined the streets and the canal running straight as a die through the centre of the town. Already the factory chimneys churned out black smoke and the roads were choked with traffic. Close by, on the edge of the Common, a tram stopped to let on mill workers bound for a day's slavery in spinning and weaving sheds in the valley bottom.

A clear head and a stout heart, Hazel vowed as she trod the cinder paths across the rough grassland to one side of the fancy wrought-iron bandstand. White lines marked out a football pitch on the grass and beyond that stood the sports pavilion, the centre of weekend activity for the young men and boys of the neighbourhood.

'It's time,' she said out loud, turning and retracing her steps down to the very bottom of Raglan Road, where she boldly knocked on Mabel Jackson's front door.

'Hazel Price – what do *you* want at this hour?' was Mabel's hostile greeting.

'Can I come in?' Hazel said. Behind her, one or two mill workers still made their way along Ghyll Road. Hooters sounded the warning for these stragglers to hurry or lose half a day's pay.

Taken by surprise, Mabel considered her options. Her overall hung loose, her hair was still in metal curlers concealed under a paisley scarf that was tied turban-style around her head and her feet were encased in felt slippers.

'I don't mean to make trouble,' Hazel explained. 'I've come to talk to you about my cousin, Sylvia.'

'Hmm. Trouble is that one's middle name, isn't it?' Mabel was taken aback by Hazel's decision to knock on her door. It took plenty of nerve – she would give her that. She looked down from the top step at the windswept, earnest figure, dressed in warm coat and headscarf, remembering the eager schoolgirl Hazel had been not so many years before – the type who read a lot and kept to herself, not the sort to play hopscotch on the pavement or to join in skipping games with the other girls.

She got that from her mother, Mabel thought sourly. *Jinny Drummond was just as stand-offish when she was a nipper.*

'It's important,' Hazel insisted, her heart racing.

Mabel made her decision. 'I don't know what Dorothy will think about me making time for you, but you'd better come in out of the cold.' Her face was blank, her voice expressionless, but she stood to one side and let Hazel pass.

'Ta.' Hazel followed the long, narrow hallway into the kitchen at the back of the house. The hall bore the musty smell of old stair carpet overlaid with lavender floor polish. The kitchen itself clearly hadn't moved with the times, from the black range where Mabel still boiled her kettle and did her baking to the stone sink and the plain Welsh dresser along one wall displaying blue and white crockery.

'Sit down.' Mabel pointed to a wooden rocking chair next to the fire.

'No thanks. I'd rather stand.'

194

'Suit yourself.' Mabel's owlish gaze didn't waver. She waited for Hazel's next move.

'Sylvia,' Hazel began again. 'You went to see her.'

'I did, because she asked me to.'

'To tell you she was pregnant and to ask you for an abortion?' There – it was out in the open, the topic that had gnawed at Hazel for days.

Mabel didn't blink. Her expression didn't change.

'I've tried to talk to her about it,' Hazel said in a rush. 'But once she realized I wouldn't help her she sent me packing. I told her she should talk things through with Norman.'

'Oh, Norman,' Mabel said with a slight nod of acknowledgement.

'It's as much his baby as hers. He has a right to know.'

'I knew his mother before she married Dick Bellamy. And look where that got her – seven babies on the trot before the worthless so-and-so did a midnight flit. He left her without a brass farthing.'

'It's not really Norman I want to talk to you about.' The heat from Mabel's fire made Hazel's cheeks feel flushed and her heart was still thudding away at her ribcage. 'It's Sylvia. We're agreeing she came to you for help to get rid of the baby, aren't we?'

After a pause, during which Hazel prepared herself for a barrage of the usual criticism, Mabel nodded again.

'Thank you.' Letting out a long sigh, Hazel's shoulders sagged and she lowered her head.

195

'For what?'

'For not trying to pull the wool over my eyes.'

'Sit,' Mabel said again, and this time Hazel obeyed. 'We won't see eye to eye on this one, I know that much.'

'No,' Hazel agreed.

'I don't have to remind you how long I've been at this game. There's nothing I haven't seen.'

'I appreciate that. And I know you think I'm wet behind the ears. But Sylvia is my cousin and I'm worried about her.'

'Quite right.'

'I mean – I can't help wondering why a young girl who has managed to persuade the father to marry her and set up home suddenly wants to back out of having the baby?'

'Maybe she thinks she's made a mistake.' Mabel's deep, unhurried voice had the unexpected effect of calming Hazel's nerves and making her listen rather than rush on with her own thoughts. 'It happens, you know. Perhaps she's realized that Norman isn't the one for her after all.'

'She did say there was a part of marriage that she was finding hard.' Hazel remembered Sylvia's awkward confession. 'I thought lots of girls probably did. I'm no expert.'

A faint smile crossed Mabel's face before she continued. 'Let's say Sylvia has seen her mistake. It's too late to be unmarried but it's not too late to change her mind over the baby. So she turns to someone like me. That's the sensible thing to do.'

'You're right – we don't see eye to eye,' Hazel

said in a louder, firmer voice than before.

'You said it yourself– you're no expert. That much was obvious when you stepped into my shoes on the night Myra died.'

Hazel flinched but decided to bite her tongue. After all, she was here for Sylvia, not to stand up for herself and enter into a bitter argument.

'And you haven't been through anything like what that young cousin of yours is going through either.'

'Fair enough. But I do know that Sylvia is far from being "sensible", as you put it. I'd say she's the exact opposite.'

'So you'd like me to say no to her request?'

'Yes, I would. That's why I came here – to ask you to try to talk her round. She wouldn't take any notice of me but she might listen to someone from outside the family.'

'And if I refused to help her, what then?' Mabel drew a chair from under the table and sat down on the opposite side of the fireplace. She looked Hazel in the eye. 'Do you suppose that Sylvia would lie down like a little lamb and do as we say?'

'Yes, if the advice was put in the right way.' Hazel sounded uncertain as a fierce new fear began to knock at her heart.

'She wouldn't move on from me to the next one and the next until she found the help she's after?'

'Oh, God.' Hazel gasped as the door to her imagination flew open and in rushed images of hot baths and gin, deliberate falls, cannulas, glass rods or curling irons.

'Quite.' Mabel read Hazel's expression. 'A girl

197

in Sylvia's predicament doesn't deserve that.'

Hazel shook her head violently but the images stayed with her.

'That's what we have to take into account,' Mabel explained patiently.

'So you agreed to help her?' This was the only conclusion Hazel could draw and now she saw not in black and white but in shades of grey. What if, after all, Mabel was right?

'I didn't turn her away.' Mabel's reply was guarded. 'On the other hand, I didn't offer to help – not right away.'

'Meaning what?'

'I saw how she was – like a little girl on her knees begging me for help, beside herself. I lifted her up and told her to pull herself together – that was no way to carry on. I said I would only consider our next move if she calmed down, which she did in the end. My advice was for her to think things through for a few days then get back to me. I think I managed to persuade her.'

Slowly Hazel nodded. 'Thank you,' she murmured. Mabel's kinder-than-expected view of Sylvia's predicament had surprised her and she reached out to shake her broad, work-worn hand. Now they had those few days for Sylvia to come to terms with her situation instead of rushing ahead with a back-street abortion in a frenzy of fear and desperation. 'That's good.'

'Don't thank me yet,' was Mabel's stolid response. She freed her hand to grudgingly pat Hazel on the shoulder then stood up to show her out. 'You can do that when it's all come out in the wash.'

198

Before Hazel knew it, the weekend arrived and with it an arrangement with Gladys to meet up and begin their search for a flat.

'Nothing's definite,' she assured Jinny as she set out late on Friday afternoon. Days were shortening and fog still wound its way through narrow streets, dimming street lamps and seeming to cushion footfall on greasy pavements.

'Don't worry – I haven't mentioned it to your dad,' Jinny said, silently envying Hazel's freedom to choose how and where she lived. *If I was her age I'd jump at the chance of branching out,* she thought as she methodically laid out Robert's tea of pork pie, pickle and two slices of bread and butter.

The front door clicked shut and the noise of traffic soon drowned out the sound of Hazel's quick footsteps.

Yes, there's a lot I'd do differently if I got the chance. Jinny stared wistfully at the window, catching her own shadowy reflection, then hurried to close the curtains.

Meanwhile, Hazel made her way to the far end of Ghyll Road – the starting point for her and Gladys's search.

'It would be handy for my work at the clinic,' Hazel had decided. 'And it's on the bus route to the hospital for you. Plus there's Clifton Market only a stone's throw away and the Assembly Rooms if we're ever short of entertainment.'

Gladys had turned up her nose. 'The Assembly Rooms are old hat,' she'd complained. 'Give me the jazz club any day.'

199

But they'd agreed that Ghyll Road offered plenty of possibilities and Gladys showed her eagerness to go ahead with their plan by showing up early for once. She stood outside the Chinese laundry on the corner of Ebeneezer Street, stamping her feet against the cold and tapping her watch as Hazel approached.

'Good heavens, I hardly recognized you,' Hazel exclaimed, taking in Gladys's latest hairstyle – more blonde than ever and even more closely cropped. She wore a navy blue clutch coat teamed with a printed yellow silk scarf and matching beret.

'Where've you been?' Gladys chided. 'I'm freezing.'

'Why – I'm not late, am I? Anyway, I went to Morrison's estate agency for the addresses of flats to rent. They gave me three here on Ghyll Road and one at the top of Ebeneezer Street.'

Armed with the list, Gladys immediately discounted the one on Ebeneezer Street. 'Too close to the gas works,' she said.

Then it turned out that the first address on Ghyll Road was next door to Pickard's butcher's. Gladys wrinkled her nose. 'All that smelly offal being cooked on the premises! But the second address might be worth a look,' she decided.

'Perhaps beggars can't be choosers,' a dispirited Hazel pointed out, trudging along in Gladys's bright wake. She bore in mind the fact that her savings might soon run out unless there was an upturn for her at the clinic.

'We're not beggars.' Gladys's retort was true enough. 'We're two respectable young women

with good jobs and references to whit. Any landlord would jump at the chance of having tenants
like us.'

'So what about this one?' Referring to the estate
agent's list, Hazel stopped outside an ornate stone
terraced house with three storeys plus a cellar that
was approached from the pavement by narrow
stone steps. A row of nameplates to one side of
the front door showed that the house was split
into six separate residences. 'It says here that the
landlord lives on the ground floor,' she pointed
out to Gladys.

Gladys stood back to inspect the somewhat
shabby building. 'I bet it's the cellar that's empty,'
she predicted, venturing down the worn steps to
peer through the window at a dark, bare room.
'Just as I thought.'

'That's the third one crossed off the list, then?'
Hazel asked. At this rate, nothing short of a
palace would satisfy Gladys.

'Yes. Who wants to live in a mouldy old cellar?
We'd be like a pair of moles scratting about in the
dark.'

They walked on down the street to the final
address on the list – a detached house set behind
a high laurel hedge in large grounds. Straight
away Gladys viewed this with more interest.

'Finally, your majesty!' Hazel teased her hard-
to-please cousin.

'Who lives here?' Gladys wondered as she set
off up the drive.

Hazel followed, noticing a yard to the side with
a coach house and other outhouses. Approaching
the stained-glass front door, she saw a wide

201

porch containing wellington boots of all sizes and a child's bike carelessly thrown down and partly blocking their way. To either side of the entrance were well-lit rooms with large paintings on the wall, a grand piano in one corner and more children's toys scattered across oriental carpets.

'Do you really think this is the right address?' Gladys sounded less sure of herself now they were on the doorstep and she hesitated before pressing the bell.

Hazel consulted her list. 'This is number 120, isn't it?'

Their voices must have attracted the attention of someone crossing the wide hallway because a woman's figure could be made out through the glass panels and a muffled, short-tempered voice called out, 'There's someone at the door!'

Soon after, the door was opened by a man they both recognized.

'Bernard!' Taken aback, Gladys's pre-rehearsed speech disappeared from her head.

Hazel realized it was the philandering doctor from King Edward's.

He stepped out into the porch, closing the door behind him. 'Hello, girls,' he began with a mixture of suspicion and pleasure. 'What brings you to my neck of the woods?'

Hazel was the first to get over their shock and explain their mission – a flat for two single people, close to the bus routes and so on.

'Well, we do have rooms to let,' Bernard acknowledged. 'They're above the old coach house, which is standing there empty, doing nothing. It was Vera's idea that we should get a lodger.'

'Is there room for two?' Gladys found her voice and fixed on her chirpy smile.

'I should say so.' Bernard's tone was enthusiastic as he looked from Hazel to Gladys and back again.

'What would the rent be?' Hazel enquired, hearing children's voices arguing, overridden by the same woman's voice as before.

Bernard blithely ignored the fracas. 'Eight shillings per week. How does that sound?'

Hazel's face fell. That seemed an awful lot. After all, you could rent a whole house on Raglan Street for seven.

'Four shillings each.' Gladys turned to Hazel, whose face told her how she was feeling. 'It's worth a look, isn't it?'

In the meantime, without them noticing, Bernard's wife Vera had left off chastising the children and quietly opened the door. She was tall, with chin-length dark hair styled into a central parting and carefully crimped. Her face was inscrutable as she took in the scene.

'It was once the groom's quarters, in the days when people had them. Horses and carriage on the ground floor, groomsman above.' Bernard was in full swing, putting a good gloss on the rooms in questions. 'There's a kitchen and two other rooms – a bedroom for each of you. Plenty of space.'

'Bernard,' his wife said in an undertone as she drew him back into the hall, frowning now and unyielding. 'I'd like a word in private.'

'Oops, that's torn it!' Gladys suppressed a giggle as the pair retreated. 'Did you see the sour look on her face?'

'Yes. I don't suppose we're the sort of lodgers she had in mind,' Hazel agreed. This was embarrassing, to put it mildly.

They waited less than a minute before Bernard reappeared. 'Vera's had a change of heart, I'm afraid,' he said through gritted teeth. 'It seems the coach house is not to let after all.'

'Oh dear!' Gladys's dismay fooled no one. It was obvious that the situation tickled her.

'Never mind. Ta, anyway.' Hazel was anxious to be on her way. 'We've only just started to look, haven't we, Gladys?'

'That's right.' Gladys's eyes twinkled with suppressed laughter. 'Will you keep your eyes and ears open for us, Bernard?'

'You bet.' He gave a conspiratorial wink then mumbled under his breath, 'Sorry about that. I hope to see you girls in town later tonight.'

'If you're lucky.' Gladys winked back at him.

Hazel turned away and started back down the drive. 'Really!' she told Gladys crossly when they were safely back on the pavement.

'I didn't do anything – what did I do?'

'You winked at him!'

'He did it first.'

'Honestly, Gladys! All right, if you must know – he's someone I can't stand.' There was something wolf-like about Bernard – a glint in his yellowish eyes, a hint of saliva at the corner of his mouth. 'What now?' she asked, stuffing her list into her pocket.

'Now we go home and get changed for the jazz club,' Gladys decided gaily. 'I'll see you at the tram stop, seven o'clock sharp.'

CHAPTER TWELVE

Everyone except Sylvia was there that night – Gladys and Hazel, Norman, Eddie and Dan and eventually John, who joined the gang at nine o'clock, accompanied by Reggie Bates, a fellow player from John's cricketing days.

'Hello, Hazel. We haven't met.' Reggie stood at the bar offering to shake her hand and enjoying the introduction made by Dan on John's behalf. 'I've heard a lot about you, though.'

'Oh dear.' Hazel tried to laugh away the embarrassment she often felt at meeting new people. 'All good, I hope.'

Taking a drink from John, Reggie carried on with more along the same lines. 'Oh yes, Dan and John both sing your praises, don't you worry.' Shorter than John, Reggie was square set, with reddish hair swept back from his high forehead and a pale, freckled face. He looked smart in a wide-shouldered grey suit and dark blue tie with a white rose county logo. 'Even so, they didn't do you justice.'

Hazel's smile was uncertain and she quickly drew Gladys into the conversation. Above the soaring notes from a band she hadn't heard before – creating a smoother and lighter mood than Earl Ray's ensemble – she explained to Reggie that this was her cousin's favourite weekend haunt and that it was due to her that she was here at all.

'Listen – I think we can do a quickstep to this music!' Without further ado, Gladys seized her chance to lead an unsuspecting Reggie onto the dance floor, while Dan picked out his own partner. This left Hazel with John at the bar.

'I did warn him he'd be forced to trip the light fantastic if he came here,' John said as he watched Reggie stumble then collide with another couple. 'I take it Gladys doesn't mind that he's no Fred Astaire.'

'I don't suppose so. I hope he's better at cricket than he is at dancing the quickstep, though,' Hazel commented wryly.

'You can bank on that. Reggie's wicket keeping takes a lot of beating.' Keen to praise his friend, John went into detail about Reggie's bulldog tenacity, behind the wicket. 'He's still in the first team, doing his bit for Yorkshire and decent enough not to forget his old pal.'

'You're not old,' Hazel argued. 'What are you – twenty-seven, twenty-eight?'

'Twenty-nine. But I've been out of the first-class game for four years now. Reggie could easily have dropped me if he'd wanted.'

'Dan says you had to give up because of an accident?'

'I jiggered my knee – fractured the kneecap and tore a ligament and that was that.' He spoke plainly and without bitterness.

'Playing cricket?'

'No. I crashed my car – my own daft fault. One day I was the season's top scorer, the next I was laid up in a hospital bed with a bandage around my bonce and my leg in plaster.' Tilting his head to one side, John paid attention to the music for a while and Hazel was diverted by a tap on her shoulder.

She turned to find David Bell greeting her with a smile.

'Don't look so surprised.' Dressed in an open-necked shirt and grey V-necked pullover, he jerked his thumb towards a table close to the stage where Bernard and a couple of other hospital doctors sat. 'They invited me along.'

'That was nice of them.' Regretting as ever her tendency to blush, it took Hazel some time to get used to seeing David in this fresh setting.

'Yes. They must think there's life in the old dog yet.'

'I should say so. Are you enjoying yourself?'

'It makes a change to get out and about. I take it this is one of your regular haunts?'

'Yes, I like it here.' Aware that Reggie had given up on the quickstep with Gladys and returned to the bar, Hazel settled into the conversation with David. The band eased from one number to the next and there was a flurry of people exchanging partners or ordering drinks, which edged her and David closer to the dance floor.

'Shall we?' he said impulsively.

'Why not?' Before she knew it, her hand was in his and his arm was around her waist. She felt him guide her expertly between couples, feet gliding across the floor and shoulders swaying to the rhythm of the music. 'You've done this before,' she said with a smile.

'Back in the dim and distant past,' he agreed. 'When I was a lad back in Durham we had a

207

wind-up gramophone and a stack of records – mostly old-fashioned dance tunes. My sister Ursula is two years older than me. She used to roll back the living-room carpet and bully me into helping her practise her dance steps. I must have been the only boy in the county who knew my Military Two-step from my Gay Gordons.'

'It paid off,' Hazel said with a laugh, growing used to the lean, taut feel of David's shoulder under his woollen sweater and enjoying the sensation of him being in control. As usual, the music brought down her guard and allowed her to relax in his arms.

'Bernard tells me you paid him a surprise visit earlier today,' he mentioned with an edge of curiosity in his voice.

'I was flat-hunting with Gladys. We didn't know it was his house.' Glancing towards the bar, she noticed that her vivacious cousin had drifted back there and was in conversation with Dan, Norman, Reggie and John. 'Anyway it turned out it was no good.'

'Bad luck,' he commiserated. 'If you're serious about finding somewhere to live, I could keep my ears open for you.'

'We're serious all right.' November was slipping away and Christmas was on the horizon. 'We'd like to find somewhere before the New Year. Anyway, is it true that you've asked Irene Bradley to be your housekeeper?'

'Guilty as charged. The poor woman's husband turned out to be unreliable – he took one look at the bouncing baby and vanished into the ether. As if things weren't bad enough for Irene already, they were set to get ten times worse.'

'So you rushed to her rescue.' It came as no surprise really – she already knew that David's sympathy for the underdog was well developed.

'No, it was the other way round,' he argued. 'You've seen the state of my living quarters – Irene came to mine.'

They agreed to differ and danced in ever decreasing circles as the floor grew even more crowded. At the end of the number he held her for a few moments after the music had faded then released her with an oddly formal little bow. Then he led her back to the spot where he'd asked her to dance.

'Thank you,' he said, relinquishing her hand and acknowledging Gladys and her companions before going off to rejoin Bernard.

Gladys raised her eyebrows at Hazel. 'What did I tell you?'

'Hush, leave off!'

If it turned out that Gladys and Eleanor were right and David really did have a soft spot for her, how would she feel?

'Confused' was the answer. David was a kind man – there was no doubt about it. And she held him in great respect. But she doubted that respect could lead to romance and she knew that her heart should have fluttered more than it had when he'd asked her to dance.

Next to her at the bar, John stopped listening to Reggie, who was telling a joke. He caught Hazel's eye as Dan and Norman laughed loudly at the punchline.

'What do you think of the band?' he asked,

letting his gaze flick from Hazel's face to David's retreating figure and back again. 'As good as Earl Ray or better?'

'Good, but there's something about Earl Ray...'

She hadn't got far into her sentence before Reggie claimed her for the next dance and the one after that. An hour later, with her head in a whirl from turning and swaying and having her feet trodden on, she made her excuses then escaped to the ladies' toilets where she looked in the mirror at her flushed complexion and faded lipstick. Dipping a corner of her handkerchief under the cold tap, she dabbed her cheeks, ran a comb through her hair but decided not to bother with her lipstick. She'd enjoyed her evening but she decided she'd had enough of Reggie's relentless flattery and clumsy plates of meat and so it was time to go home.

Out in the tiny foyer, she reclaimed her hat and coat from the cloakroom and headed up the narrow steps out onto the foggy pavement where she joined a short queue at the tram stop outside Merton and Groves. She breathed in the cold, damp air, buttoned up her coat and reflected on the evening's events.

'What's this? We can't have you standing here in the cold,' a voice at her shoulder said.

It was John, jangling his car keys and offering her a lift home. 'Come on – you might as well take me up on it. At least you'll be warm.'

The lights from the department-store window outlined his tall figure and broad shoulders and his deep, slow voice drew the admiring attention of some other young women in the queue.

Without thinking, Hazel accepted. She left the tram shelter and walked with him down a side street to where his car was parked.

'I wanted to ask you for a dance,' he said as he opened the passenger door. 'But Reggie beat me to it.'

'Never mind – maybe next time.' She sat as gracefully as she could in the deep seats and waited for him to settle himself behind the wheel. Her heart fluttered as he started the engine. She tried to clear her head but the jazz rhythms lingered and the suspicion that John had staged his exit to coincide with hers made her feel giddy and a bit ashamed, coming hard on the heels of Myra's death. She glanced sideways at his profile – that long, straight nose over a full top lip, both in perfect proportion with his strong, closely shaven chin. His hair was combed back from his smooth forehead.

'It's nice to see you out and about,' she told him in an attempt to quell her nerves.

'Yes, but I'm not much of a night owl,' he admitted. He glanced in the overhead mirror then signalled to draw out into the traffic. 'I don't go to many of these places. I'm still a country boy at heart.'

'Where exactly did you grow up?'

'A little place called Shawcross – up in the Dales, miles from anywhere. I lived on a farm. My mum passed away when I was five, so that left me and my dad to run the place.'

'That sounds like a hard job.'

'It wasn't so bad – better than being cooped up in a spinning shed or crawling under looms, scav-

211

enging for scraps of wool any day. Not that I look down on the bobbin liggers and weft men round here – don't get me wrong. I just wasn't brought up to it.'

This was more than Hazel had expected to hear and it piqued her curiosity. As John braked and then stopped at a junction, she felt brave enough to ask more. 'When did cricket come into the picture?'

'When wasn't it?' he said with a smile. 'I've had a bat in my hand ever since I can remember. As a lad I used to chalk the wickets onto the barn door and get Dad to bowl me spinners. Poor bloke – he'd be worn out after a day rounding up sheep on the fell, but he always made time for a game of cricket.'

'Happy memories,' she murmured.

'Right enough.' Reaching the end of Ghyll Road, John had to stop once again for the traffic. 'What about you, Hazel? What gave you the idea to do what you're doing?'

'I don't really know.' The question silenced her for a while. 'No one in my family has gone into anything like this before. The women have worked in the mill or on the market like my mum, except for Rose. She hasn't been strong enough for full-time work so she does millinery and a bit of up-holstering. I just knew I needed to do something different. I wanted a job where I could be of use.'

'Good for you,' he said without irony. 'A lot of women couldn't face what you sometimes have to.'

The comment jerked her back to the terrible scene of Myra struggling to breathe, of the still-

212

born baby and the slack weight of him as Hazel had laid him in his crib. John too must be remembering it – not just every now and then, but many times a day since it had happened.

'And how is it working out with Dr Bell?' He went smoothly through the gears as they pulled out from the junction.

'Tip top. We get on swimmingly. We could do with more patients attending my antenatal clinic, though.'

'Well, good luck with that.' Turning off from Ghyll Road onto the cobbled surface of Raglan Road, he slowed down outside Hazel's house. 'I was wondering, would you like to drive out to Shawcross with me some time?' he asked as casually as he could manage, tapping his forefinger against the steering wheel while he awaited her reply.

Hazel breathed in deeply. She saw a light on in the front bedroom – that would be her mother and father lying awake, waiting for her safe return. 'When?' she murmured.

'How does Sunday morning sound?'

'Sunday morning it is,' she said, fumbling with the door handle then making a hurried exit. The door closed with a heavy clunk. She didn't look back or wave goodbye as she went up the steps and turned her key in the lock. John's car purred on up the hill.

'Remember to bolt that door before you come up,' her mother called sharply from the bedroom.

'I will.' Hazel kicked off her shoes then sat a while beside the fire. The room was silent and she enjoyed the peace and quiet, and the way her

213

thoughts glowed, shifted then settled like the embers in the grate.

The next day Jinny left instructions for Hazel to take sandwiches to Robert in Nelson Yard.

'Your father's helping Norman with a few odd jobs,' she explained on her way out of the house. 'You'll need to buy some boiled ham from Hutchinson's.'

Still in her dressing-gown, Hazel followed Jinny to the door and watched her make her rapid way up the street. She was dressed for work in a paisley-patterned wrap-over apron under her dark green coat, wearing a woollen headscarf and brown laced boots with a fur lining. Even in this workaday outfit, her mother managed to attract glances from the men digging up the cobbles outside number 30, Hazel realized with a pang.

She thought of the times she'd heard Jinny wish that she'd had the chance to make more of herself by finding office work after leaving school at fourteen. 'A typist or a telephonist – that would have been the job for me.' Then she would quickly sigh and dismiss the notion as a fairy tale.

'Count yourself lucky you've got a decent husband,' Ada would chide, one eye on young Hazel who soaked up every word. 'There's a lot of war widows around here who would give their eye teeth to be in your position – a steady new husband, a nice house and a little girl growing up to be your spitting image.'

It hadn't been enough, though, Hazel knew now as her mother disappeared around the corner and she went back inside. She got dressed and spent the morning dusting and polishing then slipped out to buy the ham – enough for Norman and Sylvia as well if they happened to be in. At twelve o'clock she made the sandwiches and set off for Nelson Yard.

With luck, Sylvia would be there. Hazel would find her on home territory and she would perhaps be calmer. There was even a chance that she would have talked things through with Norman and settled in her mind to go ahead and have the baby after all. This at least was what Hazel was hoping as she headed down the dank alley into the yard.

As it happened, she crossed paths with her father on his way to the ironmonger's on Ghyll Road for a bag of screws and some rawl plugs.

'I'm helping Norman put up shelves in the kitchen,' he explained. 'Everything is in a right mess. Best leave the sandwiches on the draining board, out of harm's way.'

So Hazel went on and found Norman alone in the comfortless house, sawing planks of wood to fit an alcove. There was sawdust everywhere, parts of an iron bedstead waiting to be carried upstairs and a tea chest full of borrowed pots and pans in the corner next to the sink.

'Hello – somebody's hard at it!' she said cheerily as she stepped through the open door.

Norman was in shirtsleeves and braces and was clean shaven, having given up his attempt to grow a moustache. He had the stump of a pencil tucked behind his ear and a list of scribbled measurements tacked to the wall. 'You don't say. Your dad's a stickler for getting things right. Not that I'm complaining, not when he's given up his

215

weekend to lend a hand.'

'So I take it Sylvia isn't in?' Hazel plunged into the topic that troubled her more with each day that passed. 'I haven't seen much of her lately. Is she trying to avoid me?'

Norman frowned then laid down his saw. 'She's never in, to tell you the truth. What with me being out at work and her gadding out and about in the evenings, we hardly ever see each other.'

'Where is she now?'

'At the shops, so she said.'

Norman's unhappy expression brought out the protective side of Hazel's nature. 'Never mind. I expect she wanted to keep out of the way while you and Dad got to grips with things.'

He shook his head. 'Why would she go shopping without any money in her purse?' he asked. 'It was only an excuse. I'm worried about her, if you must know.'

'Why, what's wrong?'

Norman had taken to Hazel as she had to him and his open nature meant that he saw no reason not to come clean. 'Half the time she's avoiding me, the other half she's crying on my shoulder. But she won't talk to me so how can I get to the bottom of it?'

Hazel sighed. 'Doesn't she say anything at all?'

'Not about why she's upset. When she does open her mouth, it's to tell me off for being on short time at Calvert's and getting under her feet here in the house. She wants me to go around looking for more work, but it's not easy. I'm only a packer in the warehouse – we're ten a penny when it comes down to it.'

'Don't give up on her,' Hazel urged. 'Sylvia's had things her own way for most of her life. Now she's having to come down to earth with a bump. It'll take time for her to learn how to make the money spin out, to keep the house tidy, and so on.' Aware that she was skirting around the main issue, Hazel trailed off and tried to read Norman's expression. He looked weary and dispirited, totally out of his depth.

'She was blubbering all last night,' he confessed. 'I've never heard anything like it – crying non-stop until by morning she made herself poorly.'

'Was she sick?' Hazel wanted to know, her mouth suddenly dry and her heart racing. If so, it could mean one of two things – either Sylvia was suffering from common or garden morning sickness or else she'd taken a strong purgative to try to rid herself of the baby.

'As a dog,' he confirmed. 'Then she got dressed and rushed out without any breakfast. That was four hours ago and I haven't seen hide nor hair of her since. It's not the first time she's done it either.'

'Rightio, I'll try to have a word with her if you like.' Anxious to be off, Hazel made her way to the door.

'I doubt that she'll listen,' Norman mumbled before stopping to think then following her onto the doorstep. 'Unless there's something you're not telling me?'

Hazel groaned inwardly. Lying didn't come easily, yet David had been adamant that knowledge of Sylvia's condition mustn't be shared. 'Let me have a word with her,' she said again before

217

hurrying off.

Crossing the yard, she saw Betty Hollings tucking Daisy into her pram and perching Polly at the bottom end while Keith picked up a stone and chucked it at a pigeon sitting on the ash-pit roof. Next she spotted her grandmother, who sat at her window surveying all. *Can't stop!* she mouthed, waving at Ada. She said the same to her Aunty Ethel, who was labouring down the ginnel with a heavy bag of groceries.

But Ethel collared her. 'I was wondering – have you seen Sylvia?' she asked, blocking Hazel's exit onto Raglan Road.

'Not lately,' Hazel confessed. 'Why?'

'I don't know what's got into her. She snaps my head off before I even open my mouth. And she looks downright peaky.' Plain-speaking Ethel came quickly to the point. 'Sylvia can scowl and stamp her foot all she likes when me and your nana and Aunty Rose knock on her door, but she can't kid us that she's not three months' gone. That's why I was hoping she'd stay in touch with you.'

'She hasn't,' Hazel said, looking Ethel in the eye as best she could. It came to her how lonely Sylvia must be – talking to no one except Mabel, unhappy in her new marriage and desperate to end her unwanted pregnancy.

Mabel. The name stayed with her as she managed to sidle past Ethel. Before she knew it she'd walked the few yards down the street and was knocking at the door of the corner house.

'Before you ask – no, Sylvia hasn't got back to me,' Mabel said the moment she opened the door.

218

Hazel bit her bottom lip and was about to turn away. But she hesitated. 'How did you know...?'

'Why you were hammering on my door?' Mabel stood full square, chin jutting out, feet wide apart. 'She's the only reason you'd be here, isn't she?'

'Yes. She's keeping out of the way of everyone except you. I'm worried about her, and I'm not the only one. I was hoping you'd have some news.'

'No news.'

'Are you sure?' Sixth sense was telling Hazel otherwise. Mabel's voice was edgy and defensive. Besides, she'd jumped the gun over Hazel's enquiry.

'Are you calling me a liar?' Hackles rising, Mabel made as if to close the door.

'No. Wait. From what I can gather, Sylvia's reached the end of her tether. I know for a fact she didn't take your advice about talking things through with Norman.'

Mabel clamped her lips tight shut and grunted in acknowledgement. She relaxed her hold on the door.

'He still hasn't got a clue about what's going on and Sylvia makes every excuse she can find to vanish for hours on end. I can't help thinking the worst–'

'All right, all right,' Mabel interrupted with a sigh of resignation. 'You'd better come in.'

So, rehearsing her next set of questions, Hazel walked down the hallway then turned into the front room where there was a low fire and the curtains were drawn against the daylight. After her eyes had adjusted to the gloom, she saw Sylvia lying on Mabel's horsehair sofa, covered by a patchwork blanket, her dark eyes glittering in her pale, exhausted face.

'Good heavens above!' Hazel exclaimed, feeling as though someone had punched her in the pit of her stomach.

Mabel thrust her further into the room then closed the door behind her, standing with her arms folded while Hazel recovered from the shock.

Sylvia raised herself onto her elbows then fell back. She groaned and turned her head away.

Hazel knelt beside the sofa. 'What have you done?' she whispered as she put her hand to Sylvia's forehead and found it damp and cold.

'Don't...' Sylvia whimpered.

'How long has she been like this?' Hazel asked Mabel. 'Have you examined her?'

'She won't let me near,' Mabel explained. 'I found her half-dead on my doorstep. I brought her in but I couldn't get a word out of her, except for her to say I shouldn't fetch help.'

'And you agreed!' Exasperated, Hazel found Sylvia's wrist under the blanket and felt her pulse. 'Have you taken something?' she asked. 'Tell me – what was it? Was it from the chemist?'

Weakly Sylvia pulled her hand away. 'Leave me alone.'

'I found these in her coat pocket,' Mabel told Hazel. She handed over a small round box labelled *Renovating Pills,* and underneath the words For Female Ailments. 'They're the sort you send away for.'

'Sylvia, listen to me.' Leaning in and stroking

220

her cheek, Hazel spoke gently. 'The box is empty. Does that mean you took them all?'

Sylvia groaned and placed her hands on her belly. She shivered violently and yet her whole body was drenched with sweat. 'I had to,' she whispered. 'I can't have this baby. I won't!'

Hazel folded back the blanket to reveal Sylvia's bare shoulders. She was in her brassiere and petticoat. Her dress was draped over the back of the sofa. 'Listen, Sylvia, I have to find out what's happening to you. Will you let me examine you?'

'No. Leave me alone,' she insisted, drawing the blanket back up.

Turning to Mabel, Hazel asked for a damp flannel to wipe Sylvia's face and a glass of water. 'She needs to drink as much as possible,' she explained.

'I've tried that. She can't keep anything down – not even water.' Mabel's attitude had changed – no longer defensive but resigned. 'We just have to wait until the pills do what they're supposed to do.'

'No.' Hazel was adamant. 'We don't even know what's in them or if they will work. All we know is that they've made Sylvia very sick.'

'What do you suggest instead?'

'You must go out to the telephone box on Ghyll Road and call for an ambulance.' Hazel overrode Sylvia's feeble protest. 'Ask them to get here as quickly as they can. I'll wait here and do whatever I can.'

Mabel grunted and shook her head. 'You're sure? Remember, this kind of thing goes on hundreds of times every day, up and down the country.'

'Do it,' Hazel insisted, waiting until Mabel had fetched her hat and coat then plodded off down the hallway. Left alone with Sylvia, she persuaded her to allow the examination to take place. 'Let me at least see if you're bleeding. It won't hurt, I promise.'

Weak and dazed, Sylvia agreed. With hardly the strength to turn onto her back and raise her knees, she cried softly when Hazel told her that there was no sign of blood or any discharge. 'That means it hasn't worked, doesn't it?'

Hazel agreed. 'But you still have to go to the hospital. What you've taken is poisonous – it may have lead in it, or turpentine. That's what's made you sick.'

'Oh!' Sylvia sighed, her cheeks wet with tears. 'This means everyone will know.'

'Yes, you can't keep it a secret any more. Anyway, most of us have already guessed.' Sylvia's look of fraught concentration reminded Hazel of a child trying to work through her times tables. 'All except Norman,' she added.

Sylvia groaned again and she grasped Hazel's hand. Her dilated pupils made her eyes seem huge. Her damp hair lay flat against her head. 'I'm not going to die, am I?'

'No. The doctors and nurses will look after you.' Hazel prayed silently that she was right.

As Mabel returned with the news that the ambulance would soon be there, Sylvia's grip on Hazel's hand tightened. 'Remember we're flesh and blood,' she wailed from the depths of pain and distress. 'If you don't stick by me, I don't know who will.'

CHAPTER THIRTEEN

The word was out. Sylvia was in hospital at risk of miscarriage. Norman was at her bedside.

Rose was the first to praise the part Hazel had played in events. 'It's a good job you stood up to Mabel and made her call the ambulance when you did,' she told her amongst the sawdust and make-shift furniture of Sylvia and Norman's kitchen. 'Goodness knows what would have happened otherwise.'

'Let's all keep our fingers crossed,' Robert added, still at work with saw and screwdriver. He'd stayed on after Norman had got the call to go to hospital, determined to get the place shipshape.

No one knew the real reason why things had gone wrong for Sylvia and, as always, Hazel kept her own counsel. She'd simply handed over the empty pill box to the ambulance driver and watched him take the patient away. Now it was in the hands of the doctors and all she could do was hope and pray.

'What was Mabel thinking?' Rose handed out the tea after she'd poured it from a vacuum-flask. Then she picked up a broom and started to sweep. 'Anyone could see that poor Sylvia was in a bad way.'

'That's the trouble with these old girls.' Rarely one to criticize, on this occasion Robert considered their neighbour to be in the wrong. 'They

223

reckon they know everything and they're too stubborn and set in their ways to call the doctor. But they only have herbal remedies and such like. What's the use of them in this day and age?'

Hazel smiled warmly. It was a long speech from her father and showed touching faith in the training she'd gone through.

'That's right,' Rose agreed. 'I'll make sure everyone knows how lucky it was for Sylvia that you were passing.'

'I didn't do much,' Hazel pointed out. She looked out of the window at the gathering dusk and at a stray ginger cat weaving its way between over-filled dustbins. Through the open door she heard the sound of approaching footsteps then voices exchanging goodbyes. Soon after, a weary-looking Norman appeared in the doorway.

'How is she?' Rose rushed to greet him and made him sit down. 'What did the doctor say?'

'He gave her something to stop her being sick. They're going to be all right – both her and the baby.' Norman spoke the word 'baby' with an air of disbelief. 'She just needs to rest.'

'Was that Ethel we heard outside?' Robert asked. 'Was she at the hospital with you?'

'Yes, there were three of us there – me, Sylvia's mother and Gladys – all crowding round the bed. In the end they chucked us out so Sylvia could get some sleep.'

'Right you are; I'll make myself scarce.' Deciding that Ethel would be a better source of more detailed information, Rose hurried away.

Hazel was about to follow her but was only a few steps across the yard when Norman came after her. 'I want to say thank you,' he began stiffly.

'There's no need – honestly.'

He chewed his lip and frowned. 'You knew, didn't you? That she's having a baby, I mean.'

Hazel nodded.

'So did every blighter except me, I reckon,' he said with downcast eyes. 'That must make me a laughing stock around here.'

'No, it doesn't,' she argued hastily. 'It was Sylvia's job to tell you, not anyone else's. Anyway, we're women – we pick up on these things sooner than you men.'

'Maybe I did know it, thinking back. I've seen it with Mum often enough. Only, Sylvia didn't say anything, so I pushed it to the back of my mind.'

Norman's misery on what should have been a happy occasion made Hazel sad too. 'Come on, do you fancy a walk on the Common before it gets dark?' Without waiting for an answer, she led the way down the ginnel and up the street. 'Let's look on the bright side,' she continued, crossing Overcliffe Road and striding out towards the bandstand where the Whitsuntide gala took place. 'With luck Sylvia will be out of hospital in a couple of days and we'll all be on hand to help her. By that time you and Dad will have got things straight in the house. Today has been a shock, but everything will settle down now, you wait and see.'

Norman walked by her side, hands in pockets, a thick scarf muffling the lower half of his face. 'I'm not as daft as I look,' he said suddenly.

'What do you mean?'

'I don't buy it,' he insisted. 'There has to be a

225

reason why she wouldn't let me in on it.'

'Maybe not.' Hazel comforted Norman as best she could. 'It could just be Sylvia seeing her life changing too fast then panicking and burying her head in the sand.'

'No. There's more to it.' As he reached the bandstand he sighed deeply and sat down on the top step, hunched forward, arms resting on his thighs. 'She's been different since we got married. She's not the girl I knew.'

Hazel's heart sank but she sat down beside him, ready to hear him out.

'I first met her by chance at the flicks. She was with a bunch of girls and she made a beeline straight for me, don't ask me why. A proper little whirlwind – I hardly knew what hit me.'

'That's Sylvia,' Hazel agreed.

'*Was,*' he corrected. 'Not any more. Anyway, before I knew it we were courting. There was I, plain old Norman Bellamy, swanning around town with the girl of my dreams, not listening to anyone's advice about slowing down and taking a cool, calm look at where we were headed. You don't, do you?'

'Not when you're in love.'

'I was. I still am. My mother was the one telling me to think twice.'

'Is that why she didn't come to the wedding?'

'Yes. She met Sylvia just the once, at our house in Hadley, and straight away she said it was too soon to think about marrying. She still hasn't come round to the idea.'

'I'm sorry to hear it.'

'She relied on me, did Mum.' Lost in thought

226

and with his head bowed, Norman fell silent.

A boy on a bike rode by, whistling a tune. Behind them, the blackness of the moors threatened to envelop them.

'Why did she pick me out from all the rest?' Norman's mind was fixed on this one point.

'Why not?' Hazel murmured, sitting with him under the octagonal bandstand roof. 'You're nice-looking and you have a good heart. What more could a girl want in a husband?'

'Five quid a week and a car to drive around in,' he quipped. 'That would go a long way towards keeping Sylvia happy.'

The sudden change of mood took her aback but she willingly went along with it. 'Ah,' she said, 'now you're talking.'

He laughed then stood up. 'Ta, anyway, Hazel.'

'What for?'

'For letting me get it off my chest.'

They began to walk back towards the town, facing a spider's web of twinkling street lights in the gloomy valley.

'I'm only sorry I haven't got the answer,' Hazel told him as she thought about the desperate measure that Sylvia had taken and the rocky road that still lay ahead for her and her new husband. 'Let's get her home and hope for the best, shall we?'

All might now be well, Hazel decided. After all, Norman was devoted to Sylvia and he seemed a steady type. In any case, there was nothing more she could do. Instead, she got up next morning with butterflies in her stomach about the forthcoming trip up the dale with John.

'How do I look?' she asked Jinny, appearing in the kitchen in her pink blouse and a grey skirt. She'd taken care with her hair and put on lipstick for the occasion.

'You'll do.' Jinny's reply was predictably downbeat as she went on spreading marmalade on her toast. Robert had already left for Norman and Sylvia's house so an uneventful Sunday doing housework lay ahead of her unless she and Hazel arranged something nicer. Now it seemed that Hazel had made other plans.

The answer was much as Hazel had expected – a cool glance of approval and a curt remark. She picked up her flat brogues from the row of shoes placed neatly by the door. 'Say ta to Dad,' she said as she put them on.

'What for?'

'For polishing these for me.' Then it was on with her best coat and hat, her leather gloves and silk scarf.

'Anyway, who are you getting all dressed up for?' Jinny wanted to know.

Hazel resisted the temptation to brush the question aside. 'John Moxon has offered to drive me out into the countryside. Why?'

'Has he, by Jove?' Jinny's surprise was genuine. 'Just the two of you?'

'Yes, but it's nothing,' Hazel assured her. 'He's only being friendly.'

'John Moxon,' Jinny echoed quietly as Hazel was on her way out. The door closed. Jinny frowned and put down her piece of toast. 'That was quick,' she muttered, cutting the uneaten toast into small squares to put out for the birds in the back yard. 'Let's hope you haven't made poor Myra turn in her grave.'

Hazel's butterflies increased as she walked up the hill. For two pins she would have backed out if John hadn't already been waiting on the pavement, nattily dressed in a tweed sports jacket, brogues and twill trousers. He was bareheaded in spite of the cold, holding open the car door for her as she approached.

'I thought you'd changed your mind,' he said as he got in beside her.

'Why – I'm not late, am I?'

'No, bang on time, as it happens.'

The car's gleaming dashboard with its mysterious dials and switches seemed to invite her into a more sophisticated world. 'I could get used to this,' she joked as they set off onto Overcliffe Road, gathering speed as they left the town behind. They were soon on the open road, bowling along under grey winter skies with heather moors to either side, then taking winding lanes through villages tucked away in narrow valleys between craggy hillsides.

'I'd better hang onto my hat!' Hazel laughed nervously as the lanes grew narrower, the villages more remote. 'Anyway, where are you taking me?'

John drove carelessly through puddles, fairly zipping along between rough stone walls, barely avoiding a cock pheasant that pecked for seeds at the roadside. At the last second he braked and the bird flew up and away over the wall, clattering its wings as it went.

'It's all right – I know these lanes like the back of my hand,' he assured her. 'I used to cycle them every day on my way to school.'

He finally slowed down when they came to a hamlet with a church overlooking a fast-flowing stream and a village green bordered by poky grey cottages and a pub with a low, stone-slated roof.

'This is it,' he announced. 'Shawcross.'

'It's small.' It was tiny, in fact. A huddle of houses, a worn memorial cross on a plinth in the middle of the green, mossy gravestones in the church yard and a wild rush of water at its feet.

'There's not much here,' he acknowledged. But he seemed proud of the place nonetheless and anxious for her to approve. 'There's a post box on the wall of the Red Lion – that was my only link with the outside world when I was growing up. Me and my mate, Alfred Jennings, we used to send off for stamps and stick them in an album. Stamps from France and Germany, even Africa – they were the colourful ones with birds and flowers on them that we'd never seen before.'

'So you didn't spend all your free time playing cricket?'

'Hmm, let me think. No – only ninety-five per cent, I'd say. I squeezed in the stamp collecting in the remaining five per cent, in between scoring a century for England, close on the heels of Jack Hobbs and the great W. G. Grace. Only in my dreams, mind you.'

'So where was your farm?' Hazel asked. John had parked next to the church and so far they'd stayed in the car, looking out at the humble land-marks of John's childhood. 'Will you show me it?'

'We'll have to reach it on Shanks's pony,' he warned, leaning over to look down at her shoes. 'Do you mind getting mucky?'

'Not a bit. These can always be cleaned.' She braced herself to face a biting wind and muddy tracks. 'Lead on.'

So he walked her out past the pub, up an ancient lane used by drovers leading their flocks to market. They went high onto the fell, beneath a craggy overhang colonized by gulls, and on again to where the valley widened and stone barns were scattered across the hillsides. The wind blew in from the west and they had to lean into it, John going slightly ahead to shield her.

'I'm not used to this,' she confessed. The space and the wind made her shiver. 'Dad used to bring me out on bike rides but we never got this far.'

'Would you rather go back?'

Hazel shook her head. Despite the lowering clouds and the wild horizon, she was determined to carry on.

'It's not far now.' On they went, battered by the wind, along the green lane with fields to either side until they came over the brow of a hill and looked down at a solitary farmhouse backed by three tall ash trees that leaned with the wind and provided the only shelter in the lonely landscape. 'This is it – Dale Head Farm,' John said quietly.

Hazel stood for a while without speaking, trying to picture what it must have been like to grow up here, without buses and trams, shops, factories, railways and canals – all the familiar sights and sounds of modern life. She shook her head and looked at him wide-eyed.

231

'It's not that bad.' He made a joke of her amazement.

'No, but it's ... different. I don't know how you managed it.'

'Up in all weathers – lambing in spring, digging sheep out of snow drifts in winter. That's how it was.'

'Honestly?'

'Scout's honour. I didn't mind it. On the other hand, I didn't want to stick around. As soon as I got the chance to leave, I grabbed it with both hands.'

'And your dad?'

John glanced up at the sky then looked her steadily in the eye. 'He had a heart attack. That was my chance. It sounds harsh, but Dad dying gave me my let-out.'

'How old were you?'

'Fifteen. I'd left school by then and was helping him here on the farm, fitting in the cricket at weekends.'

'My own father died in the war just after I was born,' she confided in turn. 'I was five when Mum married again. Of course I don't remember him.'

'Is that right?' John took the news and chewed it over before he spoke again. 'Robert has made a good job of stepping into your dad's shoes, I have to say.'

'He has. We were lucky. Mum might not admit it, but we were.'

'So was Robert. He had a ready-made family.' *Not like me,* he thought. *I've just lost mine.*

'Oh yes – me and Mum, Nana, Aunty Rose ... need I go on?'

'The Drummond family is a force to be reckoned with, eh?' Pulling himself together and linking his arm through hers, John drew her close to shelter her from the wind. 'Have you seen enough? Shall we go back?'

'Yes, if you promise to fill in the gap between leaving Shawcross and playing for Yorkshire.'

Setting off arm in arm the way they'd come and with the wind behind them, John was happy to carry on talking. 'You mean, how does a country bumpkin end up leading his team out to bat at Headingley? Hours of practice and a big dollop of luck – that's how.'

'I don't know much about cricket, but Dan says you were one of the best.'

'Hold on – don't go making me a worse bighead than I already am.'

'You don't strike me as big-headed,' she objected, steadying herself against him as they came to a narrow, rocky section of the track.

'Not any more – maybe once upon a time I had ideas above my station.' He concentrated on helping her find her footing. 'These days there's no reason to think I'm any better than the next chap.'

'You still teach the youngsters, though.'

'In the spring and summer. I drive to Leeds on a Tuesday and a Thursday after work, and sometimes on a weekend.'

'So you're passing on what you know. That's worth doing, isn't it?'

'Maybe.' As the village of Shawcross came into view, John's high spirits seemed to sink. 'I'm not sure if I'll carry on with it next year, though.

Things are different now.'

Did he mean Myra dying? Hazel wondered. Is that what had brought doubt into his mind? 'Oh, I would if I was you,' she urged.

'Maybe,' he said again, looking at her then changing the subject. 'Tell me – have you had a nice time?'

'Yes, it's been worth getting clarted up with mud for,' she assured him, judging that teasing would be the best way to bring the smile back to his face. 'I'm not sure that Dad will be happy, though.'

'What's it got to do with your dad?'

'He's the chief shoe cleaner in our house.'

'Take them off,' John commanded suddenly as he opened the car door and made her sit down. 'You're right – I can't send you home in this state. Come on – unfasten the laces, hand them over.'

She did as she was told, kicking off her shoes and watching him use a stick to scrape mud from the soles then wipe them on the grass. Her feet dangled sideways out of the car – a silly position that made her feel embarrassed.

'We'll have to do this again,' he said as he handed the shoes back one at a time.

Hazel bent forward to tie her laces. When she looked up, he was still crouching beside the car and his eyes met hers. They were light brown, flecked and striped like hazelnuts in their shells. Her face felt flushed and she was unsure how to strike the balance between rushing headlong where her heart was leading and holding back for propriety's sake.

'That would be nice.'

'In a week or two? Or is that too near Christmas?'

'No. I'd like to meet up again soon.'

'Same time next week, then?'

'No – let's say the week after.' There – she'd established the compromise.

John's smile was back. He stood up and walked around the front of the car, tapping the bonnet as he went. Then he stooped to ease his tall figure into the driving seat.

'In two weeks' time,' she said, a flurry of strong feelings flitting around her fast-beating heart.

'Welcome to the new regime.' Eleanor greeted Hazel with a disgruntled nod towards Irene Bradley who carried a tray laden with cups and saucers up the stairs to the clinic. 'Irene has moved in and I've been taken off tea duty.'

'How is it working out?' Detecting a hint of jealousy in the receptionist's voice, Hazel set down her bag then took off her hat and gloves.

'She's got a lot to learn,' Eleanor grumbled. 'This morning I caught her emptying the contents of the carpet sweeper into the waste-paper basket in your clinic room. There was dust everywhere. Luckily there was time for her to clean up the mess before your ladies arrived.'

My ladies. Hazel smiled and puffed out her chest at the idea. 'How many have we got today?'

'Five so far.'

Relieved that attendance was slowly returning to its original level, Hazel was eager to start. She went quickly upstairs and counted heads – five women and three children – and decided to ask

235

Irene to bring orange squash and beakers for the little ones. 'It can wait until tea break,' she added above the chatter.

Dressed in a grey blouse and serge skirt with a blue cotton apron over the top, Irene made a mental note. Nervous of getting things wrong, she nevertheless seemed less cowed than when Hazel had first met her and her face and figure were gradually fleshing out.

'How's little Grace?' Hazel found time to ask.

Irene stood a full inch taller at the mention of her baby and her face broke into a tender smile. 'She's a good little thing, touch wood. No trouble at all.'

'Where is she now?'

'Fast asleep in my room,' Irene reported. 'She won't wake up until it's time for her feed.'

'Why not bring her to clinic when she's awake? We'd all love to see her, wouldn't we, ladies?'

There was a chorus of yeses followed by a cheeky remark addressed to Hazel from Cynthia Houghton at the head of the queue.

'There you are, slow coach. We've been sitting here twiddling our thumbs for ages.'

'You must have been early, then. I'm bang on time.' Carefully avoiding two toddlers and one crawling baby, Hazel crossed the room and laid out her instruments behind the green screen. 'Anyway, I'm here now. Come in please, Cynthia. Let's see how you're getting along.'

'Couldn't be better,' Cynthia assured her as she got undressed and lay down to be examined.

'Yes, you look as if you're blooming. Being pregnant suits you.'

'And I've started reading about it, getting myself up to speed.'

'About what happens when you have a baby?' Hazel took Cynthia's blood pressure then checked her ankles and fingers for signs of swelling.

'Yes, all that malarkey. It was Tilly's idea. It's fascinating – there are books that show you pictures of a woman's insides and how the baby grows.'

Hazel smiled and made encouraging noises before listening with her stethoscope. 'Next time, can you bring in that urine sample I mentioned? And I'd like you to start noticing baby's movements – perhaps count how many kicks you feel during an hour – in the morning and again in the evening. Write it down if you like.'

'This one is kicking non-stop,' Cynthia told her cheerily. 'I swear he's wearing clogs. My old man is convinced I'm giving birth to a second Stanley Matthews.'

'Champion. Everything looks fine.'

'Can I go now?' Cynthia hauled herself into a sitting position then swung her legs over the side of the table.

'Yes. Just remember to rest – and eat well.' Already thinking ahead to her next patient, Hazel wrote swiftly in Cynthia's file.

'I'm eating for England, don't you worry.' Clothes back on, she thanked Hazel and departed.

'Next, please.' Hazel popped her head around the screen and invited a new lady in. This meant there was extra paperwork to fill in before they got started – Barbara Baxter was the wife of Philip Baxter, John's garage-owning boss. She was thirty-five years old and this was her first baby.

She obviously took pride in her appearance – her shiny dark brown hair was carefully waved and pinned back from her forehead and she wore a navy blue dress with a pert yellow bow adorning the neckline. She was in early pregnancy – hardly showing as yet.

Hazel waited for her to take off her clothes and took her time with the newcomer, explaining in detail everything that would happen. 'Everyone is nervous first time around,' she reassured her as she noted down Barbara's weight and height. 'But don't worry – you've come to the right place.'

'I do worry, though,' Barbara said. 'I can't help thinking of all the things that can go wrong, especially at my age.'

'You're through the first six weeks – that's a good milestone for us to reach. If you keep on coming to clinic, I'll make sure that everything is progressing as it should be.'

'They said you were young to be doing this job and they were right.' Submitting to her first examination, Barbara chatted nervously. 'Does Dr Bell keep a close eye on what you do?'

Hazel tried not to mind what she interpreted as a slight and answered confidently. 'He does. In fact, you're still his patient. Both he and I will be involved nearer the time.'

'Let's hope it won't turn out the way it did with poor Myra Moxon.'

Hazel's heart sank as she made the connection between her new patient and John's workplace.

'I called in at the garage and saw John two days after it happened. He was like a ghost – there in body but not there, if you know what I mean. I've never seen anyone look so pale and miserable.'

Hazel swallowed hard and tried not to react. 'Something like that is very rare,' she explained. 'It might not have happened if Myra had asked for help earlier.'

'That's as may be. At any rate, that's why I'm here – to check everything is as it should be.'

'And it is,' Hazel assured her. Struck by what Cynthia had said about teaching herself the basic facts of pregnancy, she recommended that Barbara go to the library and read up about it if she had time. 'Only if you think it would help you, though.'

'Ta, I will.' Relieved that the examination was over, Barbara slipped her dress carefully over her coiffured head. 'Philip has promised to drive me into town tomorrow to buy knitting wool for a matinée jacket. I can call in at the library at the same time.'

It was settled and Barbara left feeling happier than when she'd arrived. Hazel went on briskly to her next patient when there was a knock on the door and Irene came in with the tea trolley.

Then there was a break in proceedings and jovial cries of, 'Come on, Irene, let's see the littl'un.' Irene protested that she couldn't wake Grace up just for that. 'Yes, you can. Go and fetch her.' And so it went on until Irene went away and brought back a happy, gurgling infant swaddled in a soft white blanket. She sat with the baby in her arms amongst the mothers-to-be, glancing happily at Hazel, who hadn't the heart to start clinic again until everyone had had their fill of Grace.

Dusk was falling before she picked up the baton

239

again – another hour and a half of weighing, listening to heartbeats, inspection of varicose veins and talking through the advantages of breastfeeding over bottle before her last patient was seen and dispatched.

'You look done in,' David told her when she finally came downstairs. He too had just finished a busy surgery.

'I am,' Hazel admitted. She reached for her coat, picturing a quiet night in, soaking her feet in hot water and catching up with family news.

'Can you spare a minute?' He opened the door into his examination room and ushered her in. 'I see your numbers are going up nicely,' he began without preliminaries.

She nodded. 'I was afraid they might not – not after Myra.'

'I had every faith,' he insisted. 'And I know you've worked your socks off to regain lost ground.' He stood with his stethoscope around his neck, looking intently at her. 'How many patients did you manage to see this afternoon?'

'Seven in total. Two more came along from Hadley on Cynthia Houghton's say-so. The chances are they live too far out of town to have picked up the gossip.'

She glanced out at the receptionist, who was listening in as usual from behind her desk. 'On top of that, Eleanor has two new names on our list for next Tuesday if I can fit them in.'

'And all for three shillings a week.' He smiled wryly, thrust his hands in his jacket pockets and rocked back on his heels. 'What would you say if I put your money up to five shillings?'

240

'For half a day's work, I'd be more than happy. As long as giving me a rise doesn't mean we have to start charging.'

'It's still a free service,' he confirmed, ignoring Hazel's offer to shake hands on the new arrangement. 'Wait, I haven't finished yet. What would you think to working here on a Thursday as well as a Tuesday?'

'An extra clinic?' Her eyes lit up. 'Are you sure?'

'On a trial basis,' he suggested cautiously. 'Starting in January and going through to the end of February. That would give us a fair chance to see how it goes. What do you say?'

'I say yes!' This time she seized his hand and shook it warmly. She envisaged extra posters and more foot-slogging around the streets. She could ask the women who attended her Tuesday clinic to spread the word, too. This was already three ways that she could increase numbers, even before she'd put her thinking cap on. Besides, it seemed that the coven's hold over local opinion was loosening at last.

'I can make it pay off – I'm sure I can!'

She shook hands so enthusiastically that David laughed and took a step back. 'I have faith in your ability to reach any goal you set yourself, Hazel Price.'

'You do?' For a moment she forgot herself and almost planted a kiss on his cheek. Excitement coursed through her like electricity. Her career was on the up, make no mistake. 'Thank you!' she beamed. Instead of kissing him, she turned and dashed out into Reception to glean Eleanor's reaction.

241

'So there'll be no licking envelopes and changing typewriter ribbons for you, then?' The receptionist cast a telling glance at David who hovered in the doorway to his room. 'At this rate, she'll be working full time before we know it.'

'You don't say,' David replied, inwardly regretting the passing moment when he had wondered if Hazel might have been on the verge of kissing him.

Sharp-eyed Eleanor had picked up on it too. She was wearing her sentry look, guarding him on this occasion from the foolishness of falling in love with Hazel. Too late, as it happened. He sighed and unhooked his stethoscope from around his neck.

'There are five letters for you to sign before you go home,' Eleanor told him briskly.

'Goodnight!' Hazel's rich voice faded as she made her way out of the building. She couldn't wait to go home and tell her mother and father the good news, then her nana and Aunty Rose. 'And thank you!'

CHAPTER FOURTEEN

Robert beamed at Hazel across the kitchen table. 'By Jove!' he said, almost speechless with delight. He held his knife and fork poised over his tea of Welsh rarebit.

'I know! Can you believe it?' Hazel's smile went from ear to ear. 'David thinks enough of me to offer me this extra work.'

'And extra pay,' Jinny observed.

'There's that as well.' Too excited to eat, Hazel planned ahead. The pay rise would be more than enough to cover her rent once she and Gladys had settled down somewhere suitable.

Robert found his voice. 'I knew it – the sky's the limit for you, my girl.'

Hazel jumped up and skipped around the room, hugging first him and then her mother.

'Steady on,' Jinny grumbled as she submitted to the embrace. 'It won't all be plain sailing. You still have to keep your feet on the ground.'

'Once – just once – tell me you're pleased!' Hazel demanded. She was like a kite, sailing so high that she could afford to risk a small tug of disapproval.

There was a long pause while Jinny pursed her lips and carefully placed her knife and fork on her empty plate. It was a big moment and she knew it.

Robert looked from one to the other, at the irrepressible joy on Hazel's face and Jinny's struggle to control her feelings. He willed his wife to give Hazel the praise that she deserved.

'I am pleased,' Jinny said with tears in her eyes. 'But someone has to point out the pitfalls.'

Hazel crouched beside her and spoke gently. 'I'm not daft, Mum. I know it'll be hard work.'

Jinny gave a single nod. A slow tear trickled down her cheeks. 'You've never been afraid of hard graft, I'll give you that.'

'Why are you sad?'

'I'm not. I'm all right.'

'Then why are you crying?' Moved by Jinny's show of emotion, Hazel lowered her voice to a soft whisper.

Jinny's lip quivered as she took her daughter's hand. 'This is me being happy for you,' she confessed. 'And proud, too.'

'Honestly?' Hazel looked deep into Jinny's eyes. In her mother she saw herself as she would have been without love and support throughout her childhood, without the backing she'd received to make something of herself. 'Thank you,' she breathed, clasping Jinny's hand and squeezing it. 'That means the world to me.'

The new harmony in the house carried Hazel through the next few days with a glow of happy expectation. There were talks with David and Eleanor about getting proper posters printed to advertise the new clinic times, post-natal visits to be made and two consecutive evenings spent in the town library extracting information from medical books for Hazel to use in writing leaflets that she intended to hand out at clinic.

'Excellent idea,' was David's verdict when she made a special visit to the surgery to talk through her latest plan. It was Friday; the end of a long week for him of treating bunions, sore throats, psoriasis and bad backs. Then there were two cases of scarlet fever within one family on Over-cliffe Road when David had had to call for the dreaded van to stretcher the two hapless victims, wrapped in the tell-tale red blankets, to the children's isolation hospital – a move that upset him almost as much as it did the family involved.

Now he had to meet and match Hazel's enthusiasm. 'A leaflet to advise pregnant women on what to eat.'

'And what *not* to eat,' Hazel pointed out, showing him her handwritten draft. 'Plus, the need for exercise, but not too much. And the signs to watch out for if something is going wrong.'

'Oedema,' David agreed as he read her notes. 'We know that's the main symptom to look out for.'

In the privacy of David's examination room, Hazel got into her stride. 'Yes, but we have to keep it simple and concentrate on the up-side. This leaflet should be a guide on what to do for a healthy pregnancy: a list of good foods, the changes to expect in your body, and so forth.'

'I agree.'

'Shall I talk to the printer about how much it will cost? He's already given me the price for the posters. Maybe we could get a reduction from him for doing the leaflets as well.'

'It's worth a try.' David suspected that Hazel's natural charm and enthusiasm could work wonders, even with a hard-headed local businessman. *If they're anything like me,* he thought ruefully. Though he tried his best to keep his feelings in check, he found that every time Hazel walked into the building he was smitten all over again. Like now – she'd breezed in out of the damp, dark evening bringing what he could only describe as a bright light with her. She shone with energy – it came off her creamy skin and her gleaming fair hair and glowed in her dark blue eyes.

'It's as good as done,' she promised before

245

moving on to ask about Irene and her baby.

'Both well,' he reported. 'Irene is a doting mother.'

'But a so-so housekeeper, by all accounts.'

'Ah, Eleanor's been tittle-tattling,' he guessed as the conversation wound down and Hazel got ready to leave. 'What are you up to later? Will I see you at the jazz club?'

'Not tonight. I'm having a quiet night in.'

Off she rushed, oblivious to his disappointment, out through Reception, past an ever-watchful Eleanor and down the steps onto the street. 'If you go into town, say hello to the others from me,' was her breezy parting shot.

The next day, Saturday, was the time set aside for Hazel and Gladys to continue their flat-hunting. They met at ten in Nixon's café, fortifying themselves with tea and toasted teacakes, armed with lists from two new estate agents.

As usual, Gladys was full of gossip.

'You missed a good night last night,' she told Hazel as she tucked into her snack. 'I danced the night away with the usual crowd.'

'From the hospital?' Hazel asked, without paying much attention. In her mind, the quest to find a flat came before hearing about Gladys's social life.

'Yes, and your David was there too.'

'He's not *my* David.' Gladys's quip was so cheeky and blatant that for once Hazel didn't blush.

'Says you. Anyway, our old friend Bernard is becoming quite a pest. He wouldn't leave me

246

alone for one minute, always on at me to dance with him. And he made remarks that I didn't like. In the end I had to put him in his place. Oh, and something is going on between my friend Mary Fenning and John Moxon, I'm sure of it.'

A jolt of unpleasant surprise ran through Hazel. 'So he was there last night?'

'Yes – with Dan and Reggie, propping up the bar as usual until Mary inveigled him onto the dance floor. He went off with her at the end of the evening.'

Hazel remembered Mary, Gladys's fellow secretary at the King Edward's – a self-possessed, striking-looking, auburn-haired woman who was obviously at ease in male company. Ignoring a small stab of jealousy, she concentrated on her list once more.

'And there's bad news to do with Dan,' Gladys prattled on as she leaned sideways to wipe the steamed-up window then peer out onto the street. She pulled a sour face at Hazel as Doreen, Mabel and Dorothy walked by armed with shopping bags and umbrellas. 'By the way, Mabel's been on at Mum to sort Sylvia out,' she muttered.

'Sort her out – how?'

'I don't know – get her organized for when the baby finally comes, I suppose. Anyway, Dan–'

'Yes, what's he done now?' Hazel asked.

'You remember he went off to the bookmaker's at Blackpool and came back with a face like a wet weekend? It turns out that he'd entered into a big betting syndicate with Reggie and John a few days earlier, using money that he hadn't got. Of course, their horse lost that day and Dan knew he would have to scrounge more cash from somewhere if he wanted to carry on being part of the group. That's why he looked so glum.'

'What about John? Could he afford to lose the bet?'

'I doubt it – not on a garage mechanic's wages. Reggie's different. I expect he can splash out whenever he wants.'

'So what will Dan do?' Telling herself that what John got up to was none of her business, Hazel steered the conversation back towards her ne'er-do-well cousin.

Gladys shrugged. 'Dad wouldn't give him any money and he's not getting a penny from me. He says he'll have to work overtime to pay it back. The thing is, Dan and John borrowed from Reggie to get themselves into the syndicate in the first place. It's him Dan owes the money to.'

'That's the way to ruin a friendship,' Hazel commented. 'I don't know much about Reggie, but he doesn't strike me as the type you should cross. And I'm surprised at John.'

'Yes, but we don't know him very well. Perhaps he's easily led.' Gladys had finished her tea and was pulling on her gloves.

'No,' Hazel argued, 'I don't get that impression.'

Gladys caught her earnest tone and gave her a sharp look.

'He seems decent, that's all.' Feeling a strong urge to spring to his defence, Hazel put on her gloves to avoid looking directly at Gladys and to give herself time to settle some qualms about John's behaviour. 'If you must know, he went out of his way to let me off the hook after Myra died.'

'And?'

'And nothing.' This was not the time to tell Gladys about last Sunday's drive out to Shaw-cross, Hazel decided. 'Come on, slow coach – we won't find somewhere to live by sitting on our backsides. And by the way, how is Sylvia now that she's back home?'

They left the café and walked briskly across Ghyll Road down steep steps onto Canal Road, where their figures were dwarfed by the three-storey, grimy walls of Kingsley's and Calvert's mills and Brinkley Baths beyond. There was a constant rumble of traffic and a frenzy of activity as cars and buses pulled up at kerbs and trams trundled by.

'As far as I know, it's all quiet on the western front,' Gladys said in reply to Hazel's question about Sylvia. 'My dad took over from yours at the start of the week – lending a hand with the decorating and such like. Now Sylvia and Norman have at least got a bed to sleep in and a table to eat off. Mum's keeping Mabel at arm's length, saying Sylvia isn't ready to think that far ahead. I told her that the first thing she should do is sign up to your clinic.'

'Ta for that.' Hazel was relieved that Sylvia was now getting some family back-up. 'I hope she listens to you.'

Gladys breathed out and popped her lips. 'Pah! When did she ever do that? What number Canal Road are we looking for?'

'102. It's past the Victory, on the right-hand side.'

The address they'd been given by the agent

249

turned out to be one of a long row of large terraced houses that had once belonged to wealthy merchants and factory-owners but had now gone to seed. Stone steps led up to porticoed entrances with fan-shaped windows above wide, panelled doors. They were blackened by soot and weeds wilted in the high gutters. Most of the paintwork was faded and flaking.

'Not very promising,' Gladys commented. '98 ... 100 ... 102. Ah, this is better!'

Indeed, the door to 102 was painted a shiny black, with a polished lion's-head knocker. The worn steps were freshened by donkey-stoned edges.

'Worth a look,' Hazel agreed.

Gladys went ahead up the steps and lifted the knocker. They waited a long time without a reply and were about to give up when the door was opened by a nattily dressed black man whom Gladys thought she recognized.'

Busy lighting a cigarette, he looked them up and down. He wore a trilby hat at a cocky angle, a pinstriped suit with broad shoulders and lapels, two-tone shoes and a yellow cravat – in other words he was bang up to date, as Gladys recounted later.

'Don't I know you?' she asked with a cheeky grin.

'I have no clue – do you?'

'You're in Earl Ray's band. You play the saxophone.'

'That's right,' he said, nonchalantly slipping his silver lighter into his top pocket. His lazy American accent stretched out his vowel sounds – different to the flat, clipped dialect they were used to. 'The name's Sonny – Sonny Dubec. I guess you're looking for the lady of the house?'

'Yes. She has rooms to rent.' For once Gladys was thrown off balance so she kept her answer prim and to the point.

'Miss Bennett!' Sonny called in his low, lilting voice, still unashamedly weighing up the visitors.

A middle-aged woman emerged from a room at the end of the tiled hallway, drying her hands on a towel and hurrying towards them. 'Thank you, Mr Dubec.'

'The pleasure is mine, Miss Bennett,' he intoned, drawing hard on his cigarette then directing a plume of blue smoke upwards to the ceiling. He smiled broadly as he brushed past Hazel and Gladys and went on his way.

'I'm sorry you had to wait. I was busy in the kitchen,' the woman said. 'I'm Miriam Bennett. Have you come about the rooms on the top floor?'

As Gladys introduced herself, Hazel took in details of the landlady and their surroundings. Miriam Bennett was a trim woman with mid brown hair going grey at the temples. She wore a black jumper and matching skirt, teamed with a string of pearls and black shoes with a small heel. Hazel noted with approval that she took care to keep the intricate mosaic of terracotta tiles polished and the patterned stair carpet clean, its brass stair rods gleaming. Overhead, a plain skylight lit the stairwell that ascended three storeys to a high attic landing.

'Follow me,' the landlady told them, explaining

251

the situation as they climbed the stairs. 'Most of my rooms are rented out to people from the theatre and the clubs – like Mr Dubec. They come and go from week to week. But I prefer to have permanent lodgers on the top floor. That way I can be sure of one steady rent and some familiar faces.'

'That makes sense,' Gladys agreed. She too seemed impressed by the standards of cleanliness.

'There's a young couple in here at the moment – Mr and Mrs Jackson. They've gone away to Scarborough for the weekend. They leave for good at the end of the month.' Reaching the spacious top landing, Miss Bennett opened a door onto a living room with easy chairs to either side of a small fireplace, made cosy by the current tenants' ornaments and pictures.

'Plenty of headroom, you see – exactly the same as the room on the other side.'

Gladys and Hazel found themselves peering into an attic room that was a mirror image of the other, only this time with a double bed and a dressing table.

'There's only one bedroom,' Hazel pointed out.

Gladys quickly worked out that they could convert both rooms into single bedrooms and turn the landing space into an open, well-lit living area.

'There's an inside bathroom down on the first floor with hot and cold running water, and a separate WC. They're shared between all my lodgers.' Miss Bennett listed the facilities then went downstairs to give Gladys and Hazel time to talk things through.

'What do you think to being woken up every day

by strains of saxophone music?' The gleam in Gladys's eye that had appeared when she'd recognized the jazz player was still there. 'Or an actor rehearsing lines? "It is a far, far better thing I do..."! You know – the smell of the greasepaint and all that.'

Hazel couldn't help but smile. 'I do like the place,' she conceded. 'And it's handy for you that it's close to town. But maybe we should look at others on the list before we decide.'

'But then we'd risk losing this one.' Gladys paced out the space on the landing. 'We can easily fit two armchairs in here and plug in one of those two-bar electric fires. Or if we want peace and quiet, we can each go to ground in our own rooms.'

'I know you – you'll be hanging over the banister calling coo-ee to those handsome actors, inviting them up for cups of tea. There'll be no stopping you.'

'Does that mean yes?' A gleeful Gladys was on the point of running downstairs to tell the landlady.

'Yes.' Hazel's agreement took even her by surprise. But life would never be dull here – two girls jumping into the swing of things, living a modern life. Privately she thought that she wouldn't mention the likes of Sonny Dubec and Earl Ray to her mum and dad, who would no doubt consider them too racy.

As if summoning him by her thoughts, as Gladys and Hazel descended the stairs a door on the first landing opened and out stepped the great man himself. Earl Ray was an imposing

253

figure dressed in a light grey three-piece suit with a camel-hair overcoat hanging from his shoulders like a cape. He was on his way out, but he stopped to say hello.

'It's a thrill to meet you,' a star-struck Gladys gushed. 'Isn't it, Hazel? My friends and I love to listen to your band and my little sister is your biggest follower.'

Earl Ray soaked up the admiration. He was glad to learn that they would soon be neighbours and hoped that Gladys and Hazel would settle quickly into number 102. 'We're a free and easy bunch,' he assured them. And to prove it he offered them two complimentary tickets to a January concert at the Town Hall. 'Front-row seats,' he told Gladys as, with a flash of gold rings, he pulled the tickets from his waistcoat pocket.

'It's our lucky day,' Gladys cooed after Earl Ray had said goodbye and left them overcome with excitement.

Hazel heard his footsteps cross the hall and then the click of the front door closing. 'Let's find Miss Bennett and tell her we want to take the rooms,' she said once she'd got her wits about her. 'We'll arrange to pay her a deposit. Come on, Gladys – stop catching flies.'

'Oh, but this is wonderful,' Gladys sighed, waving the concert tickets in the air. 'Pinch me and tell me it's true.'

Life was nothing if not varied for Hazel. The arrangement was made with Miss Bennett for her and Gladys to move in at the start of January and with it came the promise of glamour and excitement for the two cousins from Raglan Road and Nelson Yard. The following Tuesday Hazel was back running a busy clinic, sleeves rolled up, rubber gloves on.

'Take a look and see what you think,' Cynthia Houghton told Hazel as she lay back on the examination table. 'I've had so many aches and pains this last couple of days that I'm sure baby is on its way.'

Hazel consulted Cynthia's record card. 'It's a bit early. The pains are probably Braxton Hicks, but let's see.'

'What's that when they're at home?'

'It's what we call false labour – you'll have read about it, I'm sure.' Waiting until Cynthia was comfortable on her back with her knees crooked, Hazel began her examination. 'Where do you feel the pain – in your back or in your abdomen?'

'All over,' Cynthia groaned. Up till now she'd been glowing with health through each stage of her pregnancy but today she was slow and listless. 'Mostly low down in my back then it works its way round to the front.'

Hazel felt her way carefully. 'How long do the pains last? A few seconds or longer?'

'Usually longer.' Seized by a new twinge, Cynthia let out a groan. 'I'm right, aren't I? This is the real thing.'

'I'm not sure yet. Tell me – is there any way you could have missed your waters breaking?'

'Lord only knows. I've been dashing to the WC a lot, though.'

As Cynthia described her symptoms, Hazel grew convinced that her patient was right. Beyond the

255

screen, the other women chatted over their cups of tea and children played noisily with building bricks and plasticine. Luckily Irene was still there, overseeing the teapot. 'Irene!' Hazel hissed as she poked her head around the edge of the screen. 'We might need Dr Bell. Can you ask him to come up, please?'

'He's out on a house call,' Irene told her.

'Rightio. Ask Eleanor to pass on the message as soon as he comes back, then.'

Sensing that something was up, the chatter in the room died down and Cynthia's labour went ahead with an audience of avid listeners.

'Ouch, that hurt,' one of the women commented when Cynthia let out a groan followed by a loud cry.

'Rather her than me,' another added as Hazel urged Cynthia to turn onto her side and gave calm advice about breathing.

Behind the screen it was now obvious to Hazel what was happening. The baby's head was fully engaged and the cervix dilated. She drew boiling water from the gas geyser above the sink then slid towels under the patient. 'Can you manage?' she asked Cynthia. 'Or would you like something for the pain?'

'Nothing,' Cynthia's predictable reply came through gritted teeth. She breathed in sharply at the start of another contraction.

Hurry up in there,' someone called. 'I haven't got all day. I've to be home in time to make Harold his tea.'

This raised a titter and drew a sympathetic smile from Hazel. 'Take your time, Cynthia. Deep breaths – that's right, nice and easy.'

Half an hour went by without much progress so Hazel decided it was best to move the weighing scales out from behind the screen and carry out some routine checks on the women who had chosen to stay while Cynthia rested and waited. 'Call if you need me,' Hazel told her.

'That's the ticket.' The woman at the head of the queue jumped onto the scales with alacrity. She lifted her dress up around her chest for Hazel to listen to her abdomen, giving everyone a clear view of voluminous knickers and stout legs with skin that was mottled from sitting too close to the fire. 'Take a good butcher's,' she invited her fellow sufferers. 'And don't you worry – before you know it I'll be back to my sylph-like self!'

Noting down figures amidst a round of friendly laughter and ribald comments, Hazel reassured her that all was well then moved on to the next.

'Who'd have thought one young girl could get through us lot at the same time as keeping an eye on Cynthia?' Approval for Hazel rose and was voiced by the next in the queue.

'Don't speak too soon,' her neighbour warned as Cynthia let out a full-throated yell and Hazel disappeared once more behind the screen.

'Deep breaths,' Hazel reminded her patient, registering the presentation of the dome of the baby's head. She mopped Cynthia's brow as they waited for the contractions to ease. They began again almost immediately, making Cynthia grasp the edge of the examination table until her knuckles were white. She clenched her teeth and moaned. 'Now breathe in and out quickly,' Hazel instructed. Here came the head in exactly the right position – a steady, smooth birth during which the shoulders eased out and the worst was soon over. 'Marvellous, wonderful, Cynthia – you're doing beautifully! It's a little boy.'

Out in the room a cheer went up followed by a spontaneous chorus of 'For She's a Jolly Good Fellow.'

'Let me hold him.' Cynthia could hardly wait until the cord was cut and the mucus cleared from her baby's face. 'Is he all right? Why isn't he crying?'

'He will,' Hazel assured her as she held the infant upside down and gave his bottom a sharp tap with her fingertips. He took his first breath then gave a long, high wail.

'There's nothing wrong with his lungs at any rate,' was the general opinion.

'Give him to me, please,' Cynthia pleaded.

Hazel wiped the baby's face with cotton-wool swabs then wrapped him in a blanket. The little boy's eyes opened on the outside world for the very first time. 'Here he is,' she murmured, as, with infinite care, she nestled the precious infant in his mother's arms.

CHAPTER FIFTEEN

A weak sun broke through the clouds as Hazel got out of bed and stood on tiptoe-to peer out of her attic window on the day of her second planned drive with John. The slate roofs were white with frost.

The fine weather was a good omen, she decided. She chose warm clothes – a Fair Isle sweater knitted by Rose teamed with her dark blue slacks – and took special care to brush her hair until it shone. She went downstairs, bracing herself for the inevitable cross-examination.

'Where are you off to, as if I didn't know?' Jinny asked, her back to Hazel as she timed Robert's two boiled eggs, ready for his return with his Sunday newspaper.

'Nowhere special. John's invited me out on another drive.'

Hazel's airy reply cut no ice with her mother. 'I knew it. You should watch what you're doing if you don't want folk talking behind your back.'

'Why would they?' Reluctantly Hazel sat down to a slice of toast and marmalade, no doubt accompanied by a big dollop of her mother's disapproval.

'Because they will,' Jinny said, turning and arching her eyebrows.

'Well, let them.' Hazel dug in her heels. 'There won't be a word of truth in what they say. My

259

jaunts out into the countryside with John are open and above board.'

That was it – a dead end. Neither would say more.

Hazel pushed her plate away then hurried to put on her coat and hat, bumping into her father on her way out of the house.

'What's the rush?' One glance at Hazel then at Jinny made Robert sense an atmosphere. 'Never mind – your mother will fill me in. Have a nice time, wherever it is you're going.'

So Hazel was off-kilter when she set out up the empty street. *As if my nerves weren't bad enough already,* she thought. *Do I really know what I'm doing here? What if Mum's right and there is more to it on both sides than a jaunt in John's car?*

So what? the stubborn voice said. *We're both free agents. We're not harming anyone.*

As on the previous occasion, John was waiting for her at the top of the street, seeming not to feel the cold in his sports jacket and open-necked shirt. He greeted her with a relaxed smile then moved quickly to open the car door. 'You'll soon warm up once I get the engine running,' he predicted.

See! In case anyone was peeking through their net curtains, Hazel cast a defiant glance out of the side window as the car set off. *Open and above board.*

It was a morning of glorious blue skies, of sweeping, frosty hillsides and bare winter trees, of wide-open space and fresh air, accompanying them up hill and down dale, as the railway posters and guidebooks had it. They drove along winding byways that Hazel had never seen before then all of a sudden, in the distance, she saw a wondrous viaduct striding across a rugged valley with a train crossing. John stopped the car so they could watch the plume of smoke dissolve into the sky and the dark chain of carriages snake out of sight.

Where would that train carry its passengers? she wondered. Perhaps north to Carlisle then on across the border to Edinburgh – a world opening up into mountains and medieval castles, away from the mills and factories.

As they drove, John and Hazel chatted easily – him taking the lead to put her at her ease. 'We won't talk about the weather or Christmas,' he promised.

'Or work,' Hazel added.

'So what's left? I know – I want to find out why I haven't seen you at the jazz club for a week or two.'

'I've been busy.' A flutter of nerves made her turn to teasing him. 'Anyway, a little bird tells me you didn't miss me.'

'Oho! So you've been keeping tabs on me.'

She tossed her head then tutted. 'I walked into that one, didn't I? No, as a matter of fact it was Gladys – she doesn't miss a trick.'

'I'll remember that in future. Hang on a second, I need to get out and open this gate.'

But before John had time to put on the hand-brake, Hazel was out of the car and opening the farmer's gate that blocked the road and kept sheep off the moor top. The wind caught her silk scarf, tugging it free and sending it off, whirling

261

and twirling across the heather. Now John leaped out and chased it down, stooping to pick it up off the ground then running back with it.

'Here.' He made her stand while he tied it around her neck.

Then they drove on, over the top to Shawcross.

'Are you ready for a pit stop?' he suggested as he pulled up outside the Red Lion.

Inside the pub, four or five weather-beaten men in worn jackets and moleskin trousers stood at the bar drinking pints of bitter, their backs to the newcomers. A black-and-white sheepdog dozed by the open fire.

'Now then, John, long time no see.' The barman smiled and reached across the bar to shake hands.

'How are you, Fred? Hazel, this is my old pal, Alfred ... Fred Jennings.'

She too shook hands. 'I've heard about you. You're John's fellow stamp collector.'

'That's right – philatelist and long-serving bowler to Yorkshire cricket's star in the making. What'll it be, Hazel?'

'I'd like a Cinzano with lemonade, please.' Responding to Fred's lively manner, Hazel understood how the two young lads had got along, with fair-haired, lightweight Fred acting as a nippy foil to John's sturdier, stronger athleticism.

'I was handy with a cricket bat but I never had a hope of reaching John's dizzy heights,' Fred admitted. 'Look at me now – pulling pints for these old reprobates.'

His comment drew little reaction from the down-to-earth farming types nearby. One glanced in John and Hazel's direction, muttered to his neighbour then carried on drinking.

'Is John taking you on a tour of his old haunts?' Fred asked, his curiosity making up for the others' dour disinterest. Of course, news had reached Fred of Myra's tragic death and he hoped with all his heart for better things for his old pal in future – especially since it had never seemed to Fred that Myra was quite the right one for John. Not that Fred had ever said this to his friend's face – and never would, now that the poor girl had passed away. 'I hope you're not letting Hazel in on our guilty secrets,' he said with a wink.

'You speak for yourself,' John bantered. 'I was too busy skying a cricket ball to get up to no good.'

Fred winked at Hazel. 'If you believe that, you'll believe anything.'

As the two men launched into a string of reminiscences, Hazel sat contentedly on a bar stool, only half listening and taking in the rows of dull pewter jugs on a shelf behind the bar above bright advertisements for beer and cigarettes. She was aware now and then of Fred stealing glances at her mid-anecdote – looks that seemed to size her up as John's new girl and end with a warm smile of approval. Apparently oblivious to the undercurrent, John enjoyed his walk down memory lane until at last he tapped his watch.

'We'll love you and leave you,' he told Fred, explaining to Hazel that there was only an hour of daylight left. 'We won't have time to walk out to Dale Head today,' he told her as they left the pub. 'We could take a stroll through the churchyard instead.'

So they walked arm in arm across the green then down a short lane leading to a lich-gate and through this into a mossy churchyard thronged with ancient gravestones. The stone church, with its round-arched Norman entrance and squat, square tower, overlooked the river and a steep bank beyond.

'This whole churchyard will be covered in snowdrops in a few weeks' time.' John's voice was low, hardly audible over the rush of water.

Reading inscriptions on nearby graves, Hazel found one for a child – Sarah Winters aged eight – and next to it a smaller one for her sister, Lucy, who departed this life on 3 September 1823, aged just three years. There was an angel carved in stone watching over them both.

'This is where my lot are buried.' John took her to a quiet corner and showed her the Moxon family plot – his grandparents, Sarah and William, then Elizabeth, his mother, who died in her thirty-sixth year, resting alongside Thomas, his father, who had died aged fifty-two. Their white marble gravestone stood out from the more ancient memorials and was in the shape of a cross. The inscription read 'In loving memory' – plain and simple.

'We buried Myra in St Luke's churchyard,' John reminded Hazel in a low voice.

She felt her heart flutter. 'I know. I'm sorry I didn't come to the funeral.'

'No, that's all right, I understand. You'd have been welcome if it had been up to me, but we both know her mother would've kicked up a fuss.'

'I am very sorry,' Hazel said from the bottom of her heart. His mention of Myra's name had built her a bridge that she felt bold enough to venture across. 'Should you have liked to bury her here?'

He answered slowly. 'No. St Luke's was the right place for her. It's handy for her mother and father. And you know something – being married to Myra is already beginning to feel like a dream.'

'Like it never happened?' It shook her to think how quickly solid reality – a beautiful wife and a baby – shifted and faded.

'It did happen – I know it did. I'm left with the pain of losing it – that's how I know it was real.' John stood in the corner of the graveyard in the gathering dusk as if suspended, lost in the moment, staring up at the black yew tree over-head. 'But when I look back and try to grasp hold of it, I can't.'

'Give it time – perhaps you will.' When the pain eased and memories re-emerged like snowdrops from the frozen earth. 'You'll remember the good times.'

He nodded and seemed to come back from wherever he'd been. 'I can talk like this to you. I know you'll understand.'

'Let's walk on,' she suggested quietly, retracing their steps through the lich-gate and finding an overgrown path along the riverbank. Crows rose from tall elms and flapped across the fields – the only movement in the sheltered landscape. After a while their way was blocked by brambles and she turned to see what they should do.

John was close behind – near enough to reach out and lay his hand on her shoulder. He looked intently at her, silently questioning and searching for answers.

She felt the weight of his hand and didn't flinch from his gaze. He leaned forward until his face was a blur then he kissed her on the lips, softly at first then more strongly. Melting into the moment, she put her arms around his neck and kissed him back.

'You didn't mind?' John asked once he and Hazel had retraced their steps to the village green. He sounded unsure of himself and avoided looking Hazel in the eye as he held open the car door.

For her the kiss had come out of the blue. It had been like no other she had ever experienced – slow and measured at first but then, as she'd flung caution to the winds, it had grown passionate. For what seemed like an age, she'd hardly known where she was or what she was doing. Coming out of it had been like floating up to the surface after a sudden plunge into a deep, dark pool.

'No, I didn't mind,' she said now. Words couldn't convey how she felt. Thrown off balance, over-joyed, fearful, uncertain – it was a mixture of all these.

'You looked so ... lovely,' he explained. Again, the words didn't do justice to his feelings. It was her eyes that had captivated him, he realized. Deepest blue, heavily lashed and shining.

Her head began to clear – she took in the row of stone cottages bordering the village green, the sound of the car engine turning and choking into life – but the ground under her feet still didn't feel solid and her world was transformed. John's kiss had changed everything.

John too was knocked off balance by the kiss. 'I don't know what to say to you,' he admitted as they drove off. 'I can't shake off the feeling of wanting to say sorry.'

'For what?'

'For springing that on you. It was when you suddenly turned around – I couldn't help myself.'

'I didn't mind – honestly.' Hazel had found real delight in that moment when their lips had touched but the emotion had been so strong it had scared her. Then there was the eventual pulling back and letting go, returning along the overgrown path and trying to get back to normal when she was sure nothing was the same between them or would ever be again.

John drove the car, staring straight ahead. He pointed out the sun sinking behind a rugged, dark horizon then the landmark viaduct crossing the valley, followed by details closer to hand – trails on the frosty verges made by foxes and the sight of a red kite soaring overhead.

Hazel minded that he didn't look at her. He seemed to grow tense, determined to keep the conversation neutral. What did she care about foxes and birds when all she really wanted was for him to kiss her again?

The return to town put paid to that. Houses, street signs, traffic lights, other cars – these were familiar, belonging to the real world. By the time they reached Overcliffe Road, the conversation had dwindled almost to nothing.

'I hope I've got you back in time for your tea,' John said as they turned onto Raglan Road.

'Plenty of time, ta. Why don't you park outside your house? I'll walk down the hill from here.'

'Right you are.' He pulled into the kerb, still without looking at her. He shouldn't have acted on impulse, he thought. It had tipped him too far off balance and would lead who knew where. He should have taken things more slowly and worked out how Hazel was feeling first. Best to keep it neutral for now. 'Have you enjoyed yourself?'

'Yes, ta.' Hazel had the strange sensation of being an excited child who had opened a birthday present only to find that there was nothing inside. The main thing was to stay polite, not to let her disappointment show.

'I have too.' Ever the gentleman, John opened Hazel's door.

As she stepped out onto the pavement and buttoned her coat, she glanced up towards the corner of the street and was dismayed to see two figures in Pennington's shop doorway. In the yellow glare of the street lamp she recognized them straight away – it was Mabel with her rolled umbrella over her arm, dressed in her unmistakable brown coat and hat, presumably calling on Dorothy before they wended their way to the evening service at St Luke's.

The women must have heard the click of John's car door. They glanced down the street just as Hazel stepped out of the car.

'Uh-oh – looks like we've been caught red-handed.' Wrong-footed by his erstwhile mother-in-law, John's lame attempt at a joke struck the wrong note and he cursed himself the moment

268

the words were out of his mouth.

Hazel wilted under the force of Mabel and Dorothy's glares. 'Ta again,' she told him hurriedly as she walked quickly down the street.

Gladys came to Hazel's house the following evening. She breezed in and demanded tea. 'Hot and strong, please, Aunty Jinny. I've come to ask Uncle Robert to help us move our furniture into the flat in the New Year. Is he in?'

'No, lucky for you. He's playing in a darts match at the Green Cross.' Jinny busied herself with kettle and teapot.

'Why "lucky for me"?'

'Ask Hazel.'

'Because I haven't plucked up the courage to tell him I'm moving out yet,' Hazel admitted.

Gladys tutted and offered advice without waiting to be asked. 'Honesty is the best policy,' she asserted glibly. 'But then you always were a dark horse, Hazel.'

'What? Why are you looking at me like that?' Hazel coloured up under Gladys's scrutiny.

Her cousin sat down by the fire with legs primly crossed, enjoying the air of mystery that she'd brought into the conversation. 'I could mention a certain name beginning with a "J".'

Jinny handed Gladys her cup of tea. 'I take it we're talking about Hazel's car ride with John Moxon?'

Hazel groaned inwardly. She could just imagine the train of events since Mabel and Dorothy had spotted her getting out of John's car – Mabel trotting off to church and recounting what she'd seen to Berta and Doreen, Dorothy stewing over it through the night. No doubt the witches' coven had met up again today and stirred the cauldron, conjuring their wicked spell.

'Spot on as usual, Aunty Jinny. How long were you going to keep it a secret from me, Hazel?' Gladys's arch reproach was meant to lighten the darkening mood but it had the opposite effect. Hazel looked pained, her mother angry. 'Sorry,' Gladys added quickly, 'don't mind me.'

'Would you like a biscuit?' Jinny thrust the open tin under Gladys's nose.

'No ta. Honestly, Hazel, it's just me putting my big foot in it as usual.'

'Exactly what have you heard?' Hazel asked, a helpless moth drawn to the flame of gossip

Gladys hesitated and looked from one to the other. 'I could give you the nice version from Marjorie Sykes or the nasty one–'

'From Dorothy?' Jinny guessed.

The testy interruption made Gladys more apprehensive but she prattled on. 'Marjorie first. Mum was in the bread shop first thing this morning when Marjorie happened to be singing Hazel's praises to Violet Wheeler. You both know Violet – from Jubilee Dress Shop? It was "Hazel this" and "Hazel that", Marjorie saying what a wonder you were at the clinic and how you were putting Mabel in her place and no mistake.'

'Marjorie's right – she is,' Jinny said with a steely edge.

'So she said she wouldn't hear a word against you, Hazel. Dorothy could spread rumours all she liked about you and John – it didn't dent her good opinion.'

Hazel's suppressed groan came out as a sigh. 'What kind of rumours?'

'Are you sure you want me to go on?'

'Yes, I'm sure.' The flame flickered, Hazel couldn't resist.

'That you and John were "carrying on" behind her back. That's how Dorothy put it.'

'What does she mean, "carrying on"?' The silly expression suddenly infuriated Hazel and she rose to her own defence. 'Am I skulking in dark alleyways, making secret assignations? No. I'm going out for a drive in the country with a friend, that's all!'

'I wish I'd never started this,' Gladys complained. 'I only meant it as a joke.'

'It's not funny, Gladys. Dorothy has set out to make it look as if I'm doing something I shouldn't.'

'Egged on by Mabel,' Jinny surmised.

'I see.' Slowly Gladys began to get the point. 'Mabel has a grudge against you because of the work you do – you've set up in competition. And Dorothy – well, she still has it in for you because of what happened to Myra.'

'Which she has no right to do,' Jinny reminded them sharply. She jammed the lid on the biscuit tin and put it back in the cupboard. 'And it's not as if Hazel had anything to do with John before his poor wife died.'

Myra again! Her ghostly presence loomed everywhere – in Hazel and John's minds and now in the hateful rumours flying around the neighbourhood. To Hazel it seemed as if there was no

271

escape. 'Is there anything else I should know?' she asked Gladys with a sinking heart.

'Not really. Mum swears she stuck up for you. She bought her loaf of bread and told the whole shop that you had every right to walk out with whoever you liked. It was none of their business.'

'There *is* more,' Jinny insisted reluctantly as she took the teacups and rinsed them under the tap. 'I was keeping quiet, but now Gladys has had her say, I'd better have mine.'

Hazel braced herself, her knowledge of the kiss and its aftermath weighing heavily. If only life were simple and she could hold her head high and truthfully rebut the charge.

'As luck would have it, I ran into Dorothy myself earlier today,' Jinny explained as she finished at the sink and dried her hands. 'I was serving on the stall so there was no avoiding her. She bought her pound of carrots and as I reached out to take her money, she grabbed my hand and wouldn't let go. "Tell your Hazel she should have more sense," she said, and she gave me one of her looks.'

'I knew she didn't like it,' Hazel admitted. 'I saw that same look yesterday, when I got out of the car.'

'There was more. She said: "And tell her she'll keep her wits about her if she knows what's good for her."'

'Whatever did she mean?' Aghast at what sounded like a threat, still Gladys thrilled to the drama of the occasion. 'Surely Dorothy doesn't intend to do Hazel actual bodily harm?'

Jinny shook her head. 'No, I got the feeling it

was more to do with her not being sucked into something she couldn't easily get out of.'

'Sucked in by John?'

'Yes.'

'Why? What does Dorothy know about him that we don't?' Gladys urged.

'Plenty, I should think.' Jinny's restless activity ceased and she looked thoughtfully at Hazel. 'Whatever daughters tell their mothers about their new husbands – that's what Dorothy is holding in reserve.'

CHAPTER SIXTEEN

How could a single kiss send Hazel reeling?

The question went round and round in her head as she got up next morning and planned the day ahead. She had three post-natal visits on her list, plus a visit to Barlow's to pick up rubber gloves and a carbolic spray.

There I was, going along nicely in my midwifery work, slowly building up numbers. The same in my private life – sailing on without a care.

And now that one kiss has undone all that.

She relived the moment – the sound of the rushing stream at their feet, the barrier of brambles, rooks rising from the bare trees. Most of all, the tingle in her spine as John's lips touched hers, the darkness at the centre of his glistening, light brown eyes.

Had it been a moment of madness with some-

273

one she hardly knew – a moment that she would live to regret?

'Have you told your dad yet?' Jinny's question as she came downstairs and into the kitchen broke Hazel's train of thought. 'Hazel, did you hear what I said?'

'Sorry, I was miles away.'

Her hair still trapped beneath an unflattering hair net, Jinny was yet to put on her public face. She was pale and there were worry lines between her brows. 'Have you told your father that you're moving out?'

'Not yet. He was in a rush this morning. I will, though.'

'When?'

'As soon as I get the chance.' Hazel reached for her coat. 'Don't go on at me, please.'

'Make it sooner rather than later.' Jinny's tone was stern. 'I could break the news to him myself, only you're the one who's moving out so you ought to be the one to tell him.'

'I will!' Hazel insisted as she fled the house and rushed into the back yard for her bike. Barlow's wouldn't be open until nine o'clock so she had half an hour to kill – enough time to cycle up to the Common and try to clear her head. Deliberately avoiding Pennington's at the top of Raglan Road, she cycled up Albion Lane instead, going against a tide of schoolchildren and shop workers who crowded the pavements and spilled over onto the road.

'Watch where you're going!' a young wag in a green school cap cried as he pretended to fall sideways across Hazel's path then leaped out of her way. 'Ouch, that was my foot!'

His pals, filled with pre-Christmas high spirits, copied the pantomime.

It was no good – the street was so crowded that Hazel had to get off her bike and walk. When she reached the junction with Overcliffe Road, the sight of a yellow and brown tram whining to a halt at a nearby stop gave her an idea and she changed her mind about where she would go. Instead of crossing the road onto the Common, she turned right and followed the tram towards its depot on Westgate Road, in the hope that she might run into Dan there.

He's the person to talk to if I'm serious about clearing my head, she decided on a sudden impulse. *I need to know what lies behind Dorothy's warning and I'm sure Dan knows more about John than the rest of us. He won't mince his words, I can bank on that.*

Soon the tram depot hove into sight. It occupied a large, flat area of land at the far end of the Common. There was a smooth, tarmacadam approach to several large, high sheds made out of corrugated iron. The windswept area was criss-crossed by steel tram lines, with electric wires overhead – a busy, humming centre of activity dedicated to maintaining the town's main system of public transport.

Hazel arrived just as the men and women from the early morning shift began their tea break. As they came off duty and sauntered towards the small, brick-built canteen, others took their place on board the trams – one regiment of uniformed drivers and conductors replacing another. This made it difficult for Hazel to pick out her cousin and she was on the point of giving up when Dan himself spotted her and strode across.

'Hello, Hazel. I take it it's me you're looking for,' he began as he rolled himself a cigarette. 'To what do I owe the honour?' Dressed in his brown tram driver's jacket but without his cap and with his tie loosely knotted, he looked considerably less dapper than when Hazel saw him out and about in town on a Friday night. What's more, he was in need of a shave and a short back and sides.

'Have you got time for a chat?' Propping her bike against the side of the nearest shed, Hazel began to wonder if she was making a wise move. What Dan knew about John might turn out to be the very things that she didn't want to hear.

'For you, Hazel, any time.' With a gallant flourish, Dan invited her to step into a stationary tram inside one of the sheds. They sat down in seats close to the rear platform, ignoring used tickets on the floor and the smell of stale tobacco smoke given off by the leather upholstery. 'Don't tell me – this is about the best batsman England never had!'

Hazel stiffened. 'How did you know?'

'Why else would you be here?'

'So what if it is? Have you spoken to John lately?'

'Last night, down at the Green Cross, as it happens.'

'Did he say anything about me?' Hazel knew the question gave too much away but she couldn't help herself.

Dan blew out a plume of cigarette smoke then threw his head back and laughed. 'You girls – you

276

always suppose that blokes spend all their time yakking about you.'

'But did he?'

'Not a dicky bird. There, now I've put you down in the dumps.'

Dan's manner raised the fighting spirit in Hazel, recalling the times when he'd tormented her as a child. In those days there'd been jibes about her neat clothes (little Miss Prim and Proper), her long fair plaits (Rapunzel, Rapunzel, let down your hair) and her bookishness (Miss Clever Clogs) and she had learned not to take them lying down. 'You'll be sorry you didn't knuckle down,' she used to retort, fulfilling her prim and proper tag. 'One day you'll wish you had.'

'I'm not down in the dumps, Dan. You know me better than that, I hope. Yes, I've come to talk to you about John. Why not, since the whole neighbourhood is gossiping about us?'

'Fire away,' he said and grinned.

'I have to keep my wits about me,' she told him. 'That's what Dorothy Pennington recommended as far as John is concerned. So this is me asking you to tell me honestly – why would I need to do that?'

'Keep your wits about you?' Dan threw his cigarette butt to the floor and ground it with his toe. He laughed again. 'I really have no idea.'

'But why would she say it?'

'Again – I haven't a clue. Except that Dorothy never held a high opinion of her son-in-law.'

'Oh!' This was news to Hazel. 'I would've thought the Penningtons would welcome John with open arms.'

277

'John told me they thought Myra was too young...' Dan explained. 'And they didn't know much about his family. You know how Mum and Dad were with poor Norman – it's what people are like around here.'

'Can we please stop calling Norman "poor Norman"? He's a decent young man, if only you take the trouble to get to know him.'

'All right, I take it back. But it doesn't alter the fact that Mum and Dad took a while to come round to the idea of him marrying Sylvia. Things only changed when a shotgun entered the affair, if you get my meaning.'

Hazel frowned. 'But there was nothing forcing John to marry Myra, was there? She didn't fall pregnant until after they got married.'

Dan reply was cagey. 'I don't know. I never asked.'

Hazel sighed. 'Thanks anyway, Dan. I didn't realize Dorothy was against the wedding. It's given me food for thought.' Guessing that his tea break was coming to an end, she got ready to say goodbye. 'I was dreading the worst,' she confessed.

'Why was that? Oh, you're on about us being part of the gambling syndicate ... and the women?' Winking then grabbing the pole to swing from the platform onto the concrete floor of the hangar, Dan turned to help Hazel alight.

She gasped then did a double-take. 'Dan!'

'I'm joking,' he said, deadpan.

Women and gambling. Dan's flippant remark threw Hazel into a fresh turmoil. He'd teased her with unanswerable questions – which women and how much gambling was he talking about? Then he'd acted as if he'd plucked the words out of thin air as a joke. In which case, there were no women in John's life, Hazel decided – except for Mary Fenning from the King Edward's, who, according to Gladys, had left the jazz club with him one Friday night. And did it also mean there were no bets placed and lost on horses, except for the time Dan and John had run up debts to Reggie Bates the day of the trip to Blackpool?

Cycling from the tram depot down to Canal Road, Hazel couldn't disentangle truth from lies or concentrate on the task in hand. She stopped at Barlow's to buy two dozen pairs of surgical gloves but forgot the carbolic spray and had to backtrack, which made her ten minutes late for her first post-natal visit to Cynthia Houghton on Chapel Street.

Luckily, Cynthia proved to be as easy going about the business of caring for her infant son as she had been about her pregnancy – Bertie was the perfect baby, she insisted, as Hazel apologized and proceeded to weigh him. A touch of wind after feeding, maybe, but that was to be expected. And good as gold during the night – only waking twice at the most. 'Tilly is green with envy,' Cynthia announced. 'She's two years older than me, but still no chap in sight, and I'm not surprised, with her stuck behind the counter in that dusty library. I don't suppose you've got a spare one tucked away somewhere?'

'A spare chap?' Hazel laughed and self-consciously told her no.

'Pity. Tilly's grown broody ever since she clapped

eyes on Bertie.' Cynthia pinned the baby's nappy back in place then hoisted him over her shoulder to show Hazel to the door. 'What's holding you back anyway?' she chipped in cheekily as they said goodbye. 'A good-looking girl like you – surely they're queuing up at the door?'

'If only!'

'Don't tell me – you're wedded to your work.' Cynthia's parting shot was accompanied by a sly wink. 'So if you do happen to come across a chap going spare, be sure to let Tilly know.'

Laughing to herself, Hazel promised she would then made her next two visits and was finished in good time to call in at home before she set off again for clinic. She found the house empty and a small white envelope on the door mat. There was no stamp or address – simply her first name in a cramped, forward-sloping handwriting she didn't recognize – and when she opened it her eyes went straight to the signature: *John.*

The sight of it made her hand tremble so much that she had to sit at the table and flatten the letter onto it. 'Dear Hazel,' she read, 'I hope you don't think I'm being too pushy in writing to you. I've had a lot on my mind since we drove out to Shawcross at the weekend. On top of which I've had Dorothy coming down on me like a ton of bricks. To cut a long story short, she's against us having any more to do with one another.'

Lacking the courage to read on, Hazel laid her hand over the rest of the letter. In that moment she was sure that the next paragraph would put an end to her own dilemma by telling her that it was best for them not to see each other again.

The flame that had been lit by the kiss on the riverbank would flicker and die.

Better get it over with, she thought with dread, lifting her hand and reading on.

'I put her right on that score, don't you worry. I told Myra's mother a few home truths and sent her away with her tail between her legs.'

'Oh!' Hazel gasped. Now her whole body was shaking as she imagined John's deep, sincere voice speaking the words that he'd written.

'The point is, Hazel, no matter what Dorothy and everyone else thinks, do you [this word was underlined three times] want to have any more to do with me [more underlining]?'

She paused again to let the question sink in.

'If the answer is yes, would you like to come to the pictures with me this Friday? If not, just drop me a note anyway to let me know.'

The letter was signed 'John' – no 'Love from', no kisses after the name.

'Yes!' she said out loud, instantly casting aside her worries. Her heart soared. She scribbled her reply and posted it through John's letter box on her way to clinic. She would knock on his door at six o'clock on Friday night and she didn't care who was looking or what they said.

If Hazel imagined that John's invitation was the only surprise of the day, her arrival at Westgate Road proved her wrong.

'Betty, what are you doing here?' she asked when she spotted her neighbour from Nelson Yard at the head of the queue. As usual, Eleanor had directed Hazel's ladies upstairs and they'd settled into the row of chairs to await her arrival.

With a wry smile and a wink, Betty patted her stomach. 'What do you think?'

'Come in.' Inviting her behind the screen, Hazel got to work. 'I take it breastfeeding Daisy proved too much for you?'

'My milk dried up, that was the truth of it. So I had to turn to the bottle. And now – hey presto – here I am again!'

'Who's looking after the little ones?' Hazel asked. Examining Betty, she found there was no doubt about it – all the signs of early pregnancy were there.

'Doreen. Say what you like about her, she'll always step in and lend a hand.'

'I'm sure she's good to you,' Hazel agreed. 'Now this time, Betty, I want you to start the pregnancy as you mean to go on. You know what I'm going to say – that includes regular meals and plenty of rest.'

'By what miracle is that going to happen, pray?' Behind Betty's usual chirpy words, Hazel detected a weariness. In fact, she looked more worn down than ever – her hands were rough and red, her thin features pale and peaky. 'You know how it is. Keith's five now and not much trouble, touch wood. But Polly is still under my feet and Daisy – well, what can you expect with a baby that age?'

Hazel thought hard about how Betty could improve her lot. 'Is Leonard there to lend a hand some of the time?'

Betty's eyebrows shot up. 'We're between the devil and the deep blue sea in that regard. If he's at home to help me, there's no money coming in. So he joins the queue outside Kingsley's for every extra shift he can get.'

'I see.' Hazel's smile was sympathetic.

Betty swung her legs over the side of the examination table and put on a pair of thick stockings, hitching them onto elastic suspenders that had seen better days. 'Leonard has his faults,' she confided, 'but he works hard for his family and you can't say that about every man on the Yard.'

'No, you can't. What about your mother over in Welby? Can't you patch things up with her?'

'Hah!' Betty's reply conveyed deep scorn. 'She hasn't even bothered to come and see Daisy yet, has she? Not once.'

'Then you'll have to rely on Doreen all you can,' Hazel concluded. 'And take one of these leaflets. It shows you which foods are best for you while you're pregnant, and all the other dos and don'ts.'

'Starting with a cup of tea and biscuits, I hope!'

Hazel thought that Betty's bounce back from the edge of despair was remarkable under the circumstances. 'Two cups for Betty, please, Irene,' she insisted, escorting her from behind the screen. 'And while you're at it, why not pop some custard creams in a bag for Keith and Polly? No one heard me say that, did they?'

'No-o-o!' came the high, lilting chorus from the women in the room.

'You'll have them all at it,' Irene grumbled. 'At this rate we'll run out of everything before the end of clinic.' But she put six custard creams in the bag and added two rich teas for luck, making

283

Betty a happy woman and, by rights, Dr Bell eight biscuits short. Not that her kindly employer would mind about that, Irene was sure.

In any case, Hazel tackled the subject of refreshments when she went to David's room at the end of clinic. 'I've been thinking,' she began.

'Oh dear – never a good sign.' He welcomed her in with a gesture for her to sit down, which she ignored.

'Seriously – now that we've settled on two clinics a week and my earnings are due to rise, why not let me buy the tea and biscuits instead of you?'

Shaking his head and arranging papers on his desk, David was prepared to argue the case. 'I assure you, there's no need.'

'But I'd like to. That way, I can be as generous or stingy as I like with what I offer.'

Her earnestness amused him, making the corners of his mouth twitch. 'I've no doubt it'll be the former. And that would be fine with me. But yes – yes, by all means, if it's what you want.'

'Consider it done.' A bright, dimpled smile concluded the business and she turned to go.

'Hazel – before you go – the surgery is closed next week for Christmas. I take it you've cancelled your clinic?'

'Yes, but everyone knows where I live in an emergency – if they can't get hold of you, that is.'

'I'm not going far over the festive season,' he assured her, taking a small, brightly wrapped parcel from the top drawer of his desk. 'Oh, and in case I don't see you beforehand, let me give you this and wish you a Happy Christmas.'

The gift flustered her. 'You shouldn't have...' was all she managed as she backed towards the door.

'It's not much,' he said at the same time.

They both smiled. She looked awkwardly at the floor while he cleared his throat and shuffled more papers.

He was the first to speak again. 'They say you shouldn't mix business with pleasure and as a rule I'd be the first to agree.'

'No, honestly, ta very much.'

'But I believe on this occasion a little something won't go amiss.' Underneath his mild words there was an ever increasing pressure of stronger feelings struggling to rise to the surface. *Business and pleasure do not mix,* he repeated firmly to himself as Hazel hovered by the door, a picture of loveliness. 'It's my way of saying thank-you,' he continued. 'You've made a big difference here, Hazel, in many ways.'

She balanced the parcel in the palm of her hand. The paper was covered in festive sprigs of holly and the object inside was heavy. 'Happy Christmas, then.' She murmured the inadequate words as she looked up and registered the seriousness of his gaze.

There he sat in shirtsleeves, waistcoat unbuttoned and stethoscope still hanging from his neck. Racing pell-mell towards Christmas, mopping up ailments and hospital appointments before the holiday, David looked tired. And yet he'd found the time to buy her a present and say a genuine thank-you. She felt a mixture of fondness and embarrassment as she made her exit.

'Happy Christmas,' he replied with a nod and a smile.

'Hold onto this end while I fetch a drawing pin,' Robert instructed Hazel.

It was Thursday evening and time to put up decorations. There were paper chains to be hung from one corner of the ceiling to the other, holly for the mantelpiece and a tree awaiting baubles in its tub by the window.

Holding the end of the fragile chain, Hazel watched her mother bring down the box of glass balls from the wardrobe shelf and set it on the table. Each was wrapped in tissue paper and was taken carefully from the box then rethreaded with black cotton ready for hanging.

For as long as Hazel could remember this family ritual had marked the start of the festive season. Jinny would choose a tree from her market stall – exactly the right size and shape – and Robert would stop off on his way from work to collect it. He would ride home on his bike with the tree slung over his shoulder.

'Turn it this way,' Jinny would suggest after he'd anchored it in the tub with sand kept in a sack in the cellar and set it down in position. 'A bit more – no, back again. Further – yes, that's good.'

Inside the box there were glass decorations in the shape of icicles as well as the brightly coloured balls. And this year they were joined by an innovation seized upon by Jinny when she saw it on a neighbouring stall: a perfect miniature replica of a flying swan with Father Christmas perched astride, which she put in pride of place at the front of the tree.

'All right, Hazel, now give me that other end,' Robert told her. With the stepladder in place, he finished pinning the paper chain to the ceiling.

'How does it look so far?' Midway through the hanging process and enjoying every minute, Jinny stood back from the tree.

'Lovely,' Hazel said with a sad sigh.

'Try to sound a bit more enthusiastic.' Her mother laughed then thought better of it. 'What's wrong? Are you worried about something?'

'No. Well, yes. David gave me a present, that's all.' She pointed to the small parcel on the window sill. 'I didn't buy one for him.'

'I'm sure he didn't expect one,' Jinny said, hesitating slightly.

Robert clattered the two sides of the stepladder together then rested it against the cellar door. Then he stood back to admire the festoons strung across the ceiling. 'This looks more like it,' he murmured.

'Dad,' Hazel began in a serious tone that alerted her mother, 'there's something else I've been meaning to tell you.'

'Fire away.'

'Gladys and I – well, we – we're both twenty-two now...' She ground to a halt and looked to Jinny for help.

'Don't tell me – you want to move out into a place of your own,' Robert said, quick as a flash. He stood with his arms folded, looking steadily at her. Whatever he was feeling beneath the surface, he was determined not to let it show.

287

Hazel stared at him wide-eyed. 'How did...? Yes, that's it.'

'Where to?'

'To a flat on Canal Road. It's at the nice end near the town centre. Miss Bennett is the name of the landlady. She seems very respectable.'

'You've made up your mind, then?' He glanced at Jinny to see how she was reacting. 'I gather you know all about it?'

'Don't blame Mum, blame me,' Hazel begged. 'I've been dreading telling you and we've all been so busy. Besides, it's not the end of the world, me moving out. I'll still be visiting and getting under your feet as usual, don't you worry.'

'Well?' Jinny prompted, accidentally knocking the tree and making the glass baubles quiver.

Robert took a deep breath. 'It's the end of an era,' he murmured. There was no need to remind them how he'd poured his hopes and dreams into Hazel. He called to mind the musty smell of the library books that they brought home each Saturday and the diminutive size of the shoes that he'd polished to get her ready for primary school. 'Come here, love.' He opened his arms to her and she rushed into his embrace. 'Promise me one thing.'

'Anything,' Hazel murmured, feeling a flood of relief.

He tipped her chin up and waited for her slow smile. 'You'll let this old-timer help to move you into your new flat when the time comes.'

CHAPTER SEVENTEEN

If anyone had asked Hazel the name of the film John took her to see that Friday before Christmas, she could scarcely have told them.

The evening was a blur from the moment she'd knocked on his door, through the smooth car journey into town and all the time they'd spent holding hands in the plush red seats of the new Odeon cinema. She only knew for certain that they sat in aisle seats to watch a musical extravaganza starring two Hollywood actresses at their glamorous best. It also had the charming William Powell as a theatre impresario. None of the razzmatazz – not the dancing beauties in their sequined costumes nor the trained lions and prancing ponies – mattered to Hazel; she only had eyes and ears for John.

'Would you like an ice cream?' he asked her during the interval, when the lights went on and usherettes carried their illuminated trays down the aisles.

She shook her head. 'No, ta.'

'Are you sure?'

'Quite sure, thanks.'

He smiled and rested his arm along the back of her seat, listening to Hazel's chatter about the build-up to Christmas. 'I won't be ordering a turkey this year,' he commented.

'No, I suppose not.' She could have kicked

herself for forgetting that John would be spending this Christmas alone.

The lights dimmed and the film started again. The words of the song 'A Pretty Girl Is Like a Melody' made them look at each other and smile, then Hazel felt John's arm shift from the back of her seat to her shoulder. But soon the overblown, on-screen spectacle palled and he grew fidgety. He leaned across to whisper in her ear, 'Shall we get out of here while the going's good?'

She nodded. 'That's fine by me.'

They stood up and heard their seats snap upright with a loud clunk.

'Ssshh!' voices tutted at the disturbance.

Bowing their heads, they crept up the dark aisle and through the swing doors, across the foyer and out into the street.

'I'm sorry – there're only so many ostrich feathers a chap like me can take.' John's apology came with a wink.

'Even when pretty girls are wearing them?' Hazel hummed a few bars of the famous Irving Berlin tune. 'Perhaps you'd have been happier with cowboys and Indians?'

'Yes – six-shooters are more my style.' John laughed with a distracted air. 'Never mind, the night is still young.' Steering her down the hill past the gleaming windows of Merton and Groves, then glancing quickly up and down the broad street, he stopped outside the jazz club and jerked his thumb towards the entrance. 'What do you say we pop in here?'

Hazel's smile of agreement was the signal for him to lead her down the steps into the low-lit room where they went straight to the bar.

'Cinzano, if I remember rightly?' he said before ordering and paying.

Hazel nodded. 'I've spotted two empty seats at the back,' she said, pointing them out.

'Lead on,' he told her, a glass in either hand. However, as soon as they reached the seats and he'd put down the drinks on the nearest table, he was off again – to see a man about a dog, as he put it. 'If you don't mind,' he added. 'I'll be back in a tick.'

'I'm fine here, thanks.' Assuming John had caught sight of someone he knew, Hazel tried to get herself in the mood by watching the couples on the dance floor and listening to the music. She started to tap her foot to Earl Ray's version of Duke Ellington's 'It Don't Mean a Thing' and sipped her drink until Gladys suddenly emerged from the crush with Bernard in tow.

'Save me!' Gladys muttered under her breath, the corners of her mouth turned down in a comical grimace.

Cottoning on, Hazel sprang up from her seat. 'I need to go to the little girls' room!' she declared. 'Come along, Gladys, time to powder our noses.'

'Excuse us,' Gladys told her unwelcome suitor, following close on Hazel's heels.

They left Bernard high and dry and made their way out into the foyer.

'That man is a limpet,' Gladys complained. 'He had his paws all over me during that last dance.'

'Limpets don't have paws,' Hazel observed. She was keeping an eye out for John and was taken aback to see him standing on the stairs having a

291

heated conversation with Reggie Bates and her cousin Dan. Backed against the wall, Dan seemed the most animated, while Reggie listened with a dour, unreadable expression until John chipped in with a comment that seemed to enrage Dan. With two hands he took hold of John's lapels and shoved him roughly down the stairs. John lost his balance then regained it and sprang back at Dan but Reggie intervened, stepping forward and easily pulling the much slighter Dan away from John.

Unaware of the altercation, Gladys sailed on into the ladies' cloakroom, still giving Hazel the low down on the wretched Bernard. 'If there's one thing I can't stand, it's being mauled by a man on the dance floor,' she complained as she stood in front of the mirror and patted her hair. 'I made it clear to Bernard that it wasn't on. I even dropped the name Vera into his shell-like ear to put him off his stride but it made no difference.'

Hazel laughed uneasily, unable to rid herself of the image of Dan squaring up to John. 'What's Dan been up to lately?' she asked Gladys, hoping for enlightenment.

'In hot water as usual.' Gladys took a lipstick from her handbag. 'Why?'

'I just saw him out there. He was in an argument with John and I wondered why.'

'Don't ask me.' Gladys ran the red lipstick over her mouth. 'Right now Dan would argue with his own shadow.'

'Could it be about money? Are they still in that betting syndicate with Reggie?'

Into the handbag went the lipstick, out came

292

the powder compact. 'Not any more. As far as I know that all fell through a while back.'

Hazel was thoughtful. Despite Gladys's answer, it seemed to her that money was probably the reason behind the fracas on the stairs.

'Ready?' Finishing at the mirror and pleased with the result, Gladys held the door open for Hazel. 'Hopefully Bernard will have given up by now. Come along, Miss Head-in-the-clouds – back into the fray.'

There was no sign of Reggie, Dan or John out in the foyer, so Hazel and Gladys made their way back into the club to reclaim the two empty seats and listen to the band, now swinging along, Louis Armstrong style, with 'On the Sunny Side of the Street'.

'Don't you love this tune?' Gladys sighed as she took a sip from Hazel's glass. 'However down in the dumps you are, it takes you out of yourself. Uh-oh, here comes trouble!' Intent on giving the persistent Bernard the cold shoulder, she jumped up and made a beeline for the stage, adopting Sylvia's trick of standing in the band leader's eye-line until the number came to an end.

Hazel had to admire Gladys's front – the way she smiled up at Earl Ray through a haze of cigarette smoke, no doubt re-introducing herself as his soon-to-be neighbour on Canal Road, then putting in a request for a favourite song.

Earl stooped towards her, said a few words, smiled then nodded and backed away from the edge of the stage.

He led the band in two more numbers and still there was no sign of John. Sitting alone at the table, Hazel felt her mood plummet. Gone was the feeling of floating on air when she and John had entered the Odeon; now she felt only jittery uncertainty about why she was here at all. The longer she sat wondering what had been going on between John, Dan and Reggie, the larger her doubts loomed.

She stared morosely at the crowd of dancers, waving briefly at Gladys who was by now dancing with a stranger whose hands didn't roam and then at David Bell, on his way to the bar.

Seeing her sitting by herself, he made a deliberate detour.

'All on your ownio?' he enquired with his usual warm smile, raising his voice to be heard over the saxophone and drums.

'No, I'm with ... someone.' She pulled back from naming John then grew embarrassed and quickly set the record straight. 'With John Moxon, as a matter of fact. We went to the pictures then came here.'

'Oh.' David's smile faltered and he glanced around the room. 'What's happened to our famous cricketer? Has he got lost?'

'No. He's here somewhere.' *But where?* she wondered. John seeing a man about a dog was one thing, but having an argument with Dan and then clean vanishing was quite another.

'So now's my chance.' On an impulse David offered Hazel his hand. 'Would you like this dance?'

'Why not?' Equally impulsively she took it and followed him onto the floor. Before she knew it, he was holding her tight and leading her in one

294

of the band's slower, earthier numbers – a song by Cole Porter called 'Love for Sale'.

'Old love, new love, every love but true love' – the words of the street girl's lament insinuated themselves into Hazel's mind and raised the questions she would rather not face about the feelings she'd had for John ever since they'd kissed on the riverbank.

Where did she really stand with him? True he'd written her the note and asked her out, but things were not straightforward – not with Dorothy leading the gossipmongers and Myra's name still writ large in all their minds.

Was it rash to have said yes to him – for her heart to have lifted and soared the way it did? And what did John have in mind for the future? Where, if anywhere, was all this leading?

'A penny for them?' David said with a sympathetic smile as the music ended and the band put down their instruments.

She made the effort to smile back. 'They're not worth it.'

He noticed John in the doorway, taller than most, surveying the room. 'The wanderer returns,' David said with a nod in the other man's direction.

Hazel smiled again, wishing David a happy Christmas as she slipped away.

Ridiculous! Swallowing a dose of stone-cold reality, David was left to measure himself up against the darkly handsome John Moxon. *Face it – you're an average-looking, over-the-hill GP up to your ears in diphtheria, measles and chicken pox. And widowed to boot.* 'Hmm,' he grunted as he

295

straightened his tie and made his way to the bar. The race was over before it had even begun – a foregone conclusion. Better let it go.

'Sorry about that.' John's apology to Hazel was brief and without explanation. Retrieving his drink and resuming their seats during the musicians' break, he didn't mention his recent spat with her cousin.

His abrupt manner unsettled her further. She fidgeted with her almost empty glass, crossed and uncrossed her legs and, spotting Gladys talking with Earl Ray and Sonny Dubec at the bar, attempted some small talk. 'Did I tell you that I'm moving into a flat with Gladys in the New Year? It's on Canal Road. I was dreading breaking the news to Dad, but it turns out that he didn't mind, thank goodness.'

John listened with a distracted air then, as the band took the stage again, he suggested that it was time to go. 'If you don't mind,' he added.

Hazel's heart sank. Whatever had happened between him, Reggie and Dan had altered the mood of the evening for the worse and she saw there was no hope of rescuing it. 'Of course not,' she replied primly.

They left in a hurry and returned to the car but when John pulled out the choke and turned the ignition key, the engine coughed and refused to start. He tried again, stamping his foot hard on the accelerator without success. 'I warned Dan not to flatten the battery, the silly sod.'

'Dan borrowed your car?'

'Yes, earlier this week.' John tried a third time.

'Hang on a sec. Let me get this engine started.'

With nothing to lose, Hazel seized her chance. 'Ah, so that's what you two were arguing about.'

'When?' The engine coughed again and this time spluttered into life.

'In the club. I saw you. Reggie was there too.'

John revved the engine then sat a while, allowing it to tick over. 'Yes, sorry about that,' he muttered. 'Dan doesn't listen – that's his problem. But never mind – it's time I got you home.'

So they set off out of town and along Canal Road, with Hazel pointing out number 102 as they passed it. John said very little until he turned onto Ghyll Road and unexpectedly stopped the car beside a lamp-post outside Thornley's Brewery.

He killed the engine and turned to Hazel with a troubled look. 'This isn't like me, you know.'

Her heart missed a beat. 'What isn't?'

'Going off and leaving you on your own like that. You must think I'm a blithering idiot.'

'No, I don't. And there's no need to explain if you'd rather not.' She took a deep breath and tried to adjust to yet another sudden turn of events.

'Sorry – I can't go into details.'

Hearing the sincerity in his low, hesitant voice, Hazel felt the ice between them melt. 'Honestly, there's no need.'

'There is. It spoiled our night.'

'The evening hasn't been a roaring success,' she admitted with a sigh.

Her comment drew a faint smile from him then he turned further in his seat towards her with an earnest air. 'Listen, Hazel, I hope this won't put

297

you off coming out with me again. I wouldn't blame you if it did. But if we do carry on, I promise not to abandon you next time.'

She nodded slowly, drawn in by the graceful twist of his body, the symmetry of his strong features illuminated by gaslight and the touch of his hand as he placed it on her arm.

'And I won't be allowing Dr Bell any more chances to step into my shoes either,' he added, giving that upwards twitch at the corner of his mouth that suggested a joke, this time at his own expense.

'David's a good dancer,' she protested archly.

'A right little Nijinsky, eh? Not like me. I can hardly put one foot in front of the other.'

'I never said that.' The night had certainly had its twists and turns and they weren't over yet, Hazel realized. Inside the car, with its gleaming dashboard, she waited with bated breath.

'So will there be a next time?'

And here it was again – the sudden rush of feelings that quickened her heartbeat and twisted her stomach into knots. 'That depends.' By stalling she hoped to steady herself and keep control.

'On what?'

'On whereabouts you want to take me.'

'Where would you like to go? Out to Shawcross again – once your family Christmas is over and done with?'

Heart racing, eyes widening, she yielded. 'That would be nice.'

'Honestly? We'll fix a date in the New Year.' He slid his hand down her arm onto her knee. 'I don't deserve any more chances after the way

I've behaved. But I'll keep my promise – it won't happen again.' Leaning forward, he brushed his lips against hers.

His features fell out of focus as he came close, his lips were soft. Hazel closed her eyes and gave way to sensation. Inside the warm car, under the gas lamp, she thrilled to John's kisses and sank into his embrace.

'It's a lot of palaver over nothing.' Ada's customary, bah-humbug grumble as the family gathered on Raglan Road on Christmas Day didn't fool anyone.

'You like it really, Mum,' Rose chided, taking her coat and hanging it on a hook at the cellar head. 'Sit down by the fire. I'll help Hazel to set the table.'

'Have we got enough chairs?' Jinny counted five, including two brought down from the bedrooms. 'Are Dan and Gladys coming?' she asked Rose.

'Yes, they'll be here any time. But not Eddie and Joan – they've gone to her mother's.' Fussing with knives, forks and place mats, Rose calculated that they were one chair short.

'How about Sylvia and Norman?' Jinny asked. The turkey in the oven would just about stretch to nine people if necessary and there were enough roast spuds to feed a small army.

'Sylvia has decided to stay at home and have a quiet Christmas.' Peacemaker Rose hoped that the bland explanation would pour oil on troubled waters. She didn't tell the others about the blazing row Ada and Sylvia had had two days earlier,

299

where Sylvia had declared that wild horses wouldn't drag her and Norman round to the Prices' for Christmas dinner, not after the way people had gossiped behind her back. And she wouldn't go to her mother and father's house either. She said she washed her hands of everyone.

'Can't Ethel and Cyril persuade her to come round with them later on?' Jinny didn't like the idea of Sylvia and Norman being left out completely.

Taking up position in the fireside chair, Ada cut the conversation short with a chilly, 'That's up to Sylvia.'

'Back to the question of chairs – I can nip round to Nelson Yard and fetch one,' Robert offered as he reached for his jacket and cap. 'It's no trouble.'

'Yes, do that. You won't need a key – the door's open,' Rose informed him.

Making a quick exit, he bumped into Gladys and Dan on the doorstep. 'Go on in,' he invited before explaining his errand and hurrying off.

'Something smells good,' Gladys exclaimed. She was warmly dressed in a pale blue sweater and dark slacks, handing over brightly wrapped presents for Hazel, Robert and Jinny while Dan, unshaven and already a little drunk, sat down at the half-laid table. 'Happy Christmas, everyone!'

Taking her present, Hazel gave Gladys a peck on the cheek. 'Happy Christmas to you too.'

'This is a milestone – the last time everyone will be living cheek by jowl,' Gladys reminded her. 'Come January, you and I will be all set up on Canal Road in our own little flat.'

'Bully for you,' Dan remarked bitterly. 'Some of us can't afford the luxury.'

Gladys took up the cudgels. 'You could if you didn't throw all your money down the drain.'

'Now, now,' Rose warned. 'No bickering, please.'

Hazel worried that the festive gathering was getting off to a lukewarm start despite the paper streamers and the daintily decorated tree. But when Robert came back with the extra chair and once they were all seated around the table, differences were laid to one side. Jinny produced a plump turkey that was done to a turn, together with all the trimmings. These included the savoury pudding brought along by Ada that followed a traditional recipe containing sage and dripping. Robert picked it out for special praise, which mollified Ada and brought a relieved smile to Rose's anxious face.

'And God bless the cook,' Robert added, looking down the length of the table at a red-cheeked, flustered Jinny.

'What does God have to do with it?' bleary-eyed Dan objected.

'Everything!' Gladys's trilling laughter helped them skim over another sticky moment. 'After all, where would Christmas be without Him?'

Hazel agreed. 'No Baby Jesus, no Wise Men, no presents.'

Gladys didn't pursue the argument. 'And thank you anyway, Aunty Jinny.'

'Now can we please tuck in?' Ada's knife sliced through a piece of tender breast meat.

Food was eaten, verdicts given on the turkey –

301

lovely and moist; very tasty; better than last year –
Christmas pudding was produced. *No, I couldn't.
Go on then – just a spoonful. Who's got the sixpence?*

'Me,' Dan said, pulling it from his mouth
between thumb and forefinger.

'Good – that'll help you out of your next tight
spot,' Gladys quipped.

Even Dan joined in the laughter at this one and
by the time the dishes were cleared away, they
were all ready to get out the games and settle into
a late-afternoon session of dominoes, whist and
tiddlywinks.

'You're never too old...' Robert avowed, chal-
lenging Hazel to 'tiddle the winks'. He cleared a
space at the end of the table and they began.

As she threw herself into the Christmas spirit,
Hazel couldn't help but give a thought to the
people unable to indulge in a spot of family
bickering, as Rose had called it.

There was David for a start, whose present had
been a small volume of poetry by Robert Burns.
He would be at home above the surgery with
only Irene and baby Grace for company. No
doubt he would enter into the spirit for their
sakes. Still, she felt a twinge of sadness for the
man whose dead wife's framed picture graced his
bureau. He'd been willing to take a risk on a
newly qualified midwife and give Hazel the
chance she needed and because of this she admired him more than she could say.

Then, of course, there was John. She thought of
him again – alone in his silent house – and her
heart ached. She longed to run up the street, to
knock on his door and invite him to join them.

302

Who cared if Dorothy got to hear of it and cast sour aspersions? What did it matter if Nana and Aunty Rose were taken aback?

'Your turn, Hazel.' Her dad's reminder drew her back into the cosy present. She took aim, fired her tiddlywink towards the small Bakelite cup and saw it land with a triumphant chink. The moment had passed.

At four in the afternoon, as darkness fell, there was a knock at the door announcing the customary arrival for Christmas tea of Ethel and Cyril.

'Guess who we've dragged out of their love nest,' Ethel announced as they all made space for extra visitors.

'Come in, come in and shut that door behind you,' Jinny told Sylvia and Norman, who lagged behind.

They shuffled into the kitchen, Norman in shirt-sleeves and a fawn pullover, Sylvia without a coat and done up in the one dress that still fitted her towards the end of her fifth month – a crêpe de Chine wrap-over in deep red with navy piping around the neckline. Her dark hair was neatly crimped and she'd dabbed on rouge to disguise her pale cheeks.

'You two will catch your deaths if you're not careful,' Ada warned from her privileged fireside chair.

Rose drew the new arrivals to the fire then fussed over an irritable Sylvia. 'Fetch the girl a chair,' she told Dan, who was deep into his fourth bottle of pale ale.

Clumsily he pulled a stool from under the sink

and scraped it across the lino.

Ada tutted. 'Not a stool, Dan – fetch Sylvia a proper chair.'

There was much shifting and shuffling in the confined space as one was produced.

'A stool would have done.' Sylvia sat down with a frown. 'We haven't come for long, Aunty Jinny. And we haven't bothered with cards and presents this year – I hope no one minds.'

Watching from her side of the room, Hazel tried to work out how Sylvia was coping. She'd made an effort to dress up nicely and this was a reassuring reminder of the old, carefree times. But her face was pinched and peaky and she seemed to ignore Norman, who was boxed into a corner, forced into exchanging pleasantries with Rose. She also seemed determined to ignore her condition, talking instead about a second-hand gramophone that she'd picked up for a song on a stall at Clifton Market.

'I couldn't believe my luck. It came complete with a box of needles and three Count Basie records,' she boasted across the room to Gladys and Hazel, who decided to join her.

'Count Basie comes before baby clothes, eh?' Gladys said with deliberate lack of tact and openly critical of the way Sylvia was carrying on. 'What are you going to dress this poor child in, come April? Has it even got a nightie?'

There was an uncomfortable silence, covered up by Jinny's offer to make tea and sandwiches.

'No, ta!' Dan slurred his words. 'We're still full to bursting from turkey and savoury pud.'

'But a cup of tea would be nice,' Ada said with

a pointed look at Dan.

Ignoring Gladys's disapproval, Sylvia turned to Hazel. 'Never mind about baby clothes – no one's interested in that. Tell me – when's the big move to Canal Road?'

'In a week's time,' Hazel replied. Now that she had the opportunity, she made a close-up, professional assessment of Sylvia, noting the thickening waist and reassured that there was no sign of oedema or excessive fatigue. Nevertheless, she had to resist the urge to ask Sylvia to attend clinic. *Now's not the time or the place*, she reminded herself.

'She turned green with envy when I broke the news,' Gladys remarked.

Sylvia's face reddened. 'No, I didn't.'

'Yes, you did. Especially when I dropped a certain Mr Earl Ray's name into the conversation.'

'I hear he gave you some free tickets to a concert.' Sylvia's voice was quiet and her expression rueful rather than angry, like a child hovering on the edge of a playground game.

'He did. But you can have mine,' Hazel offered without hesitating. 'I know how much you like his music.'

Sylvia shook her head. She glanced at Norman, who had broken away from Rose and was now chatting to his father-in-law. 'Gladys has got it all wrong,' she insisted. 'I'm not jealous.'

'Quite right. You and Norman have other things to look forward to.' It was as close as Hazel dared come to the topic that Sylvia seemed so anxious to avoid and it was a mistake.

'Oh, why must everyone go on about it?' She stood up jerkily, tipping Hazel sideways off the arm of the chair. 'If it's not nighties, it's matinée jackets, and if it's not matinée jacket, it's bootees.'

'Calm down, Sylvia. Hazel didn't mean any harm,' Gladys objected.

'Stop bossing me around. Leave me alone,' Sylvia snapped back.

'I'm not bossing you around. Nana, did you hear me say anything nasty to Sylvia?'

'Pipe down, both of you. A fine Christmas this is turning out to be,' Ada said with a dismissive wave of her hand.

'Your nana's right.' Cyril stepped forward with a warning look.

Sylvia pushed past him and headed for the door. 'That's right, Dad, gang up on me with the rest of them, why don't you? I knew this would happen; I don't know why I even bothered coming.'

The crowded room was already in disarray when Dan stood up and knocked over his bottle of beer. He ignored it and clapped loudly. 'Bravo, Sylvia, another fine performance.'

The beer spilled and soaked into the white tablecloth. Dan swayed then sat down heavily.

By this time Sylvia was beside herself. She clutched at Norman's sleeve. 'We're off,' she told him.

But now Ethel blocked her way. 'Not without saying sorry, you're not.'

'Sorry for what? For not knitting bootees?' Sylvia screeched then tried to push past her mother. Her face changed colour quickly from flushed to pale and she needed Norman to steady her. 'I'm sick

306

and tired of this, you hear? From now on you're all to leave me alone.'

Her mother winced then stepped aside. 'Right you are,' she muttered. 'If that's the way you want it.'

'Oh, Sylvia,' Rose murmured sorrowfully in the shocked silence that accompanied her departure with a nonplussed Norman.

Jinny stood Dan's bottle upright then mopped up the beer with a teacloth.

'I'll do that.' Hazel took over, carefully picking up the bright yellow and red tiddlywinks and dabbing them dry.

'Happy Christmas, everyone,' Dan muttered sardonically.

Hazel didn't react. She'd pushed Sylvia over the edge without meaning to and she regretted it. She was also deeply worried about her cousin's rapidly changing moods. *Please come to the clinic,* she thought as she lifted the stained cloth from the table. *Whatever you're going through, you need to talk to someone. I'm here – it's my job. You must come clean about everything and let me help.*

CHAPTER EIGHTEEN

In the dog days between Christmas and New Year, Hazel heard no word from John. She tried to distract herself by keeping busy – firstly by packing a tea chest with all the things she would need to take with her to Canal Road and then by running her clinic.

'Did you have a nice Christmas?' Eleanor asked when she arrived.

'Yes, ta. Did you?'

'Yes. I had a lovely, last-minute surprise – an invite from David to come here for tea on Christmas Day.'

As he came down the stairs, David overheard Eleanor sharing her snippet of information and readily joined in. 'Irene put on a good spread for us, didn't she?'

'Very good.' Eleanor blushed then pretended to be busy with some papers on her desk.

Oh! Caught off balance, Hazel looked from one to the other with sudden curiosity. Eleanor and David. She pictured the pair of them having a cosy festive tea, with Irene carrying trays to and fro and baby Grace fast asleep in her cot.

'No peace for the wicked, eh?' David joked as they crossed on the stairs. He'd been working as usual since Boxing Day, dealing with cases of acute angina, lumbago and bronchitis on top of run-of-the-mill childhood illnesses such as measles and chicken pox.

'You can say that again. And ta, by the way, for the book of poems.'

'You're very welcome. I hope you enjoy reading them.'

'I'm sure I will.' Clutching her list of patients, Hazel hurried on up the stairs into the lively, crowded room.

Greeted with cheery hellos from mothers-to-be and the raucous cries of toddlers at play, she spent the next three hours carrying out examinations and giving routine advice. She had a long chat with Betty Hollings, who swore she was doing her best to take things easy, but the most interesting case of the day came at the end of the afternoon when Hazel was already tidying away the toys in the playpen and was about to pack her bag. It came in the fashionable shape of Philip Baxter's wife Barbara.

'Am I too late?' Barbara looked apprehensively around the empty room.

'Hello again,' Hazel greeted her with a warm smile. 'Not at all. Come straight through and I'll take a look at you.'

Barbara went behind the screen and removed her plum-coloured jacket and skirt. She was down to her white blouse and petticoat before Hazel got the feeling that not all was well with her elderly *primigravida*. She had stopped getting undressed and stood uncertainly by the examination table, seemingly close to tears.

'What is it – what's wrong?' Hazel asked.

'The fact is, I've changed my mind. I'd rather not be here,' Barbara confessed, reaching for her skirt and stepping back into it.

'Why ever not?'

Barbara tossed her head impatiently. 'I'm perfectly all right, that's why. I only agreed to come to the clinic in the first place to keep Philip happy. But there really is no need to keep on coming.'

Studying her tearful face, Hazel trod carefully. 'Wouldn't you like to be weighed at least? And you can keep some of your clothes on if you'd prefer.'

As Barbara ignored the invitation, the reasons for her upset came swiftly to the fore. 'This is my first baby and Philip is dead set on doing things in the modern way. He says that I deserve the best care. That's why he wanted me to come here.'

'Good for him. But that isn't what you would like?' Recalling the garage owner's military appearance and blunt manner, Hazel assumed that his force of personality usually carried the day. This was why she was determined to give Barbara space to explain.

'No. I've nothing against you, you understand. But I would have gone to Mabel Jackson, the same as my mother did when she had me.' Tears were now well and truly streaming down Barbara's face, streaking her rouged cheeks. 'I was hoping it would all happen quietly at home, without me having to sit here every fortnight, listening to other women's tittle-tattle. And there wouldn't have been any men involved either.'

'You mean, when you give birth?'

Barbara took a hankie from her pocket and dabbed her cheeks. 'That's right. You said last time that Dr Bell will be in charge for that part. I went home and thought about it, and to be honest I'm dreading it.'

'I see. Why not let me have a word with Dr Bell?' Hazel said. Belatedly she recognized a strong prudishness beneath Barbara's sophisticated appearance and wished she'd picked up on it sooner. The poor woman simply didn't want a man present during childbirth.

After a while Barbara rallied. 'I'm not being awkward, am I?'

'Not at all. You must speak up about what you'd like.'

310

'That's been the way of doing it all these years – a neighbour like Mabel coming in and taking charge. Women like her – they're bona fide, after all.'

Hazel couldn't deny it. 'Yes, they're regulated to some extent. But they're not trained. And with someone in your position – that is, well, a little older than average to be having your first baby – there is an increased risk.'

'Of what?' Barbara frowned and took a sharp breath.

'Of raised blood pressure, for instance. Now, if that happens it's not necessarily something for you to worry about but we'd just like to keep a close eye on you to make sure it doesn't run out of control.' Hazel hoped that by explaining carefully and calmly she would gain her patient's trust.

'That's the way Philip looks at it. He's forever reminding me about what happened to poor Myra.'

Once again, Hazel fought to keep her own feelings out of the picture. 'He's right. By coming here you're taking good care of both yourself and the baby. We can show you what to eat, tell you when to put your feet up and carry out all the tests to keep you safe. And if in the end you'd prefer me to deliver your baby at home, I'm sure I can arrange that with Dr Bell.'

Slowly Barbara nodded. 'I *am* being awkward,' she asserted miserably. 'But I can't help the way I feel.'

'And why should you?' Hazel readily acknow-ledged Barbara's right to make a stand. She smiled as she saw her unzip her skirt again and take off her blouse. 'The main thing is you're here now and I'm standing by with my stethoscope, ready and willing to listen to baby's heartbeat.'

'Right you are.' Barbara swung her slim legs up onto the table and lay back. 'From now on I promise to do as I'm told.'

'That's the ticket,' Hazel said, warming the stethoscope then applying it to Barbara's abdomen. She leaned forward, put her ear to the instrument and listened intently to the tiny, miraculous heartbeat of a baby preparing to be born.

Hazel and Gladys's big move came on Saturday the second of January. There was still a deafening silence from John, even though she was sure that he must have spotted Napier's horse and cart waiting outside the house on his way to work.

He'll be keeping his head down until I'm settled in the flat, Hazel told herself, mentally squaring her shoulders to make herself concentrate on the task in hand.

Her father had enlisted Norman's help to manhandle her bulky tea chest down the narrow stairs. There was much grunting and shuffling to get it out onto the street and on the back of the cart.

'What have you got in here – the kitchen sink?' old Napier joked.

Hazel grinned. 'It's my textbooks that weigh the most. Anyway, you should see the amount of stuff that Gladys has.' One last return to her room convinced Hazel that she hadn't forgotten anything. The bed was stripped bare, the shelves and chest of drawers were empty and she felt a strong twinge of sadness. Her mother climbed the stairs to join her.

'Why not take this with you?' Almost shyly Jinny offered Hazel her sewing basket containing scissors, cotton reels, needles and her silver thimble.

'I couldn't,' Hazel objected.

'Don't be silly – of course you can. You'll need something to mend your stockings with, won't you?'

'How will you manage without it?'

'Don't worry about that – Rose is rummaging in her basket, sorting out spares for me.'

'Then ta – I'll take this one with me.'

Mother and daughter stood framed in the attic doorway, surveying the sloping ceiling, varnished floorboards and striped flock mattress. Both knew it was a big moment.

'The room looks bigger without all your clutter,' Jinny commented.

'Canal Road isn't far away,' Hazel said.

They glanced at each other and smiled. It was a deep, silent exchange that encompassed their years of struggle and joy together, of pride and petty jealousies, of Jinny giving birth and Hazel growing up, growing away.

'We're ready to go!' Robert called up the stairs.

'All done and dusted.' Jinny sighed. A room without possessions was nothing – just an empty space. A house without a daughter was something she would have to get used to.

'Coming!' Hazel shouted. Holding the sewing box close to her chest, she left without looking back.

'Wouldn't you just know it?' Gladys wailed. She'd run down the ginnel to greet Napier's cart, bumping into Norman as he said goodbye to Hazel and Robert. 'Dan's let me down as usual.'

'What's he done now?' an unruffled Robert asked. It was a dismal, grey day and he'd dressed for the weather in his cap and thick woollen scarf.

'He only promised to help me shift my belongings. But he went to the Green Cross with John last night and he never came home.'

'Count me in,' Norman volunteered. 'Hang on here while I tell Sylvia what's up.'

'Sylvia can say what she likes, Norman's got a heart of gold,' a grateful Gladys acknowledged.

'He's used to flitting.' Hazel remembered that his impoverished family had been forced to move house many times. 'And yes, it is good of him.'

Before they knew it, Norman was back to lift Gladys's three big cardboard boxes out of the house, across the cobbled yard and down the ginnel onto the cart, together with two suitcases and a full-length mirror that she swore she couldn't do without.

'What happens at the far end?' Jim Napier mumbled. The scrap dealer didn't mind lending his horse and cart but made it plain that, with his bad back, he had no intention of lifting heavy boxes.

'Don't worry – I'm yours for as long as you need me,' Norman promised.

All told, Gladys's leave-taking from Nelson Yard was as noisy and disorganized as Hazel's departure from Raglan Road had been calm and considered. Twice she forgot vital things and had to go back into the house where she begged spare pillow cases and a teapot from her mother. Then she had to fight her way through wet towels and sheets flapping from criss-crossing lines to say tearful goodbyes to her grandmother and Aunty Rose. A dustbin lid clanged, boys shouted and ran flat-footed along the echoing alleyway.

'That's that,' Gladys declared at last, brushing the palms of her hands together. 'All done and dusted.'

'Ready?' Robert asked.

'Ready,' Gladys and Hazel confirmed. They sat on the back of the scrap man's cart, legs dangling and calling out to the plodding grey cart horse in high, excited voices. 'Gee-up, Ned, clippety-clop!'

After an afternoon of fetching and carrying, the new lodgers at number 102 Canal Road were cosily installed. Hazel's dresses hung neatly on a rail in an alcove by the chimney breast and her books were lined up on the window sill. She sat on the bed and ran her hand along the sleek wooden headboard chosen by Miss Bennett and reflecting the house-proud landlady's intention to move with the times. So too did the geometric designs of the green and gold rug and co-ordin-ated curtains and wallpaper.

'Hazel, come and help me decide where to put the mirror,' Gladys called from her own room across the landing. 'Should it be under the skylight or tucked away in the alcove?'

'Skylight,' Hazel told her. 'That way you can see what you're doing.' She noticed that Gladys had

315

already made her mark on the room. There were framed pictures on the cast-iron mantelpiece – holiday snaps of a young Gladys and Sylvia riding donkeys on Blackpool's Golden Mile, together with a glamorous studio shot of Gladys taken in more recent days. Her clothes were strewn over the bed – a colourful riot of rayon blouses and dresses, velour jackets and lacy underwear.

Gladys placed the mirror in the recommended position, studied her reflection, then gave a twirl. 'Perfect. Now, how about a cuppa?'

To make tea they had to go down to a first-floor kitchenette equipped with a gas ring and a sink. It was at the far end of the corridor, opposite the shared bathroom, and had a cupboard where Gladys and Hazel would store their cups, teapot, tea caddy and so on.

'Isn't this grand?' Gladys beamed at Hazel as the kettle came to the boil.

'Yes. We've really landed on our feet.' Hazel was tired but exhilarated. This was how freedom felt – an attic flat close to the buzz of the town centre, perched high above the canal and the main tram routes, ready for any excitement that came their way.'

Along the corridor a door opened and a man's voice was heard, talking about new reeds for a clarinet and venues for forthcoming shows. 'Three more nights here, then after that, Leeds then Manchester.'

Gladys's eyes lit up as she recognized Earl Ray's drawling accent and gravelly tone. She rushed out into the corridor, dragging Hazel with her. 'Hello. Remember us?' she cried.

316

The off-duty band leader was dressed in a sleeveless pullover with a bold black-and-white zig-zag pattern, teamed up with wide black trousers. 'Ladies, how could I forget?'

Gladys basked in his admiring glance. 'We've spent the day moving in upstairs, getting the place nice and cosy.'

'I'm glad you made it. Saying hi to two new, pretty neighbours sure makes my day.'

While Gladys and Earl chatted on, Hazel summed him up. Despite the ease and friendliness, she found his warmth insincere. It was difficult to put her finger on it – only that the compliments came too readily and followed a formula that he must use a dozen times a day, whenever he met an ardent young fan. On top of which, his physical presence intimidated her – again, it was hard to define, but had something to do with the way he used his height to lean in too close while he was speaking.

Gladys, however, was enthralled, smiling and fluttering her eyelashes for all she was worth. She offered Earl a cup of tea, which he smoothly declined – unless it came with a splash of Jack Daniel's whiskey, he added with a chuckle. She praised his playing and his singing, putting it above anything she'd heard. He smiled back and admired her baby-blue eyes.

'Did you hear that?' Gladys swooned after the great man had said goodbye and gone downstairs. He was hardly out of earshot but she didn't seem to care. 'Isn't he the bee's knees? Oh Hazel, I'm so excited!'

'Hush, I think he's coming back,' Hazel warned

317

as she heard footsteps on the stairs.

But it was only Miriam Bennett in a sober grey house dress adorned with a silver brooch in the shape of a galleon in full sail, coming to ask if there was anything they needed.

'A new light bulb for the ceiling light in my room, please,' Hazel replied.

'Everything else is tickety-boo, Miss Bennett. We're thrilled to be here.' Gladys still bubbled with naive excitement. 'Living cheek by jowl with famous musicians and actors and all.'

The landlady chose to ignore this and instead ran through a few house rules. 'I don't allow pets – no cats, no dogs, no budgerigars, not so much as a goldfish. And I don't encourage visitors after eight o'clock in the evening. Oh, and if there's any damage to furniture and fittings from spilt drinks, for example, I expect to be informed immediately.'

The strict instructions failed to bring Gladys down to earth. 'Musicians and so on – they live in a different world from us mere mortals, don't they? We trudge along in our workaday lives while they travel all over the country playing their jazz and soaking up applause.'

A frown creased Miriam Bennett's smooth brow. 'I think you'll find they're not so very different,' she said with a hint of acid in her voice. 'After all, they're men – with all their foibles and failings.'

Gladys flashed a glance at Hazel and waited impatiently for the landlady to retreat to her own quarters. 'Fancy that. I wouldn't have put her down as a man hater, would you?'

'"Men – with all their foibles and failings",' Hazel echoed as she went back into the kitchen to pour the tea. 'I wonder what she meant by that.'

'Yes. And what makes her think that way.' Gladys giggled at the older woman's cynicism. In her mind she sketched a history of betrayal and lost love for their refined, buttoned-up landlady.

Hazel added milk to her cup of tea then took a first sip. 'Maybe she intended it as a warning for us to stay away from Earl Ray.'

'Oh Lord, no!' Gladys laughed away the idea. Cradling her cup, she led the way upstairs. 'Miss Bennett doesn't have to worry – we're not in any danger.'

'Still.' As they settled into the armchairs in their improvised sitting room on the top-floor landing, Hazel remained thoughtful.

'Honestly, we're not a pair of silly geese who know nothing of the world,' Gladys insisted. 'And talking of warnings, there's something – some-body – I meant to mention to you.'

'Hmm. Who's that?' Still caught up in the after-math of their conversation with Earl Ray, Gladys's change of subject took Hazel by surprise.

'It's John Moxon,' Gladys said with a roll of her eyes.

In an instant, Hazel's mind became razor sharp. 'What about him?'

'It may be nothing. Dan mentioned it a couple of days ago, that's all. He said John and he had had a falling-out.'

'We know they did,' Hazel reminded her. 'I saw them at the jazz club before Christmas. Reggie

319

Bates had to step in between them.'

'No, I mean there was another time after that, at the greyhound track on Boxing Day. According to Dan, this time it came to actual fisticuffs.'

'Did he say what it was about?'

Gladys shook her head. 'You know Dan – getting anything out of him is like squeezing blood out of a stone. He had to admit he'd been in a fight because he came home with a shiner of a black eye. But he clammed up about what had caused it, except that John had lost his temper and called him all the names under the sun.'

Hazel narrowed her eyes and thought it through. 'Which Dan probably deserved. Anyway, they must have patched things up because you said the two of them went out together to the Green Cross last night.'

'They did. But Dan didn't come home – remember. To my mind that must have been John leading him astray.'

'Or the other way around.' Despite sticking up for John, however, Hazel felt riddled by fresh doubts. 'But you think I should steer clear of him in any case?'

'I do. I know you have a soft spot for him, but I'm afraid he spells trouble. Don't get me wrong – I've no axe to grind. I'm not a fully paid-up member of Dorothy and Mabel's coven or anything like that.'

'Why? What are they bad-mouthing him about now?'

'The same old things.'

'Including the fact that he asked me out?'

Gladys nodded. 'And to cap it all, Dorothy

won't hear a bad word about Myra, even though it's common knowledge that the marriage was rocky from the start, thanks to poor Myra's habit of weeping and wailing and running to her mother over the least little thing.'

'I didn't realize that,' Hazel said quietly. She paused to consider the new picture this presented, then went on.

'I do like John,' she confessed shakily. 'And I was sure he liked me too...'

'But?'

'He blows hot and cold. One minute he writes me a note asking me out to the pictures, and I went. He promises to take me out again, but then he goes to ground and I haven't seen hide nor hair of him since before Christmas.'

'Poor you,' Gladys commiserated. 'I can see that he's got you hooked.'

Hazel bridled. 'No – I don't intend to be at anyone's beck and call.'

'Definitely not.' Gladys was firm, setting down her cup and leaning earnestly forward as she counted on her fingers the reasons that Hazel should stay away from John Moxon. 'Firstly, he keeps you dangling and no decent man would do that. Secondly, we know he gets into fights, which means he has trouble controlling his temper. Thirdly, he throws his money away on gambling–'

'Stop!' Hazel pleaded. 'I know all this but I still can't stop thinking about him.'

'Oh, dearie me.' When she realized how seriously Hazel was smitten, Gladys heaved a sigh.

'Every morning I get up hoping that today will be the day he'll be back in touch. As a matter of fact, I'm on the point of knocking on his door to find out what's wrong.'

'No, you mustn't do that.' Gladys was adamant. She thought for a while, trying to put herself in John's shoes. 'Setting all that to one side – the gambling, the broken promises and the fights – maybe it's just too soon.'

'Don't say that, please.' The ghost of Myra reared up once more and couldn't be banished.

'Yes, that's it. All this is to do with John losing his poor wife. That's why he's acting the way he is.' The conclusion satisfied Gladys and she sat back in her chair. 'Take my advice, Hazel, and think no more about him.'

CHAPTER NINETEEN

Next morning, the sluggish winter daylight didn't creep through the chink in Hazel's curtains until well after eight o'clock. It was a Sunday and she luxuriated in the knowledge that she could lie in until at least nine, when she would stop listening to the patter of raindrops gusting against the windowpanes and get up and tidy the top drawer of the tallboy in the corner of the room. She would separate stockings from brassieres and petticoats and establish a system that satisfied her need for order.

She was still in her nightdress carrying out this task when she heard Miss Bennett call her name from the foot of the stairs.

'Miss Price, are you there? There's someone here to see you. Shall I send him up?'

Hazel opened her door and peered out. 'I'm not decent,' she called back, wondering who would visit at such an odd time. 'I'll be down as soon as I'm dressed.'

John! For a split second she thought it might be him then quickly dismissed the idea. Perhaps it was her father, come to see how she'd settled in. Or else the husband of one of the ladies from her clinic, to announce the inconvenient fact that baby was on its way. In which case, she'd better hurry.

Quickly she slipped into her most practical outfit of slacks, jumper and brogues then ran a brush through her hair. She grabbed her coat and an umbrella just in case then rushed downstairs to find Norman, ashen faced, wild eyed and soaked to the skin, waiting for her in the hallway.

She saw straight away that something was badly wrong. 'Whatever is the matter?' she gasped.

'It's Sylvia,' he muttered. 'She's gone missing.'

'Not again!' Hazel's heart sank. 'What do you mean – missing?'

'We went to bed as usual last night but when I woke up this morning she'd clean vanished.' Norman caught his breath and the words tumbled out.

It was clear to Hazel that he'd run here all the way from Nelson Yard in the pouring rain. 'All right, take your time. Did you check with Aunty Ethel to see if Sylvia got up early and paid them a visit? Or with Nana and Aunty Rose?'

'She wouldn't do that. She's not even on speaking terms with any of them, remember.' Driven

323

to distraction, the muscle at the corner of Norman's mouth twitched as he ran a hand through his thick brown hair. 'It's happened again, hasn't it?'

Hazel held his elbow and guided him through the front door, down the steps and onto the wet pavement, out of range of Miss Bennett. 'What has?'

'You know – like before, when Sylvia took it into her head that she wasn't going to have the baby. Don't think I haven't worked out what was going on when she went to Mabel Jackson.' A chilly wind blew straight through his sodden, threadbare jacket, making his teeth chatter.

Hazel closed her eyes and groaned. Though she didn't want to believe it of Sylvia, she suspected that it was true. 'Has she said something to you?'

'No. You know what Sylvia's like – she blows her top and accuses me of spying on her when all I'm really doing is trying to make sure she hasn't sent away for any of those so-called remedies again. Then after that – silence.'

'But she's been upset?' Already drenched, Hazel belatedly put up her umbrella.

Norman nodded. 'She's been crying buckets, moping about all day. I want to help but she won't let me near.'

'But, if you're right and Sylvia's mind is made up – why would she take it into her head to do it now? Why not wait until tomorrow, when you're at work?' To Hazel it didn't make sense, but then, on reflection, that was the point. Nothing that Sylvia did as far as her pregnancy was concerned was rational.

'Don't ask me.' Norman paced the pavement, ignoring the curious twitching of Miss Bennett's downstairs net curtain. 'But what am I going to do about it?'

Hazel was keen to reassure him that he'd come to the right person for help. 'You mean, what are *we* going to do about it? First things first – we're going to go straight back to Raglan Road and pay Mabel Jackson a visit.'

Seeing Hazel set off at a determined march past the Victory and the green-tiled entrance to the Brinkley Baths, Norman hurried to keep up. 'What for? You don't think Mabel's going to help Sylvia to ... you know.'

Why was it so hard to say the words? Hazel wondered as she fought against a strong wind for control of her umbrella. Why did the issue have to be skirted around and avoided at all costs? 'Mabel probably won't be the one to carry out the abortion,' she agreed, walking in the shadow of Kingsley's mill. 'She knows she'd get into trouble with the police if she did. But who else would Sylvia turn to if she's still dead set on doing it?'

Norman took the point. 'You think Mabel might know someone who will help her get what she wants?'

'We'll soon see.' Hazel turned left up a narrow alley leading to Ghyll Road. They came out onto Raglan Road and within seconds were knocking loudly on the old handywoman's door.

They waited for a full minute but there was no reply and they were in a quandary when Doreen emerged from the nearby ginnel. Unable to resist a mystery, Betty Hollings' busybody neighbour

325

made a beeline for Hazel and Norman.

'You can knock all you like, you won't get an answer,' she asserted from under her black umbrella. 'Mabel's not in.'

Irritated by Doreen's gloating tone, Hazel didn't waver. 'Can you tell us where she's gone?' she asked as politely as she could.

'Where she always goes at this time on a Sunday morning, come rain or shine. It's where I'm headed, right this minute.'

'To church,' Hazel realized. 'Come on, Norman. Let's try to get hold of Mabel before the service starts.'

They set off at a run, leaving Doreen to toil up the hill after them and arriving at the entrance to St Luke's at the same time as a straggle of worshippers for morning prayers.

Hazel and Norman stopped at the gate and tried to pick out Mabel's stout figure amongst them.

Unluckily for them, Dorothy and Henry Pennington soon approached from behind. Dorothy was dressed for battle in a fox fur stole and helmet-like grey velour hat fixed in place by a hatpin in the shape of a miniature dagger. 'Look who it isn't!' Her loud voice drew the attention of Philip and Barbara Baxter, halfway up the path, who stopped to listen.

'Come along, Dorothy.'

Henry the appeaser tried to hurry his wife but she shrugged him off, taking time to look Hazel and Norman up and down with an expression of scornful distaste before she continued, 'To what do we owe the pleasure?'

'She's looking for Mabel,' Doreen informed

326

her, out of breath after taking the hill at twice her usual trundle.

'What does she want with Mabel?' a suspicious Dorothy asked over Hazel's head.

They were wasting precious time and Hazel was grateful to Barbara Baxter for retracing her steps to join them.

'I saw Mabel go into church just ahead of us,' she told Hazel with an understanding smile.

Hazel and Norman thanked her, stepping off the path onto the muddy grass to circumvent Dorothy. They rushed on and caught up with Mabel in the porch.

'Well.' Mabel showed no surprise; she simply nodded as she shook raindrops from her umbrella.

Norman interpreted the look and jumped in quickly. 'Tell us where she is!'

'Where who is?'

'Sylvia, of course.'

'What are you on about?' Mabel filled the chilly stone porch with her presence. Her wide stance and steady gaze were intended to show that she wouldn't budge for the bishop himself.

'We don't have time for this,' Hazel insisted as Dorothy, Henry and Doreen sidled past. 'Just tell us – did Sylvia come knocking for help?'

'Oh, very well, yes, she did,' Mabel conceded. 'At the crack of dawn, no less.' She nodded at Dorothy to assure her that everything was under control. 'She's not there now, though, if that's what you're thinking.'

'Tell us where she went.' Norman stepped towards her with urgent intent. 'She came to see you, then what?'

Mabel sighed then went on in a confidential undertone. 'If you must know, I had all on to calm her down. She wasn't making any sense, saying she couldn't go on another minute longer and goodness knows what.'

'So what did you do?' Hazel's mind flew off in a new direction. Surely Sylvia wouldn't think of ending it, once and for all?

'We know this is the second time she's acted like this and I have to admit, I felt sorry for her. Still – I don't know whether I did the right thing or not.' Mabel's mouth twitched with indecision for once as several more worshippers filtered past. 'Come with me,' she said at last.

She led Hazel and Norman out of the porch into a flurry of heavy raindrops and down the side of the church towards a narrow door leading into the musty, whitewashed vestry where they found the vicar adjusting his surplice and Berta White assembling her musical scores.

'We'll start the service with hymn number 321,' Reverend Turner was telling Berta as the door opened and in blew wind and rain, soon followed by Mabel, Hazel and Norman.

'Berta, I need to have a word,' Mabel said in the voice that could not be disobeyed.

Small, slight and prim, dressed in her usual dowdy grey dress unrelieved by frills or lace, Berta was no physical match for Mabel. But she wasn't ready to kow-tow. 'Not now,' she retorted.

'Yes – now,' Mabel insisted, while Hazel and Norman held back in confusion.

'Ladies, please.' Reverend Turner tapped his watch and cleared his throat.

'You go ahead, Vicar – this won't take long,' Mabel promised.

So the gangling, gap-toothed man of the cloth tucked his Bible under his arm and stooped to avoid knocking his bald head on the inner doorway. He joined his congregation in the vast, gloomy edifice built with mill-owning money some sixty years earlier.

'Well?' Berta challenged Mabel.

'Come off it, Berta. You know what this is about.' The church pianist pointed at Norman.

'Who's this?'

'A certain person's husband. Look a bit closer – you'll recognize him from the wedding. And you know who this is – this is the cousin who trained up as a midwife.'

Berta White – of all people! Never for a second would Hazel have suspected that she was tangled up in the illegal abortion trade if she hadn't been here witnessing this.

'What do they want?' Berta demanded.

'They're after an address,' Mabel explained, stony faced. 'I've come clean over handing the girl on to you and now they want to know where you sent her. I reckon they have the right.'

Berta shook her head and remained silent.

'Was it to Drummond Road or Rawson Street?'

'Neither,' Berta said through clenched, un-Christian teeth. She signalled through the open door to the impatient vicar that she was on her way.

'Butler Close?'

Another shake of the head showed Berta near to breaking point.

329

'Where then?' Implacable Mabel winkled out her answer.

'If you must know, I sent her to a new woman on the other side of the canal – on Bridge Lane.' A chink in the dam allowed the vital information to trickle through. On her way out of the room, she flashed a resentful look at Hazel. 'If anyone asks, you're not to say I was the one who let on.'

'Very well.' Hazel felt the underground network of handywomen gone-to-the-bad cling like a cobweb to her face. It made her skin crawl. 'Which number Bridge Lane?' she managed to ask before Berta made her exit.

'Number 15,' came the muttered reply.

The door closed, the latch fell. Mabel's expression behind her heavy-rimmed glasses was unreadable.

'Berta didn't give us a name,' Norman reminded Hazel as they made their way through grimy alleys and down mossy steps towards the murky water of the canal.

'No, but the address is what counts.' She paused on the deserted bridge to look at her watch. 'What time did you discover Sylvia had gone missing?'

'Eight o'clock.'

'That gives her two hours' head start,' she calculated.

'Will we be in time?' Norman glanced over the parapet to the stagnant water below as if he would find his answer there. The surface was stained with rainbow patches of spilt engine oil and the tow paths littered with discarded bicycle tyres and wooden crates.

'Let's keep our fingers crossed.' Beyond the canal was a maze of back-to-back terraced streets that Hazel didn't know well. She'd heard of Bridge Lane but had never set foot there, knowing only its reputation as a place where no respectable family would want to put down roots.

'What if we do reach her in time?' As Hazel set off again, Norman lagged behind. 'Who's to say she'll listen to us? What if she won't?'

The questions hit home but she managed to shrug them off and carried on leading the way. 'We'll face that if and when it happens. First we have to find her.'

'Right you are – one thing at a time,' he agreed.

They came off the bridge and looked to right and left along a street lined by a yard stacked high with sacks of coal ready for delivery and by a round gasometer opposite the brass foundry, where Eddie worked, next door to a depot full of scrap iron – as dirty and depressing a sight as they could wish to see.

'Which way to Bridge Lane?' Norman asked a man wheeling a bike laden with old buckets and pans.

The tinker didn't reply but walked on doggedly with his clanking load, head down and coughing up phlegm.

A boy in a cap several sizes too big who lounged against some iron railings provided the answer. 'Second on your left.' He held out a grubby hand. 'Spare us a copper, Miss.'

It was Norman who dipped into his pocket and shelled out some loose change then hurried after Hazel.

If the approach promised little, Bridge Lane itself proved even worse. There was hardly a house whose windows were intact or whose gutters didn't overflow and spout rainwater down the filthy, soot-stained walls. The pavements were cracked, the greasy cobbles worn down and strewn with litter.

Hazel pictured Sylvia a couple of hours earlier, taking the address from Berta with a shaking hand and forcing herself to carry through what she'd started. She must have crossed the canal with fear clutching at her heart, breathing in coal dust and gas, avoiding puddles so as not to spoil her Sunday-best shoes. What desperation had driven the poor girl to make her way along Bridge Lane, or had she simply taken one look at her surroundings, turned tail and fled?

'Number 15.' Norman announced their arrival, his voice jittery.

This house and identical ones to either side at least looked as if they were inhabited. The glass in the windows was unbroken and smoke came out of the chimneys. Blinds were down but lights were on in the downstairs rooms.

The moment had arrived. Hazel mounted two stone steps and rapped sharply on the door. They waited. She knocked again.

A green blind was raised and a woman appeared at the window. Seconds later she answered the door.

Expecting to come face to face with someone of Mabel's age and demeanour, Hazel was surprised. This woman was younger than expected and smart, with a slim figure, crimped fair hair and pleasant, even features. She wore coral-pink lipstick, a string of pearls and a bright blue and red striped dress. Holding the door fully open, she wished them good morning.

Norman brushed aside the pleasantry. 'We've come to fetch Sylvia,' he announced.

The door closed a fraction and a note of caution appeared in the woman's voice. 'I'm afraid you've come to the wrong place.'

It was left to Hazel to elaborate. 'Sylvia Bellamy is her full name. Norman here is her husband. We've been given this address.'

'Who by?' The question came quick as a flash.

'Never you mind.' Norman made it clear he wouldn't think twice about barging past the woman and searching her house if need be. 'There's no point you shilly-shallying. We know she's here.'

Hazel put a warning hand on his arm. 'Perhaps Sylvia didn't give the right name,' she suggested carefully. 'Girls in her position often don't.'

'What is her position, pray?' As the conversation developed, there was more stiffness in the woman's manner and more artifice. The door closed by degrees until she was peering through a narrow gap.

'I'm sure I don't have to spell it out,' Hazel went on. 'Let's say we've come here because we're worried about her.' Beneath her calm surface she couldn't help but picture the room behind the green blind – a sink in one corner, an operating table, a trolley equipped with glass rods, forceps and knives. The image didn't tally with the abortionist's sleek and stylish outward appearance

333

but the trail via Mabel and Berta was clear – there was no doubt that this was where it led.

The woman thought for a while. It was obvious that her callers knew what they were about and would be unlikely to be fobbed off with excuses. This left her in a sticky position. If she slammed the door on them, they would probably go straight to the police – the last thing she needed. If she let them in right away, they would see her paraphernalia laid out in the downstairs room and the end result would be the same. 'Wait here,' she said at last.

The door was closed and bolted. The woman left them standing.

'What now? Do we break down the door?' Norman was ready to do the deed.

Hazel held him back. 'No. Let's give her a minute or two to get rid of the evidence.'

'Sylvia is in there – I know she is.'

'But we got here in time, I think.' Judging by the abortionist's cool manner, it didn't look as if she'd been caught red-handed. At least, this is what Hazel hoped.

Norman paced the pavement. 'How can she...? I mean, what makes anyone pick a job like this?'

It was a hard question for Hazel to answer. 'I know – it goes against the grain,' she admitted, waiting anxiously for further developments and thinking that she heard movements behind the green blind. 'But the truth is, in some situations and for some women, this has to be the last resort.'

'Well, I'm not waiting any longer.' Norman clenched his fists and mounted the two steps. He hammered on the door.

This time it was opened by a whey-pale, trembling Sylvia. 'What are you two doing here?' she asked, as if bearing all the burdens of the world on her slight shoulders. She clutched her coat lapels to her throat and kept the other arm crossed protectively over her stomach.

Norman didn't answer. He rushed to put his arms around her but she backed down the corridor out of reach. 'Sylvia, I've come to fetch you,' Norman said at last. 'You have to come home.'

'I don't *have* to do anything.' Sylvia's old petulance put in a brief appearance but soon gave way to helpless sobs.

There was no sign of the fair-haired woman, Hazel noticed. She felt a flood of pity towards Sylvia here in this, the worst of all situations.

Norman turned to Hazel in silent appeal.

'Let me.' Hazel squeezed past him and offered to put an arm around Sylvia's shoulder. 'You're right – you don't have to,' she said. 'No one's going to force you.'

'Why can't you just leave me alone?' Sylvia cried. She backed away again, hands over her face, body racked with sobs. 'It's taken me weeks to build up to doing this and now you've gone and ruined it.'

'Hush,' Hazel murmured. 'Norman and I ... we only want to talk to you.'

'What about? Norman shouldn't have followed me. I haven't got anything to say to him.'

'Just you and me, then,' Hazel suggested. The fact that they'd 'ruined' Sylvia's plans made her more certain that they'd arrived in time and she indicated this by a reassuring nod at Norman. 'Somewhere nice and quiet, if that's better for you.'

'In here.' Sylvia fumbled at the handle of a door leading into a well-lit room. A fire glowed in the black range and a green metal shade covered an electric ceiling light. A long, narrow table on wheels of the type used in an operating theatre was pushed hard against the far wall. An alcove cupboard was padlocked shut. At least the woman carried out her work in hygienic conditions, Hazel noted as she drew two metal chairs into the centre of the room.

'You'd better sit down,' she told Sylvia. 'Are you sure you don't want Norman to be in on this?'

Sylvia gave an exasperated cry. 'No. It's nothing to do with him.'

Hazel took a deep breath and tried hard to understand. 'I hoped we'd got past this. I know you didn't want the baby for a long time and that things between you and Norman weren't all they might be. But looking ahead to when the baby's born, I really and truly believe that it will come right in the end.'

'But that's just it – it won't.' Overcome by a fresh burst of sobbing, Sylvia collapsed forward. Her dark hair fell over her face.

Hazel put a hand on her back and waited.

'How can it?' Sylvia pleaded, her voice muffled. 'Oh, I hoped it would when I rushed headlong into marrying him. At the very least I thought it would keep the tittle-tattlers at bay for a while, once they saw I was expecting. But it wasn't long before I realized I was sticking my head in the sand.'

'Why do you say that? Norman loves you – he really does.'

Sylvia raised her head and peered out from behind a curtain of dull, dark hair. 'Don't you see? That doesn't make any difference.'

'But why resort to this, Sylvia? For a start, you must know the risk you're taking coming to one of these women. What if it goes wrong?'

'It won't. Berta wouldn't have sent me here if she wasn't any good.'

Hazel knelt beside Sylvia's chair and held her gaze as she went on. 'I'm sure Berta and Mabel meant well and there are places much worse than this, I know that for a fact. But they can't give any guarantees – no one can. The biggest risk of doing something like this is that it causes haemorrhaging because of the instruments they use – bleeding that can't easily be stopped. After that, there's infection, and if they give you Diachylon – that has lead in it and you would have blood poisoning all over again. There – have I said enough?'

Sylvia drew several sharp breaths then let out a soft groan. She grasped Hazel's hand.

'I'm not telling you this to scare you. It's because it's true.'

'That's it, then. I might as well save everyone the trouble and jump off that bridge into the canal.' As Sylvia pulled herself upright, her face took on a mask-like blankness and her voice was hollow.

Hazel stood up. This wasn't Sylvia being dramatic, she realized with a fresh jolt. This was

337

something else. 'Why? What haven't you told me?'

'Nothing.'

'Sylvia, spit it out.'

'No.'

'I don't understand. Why has this got nothing to do with Norman?'

'Because...' Sylvia tilted her head back and drew a long, jagged breath before she spoke again. 'Norman isn't the father. There – I've said it.'

Hazel took three paces towards the window then walked quickly back. She rested her hands on Sylvia's shoulders and looked her in the eye. 'Not Norman. Who then?'

Sylvia shook her off with a bitter laugh. 'You'll see soon enough.'

'What do you mean?'

'I mean – if you don't let me get rid of this baby, *everyone* will see – Norman, Mum, Nana, you, Gladys–'

'What will we see? Tell me, Sylvia, who is the father?'

'Guess.'

'Don't – this isn't a game.'

'*I* know that!' A secret that Sylvia had kept locked away for months forced itself into the open. The few short minutes that she would regret for the rest of her life sprang out of the dark corners of her mind. 'I didn't know what I was doing. He swept me off my feet.'

'Who did?' Hazel struggled to identify the man who had flattered, petted and persuaded Sylvia to give in to him.

'It was a horrid, stuffy little room.' She shut her eyes at the memory and let out a low groan. The

338

pause went on and on until she opened her eyes again and gazed forlornly at Hazel. 'Then he dropped me. I tried and tried to talk to him but he just brushed me off – he wouldn't even speak to me once it had happened.'

Hazel shook her head. Nothing she could say would make this better.

'There was no one to talk to. I just waited and hoped. Then I found out...'

'That you were having a baby?'

Sylvia ignored the tears that had begun to trickle down her cheeks. 'I said to myself, No, it can't be true. I tried to ignore it and carried on going out to dances and to the flicks with the usual crowd.'

'Which is where you ran into Norman.'

'He was always sweet on me, then suddenly he's down on his knees saying he loves me and asking me to marry him. I didn't say a word about ... about the bad thing that had happened. I hid it from everyone and jumped at the chance of marrying Norman. I kidded myself that it would make everything all right, but deep down I must have known it wouldn't – not really. I knew it even before I walked down the aisle.'

Hazel thought back to the doubts she'd harboured about the actions of the young bride-to-be – how desperate Sylvia had seemed to tie the knot and yet how strangely detached from events.

'Come on, now,' Hazel said softly, her hand still on Sylvia's shoulder, 'you can tell me the father's name.'

Sylvia took a deep breath. 'Earl Ray,' she whispered in the sterile, empty surroundings chosen to put an end to her problem. 'Now do you see?'

339

CHAPTER TWENTY

'We got here in time but Sylvia is still very upset,' Hazel told Norman as she led her cousin out of the house onto the pavement. 'Let's get her home as quick as we can.'

Inside the room, Sylvia had forced a promise out of Hazel. 'You mustn't say a word!' she'd begged. 'If you do, I'll stick my head in the gas oven the minute your back is turned – I swear I will.'

'Hush, it's all right. This is between you and me – it goes no further.' The main thing was to get Sylvia away from here. Everything else would have to wait.

'It's Sunday – there are no trams or buses,' Norman pointed out. Sobbing and incoherent murmurings were all that he'd heard from inside the room and his blood still boiled when he remembered the fair-haired woman's cool, cautious demeanour.

'Then we'll have to walk,' Hazel decided.

They made their way in the rain over the bridge onto Canal Road, with Hazel linking arms with Sylvia and sheltering her with her umbrella. Sylvia leaned against her, saying nothing and allowing herself to be steered up flights of stone steps between mill buildings and along narrow streets until they came at last to Nelson Yard.

'Do you have tea and milk in the house?' Hazel

checked with Norman as they crossed the grim courtyard. 'Give her a cup with plenty of sugar and make sure she stays in bed for the rest of the day.'

Sylvia clutched at her. 'Don't go,' she begged.

'Norman's here. He'll take care of you.' Hazel prised Sylvia's fingers from her arm. 'Promise me you'll rest. I'll be back in a little while.'

'Where are you going?'

'Home, to fetch a few things – toiletries for you to spruce yourself up.'

Reluctantly Sylvia let Norman lead her into the house and Hazel hurried away. She'd reached the ginnel leading out onto Raglan Road when the door to her grandmother's house flew open and Rose rushed down the steps, a shawl pulled hastily around her shoulders, her thick hair escaping from its loose bun.

'What's the matter with Sylvia?' Rose demanded. 'I saw you with her and Norman.'

'Nothing. She's all right.'

'She didn't look all right. She looked like death warmed up.' Rose eyed Hazel suspiciously then realized from her closed expression that she would get no information out of her niece. 'You're not going to let on, are you?'

'I can't. I'm sorry.' Hazel didn't want to keep Rose at bay, especially when she saw a hurt expression followed by disappointment flicker across her aunt's sensitive face.

'I see – Sylvia's bound you to silence.'

Hazel nodded.

'And she won't open the door to me or to anyone else for that matter. So there's no point us

341

even trying.'

'She won't,' Hazel agreed.

'And I'll bet she's got nothing to eat in the house. What will they have for their dinners?' Beside herself with worry, Rose tried to work out a way of offering help. 'I know – Mother and I can spare a few slices from our Sunday joint – it's topside of beef. I'll wrap them up in greaseproof paper and leave them on their doorstep.'

'Yes, do that,' Hazel said quietly. She smiled and squeezed Rose's hand then walked quickly down the dank, dark alley.

Back at Canal Road, Hazel found that Gladys was harder to fob off than Rose.

'What do you mean – you went for a walk? Nobody goes for a walk when it's pouring down with rain.' Gladys made mincemeat of Hazel's feeble excuse. 'Not even you.'

Hazel held steady against the barrage of questions. 'I woke up early and I felt like a breath of fresh air, that's all.'

'Ah, now who's a dark horse? It was another secret assignation, wasn't it?'

'At this time on a Sunday morning? I don't think so, Gladys.'

'Yes, that's it. It was a tryst with John.' Gladys treated Hazel to a gimlet stare. 'Haven't you listened to a word I said?'

'I haven't met up with John, I swear. I haven't even spoken to him since before Christmas.'

'What was it then? Was it connected with work?'

'Goodness, Gladys. This is worse than living at home. Isn't a girl allowed to go for a walk if she

342

feels like it?'

Luckily for Hazel, Gladys was distracted by the sound of men's voices drifting up from the downstairs kitchen. She winked then leaned over the banister and called down, 'Ooh, yes ta – Hazel and I would love a cup of tea, since you're asking! Come on, Hazel, let's show our American pals how to make a nice strong brew.'

Gladys swished down the stairs and was soon engaged in lively conversation with Earl Ray and Sonny Dubec. Hazel stayed where she was, wrestling with Sylvia's recent news.

Yes, this too fell into place. She recalled how peculiar it had seemed that Sylvia had kept on pursuing the band leader in spite of her engagement to Norman, but now it was clear that she'd been desperate to talk to him about the result of their disastrous one-night stand. Did Earl Ray even know about the baby? Hazel wondered.

Then another thought occurred to her as she looked ahead to the birth – was Sylvia right to suppose through her sobs and tears in the abortionist's room that the father's race was bound to show in the colour of the baby's skin? Hazel determined to talk to David about this as soon as she got the chance.

Hearing the laughter below, she retreated to her room and sat on the edge of her bed. For a moment she was angry. How could Sylvia have hoped to trick Norman, even for a second? And anyway, the good-hearted chap didn't deserve to be used in that way. No – it was wrong on both counts.

Then she felt guilty. *Imagine the shock,* she

343

thought. Sylvia had made a bad mistake and it had brought her whole world tumbling down. She'd told no one and imagined she could work her way towards a solution, only to make things ten times worse by marrying Norman. In fact, all she'd succeeded in doing was to build a house of straw. It had altered nothing – there was still the fact of Earl Ray and the colour of his skin.

On Sylvia had rushed, from one panicky, misguided action to the next – pushing everyone away, going to Mabel for help not once but twice and being ready to risk everything so that the truth did not come out.

Hazel felt sorry and then angry again, angrier than she had ever been – this time with the man whose loud laugh and drawling voice still floated up the stairs. Sylvia was an innocent seventeen-year-old who'd never been further than Blackpool beach. And what was he? A man of thirty-five or forty, from across the Atlantic, who frequented a world of dimly lit bars that you only ever saw on the silver screen. It was plain and simple – Sylvia had idolized him and he'd seized upon her infatuation and misused it for his own ends.

How much force had he used, when it came to it? Hazel wondered. Or had it been honeyed words and dapper charm alone? Perhaps that was something she would never know.

Pressing her lips together and coming to a decision, Hazel jumped up from the bed and packed a bar of soap, a clean face flannel and a spare hairbrush into her sponge bag. She put on her coat and hat and was out of the house before Gladys had finished her morning cuppa with the man who had destroyed Sylvia's life.

'Swear that you've kept your promise,' Sylvia begged again when Hazel took her the toiletries. She was in bed. Norman was downstairs setting out the cold meat and Yorkshire puddings that Rose had left on the doorstep. 'You haven't said anything to anyone about Bridge Lane, have you?'

'Not a word.' Hazel placed the brush, soap and flannel next to the ewer and basin on the washstand in Sylvia and Norman's bedroom. 'And how are you feeling now – better?'

'Tired.'

'That's to be expected. Tomorrow I'll bring you a pick-me-up.'

'Yes, you will carry on visiting me, won't you? You won't leave me on my own?'

Hazel gazed sadly at Sylvia propped up on pillows and cushions, covered by a sheet and a thin blanket. Her face was drained of colour and her eyes were dark. 'I'll visit every day if I can,' she promised.

'Will *she* try to find me?'

'Who?'

'You know – the woman. I didn't pay her any money. I'm worried she'll come looking for me.'

'I'll see that she doesn't.' Hazel decided to pass on the message to Mabel that Sylvia was not to be bothered. 'Anyway, Norman would soon send her packing if she did.'

'Norman,' Sylvia echoed in a faint voice and tears came to her eyes.

'Wouldn't it be better–' Hazel began.

345

'No.' Sylvia wouldn't let her finish her sentence.

'He's bound to find out in the end.'

'Don't tell him. Don't tell anyone. Go away, Hazel. I don't want to talk to you if you're going to carry on like that.'

'Can you give me a straight answer – what are the chances of a child being born to a white woman with a black father turning out to look...' Under David's direct gaze, Hazel struggled to find the right words.

'White?' he said bluntly.

Tuesday's clinic had finished and Hazel had sought him out to ask his advice. He'd taken her up to his living room where a newly laid fire burned brightly. The curtains were drawn and a tray set out with tea and sandwiches. Luckily there was no sign of Irene.

'Yes.' Hazel was sure that the conversation wouldn't go beyond those four walls, but still she trod carefully in case she slipped up. 'I feel out of my depth. I've been asked by–'

Again David swatted away the rest of her sentence. 'It doesn't matter by whom. The question is purely and simply about inheritance. Let's say, for instance, that the father is of one hundred per cent African origin, then the chance of the baby born to a white mother being completely white or completely black is very remote. Most likely the newborn will have features that show a mixed origin, though it may not be obvious in the first few minutes after birth. As we know, most babies emerge with a dark purple or reddish skin tone.'

346

'That turns paler when they start to breathe – yes.' Hazel listened intently. This was not a topic they'd covered in college and she was grateful to David for talking about it with his usual directness, displaying no personal curiosity or bias.

'Other than the most obvious difference, Caucasian babies are born with dark blue eyes, African and Asian babies with grey or brown. Hair colour is usually of no significance in determining race.'

'Back to the question of skin colour – it's not all or nothing?' she asked, still tentative.

'Quite right. There's an enormous range and besides it's not fixed. Very often the colour of such a baby's skin will grow darker during the first year of life – not always, of course.' He finished then looked closely at her, wishing that he could do more to lift her mood. 'Is that enough information for you to go on?'

'Yes, thank you.' She sat for a while gazing into the fire, absorbing its warmth and reluctant to head out into the cold evening.

'In my experience, this doesn't present a problem if the parents are settled – married, and so on.' David's remark was open ended, leaving Hazel to decide whether or not she wanted to follow it up.

She frowned and continued to look at the flames. 'And if not?'

'Then it can cause a great deal of anxiety. I remember a case in my last practice when a young mother was cut off by her whole family – not for being unmarried, though that was seen as bad enough, but for the so-called sin of giving birth to a child with dark brown skin – unmistakably the result of a brief liaison with a chap from one of the cargo boats.'

'What happened to them?'

'The mother had plenty of spirit. She took the baby away and made a fresh start in a faraway town, apparently successfully. On another occasion, a young woman came to me with a similar problem. She had not a scrap of support from her family during her pregnancy and she was adamant that she didn't want to keep the baby after it was born. I recommended a maternity home in the Borders run by nuns. She went there, had the child, and in due course the Catholic sisters made arrangements for it to be adopted by a couple in Pennsylvania – all above board and satisfactory.'

'Yes, I see. Sorry – I should have thought of that.' Hazel resolved to make up for this omission by discussing this course of action with Sylvia as soon as possible.

'I've also known a few women who stayed put and stuck it out,' David added. He looked thoughtful but still resolved not to probe. 'It depends entirely on the individual.'

Hazel stood up and straightened the creases in her skirt. 'Ta. I appreciate that.'

'You're welcome. I'll see you on Thursday.' He too stood then showed her to the door. 'Our new clinic day.'

'Yes, Thursday.' The reminder drew a faint smile. 'A new clinic to start the New Year. Fresh beginnings.'

David smiled warmly. 'Goodbye, Hazel. I'll see you then.'

'Ta-ta,' Eleanor said to Hazel as she came down

the stairs. The receptionist looked up at Dr Bell still hovering on the top landing and sighed as she put the cover on her typewriter. 'Did Irene make your sandwiches?' she called up to him.

'She did – thank you, Eleanor.'

It wasn't Hazel's place to comment on David's wistful look as she left the building, but her heart was heavy as she put on her hat and coat. 'Cheerio, then.'

'Cheerio,' he said, swept up in a whirlpool of wondering who was the mother in Hazel's story, who was the father and what would be the eventual outcome. 'I'll see you on Thursday and don't be late!'

That Thursday, Barbara Baxter, with all the eagerness of a recent convert to modern midwifery, took first place in the queue at the start of Hazel's new clinic.

'I got here nice and early,' she explained to Hazel as she lay back on the examination table. 'I've been reading up about things and there's a lot I need to ask.'

'Fire away.' Hazel jotted down satisfactory blood pressure readings in Barbara's notes.

Conscious of other women lining up beyond the screen, Barbara lowered her voice. 'This enema thingy, for a start – do you have to do that?'

Hazel was brisk but sympathetic. 'Yes, that's the routine these days. We need to empty the bowel at the start of labour.'

Barbara grimaced. 'Do I absolutely have to?'

'I'm sorry but yes. It's to help contractions.'

'And when will you be able to see that the baby

349

is in the right position and not the wrong way up?'

'Much later in your pregnancy,' Hazel assured her, glad that Barbara seemed more in charge of what was happening. 'Right now he's got plenty of room to move around. Some babies don't present head down until the very last minute.'

'That's all right, then. And did you check with Dr Bell about you being there at the birth instead of him?'

'I did and he says it's perfectly all right.' As she made more notes, Hazel told Barbara that she could get dressed. 'So, you see, you have nothing to worry about,' she concluded.

'That's a relief. I can go home and tell Philip. He could do with some good news to cheer him up.' Everything about the garage owner's wife was refined – her manner of speaking, her appearance, even the delicate way she worked her fingers to ruche up her nylon stockings before putting them on. 'Did you know that he's struggling to find a trained mechanic?'

Hazel put down Barbara's notes and methodically replaced her stethoscope on its metal tray. 'What happened to John?' she asked, failing to hide a quiver in her voice.

'Philip had to lay him off for poor timekeeping.' Barbara was matter-of-fact as she slipped her feet into her shoes then put on her jacket. 'He didn't want to, knowing what poor John went through last year, so he gave him several chances to pull his socks up – all to no avail, I'm afraid.'

'Yes, I'm sure Mr Baxter gave him every opportunity.' Hazel tottered on the brink of revealing

350

her personal interest in John's fate. Why exactly? When? How did he react? How difficult will it be for him to find a new job?

Fully dressed, Barbara took a make-up mirror from her handbag and applied a slick of red lipstick. 'Who would believe that in this day and age it would be so hard to find a replacement? You'd think there'd be men queuing up at his door, wanting the work. Anyway, I mustn't keep you from your other ladies.' Clipping her bag shut, she gave a grateful smile then made a brisk exit.

The news flustered Hazel and made it hard for her to concentrate but fortunately the rest of the afternoon went smoothly and by the end of the clinic she'd decided what to do.

'Someone's in a hurry,' Eleanor mentioned as Hazel reached for her hat and coat, ready to make a hasty exit. Nothing escaped the notice of Dr Bell's sentry who came out from behind her desk proffering a black umbrella. 'It's raining cats and dogs out there.'

'Ta. Whose is it?'

Eleanor flicked her eyes towards her employer's closed door. 'Take it – he won't mind.'

So Hazel grabbed the umbrella and was grateful for it as she left the Westgate Road surgery and hurried through the rain. The pavements were crowded with workers, heads bowed against the downpour, all intent on getting home after a weary day in the woollen mill or iron foundry, the department store or bank. No one spoke above the grind of motor traffic that swished through puddles or stopped to disgorge passengers at the

351

tram stop by the Common.

With a rapidly beating heart Hazel turned onto Raglan Road and walked past Pennington's without a sideways glance. *Once – just this once –* she thought, *I shall follow my heart.* She knew it had to be done quickly and without too much thought. Two houses down from the fish and chip shop, she went up the steps and knocked on the door.

After a minute or so, John opened it.

Hazel tilted her umbrella so that he could see her face. 'It's me. Can I come in?'

He stood back to let her enter. 'Sorry about the mess.'

Hazel found the kitchen in disarray. Pots were piled up in the sink, cinders and ash spilled out of the grate. John was in shirtsleeves, a broad leather belt buckled tight around his waist. He hadn't shaved or combed his hair. 'I hear you're out of work,' she said without any preamble.

'Blimey, who's been telling tales behind my back? Let me guess. I bet it was Mrs High and Mighty Baxter.'

'John, don't – this is serious.' She faced him across the hearthrug, determined to find out what was going on.

'I never said it wasn't.' His expression grew guarded. 'Anyway, what brings you here?'

'First of all, I wanted to find out if you were all right.'

'Well, here I am.' He spread his arms wide, inviting her to take a good look. 'What do you reckon?'

'That you're not all right,' she said quietly. She took in a row of empty beer bottles lined up at the cellar head next to an abandoned cricket bat and a set of wickets. 'I noticed your car wasn't parked outside for a start.'

'Sold it,' he said abruptly.

'Who to?'

'Never you mind.'

'John – your beautiful car!'

'A car's a car.' He shrugged.

'But that Ford meant a lot to you.' She saw in a flash that his life was indeed falling apart, that he was losing everything – not just his car and his job, but any pride that he might have had in himself and his place in the world.

'Let's just say I was strapped for cash. Sorry about that – I should have let you know. It means the ride out to Shawcross is off.'

She shook her head to show that it didn't matter. 'And your job – that's gone as well.'

'Down the Swannee,' he agreed with false bravado. 'Old man Baxter gave me the push at the end of last week and I don't blame him. If I were him I'd have sacked me too.'

'John, what's happening to you?' Hazel murmured. Filled with alarm, she took a step towards him to try to break down the barrier. 'Why haven't you kept in touch like you promised?'

He gave another ironic flourish, this time gesticulating towards the unwashed pots and the untidy grate. 'Because this is what I have to offer. Do I have any takers? No, I didn't think so.'

'This isn't you,' she insisted. 'This is what happens when you give way to feeling sorry for yourself. Everything goes to pieces.'

The barb hit home and made him drop his

353

flippant tone.

'You're right, it's true. I've been drinking far too much and throwing my money away at the race course. You can blame Dan for that.'

Hazel frowned. 'Well, I wouldn't ever hold Dan up as a good example, even though he is my cousin.'

'To be fair, it's as much me as him. We're partners in crime.'

'But Dan doesn't have the reasons to go to pieces that you do. You must have had a miserable Christmas, all by yourself.'

'Too much time to sit and mope,' he agreed.

'Is that where the drink came in – to dull the ache?' Hazel began to see his plight more clearly but she wanted to know more. 'And the fight between you and Dan at the jazz club – what was that all about?'

'He lied about owing me a few quid, that's all. It made me see red until Reggie stepped in and separated us. I'm not proud of the way I behaved.'

'No, it's Dan who was in the wrong,' she insisted. 'You'd been a good pal to him up till then. He should have paid his dues.'

'Fair enough. But none of it alters the fact that I'm on my uppers. And if you really want to know why I haven't kept in touch, it's because the more I thought about it, the more I realized I didn't want to hold you back.'

'You don't hold me back,' she protested, her voice low and soft.

'Yes, I do. You're just getting started as a midwife, setting up on your own, spreading your wings. I'm on the downward slide. Take a look around you.'

There was a gap between them that could have been closed by a single step. She could sense the shame of his situation, like heat through his skin. 'What if I said that it doesn't matter?'

Momentarily weakening, he leaned in then thought better of it and pulled back. 'It does to me.'

Hazel sighed. She imagined what would have happened if he'd reached out to touch her – the embrace, the warmth, the irresistible feel of his arms around her. 'I'd better go, then.'

He made no move to stop her, but turned away, hands in pockets, head down.

To her it felt too forlorn and empty to leave it like this. 'I moved into the flat with Gladys, by the way. Remember my new address: it's Canal Road, number 102.'

John nodded. 'Good for you.'

She went to the door and picked up her umbrella. 'I hope you don't mind me coming. I really was worried about you.'

'No need.' He'd retreated into monosyllabic, pared-down responses that gave nothing away.

'Ah, but there is,' she said with a sad look that almost broke him. She opened the door and stepped outside.

The door closed. Hours later, John could still smell the perfume of her hair, and the slow softness of her voice echoed in the desolate room.

CHAPTER TWENTY-ONE

Foggy January gave way to a bitterly cold February, which, to everyone's dismay, brought the deepest snow of the winter.

'I thought we were through the worst,' Jinny complained when Hazel wheeled her bike through the afternoon gloom into the yard at the back of the house on Raglan Road. Robert had cleared a path to the shed through snow ten inches deep. 'Your dad knew you wouldn't be able to use it in this weather so he said feel free to leave it here until the thaw comes. Now come inside and get warm.'

Gratefully Hazel accepted the offer. Over tea and crumpets, mother and daughter caught up with the latest events.

Jinny went first. 'Your Aunty Rose's bronchitis is bothering her again. Dr Bell has ordered her to stay indoors. They've laid off more warp men at Oldroyd's but your dad thinks his job is still safe for the time being. Cousin Dan lost his with the tram company, though.'

'When did that happen?' Gladys hadn't mentioned this to Hazel, even though she went back regularly to Nelson Yard to call in on her mother and father.

'He kept it quiet, apparently. The cat is only just out of the bag. Anyway, what have you been up to?'

'Nothing new. Just work.' This was not quite true. Two clinics per week plus daily house visits and night-time calls to attend births did keep Hazel's nose to the grindstone, but she still found time to gad about with Gladys and accept occasional free tickets from fellow lodgers for nights out at the music hall and clubs. The only invitations she refused came from Earl Ray, whenever he was in town.

'I don't understand what you've got against him,' Gladys would say, wrinkling her nose and vowing to give away Hazel's ticket to a friend. 'Earl is a gentleman and he's always as nice as pie to you.'

Hazel managed to fob her off with, 'Sorry – I've got too much on.' Nothing on earth would break her resolve to shun Sylvia's seducer. In fact, the sound of his voice in the hallway made her seethe with silent anger.

'Work, eh? You know what they say about all work and no play.' Jinny savoured Hazel's visits and always sent her away with a thoughtful gift – a hand-embroidered pillowcase or a pad of lavender-scented writing paper from WH Smith.

'I know – it makes Jack a dull boy.' Hazel was afraid that this was true. 'I haven't got any news, only that Sylvia is still refusing to attend my clinic.'

'She's not speaking to any of us either,' Jinny said. 'It can't be doing her any good to be stuck at home by herself.'

'No, but she's dug in her heels good and proper,' Hazel admitted with a sigh.

Her mother tutted. 'Mabel said as much when I ran into her at Hutchinson's.'

357

'How does she know that?' Hazel asked warily.

'Don't worry – she didn't get it from the horse's mouth. Mabel heard it through Ethel, who got it from Norman, I expect.' Jinny sighed and shook her head. 'That girl's still as stubborn as ever. To be honest, I'll be happy when her baby finally puts in an appearance and we can all breathe a sigh of relief. By the way, I hear Mabel has started to put business your way.'

Hazel stared in disbelief at her mother, who sat with hands folded in her lap, still wearing her flowered work overall, her shoes kicked off onto the hearthrug but still wearing her hat.

'Don't look at me like that. Didn't Ivy Garrison from Ghyll Road just start at your clinic?'

'Last Thursday – yes.' Hazel matched a face to the name – Ivy was a raw-boned, fidgety sort without an ounce of spare flesh – typical of many of the women she saw. 'It's early days – she's still in her first trimester.'

'Well, it was Mabel who sent her.'

'Get away! Ivy didn't mention it.'

'No, but that's how it came about. As soon as Ivy found out she was expecting again, she did some forward planning by knocking on Mabel's door like she did for her other three. That's when Mabel told her that she was shutting up shop, so to speak.'

'What do you mean, shutting up shop?'

'Mabel swears that, come spring, she'll be officially retired.'

'Never.' Hazel hadn't seen Mabel in weeks – not since the disastrous day when she and Norman had tracked her down in the church porch.

'That's the last thing I expected.'

'Well, as soon as Ivy heard that you and Dr Bell didn't charge any more than Mabel and her sort did, her mind was made up.'

'I see.'

'It's a sign of the times,' Jinny concluded. 'New brooms. What's the matter, Hazel? I thought you'd be pleased.'

'I am,' she said as she washed up the tea things and took in the latest development. 'I'm surprised, that's all.'

'Surprised? You could have blown me down with a feather,' her mother insisted. 'I never thought I'd see the day when Mabel Jackson admitted defeat.'

Hazel stacked cups and saucers on a shelf by the sink. 'Let's wait and see, shall we? Knowing Mabel, she'll have second thoughts and be back in harness before we know it.'

The snow lasted a week then melted over two days into dirty grey mounds by the side of the road. Happy to retrieve her bike from her parents' shed, Hazel resumed her rounds out as far as Linton Park and Ada Street, and on occasions over to Hadley. By the beginning of March crocuses on the Common opened their purple and yellow petals and basked in a pale spring sun. Four weeks later, soon after the clocks went forward, green sprigs appeared in the hawthorn hedges. Daffodils grew everywhere during the lengthening days – in ditches, dappled copses and on the grass verges of the steep hill down from the moor top.

'These are for you.' Hazel took a bunch to Sylvia.

Sylvia's eyes were listless and red-rimmed as she viewed the flowers.

'Don't worry – I've brought a vase with me.' Hazel put the daffodils in water and set them on the window sill. 'Have you had any more thoughts on where you'd like to have the baby?'

'Don't start,' Sylvia warned edgily.

Ever since the close call on Bridge Lane, Hazel had kept her promise not to leave Sylvia to deal with things alone. She'd dropped in on her cousin almost daily and bit by bit she'd sowed the seeds. There were maternity homes out of town where women could receive good care and afterwards arrange for the baby to be adopted, she'd told her. Sylvia could stay there to give birth in peace and quiet, no questions asked.

At first Sylvia had displayed predictable petulance. 'Ah, so now you're ashamed of me and want to hide me away – is that it? Ta very much!'

But Hazel had persisted. She'd given Sylvia the name of a place near Bridlington, hoping that, in time, Sylvia would see it as a reasonable way forward. 'It means that no one need find out about Earl Ray and what he did to you. I know that's what bothers you the most.'

'It is,' Sylvia said with a shudder.

'It's not a perfect solution, I know. There's Norman, for a start.' And the fact that the whole thing would remain cloaked in secrecy, which certainly wasn't ideal.

This time Sylvia didn't react.

'I'm only mentioning it again because there's not much time left to sort things out,' Hazel reminded her carefully as she turned the vase

360

around for the best view of the daffodils. 'Finding a couple who will be willing to adopt isn't something the maternity home can leave until the last minute.'

Sylvia's haunted face – drained of colour, with dark circles under her eyes – and her slow, apathetic movements told Hazel that she was only too well aware of her predicament.

'Why don't you come clean?' she murmured. 'You never know – there might be no need for adoption. Norman might stick by you.'

'No.'

'You're sure?'

'Yes. Norman mustn't know. You're right – I need to go to one of your places.'

They were inching forward at last. 'Good. I'll find out the telephone number of the place on the coast,' Hazel promised.

Sitting at the table, Sylvia fiddled with the edge of the tablecloth. 'Will you come to Bridlington with me?'

The simple appeal, plaintive and unexpected, affected Hazel. 'I suppose I could arrange it with David,' she said slowly. 'It would be the first time I've had to take time off but he could probably find someone to step in and cover my clinics.'

'Will you, please?' Glimpsing light at the end of the tunnel had energized Sylvia and she immediately regained some of her old spirit. 'We could tell Norman I had complications and you needed to get me to a special hospital where they could take care of me. He trusts you more than anyone.'

'And then what?' Hazel felt her stomach twist

into knots at the enormity of the lie that she would become part of. 'What happens when we come back without a baby?'

'It's simple. We'll fib. We'll say the complications were worse than we thought and I lost it.'

Hazel's heart thudded. 'No, Sylvia. I can come with you if you want me to, but I can't lie for you.'

'Then say nothing. If they ask you what happened in the maternity home, say your lips are sealed. You're my midwife so you can't discuss it. That would soon shut people up.'

'Sylvia, don't you know you're putting me on the spot?' Hazel wondered what David's advice would be and decided that it would be to separate personal considerations from the professional. As a midwife pure and simple, what should she do? *My duty is to make sure the baby is delivered safely without the mother coming to any harm*, she thought. *The rest is beyond my control.*

'Well?' Sylvia said with impatience that edged towards hysteria.

'Leave everything to me.' Hazel swallowed her qualms. 'In the meantime, try not to worry. Get as much rest as you can.'

Hazel's independent new life on Canal Road had one major drawback in the shape of Earl Ray. He and his band came and went without any regular pattern and Gladys's high spirits when they were in residence were hard for Hazel to bear.

So it was on a Sunday morning at the end of March that she made her escape.

'Count me out. I'm off for a walk,' she told

Gladys, who had chatted with Earl in the kitchen and eagerly accepted an invitation for them to join the band in a rehearsal session above a pub in the centre of town.

'You and your walks!' Gladys couldn't believe her ears. 'You don't know what you're missing. Earl doesn't invite just any-old-body to hear them rehearse.'

'Oh, we're special, are we?' Undeterred, a sceptical Hazel buttoned her coat and put on her hat.

Gladys ignored the jibe and declared that she would go anyway. 'Why are you such a crosspatch all of a sudden?'

'I just don't like the man. There, I've said it.' It was as close as she dare get to the real reason and she hammered the point home to Gladys before she left. 'As a matter of fact, I'd think twice before I went there on my own if I was you.'

Gladys frowned. 'You're just an old fuddy-duddy.'

'I mean it, Gladys.'

'Don't be silly. It's broad daylight. What could possibly go wrong?'

'Why not take someone with you? I'm sure Mary would jump at the chance.'

The advice gave Gladys pause for thought. 'Maybe you're right. Her lodgings are above the hat shop next to the Central Library. I'll call in there and see if she's free.'

'Good idea.' Hazel left the house and planned ahead. She would take a brisk walk along Canal Road then up Chapel Street onto the Common where, if the weather was sunny enough, she might sit on a bench and watch the world go by.

363

After that, she would catch up with her mum and dad then her nana and Aunty Rose before crossing Nelson Yard to check in on Sylvia, who, by her own reckoning, had less than two weeks to go before her due date.

Lost in thought about the ins and outs of taking Sylvia to the Bridlington home, Hazel crossed Overcliffe Road and took the footpath leading towards the bandstand. The spring sunshine felt pleasantly warm after a long winter of grey skies so she unbuttoned her coat and prepared to acknowledge a woman pushing a pram towards her – Evelyn Jagger, as it turned out.

'Hello, this is a nice surprise. How are you both?' Hazel asked, peering at baby Sally sitting up under the shelter of the pram hood with a dummy in her mouth and bouncing with rosy-cheeked health.

'We're champion, thank you.' Evelyn had put on weight and lost the round-shouldered stoop that had characterized her when she first attended clinic. 'We walked this way to call on Betty – Betty Hollings – to see how she's keeping, but it turns out she and Leonard have taken the family out to Brimstone Rocks for the day.'

Passing the time of day with Evelyn, Hazel failed to notice the figure on a bike speeding up from behind. At the last minute he put on his brakes and rode onto the rough grass to avoid them. She saw him sideways on, recognized the strong-jawed profile and felt her heart lurch.

'Sorry, Hazel – I'm an idiot. I wasn't looking where I was going.' John's back tyre skidded in the mud and he struggled to keep his balance.

Evelyn picked up the atmosphere between them immediately. 'I'll be off, then.' Minding her own business, she went quickly on her way.

'It's all right. No harm done.' Hazel took a deep breath.

'I'm late,' he explained. 'I'm due in Hadley in half an hour. This is a short cut.'

'Grand. Don't let me keep you.'

'I've started coaching the junior cricket team there.' He made no move to head off. 'Reggie knows the chap who's in charge of the Hadley first eleven.'

She nodded and waited.

'There are some handy little players coming up through the ranks – two who will soon be good enough to send over to Headingley for trials. But listen to me going on. I'm holding you up.'

'No, I'm interested. It's good to see you.' Even if he only wanted to talk about everyday things, she thought. It gladdened her to hear his voice and see him smartened up and looking more like his old self than the last time they'd met, even though his smile lacked its old teasing confidence.

'You haven't given up on me, then?'

'Not altogether.' Arching her eyebrows, she smiled back.

'Right, I'd better get on.' Unsure of his ground, John pulled his cap well down and framed a final sentence. 'Anyway, I'm glad I saw you.'

'Me too. I mean it.' This wasn't quite true – the sight of him had raised mixed feelings: she was happy yet saddened by the distance that had grown between them.

He nodded, then, without more ado, he was off, pedalling hard past the bandstand, over the brow of the hill and quickly out of sight.

CHAPTER TWENTY-TWO

A few days later, on the Friday morning, Hazel received a letter.

'First-class stamp,' Gladys remarked with interest, handing it over before she left for work. 'At least it's not a bill.'

Hazel took the envelope, recognized the forward-sloping writing and slipped it in her pocket for later.

'More like a billet-doux, eh?' Gladys guessed.

Retreating into her room, Hazel waited until Gladys's footsteps had faded and the coast was clear before, with her heart in her mouth, she opened John's letter. There were two sheets of pale blue paper, with writing on both sides, this time signed at the end with 'Love from' followed by an initial – 'J'. Slowly she turned the pages over, holding them at arm's length, as if afraid the words would bite.

'Dear Hazel,' she read. 'I hope you don't mind me writing to you again.' Her heart leaped and she scanned down the first two pages, picking out odd words – 'cricket coaching', 'bike repairs', 'don't look back'.

Slow down, she told herself. *Read it properly. Take it all in.*

Dear Hazel, I hope you don't mind me writing to you again. I've been doing a lot of thinking since I saw you on the Common on Sunday and in the end I decided to write my thoughts in a letter. You can always throw it in the bin once you've read it. There'd be no hard feelings.

Hazel drew the paper closer to bring the words into focus. She felt that at this rate her pounding heart would burst with anticipation so she forced herself to take deep breaths before she carried on.

So anyway, here goes. You already know that I've been having a rough time of it lately, trying to cope with life after I lost Myra and the baby. Anyway, I've finally decided it's high time I pulled my socks up, starting with the cricket coaching, which you already know about. On top of that, I've set up in a small way doing bike repairs and tinkering with car engines off my own bat instead of working for Philip Baxter. I don't have premises to work from as yet – just my own backyard. If things go the way I hope, I should eventually save up enough money to rent somewhere proper.

Hazel stopped reading, able to tell from the erratic slope of the handwriting that John had made many stops and starts as he worked out what to put in and what to leave out. The result was an earnest and factual account that kept his feelings carefully to one side.

Hazel, if you're still reading this, what I'm trying to

tell you is that, yes, I did reach rock bottom for a while but now things are hopefully on the up. For a start, I've stopped looking for answers in the bottom of a beer glass. If you don't believe me, ask Dan. He'll tell you what a boring old codger I've turned into.

The truth is, I'm following Dad's example when Mum passed away. 'Son, don't look back,' he said whenever he found me moping in a corner. 'There's a lot in life still to look forward to if only you know where to find it.' I was a little lad at the time but I took it to heart. 'Look forward' – that's the key.

Mind you, it's taken me a while to remember it.

About the car – I handed it over to Reggie to cancel out my debts. That might sound like a funny thing to put in this letter, when I'm concentrating on the reasons why you should think better of me. But what it means is that Reggie promised to take good care of the old girl and he says I'm welcome to borrow it any time I like.

Coming to the last page, Hazel stopped again to draw breath. Behind the written words she imagined the look of concentration on John's face as he'd filled his fountain pen from the bottle of dark blue ink, the to and fro in his mind before he decided to sign off with love and then sealed the envelope.

The thing is, I can borrow the car this weekend if you would like to come out to Shawcross with me after all.

If not, I'll understand.

I'll sign off now. The rest of what I want to say wouldn't look right written down – it'll have to wait until we meet.

Let me know what you decide. I hope the answer is yes and that I'll see you at the weekend. Love from J.

Unable to stop herself from acting on impulse, Hazel wrote her answer in an impetuous rush. Yes. Yes, of course she would love to come to Shawcross. Saturday would be best because she'd already promised to have tea with her nana and Aunty Rose on the Sunday.

'Love from J.' Before signing her note, she read John's final phrase over and over. 'Love from H', she wrote back.

It was marvellous, truly magical how a lifetime's habit learned at her mother's knee, of keeping feelings in careful check, melted away in seconds and left Hazel's hopes free to soar. Fully admitting the love she felt for John was like breaking out of chains as prison doors opened and a blue sky beckoned, like basking in the golden brilliance of the sun.

John had signed his letter with love and she had done the same.

She didn't hesitate. Flinging on her coat, she took the note and ran downstairs onto the street. It was busy with early-morning traffic. A man driving a yellow van pulled up at the kerb and threw a bundle of newspapers tied with string towards the doorway of a newsagent's shop. A noisy gaggle of schoolchildren waited with their teacher at the bus stop; car horns hooted at a man driving a motor bike and sidecar the wrong way down a one-way street.

Wondering which would be quickest – to wait for a bus or to walk to Raglan Road – Hazel was surprised to see Norman push his way through the queue at the bus stop, without jacket or cap and with his face set in determined lines.

Immediately her stomach churned. 'Why aren't you at work?' she began as he drew near.

'Come quick,' he gasped. 'It's Sylvia.'

'Wait here.' In a split second Hazel had turned around and run back into the house for her bag. Norman waited for her at the bottom of the steps.

'That's right – baby's on its way,' he gabbled, taking hold of Hazel's bag and running ahead. 'I wanted to fetch you right away but Sylvia said no, it's too early. She's wrong, though. I've seen it half a dozen times with my mother. This is definitely it.'

Hearing only snatches of what he said, Hazel suppressed a groan. She followed as best she could, avoiding workmen digging up cobbles on Ghyll Road. For a moment she blamed Sylvia – it was typical of her devil-may-care nature to get her dates wrong. But then she remembered what Sylvia had suffered. And the fact that she was just seventeen and frightened out of her wits. Who in the world would be able to think clearly at a time like that?

'When did she start her labour?' she asked Norman, who had stopped at the bottom of Albion Lane.

He'd dropped the bag and was bent double to drag breath into his aching lungs, hands on knees, arms braced. 'A couple of hours ago, just as I was setting off for work. Thank heavens it happened when it did. Five minutes later and she'd have had no one at home to help her.'

'Two hours,' Hazel noted. She would save her other questions for Sylvia herself. 'Right, there's no need to panic. Let's go and see how she's getting on.'

They were five minutes away from Nelson Yard and, in spite of her soothing words, Hazel knew that every minute at this stage could be crucial. So they ran again along the flagged pavements, down the dark ginnel into the yard where Rose and Ethel hovered anxiously in their doorways.

'Is it action stations?' Ethel demanded.

'We know it is.' Rose supplied the answer. 'We saw Norman leave the house at a gallop, didn't we? And now Hazel's here.'

Ethel came down her steps and clutched Hazel's elbow. 'I tried to get into the house but she wouldn't let me. She's all by herself.'

Hazel patted her hand. 'Well, I'm here now. Aunty Rose, can you keep an eye on Aunty Ethel? We'll let you know as soon as there's any news.' She hurried on with Norman, up the worn steps to his and Sylvia's house, only to find the door locked on the inside.

'What did she go and do that for?' Hazel was alarmed. 'How are we going to get in if Sylvia's too far gone to reach the door?'

Norman shoved at the door with his shoulder. 'Sylvia, it's me!' he yelled. 'Open up.'

They lost precious seconds while they listened to heavy footsteps on the stairs.

'That doesn't sound like Sylvia.' Norman gave Hazel a baffled look.

They both gasped in astonishment when it was

371

Mabel who unbolted and opened the door.

'You'd better get a move on,' she told Hazel, glancing back up the stairs.

Hazel was so taken aback as she stepped over the threshold that she couldn't help firing a remark at Mabel. 'We thought it was Sylvia who had bolted the door on us. No one realized you were here.'

Unmoved, Mabel led the way up the stairs. 'I only had to see young Norman shoot out of the alley like a scalded cat to put two and two together,' she explained. 'I was on my doorstep, picking up my milk. "Ah," I says to myself, "I recognize that scared-rabbit look on a husband's face – I've seen it often enough." I was round here in two ticks, and sure enough, Sylvia's waters had broken.' She stopped and levelled her gaze on Hazel. 'You don't mind me lending a hand, do you?'

Not quite trusting the turnaround, Hazel was nevertheless grateful to Mabel for holding the fort. 'Let's just concentrate on Sylvia and the baby, shall we?' she said cautiously.

'Who's there? Mabel, who are you talking to?' As a fresh contraction took hold, Sylvia's high, plaintive voice became a prolonged scream.

Mabel stopped again on the landing. 'It was her – she asked me to bolt the door,' she muttered to Hazel, while Norman halted with his foot on the bottom step. 'I've never seen a woman in labour with her mind so set on keeping folk away.'

Hazel said nothing as she brushed past but again her stomach twisted itself in knots. Entering the bedroom she saw that Mabel had built a fire in the small fireplace. She'd brought hot water up from the kitchen and towels, presumably from her own house. As for Sylvia – she was propped up on extra pillows, lying on her back with her knees crooked. 'How long between contractions?' Hazel asked the old handywoman.

'Three or four minutes at most.'

Hazel glanced at her watch and nodded. She set down her bag and talked to Sylvia in a cheerful, teasing tone. 'What are you up to, catching us all off guard like this? We thought we had it all nicely planned, and now look.'

'Hazel, why are you here? Can't you see it's a false alarm?' Sylvia's feeble claim flew in the face of the evidence and she knew it. Hit by another bout of pain, she threw her head back and let out an agonized yell.

Hazel placed her cool hand on Sylvia's hot forehead. 'Let's turn you onto your side. That's right, I'll help you. Now, bring your top leg up towards your chest.'

To Hazel's surprise, Mabel made no comment about the switch of position but she observed every detail. 'You'll need a good supply of hot water,' she said in her steady way before calling downstairs for Norman to draw extra from the copper boiler next to the sink. 'Use the white enamel basin. Make it quick.'

'All right, Sylvia, I've taken a good look and as far as I can see, everything is as it should be.' Seeing that the cervix was well dilated and palpating the lower abdomen, Hazel was satisfied that the baby was presenting normally. It was time to ask Mabel to put towels in place while

373

she set out her instruments. 'Take deep, slow breaths,' she told Sylvia. 'Now, would you like me to give you an injection? It will ease the pain but it won't take it away completely.'

Sylvia groaned then nodded. She lay still, with her eyes fixed on Hazel's face as the needle went in.

'Deep breaths,' Hazel reminded her. Then, after a few moments, 'Believe it or not, Mabel and I have called a truce.'

'Aye, miracles do happen.' Mabel raised an eyebrow.

Aware that old rivalries didn't just vanish, Hazel put in a proviso. 'A truce for the time being, at any rate,' she added. 'She's staying to help me make sure that the baby arrives safely.'

Sylvia gave a slight nod then closed her eyes. 'Yes, let her take a good look. Then she'll see what all this has been about,' she murmured hopelessly.

Ignoring Mabel's questioning look, Hazel took her stethoscope and listened to the baby's heartbeat. 'Good,' she murmured then squeezed Sylvia's hand. She smiled at Norman who had just come into the room with the bowl of hot water. 'It could happen any moment now,' she told him as he placed the bowl at the foot of the bed then backed through the door.

'You hear that, Sylvia? I'm not going anywhere. I'll be right downstairs,' he said.

Keeping tight hold of Hazel's hand, Sylvia gave a desolate cry and turned her face to the wall.

There was a lull during which Norman retreated to the bottom of the stairs and Mabel wiped Sylvia's face with a cool flannel, saying

374

little but obviously thinking a lot. Then she sat down on the rickety chair by the door.

As Sylvia rested, Hazel turned to Mabel and broached the subject that had stayed in her mind since her last conversation with Jinny. 'Mum tells me that you're ready to wind down,' she began tentatively.

'That's right – I am,' came the unruffled response.

'Hmm. I'll believe that when I see it.' Hazel checked that her cord clamps and scissors were to hand. 'I didn't think you were the type to stay at home with your crocheting.'

'I'm not.' With a wry smile Mabel folded her arms and leaned against the back of the chair. 'But it's high time I stepped aside and left it to you younger ones.'

'So you've called it a day?'

'Times change,' Mabel admitted. 'Things aren't as simple and straightforward as they used to be. These days women come to me for lots of different reasons – ever since Marie Stopes and Stella Browne and their like started poking their noses in. Birth control, making abortions legal and above board – the pros and cons are beyond me and I don't mind admitting it.'

Hazel nodded to show that she understood. A few short months ago, fresh out of college, she would have rejoiced to hear this but as she went on monitoring Sylvia and listening to Mabel she couldn't help feeling a pang of regret that this decent woman was ready to admit defeat. 'You've helped a lot of folk in this neighbourhood,' she acknowledged. 'They'll be sorry to see you take a

375

back seat.'

'Like I say – times change.' Mabel stood up and tended to Sylvia who was groaning and twisting her head from side to side. 'Anyway, my mind's made up – I sent Ivy to you and I'll do the same with the next person who comes knocking on my door, and the one after that.'

Their sporadic conversation was interrupted by Norman creeping up the stairs for a bulletin on Sylvia's progress. He entered the room just as Sylvia went into another contraction and he stayed as Hazel and Mabel got to work.

'Don't just stand there,' Mabel told him bluntly as Hazel reminded Sylvia to take deep breaths. 'Since you're here, you'd better make yourself useful.'

'How?'

'Come and hold the poor girl's hand. Stay out of the way up there at the top end while we concentrate on what's happening down here.'

Between cries of pain, Sylvia caught sight of Norman. When he took her hand she didn't pull away. 'This is too much,' she cried. 'I can't bear it.'

'Yes, you can,' he insisted, stroking strands of wet hair from her forehead. 'I'm here now. I'm not going anywhere.'

'Hang onto him for all you're worth,' Mabel advised Sylvia as the contractions came rapidly one after another.

'Breathe, don't push,' Hazel instructed calmly. Then, as the dark crown of the baby's head appeared, she said, 'Now take quick, shallow breaths and push hard. That's perfect, Sylvia.

376

Keep on pushing.'

Clinging to Norman's hand, Sylvia threw her head back and gritted her teeth. Pain was her world now – it took her in its vice-like grip. 'I can't!' she cried. 'I can't do it – I can't!'

Her agony didn't faze him. He stood steady at the head of the bed. 'You can. You are.'

'Perfect,' Hazel said again as the baby's shoulders emerged. 'Don't push any more. Nice and easy does it. Wonderful, Sylvia – it's a little girl.'

Within seconds the cord was clamped and cut. Hazel lifted the baby by her ankles and listened to her take her first breath. She handed her to Mabel who swaddled her in a white towel then cleaned her face with a lint cloth. Mabel glanced in surprise at Hazel but said nothing. Tenderly she gave the baby to Sylvia.

Sylvia's face streamed with tears. Her whole body shook as she took her newborn daughter into her arms.

Norman bent over them both. Gently he folded back the towel that half covered the baby's face. She fixed her eyes on him, pushing a tiny hand free and flexing her fingers. Her eyes were dark with long lashes, her hair thick and black. Her smooth skin was darkest brown.

Sylvia sobbed and turned her face away.

Norman looked at the baby and took a broken, shuddering breath. He gave an almost imperceptible shake of his head. Then he stood up, looked straight at Hazel and backed away. Without saying a word, he turned and left the room.

Gently, Mabel took the infant from an inconsolable Sylvia and cradled her in her arms.

377

She looked down at her and sighed. 'Poor soul,' she murmured. 'Who's going to take care of you, you poor little mite?'

CHAPTER TWENTY-THREE

Norman fled from the house. He ran across the yard, ignoring anxious questions from Ethel and Rose, and vanished down the ginnel.

Rose was the first to react. She hurried ahead of Ethel up the steps into Sylvia's house, watched by Betty Hollings from her doorstep and by Ada from her vantage point at the window of number 6. 'It's us – Aunty Rose and your mum. Can we come up?' she called from the bottom of the stairs.

Sylvia sobbed as if her heart would break. 'Why not? Let them all come,' she cried bitterly.

Rose climbed the stairs and entered the bedroom ahead of Ethel. She took in the scene – Hazel still busily tending to an exhausted Sylvia and Mabel standing by the window with the baby in her arms.

Mabel beckoned Rose then handed the baby to her. 'A girl,' she murmured with a long, meaningful stare.

'Oh, my.' Rose's sigh filled the room.

The baby's fingers flexed again. Her long-lashed eyes stared out at a brand-new world.

'Oh, but she's a beauty,' Rose breathed, won over in an instant. 'Look, Sylvia – look.'

Sylvia swallowed her sobs and took her daughter in her arms, her eyes searching the infant's face, absorbing every detail.

Rose made room for Ethel at the bedside. 'A little beauty,' she said again.

Ethel crouched beside the bed. She offered her finger and the baby grasped it. Ethel smiled. 'Oh,' she sighed. 'Oh, Sylvia, love!'

'See,' Rose told her. 'No one blames you. No one at all.'

Sylvia's tears eased. She felt the warmth of her daughter's tiny body against her breast. Their gazes locked while everyone else in the crowded room blurred then faded away.

Mabel took Hazel to one side and gave her a quiet reminder. 'What about Norman – shouldn't someone go after him?'

Hazel nodded and made a decision. 'Me. I'll go.'

'Off you go then. I'll look after things here.'

'I know you will.' Without another word, Hazel left Mabel to make Sylvia comfortable and tidy up the room. She came out of the house and crossed the yard, emerging onto Raglan Road and wondering which direction to choose.

'Did you see which way Norman Bellamy went?' she asked a freckled, tow-haired lad delivering meat to number 17.

The boy shrugged. 'I don't know him from Adam,' was his careless reply.

'If you're looking for Norman, he went that-a-way.' Cycling down the hill on his way to the Friday fish market, Henry Pennington pointed over his shoulder. 'He didn't bother to say hello.

379

It looked like he had a lot on his plate.'

Hazel thanked Henry and sprinted up the street. The door to John's house was open so, without stopping to think, she ran up the steps and called his name. 'John – are you there?'

He appeared through the back door, dressed in overalls and wiping his hands on a rag. He took one look at her face. 'What's up? What's happened?'

'Sylvia's had her baby. It's obvious Norman's not the father. He's upset. I need to find him.'

John walked towards her and put a steadying hand on her arm. 'How can I help?'

'I'd get on quicker by bike than on foot. Have you got a spare one I could use?'

Nodding, John fetched one from the back yard. 'Try this for size. Don't worry – it's in good working order. Where are you heading off to?'

'To Hadley,' Hazel decided on the spur of the moment. 'Norman's mother lives over there. I don't suppose he's got anyone else to turn to.'

'Right you are.' John carried the bike down the front steps and saw Hazel on her way. 'Good luck,' he said as she set off.

'Thanks.' Suddenly remembering her note, Hazel stopped and fished it out of her pocket. 'Here,' she said, thrusting it at him.

John took the note with a questioning look.

'My answer is yes.' She smiled briefly and was off again, turning the corner onto Overcliffe Road and cycling for all she was worth.

Norman would be bound to know the short cut to Hadley across the Common, Hazel decided.

Then again, he might have decided it was quicker to take the tram out of town then switch to the number 65 bus to reach the neighbouring village.

What would she do in his shoes? she wondered. After all, Norman had just had the biggest shock of his life, completely out of the blue. The expression on his face as he'd run from the room had been that of a man who couldn't make sense of what he'd seen – confused, hurt, angry – all of these.

He won't use the bus in case he bumps into someone he knows, Hazel decided. He'll go by foot across the Common.

So she took the footpath, passing three mighty shire horses from the brewery, put out to graze on the rough grass, and a road sweeper wheeling his cart towards the bandstand.

Norman had a ten-minute start on Hazel, but borrowing the bike from John meant she should soon catch him up, even if he ran full tilt all the way to Hadley. Head down and pedalling hard against a strong wind, she set herself the task of overtaking him and bringing him back.

She'd cycled about a mile towards the moors and the jagged outline of Brimstone Rocks when at last she spotted him – a solitary figure on the narrow cinder track bordered to either side by banks of brown heather. She heard the loud crunch of his feet on the path and saw by the hunched set of his shoulders that it would be hard to convince him to slow down and listen.

'Go away, Hazel,' Norman muttered as she drew alongside.

She got off the bike to walk with him. 'No,

381

Norman, hear me out.'

'What for?' He strode on without looking at her. 'I've seen all I need to see. Heard all I want to hear.'

'It's a shock, I know.'

'No, you *don't* know!' he countered. 'I've been made a fool of – that's the start and finish of it.'

The path narrowed and Hazel had to walk behind him. 'Sylvia should have told you the truth. I expect she wishes she had.'

'No, she's not bothered. I'm just the poor sap who put the ring on her finger. I don't count for anything.' With an angry laugh he stopped and turned. 'How long have you known about this?'

Hazel flinched under his accusatory glare. 'Not long.'

He tossed his head back, his cheeks inflamed by the cold wind and the anger that bit into him. 'You did know, though. When did she tell you? Was it when she went for the abortion?'

'Yes. That's when the truth came out.'

'She swore you to secrecy, did she? Yes, that would be Sylvia's style.'

Hazel lay the bike down across the path and prevented him from walking on. 'Wait – you have to hear Sylvia's reasons before you wash your hands of her. That's why I came after you.'

He tried to push her aside but she held on to his arm. 'Let go of me,' he warned.

'Norman, listen. You care for Sylvia, I know you do. You wouldn't have married her otherwise.'

A deep frown was etched into his brow. 'I did care,' he admitted. 'Anyone could see I did. I told you before – I could never work out why I was the one she picked. I see it now, though.'

'No, I'm sure it wasn't because she hoped she could trick you. It's because, without even realizing it, she saw something in you – something decent and true that might draw out the same things in her. That's why.'

'Well, it didn't work, did it?' He jerked away from Hazel and walked on. 'There's not an honest bone in Sylvia's body.'

She ran again to keep up. 'But it still might work – if you would give her a chance and listen to what she has to say.'

'More lies,' he said bitterly, with only one thought in his head, which was to shake Hazel off and crawl back into the old family home to lick his wounds.

Without a last-ditch attempt, Hazel saw that she would lose the argument. 'All right, here are a couple of things you should know. The father of that poor baby is a man much older than Sylvia, who she admired but she hardly knew. She might not see it like this, but from where I'm standing, the man behaved badly. He took advantage of an innocent girl.'

The frown deepened and Norman drew a sharp breath.

'Do I need to name names?'

'No.' A wild look came into Norman's eyes as he stopped and turned suddenly to face the town they'd left behind. In the distance was row after row of terraced houses lining the steep hillsides. In the smoky, crowded valley bottom, a forest of mill chimneys churned out grey smoke. 'I've heard enough.'

383

'Wait!' As he set off at a run back towards the town, Hazel picked up her bike and followed. 'Are you going to talk to Sylvia?'

'No.' Again the reply fell like a hammer blow on Hazel's hopes. Anger propelled him, turning his face dark and blocking her out completely.

'You should,' she pleaded.

'Go away, Hazel.'

She felt the wind billow through her open coat and catch at her scarf, knocking her sideways off her bike. 'Shall I tell her I've seen you?' she called after him.

'Tell her what you damn well like,' he shouted over his shoulder. 'I mean it, Hazel – leave me alone.'

There was nothing left for Hazel to do except go back to Nelson Yard and report the latest events. She cycled there with a heavy heart that lightened a little when she found a house full of cheerful women rallying round Sylvia and the newborn baby girl.

Mabel was still there, stoking the bedroom fire and quietly straightening sheets. Rose brushed Sylvia's hair and praised her while Ethel rocked the baby to sleep.

'Have we got a name for her?' Ethel asked as she returned the infant to her mother.

'Not yet.' Only just coming to terms with the reality of motherhood, Sylvia noticed Hazel observing the scene from the doorway and was caught between eagerness and fear. 'Did you find him?'

Hazel nodded.

'How was he? What did he say?'

It was best not to hide the truth, Hazel decided. There'd already been too many secrets. 'He was upset. It'll take him a little while to come to terms with things.'

Sylvia's lip trembled and tears welled up. 'Does he hate me?'

'No, I'm sure he doesn't. He hates what's happened, that's all. I gave him a few of the facts.'

'Oh, Hazel, you didn't!' Instinctively clutching the sleeping baby closer to her chest, Sylvia turned to Rose and Ethel. 'What good will that do?' she wailed. 'Tell Hazel she had no right.'

'Hazel was only trying to help,' Rose insisted calmly. She too was bursting with questions but she knew she must wait until the time was right. 'We all are. That's why we're here.'

Sylvia fought back her tears and went on quizzing Hazel. 'Did you tell Norman who the father is?'

Hazel closed her eyes and gave a small sigh. 'I didn't have to. I'm pretty sure he'd already put two and two together.'

'It's that band leader you were always going on about, isn't it?' Ethel too had worked this out for herself and she didn't beat about the bush. 'He's the father. Does he have any idea about the baby?'

Sylvia shook her head. 'No. And I don't want him to.'

'She's probably right,' Rose cut in. 'What good would it do to hold him to account? He'd only deny it. And we can do without more trouble.'

'So that's it – he just walks away,' Ethel

muttered. She left the room, went downstairs and could be heard banging pots and pans around in the stone sink.

Hazel took her place by the side of the bed and tried to reassure Sylvia. 'I do think Norman will come round. Just give him time.'

'Not after the way I've treated him, he won't.' For the first time Sylvia saw beyond her own fears. 'Was he very upset? No, don't say anything – I already know the answer. Did he say where he was going?'

'When I found him he was halfway to Hadley, to his mother's house, I expect. But then, after we'd talked for a while, he backtracked. I tried to follow him but I lost sight of him getting onto a tram on Overcliffe Road.'

'That means he could be anywhere by now.' Mabel reached for her coat hanging on the door peg. 'Anyhow, I'll leave you to it,' she decided with one last fond look at the baby and a smile for Sylvia.

Hazel followed her down the stairs. 'Ta,' she said quietly. 'I mean it – thank you very much.'

Mabel nodded. 'I'm glad I could do my bit. But this is exactly what I was talking about – nothing's straightforward these days.'

'You're right, it isn't.'

'And that's why I'm ready to bow out.' Unable to resist one last piece of timely advice, Mabel turned in the doorway. 'I'd keep on looking for that young man if I was you,' she told Hazel.

'You mean Norman?'

'Yes. He's a loose cannon and there's no telling what he'll do – he could get into a fight, or worse.'

Hazel was reluctant to believe it. 'No, not Norman – not once he's had time to calm down.'

'It's up to you,' Mabel said, solid and phlegmatic as ever as she departed. 'But I'd go after him if I were you. You know what they say – better safe than sorry.'

The day rolled on and Hazel was caught up in showing Sylvia the best way to put the baby to the breast. She let Ethel demonstrate how to put on a nappy without sticking the safety pin into baby's tender flesh and welcomed Jinny into the fold when she got back from the market and came straight away to Nelson Yard to find out the state of play. It was six o'clock – a dull, wind-swept evening that seemed to put paid to hopes that spring was round the corner.

'All's quiet on the Western Front, I see,' Jinny murmured as she ventured into the kitchen.

'Yes, but you heard about the father?' Hazel whispered.

'I did. News like that travels fast. Never mind, we'll just have to make the best of it.' Jinny squeezed Hazel's hand warmly then went upstairs. 'Oh, Sylvia, love – are you going to let your aunty have a hold?' she asked as she crossed the room with arms outstretched.

Staying downstairs, Hazel listened to the gentle flow of conversation overhead and was thinking again about Mabel's warning when she looked out of the window and saw John crossing the yard. She rushed out to meet him.

'How are things?' he asked.

She quickly explained that Earl Ray was the

387

father of Sylvia's baby. 'I haven't forgotten about the bike,' she added. 'I was about to wheel it back up.'

'Never mind about that.' He held up a small bunch of keys. 'I borrowed the car from Reggie, just in case.'

'In case what?'

'In case you didn't manage to track Norman down. I thought we could carry on looking for him together.'

'In the car?' She jumped at the chance, not even going back into the house to fetch her coat or explain to the others. 'Norman's not normally a hothead, but Mabel is worried he'll rush head-long into trouble if we don't find him.'

'She might be right.' Running up Raglan Road, they reached the parked Ford and jumped in. 'I had a word with Dan earlier. He said he bumped into Norman on Canal Road. Norman had been hammering on your landlady's door, asking for Earl Ray.'

'Mabel was right, then – Norman is looking for trouble.'

'She sent him away with a flea in his ear. But Norman found out from Dan that Earl Ray is back in town and that he's due to play at the jazz club tonight.'

'Is that where we should be heading?'

John looked at his watch. 'It's too early. The club doesn't open until eight.'

For a while they sat in silence, held up by heavy traffic and without any firm idea of what they should do next.

'I read your note.' As they waited at a crossroads,

John nudged the talk in a new direction. 'Tomorrow is fine by me.'

'That's good, then.'

'I mean what I said – I really have turned over a new leaf,' he assured her, tapping his finger on the wheel.

'You're not the only one.' Hazel relived in a rush the feeling she'd had of opening up the prison door of shyness and reticence, of stepping out into the sunshine and letting her feelings grow and blossom. 'I've seen what happens when a person tries to hide from the truth. From now on I intend to be open and above board.'

'Uh-oh, should I be worried?' he asked with mock alarm. The traffic eased forward and they crawled the length of Calvert's mill, empty now that the workers had clocked off, with the furnaces to drive the engines dying down in the back courtyard and the restless, relentless looms lying silent.

'Let's see, shall we?' Hazel took a deep breath then turned in her seat to gaze directly at him. 'Keep your eyes on the road, don't look at me. Here goes. I was thrilled when I got your letter. I'd been hoping to hear from you for I don't know how long.' There – she'd said it.

'Blimey.' He glanced sideways then straight ahead again. 'What else?'

'That's enough for a start. Now it's your turn.'

'Right. I wrote the darned thing then screwed it up and chucked it in the bin I don't know how many times. When I finally posted it, it felt worse than facing a firing squad – in case you turned me down. How's that?'

'Not bad.' Hazel gave a quick nod. 'Now me

389

again. Once I recognized your writing, I could hardly open the envelope, my hands were shaking so much.'

'"About blooming time" – that's what you thought.' He glanced again with the special smile playing on his lips.

'Yes, but now I realize that any earlier would have been too soon – for both of us.'

'Yes. Knowing that and deciding to stand back nearly killed me,' he admitted. 'Let's face it – you're a catch, Hazel. One look at you and any man in his right mind would want to make a move – Reggie for a start, and any one of those hospital doctors who hang around at the jazz club. I nearly drove myself mad thinking about it.'

Flattered, Hazel raised a rueful smile. 'We've both learned a lot about ourselves lately and now I see the timing is just right.' She felt strangely calm and confident.

With both hands on the wheel and resisting the impulse to pull over and embrace her, he drove on. 'Tomorrow it is, then.'

'Yes, but for now we have to concentrate on finding Norman. Let's turn onto Canal Road. I suppose there's a chance he's still hanging around there, waiting for Earl Ray to show up.'

CHAPTER TWENTY-FOUR

There was no sign of Norman outside Hazel's lodgings. She and John waited almost an hour, sitting inside the car with the engine turned off. Dusk thickened and the gas street lights were turned on. A misty rain began to fall.

'I know the band doesn't start playing until eight, but do you think they'll get there early to re-hearse?' Hazel broke a silence that had re-focused her mind on the problem to hand. Her mouth felt dry at the prospect of what Norman might say and do when he finally came face to face with Earl Ray.

'Yes, that's a thought.' John started the engine and drew away from the kerb. He drove the short distance into town and found a parking spot outside the library. 'You stay here if you like,' he offered. 'I can go and take a look.'

'No, I'll come with you,' she decided.

They got out of the car and walked together past the shiny plate-glass window of Merton and Groves, threading through the crowd of men milling around the entrance to the pub then pausing at the top of the cellar steps.

'I can hear a saxophone playing.' Hazel had been right – the band had arrived early and were running through parts of their repertoire.

Spotting someone he knew, John hailed him. 'Jack, you haven't seen Norman Bellamy, by any chance?'

'Sorry, pal, I haven't.' The man flicked the glowing butt of his cigarette into the gutter then turned away.

'My missis heard via Mabel Jackson that they've invented a new party game called Pin the Tail on the Real Father,' someone else quipped.

John picked up the innuendo. 'Very funny,' he muttered, leaving the gang to make smutty remarks about local lasses led astray by Hollywood glamour. 'It looks like we've beaten Norman to it,' he reported back to Hazel.

'Thank goodness.' Peering down the steps, Hazel caught sight of two women coming out of the ladies' cloakroom – it was Gladys and Mary Fenning.

'Wait here in case he turns up,' she told John hurriedly. 'Let me go and have a word with Gladys.'

She flew downstairs and accosted her cousin.

'Look who's here to watch the rehearsal!' Gladys was gleeful when she saw Hazel. 'You couldn't resist getting in on the act, after all.'

'No, honestly – I'm not here for that.'

Gladys, who had obviously not picked up the Raglan Road gossip about Sylvia's baby, would have none of it and made a beeline for the room where the band was tuning up. 'Oh, is that a fact? Come off it, Hazel, who are you trying to fool?'

Mary raised her eyebrows then sashayed ahead with Gladys, leaving Hazel no option but to follow.

The room was empty except for the four musicians onstage and two barmen with trim moustaches and slicked-back hair wiping down tables.

392

Everything looked tawdry under the glare of overhead electric lights. Instrument cases were piled carelessly against the stage, coats lay thrown over tables and the previous night's dirty glasses still cluttered the bar.

'Here comes Earl.' Gladys noticed the band leader jump down from the stage and make his way towards them, smiling broadly. 'Be nice,' she warned Hazel, giving her a jab with her elbow. 'I wangled special permission to come in early, so I don't want you putting a spanner in the works.'

'He-llo lovely ladies!' Earl swung his arms around Gladys's and Mary's waists and drew them close. 'Glad y'all could make it.'

Instinctively Hazel took a step back, out of the orbit of the man's brash confidence. He was dapper as ever – sporting a yellow checked waistcoat beneath a dark, double-breasted jacket, a glint of gold around his wrist, two-tone brogues and a diamond tie-pin as a finishing touch.

'Barman, give the gals a drink – feel free to choose, ladies.'

As the others ordered their drinks at the bar, Hazel checked all around the room to make sure that Norman hadn't slipped in unnoticed No – thank heavens, there was no sign. Now she needed to get back to John, but Earl wasn't satisfied with two pretty admirers – he wanted three.

'Hey, missy – hold it right there,' he drawled when he saw her ready to depart. 'Why not have a cocktail with a cherry on a stick? Any flavour, any colour – it's on the house.'

'No, ta.' Aware that a slow trickle of customers had started to take their seats and that Sonny

393

Dubec was calling Earl back onstage, Hazel made her excuses. 'Sorry, I'm in a rush. I've got a friend waiting for me upstairs.'

'Rightio, Hazel, see you later.' Gladys covered up the awkward moment with a quick, chirpy dismissal.

Hazel turned away, noticing Dan and Reggie among the early birds. They called loudly for her to join them. Again she refused and signalled her answer by pointing to the exit. 'John's waiting for me.'

Dan nipped across to intercept her, smartly dressed in his weekend tweed jacket and twill trousers. 'Hello, Hazel. I see you got all dolled up for your night out.'

Suddenly aware of her creased and crumpled work clothes, she frowned dismissively. 'Sorry, Dan – I really have to go.'

However, she'd only got as far as the bottom step when there was a disturbance up above. She could hear shouting and scuffling, and then a dishevelled figure pushed free of the crush. Flailing his arms and thrusting people aside, Norman stumbled down the stairs towards her. John was close behind.

Hazel didn't budge. She grabbed hold of the banister and braced her other arm against the wall, determined to stop Norman. But nothing would halt his progress. Head down, he barged into her and sent her tumbling backwards. Then he stepped right over her and ran on.

John helped her to her feet. 'Are you all right? I tried to stop him but he wouldn't listen.'

As she stood up, Hazel saw a trickle of blood

from a cut at the corner of his mouth. 'I'm fine. What happened to you?'

'He socked me in the jaw.'

She grimaced. 'Come on – we'd better go after him before he does any more damage.'

Inside the room, there was further confusion. As Dan tried to waylay Norman then tussled with him, a table crashed to the ground and the band broke off from the warm-up to their first number. Before either Hazel or John had the chance to step in, Norman had vaulted onto the stage and launched himself at Earl Ray.

'For heaven's sake – somebody do something!' Gladys's strident voice rose above the buzz of disbelieving voices.

A few men in the audience spat on the palms of their hands, rolled up their sleeves and climbed onstage to separate Norman from Earl, who had staggered back but now regained his footing and struck a boxer's pose, fists up to protect his face. In a split second, Dubec and the two other musicians had put down their instruments and moved forward with lithe, expert punches intended to knock the local men clean off their feet. Soon it was mayhem – Norman threw himself at Ray a second time, dodging under his raised fists and grappling with him while John joined the mêlée and tried to pull Norman off. Hazel watched with a racing heart.

A call went up. 'Fetch the police!'

Someone reached for the telephone behind the bar.

Locked in an unbreakable hold, Earl Ray and Norman fell to the floor. The nearby Dubec

395

seized the chance to land a hefty kick in the small of Norman's back. John toppled the offending clarinettist from the stage. Blood flowed from noses, cheeks were grazed, women screamed.

Gladys ran to Hazel's side. 'What on earth's happening? Has Norman lost his mind?' Before Hazel could reply, they were forced apart as another member of the band rolled off the stage, thudded to the floor and a barman rushed to dust him down.

'That's right – call the cops. This guy is nuts.' Back on his feet, Ray stood back and took another swipe at Norman but failed to land the punch. As the fight spread out of control, there was the sound of glasses breaking and more tables being knocked over. Again John did his best to take hold of Norman, but this left Norman exposed to a volley of punches from an enraged Earl Ray. They landed in his chest and stomach, knocking the wind out of him and bending him double.

'That's enough – he's half your size.' Angered in turn, John thrust himself between Ray and Norman. He used his weight and strength to shove Ray off the stage into a narrow corridor leading to a dressing-room and a WC.

'I get it – the kid needs a bodyguard,' Ray sneered, his brow wet with sweat and breathing heavily. He lunged towards John, who fell back against the toilet door. It flew open and John crashed down onto the wooden seat. He saw Ray slam the door shut and heard him jam it with a heavy luggage trunk that had partly blocked the corridor. Choking at the stench inside the airless cubicle, John held his breath, raised his foot and kicked at the door.

Outside, Norman caught up with Ray and they scrapped again.

'Jesus,' the band leader snarled between punches. 'What in God's name did I do?'

The question drove Norman into a fresh frenzy. He smashed his knuckles into Ray's jaw then drew back his fist and went in again, making Ray protect his face with his hands and stagger back, stumbling over lengths of timber propped against the wall, past the dressing-room door and out of an Emergency Exit into the night.

The stack of wood fell like skittles across Norman's path. He clambered over them in pursuit of Ray, while, behind him, John broke out of the WC. At the same moment, Hazel, who had caught glimpses of what was happening and had climbed onto the stage, appeared at the end of the corridor.

'Norman, wait!' she pleaded.

It was no good – he kicked the timber out of the way and disappeared through the exit.

'The idiot is going to get himself killed.' Conscious of the difference between the two opponents – Earl Ray tall and muscular, Norman slight and still boyish – John set off again, closely followed by Hazel.

It took a while for their eyes to adjust as they came out into the small, unlit area at the back of the club. The yard was roughly thirty feet square, with high brick walls and a gate leading out onto a cinder track and beyond that to the unfenced railway line out of town. Slowly John and Hazel made out the figure of Earl Ray standing astride a senseless Norman. He wielded a bottle taken from a crate by the door and had one foot on his chest. Ray glanced up, spotted John and Hazel then, with a flick of his wrist, he smashed the bottle against the wall. The glass shattered and green shards rained down.

In the time that it took Ray to raise the weapon over his head, John sprinted across the yard and grabbed his wrist. They wrestled. John tightened his grip until Ray was forced to let the broken bottle drop.

Hazel ran to Norman, who lay on his back in a filthy puddle. His eyes were closed, his face covered in small cuts from the broken glass and blood streamed from his nose. As she bent to loosen his collar and raise his head, Earl Ray broke loose. He took hold of Hazel by the wrist and swung her violently round so that she came between him and John. Then he snaked his arm around her waist.

'Let go of her.' John's jaw was clenched, his words forced out from deep in his throat.

'Stay back, John. I'm all right,' she gasped.

'Yeah, stay back, John.' A second bottle rolled towards Ray. Without letting go of Hazel, he lunged at it, grabbed it and knocked it sharply against the wall.

Once more Hazel heard the chilling sound of glass smashing and saw John, suddenly wary, crouch and take a step back.

'Get the kid out of my sight,' Ray growled, kicking at Norman with the toe of his shoe. 'She stays here with me until you do.'

Out of the corner of her eye, Hazel saw the

jagged glass inches from her face. John raised both hands in surrender.

'I have no idea what this is about,' Ray insisted. 'But if you know what's good for the kid, you'll get him out of here.'

Every inch of Ray's body was tense. Hazel felt the muscles in his forearm tighten around her waist.

'All right, but you have to let her go.' John ignored the shouts from inside the building and edged towards Norman.

'When I'm good and ready.' Ray watched John's every move as he slid both hands under Norman's armpits and lugged him towards the door.

Hazel endured long seconds in Ray's grasp – time seemed to stretch, sounds were magnified so that she noticed the slow drip of water from a broken down-pipe and the scrape of Norman's shoes along the stone cobbles as John dragged him into the building.

'Don't try to put up a fight,' Ray warned, gripping her tight and making sure she could see that he still held the bottle. 'We don't want to spoil that sweet face.'

Framed in the doorway, John propped Norman against the wall. Norman's head lolled forward, his eyes stayed closed. Crouching at his side, John looked up at Ray through narrowed eyes. 'What now?'

Warily Ray edged Hazel forward to take a closer look at Norman. 'Go back in and fetch a couple of guys to haul him out of here.'

In an attempt to calm everyone's nerves, John raised his hands again and kept his eyes fixed on

Ray's face. 'I'll do it. Just let go of Hazel.'

'No, siree. She stays here with me.'

'Go – quickly!' Hazel whispered, trembling from head to toe as she saw Norman's body twitch and his eyelids flicker open.

'You heard what the lady said.' Ray backed her away again towards the gate.

'All right. All right.' John saw that he had no choice. He stepped away from Norman and started to edge backwards down the corridor.

But then everything switched from slow to fast and furious as Dan and Reggie broke away from the fight onstage and burst into the corridor. They charged past the broken toilet door, kicking the trunk and fallen timber to one side until their way was blocked by John. They saw Norman raise his head and groan then dimly made out Earl Ray backing towards the gate with Hazel.

'What the...!' Reggie swept John aside and leaped over Norman, out into the yard, with Dan close behind.

John recovered quickly. He threw himself at Dan and felled him. They lay sprawled across Norman as yet more men piled into the corridor, shouting and picking up pieces of wood to use as clubs.

Out in the yard, Ray kept hold of Hazel and waved the bottle at Reggie. 'Not another step,' he warned.

Reggie didn't notice the weapon. He lunged at the band leader who sidestepped then dragged Hazel through the gate, smashing it shut in Reggie's face.

Hazel pulled free, stumbled, then gasped in pain

as she twisted her right ankle. While Earl Ray heaved a metal dustbin across the gateway to stop Reggie following them Hazel tried to make her escape but found that her ankle wouldn't hold her weight. The next thing she knew, Ray had caught up with her and shoved her sideways onto the banking that bordered the railway tracks.

Back in the yard, there was a surge of men yelling, wrestling and throwing punches. Dan crawled out from under them and turned to help Norman, whose eyes were now fully open. Meanwhile, John picked himself up and ran for the gate, only to find it jammed shut. He looked up at the high brick wall then called Reggie.

'Give me a leg up,' he demanded.

The sturdy cricketer formed a stirrup with his hands then braced himself to take John's weight. In one smooth motion, John stepped up and placed his hands on top of the wall. He heaved himself up, sat astride the wall then positioned himself to jump down onto the cinder track. He saw Hazel run then stumble and watched Ray drag her to her feet and deliberately push her up the banking onto the gleaming steel rails.

'What in God's name is he doing?' John hissed as he realized that Ray was taking out his anger on Hazel. He was down on the ground in a flash and sprinting towards them, seeing the glare of lights from the railway station 200 yards down the track and the soaring wrought-iron and glass canopy that housed a goods engine with clouds of steam and smoke belching from its funnel. His gut churned at the shrill sound of a whistle blowing and of brakes easing as the wheels began

401

to turn and the train pulled out of the station.

'Get off the tracks!' John yelled, waving his arms above his head.

Neither Hazel nor Ray heard him. The chugging engine gradually picked up speed. At the last minute Ray saw that it was in motion and panicked. He made a frantic attempt to drag Hazel clear but overbalanced, lost his grip and fell backwards down the bank of loose gravel.

Mesmerized by the metal beast and by the lightning speed of events, Hazel hesitated. Should she escape across the track or risk a retreat, back into Earl Ray's clutches?

The smoking juggernaut rolled towards her over the wooden sleepers, eating up the space between them. The roar of the furnace that fed the boiler filled her ears.

John sprinted towards the oncoming engine. He caught hold of Hazel around the waist with both hands and lifted her clear of the tracks. They rolled together down the banking and lay with eyes shut tight as the train thundered by.

CHAPTER TWENTY-FIVE

For as long as she lived, Hazel would never forget the ominous swaying of the goods wagons or the repetitive shunt and click of wheels turning on steel rails. The picture of that train rolling towards her would stay with her and wake her from restless sleep for years to come.

The goods wagons rattled on down the track and John helped her to her feet. Earl Ray stood ten yards away, coming to his senses at last and brushing dirt from his jacket.

John led Hazel towards the yard where the fight had subsided and recently arrived police officers were putting an end to the noisy brawl. She limped heavily. 'Take your time,' he said. 'There's no rush.'

They reached the gate just as Ray shoved the dustbin to one side. 'That crazy kid,' he mumbled. 'The cops should arrest him and throw away the key.'

Hazel confronted the smug cause of Sylvia's woes. 'You nasty, heartless so-and-so...!' Speechless with rage, her words ended in furious sobs.

John felt her tremble and saw the angry tears in her eyes. He held her hand tight.

Ray shrugged his shoulders then gestured for her to go ahead into the yard. 'Ladies first.' There was no gallantry in it – it was simply a challenge to John as their gazes locked in mutual hatred and Hazel, overwhelmed, limped through the gate.

Inside the yard, two constables and a sergeant were busy easing the rival gangs apart. Their torch beams raked across faces that were bruised and cut and their boots crunched over broken glass. In the doorway where Norman was slumped against the wall, Dan was trying to explain events to David Bell who had arrived amidst the chaos.

'Where did he get these cuts?' David asked as Hazel and John made their way across the yard.

'Search me. I wasn't here when it happened,'

403

Dan said. 'All I know is there was a fight that got out of hand.'

Reggie squeezed past. 'That's right. No one knows who started it,' he said in slow, deliberate tones.

Dan caught on and spoke loud enough for the nearest policeman to overhear. 'It was over in a flash. I don't suppose we'll ever get to the bottom of it.'

'Luckily, the cuts are superficial.' David gave his verdict then noticed Hazel limping towards him with John supporting her. He went quickly to meet them. 'Norman's injuries are minor,' he reassured her. 'What happened to you?'

'It's a sprain. I'm all right. When did you get here?'

Her answer was in tune with Dan and Reggie's desire to sweep things under the carpet, so for the time being David squashed down his own curiosity. 'Five minutes ago. I was looking forward to a nice relaxing evening. Then I walked slap-bang into the middle of this.'

'Nice and easy, lads.' Two of the police officers herded men in dribs and drabs back into the building. The sergeant asked David if Norman could be moved out of the way.

'Gently does it,' David advised as Dan helped Norman to his feet and Earl Ray strutted by.

Ray couldn't resist jabbing his adversary in the chest and glaring at him. 'Hey, kid – how does a coupla nights in a police cell sound to you?'

Still dazed, Norman swore then thrust Ray backwards and clenched his fists.

Quick off the mark as ever, John stepped between them. 'If anyone's going to spend the night in custody, I wouldn't bank on it being Norman – not after what I witnessed out there by the track.'

'You ain't witnessed nothing except a guy defending himself from a crazy kid and a gal who puts herself in the wrong place at the wrong time,' Ray drawled, all wide-eyed innocence. 'That's how the judge will see it.'

Taken aback, John allowed the smooth-talking band leader to swagger on down the corridor.

David spoke quietly to Hazel. 'Are you going to tell me what happened out there? How did you hurt your ankle?'

'I fell over.'

The guarded reply made him suspicious. 'He pushed you?'

'Yes.' The sight of Earl Ray's retreating figure made her furious, and yet...

David narrowed his eyes. 'Then John's right – they should arrest him.'

'Ray threatened her with a broken bottle,' John put in. 'I'll stand up in court and swear to it.'

'No, John. I'm not sure that's the best thing.' Yes, Hazel longed for Earl Ray to be punished, but not if it involved breaking her word to Sylvia.

'Did Norman start the whole thing? Is that the problem?' David wondered.

'Partly. But there's more to it than that. It's to do with me being a midwife.'

Her faltering answer persuaded David to leave John and Dan to look after Norman and guide her to a quiet corner of the yard. 'Come on, Hazel – spit it out.'

She breathed deeply then spoke. 'This is between you and me. I attended a birth earlier today. It's the situation I told you about. The baby's mother isn't married to the father, and though I know his name, I've made a promise to the mother not to force him to face up to what he's done. As a matter of fact, she won't even let me tell him about the baby.' The bald facts led her towards a clearer view of the muddle surrounding Sylvia's pregnancy and she was grateful to David for asking the right questions. 'That puts me in a fix with–'

'No, don't bring names into it. Remember, it's best that I don't know.' He pressed his thumb and forefinger to his forehead, thought for a while then said firmly and deliberately, 'You must keep your promise.'

'And let the father get away scot-free?'

'If that's the outcome, yes. The mother's wishes are the important thing here.'

Frowning deeply, Hazel stared down the dimly lit corridor to see Earl Ray at the far end straightening his tie while he talked to the departing sergeant. Dan and John were steadying Norman and leading him slowly towards them. She held her breath in case Norman launched another attack.

David followed the direction of her gaze. 'Remind me – there's a young husband in the case?'

'Correct.' She nodded then relaxed as Dan steered Norman into the empty dressing-room and John rejoined them.

'The truth is out and now the question is – will the husband forgive his wife?' David sighed as he

406

tilted his head back and gazed up at the dark sky. 'There, Hazel – I'm sure they didn't teach you the answer to that in your otherwise excellent midwifery course.'

Within minutes everything was back to normal. There were no arrests, the bar staff put upturned tables and chairs back in place, the band returned to the stage and picked up their instruments. The opening notes of 'Georgia on My Mind' brought couples back onto the dance floor.

'Come on, Norman, let's get you home.' John steered him up the stairs out of the club and onto the street.

Gladys insisted on helping Hazel up the steps. 'Will someone please tell me what's going on?' she demanded.

'Sylvia has had the baby.' Hazel hobbled painfully to keep up with John and Norman as they headed for the car. She sank thankfully into a back seat while John settled Norman beside him in the front.

'You don't say!' In a flash, Gladys had joined them in the car. 'What is it – boy or girl?'

'Girl.' Hazel held onto the door strap as John pulled quickly away from the kerb.

'A little girl! Congratulations, Norman...' Met by a wall of silence, Gladys's voice faded and she cast a worried look at Hazel.

'I'll explain later,' Hazel muttered.

For once, Gladys bit her lip and looked out of the window as the car sped along Canal Road. In the front passenger seat, Norman ignored the blood that continued to trickle from the cuts on his face. He waited until John pulled up at the turning onto Ghyll Road then he fumbled to open the door and make his escape.

'No, you don't.' John slammed his foot on the accelerator and took the corner with a squeal of tyres. 'Sit tight, Norman, we're nearly there.'

'At least come in and see them.' Hazel leaned forward to put a restraining hand on his shoulder.

He flinched but said nothing. As they arrived at Raglan Road, he turned his head with a questioning look.

'Sylvia will want to know that you're all right,' Hazel murmured. 'You don't need to stay long – just come in and see her.'

John parked the car by the ginnel. 'Gladys, why don't we wait here and give Norman a few minutes alone with Sylvia?'

'Yes, and I'll see to the baby,' Hazel agreed. She got out of the car and opened Norman's door, afraid that any second he would turn tail and run. 'My ankle's swollen up something rotten – do you mind if I lean on you?'

He too got out and together they made their way down the ginnel into the yard, where lights were still on in many of the houses. Rose and Ada were at their window, Cyril stood on his doorstep, cigarette in hand. They watched as Hazel and Norman made their way slowly across the yard.

'Ready?' she asked.

The corner of his mouth twitched and he hesitated. Still he said nothing.

Hazel took a handkerchief from her pocket to dab away the blood. 'Here, let me clean you up a

408

bit. Just see her, talk to her,' she urged.

He nodded slowly and let her walk up the steps into the front kitchen.

'Sylvia – Norman's here,' Hazel called up the stairs.

After a few anxious moments, Ethel came onto the landing carrying the baby, followed by Jinny.

'Is she asleep?' Hazel asked.

Jinny shook her head. 'No, she's wide awake. She'd like you to come up with Norman.'

Ethel carried the baby down the stairs with Jinny close behind, then paused just long enough to hand the baby over to Hazel. 'Take her in with you,' she whispered as she and Jinny went down into the kitchen.

So Hazel accepted the baby and led Norman up to the bedroom. She felt the warm softness of the sleeping infant and breathed in the sweet, newborn smell of her skin. Behind her on the landing, Norman glanced at the baby's face just long enough to take in her features then quickly turned his head away.

'Norman?' Sylvia's shaky voice reached them from inside the room.

He breathed in quickly and went ahead of Hazel.

Sylvia sat up in bed, her hands resting on the turned-back sheet, Rose's cream-coloured shawl around her shoulders, her hair and eyes very dark. She saw Norman and gave a startled cry. 'Your face!'

'It's nothing.' He stared down at his feet, up at the ceiling – anywhere but at her.

'This is all my fault. I should never have lied to

409

you. I was a stupid girl trying to make everything all right.' Words caught in her throat and came out strangled and wrong.

Norman took a step towards the bed. Hazel stayed in the doorway with the baby.

'I knew the minute I saw her who the father was.' His voice was fierce, his knuckles white as he formed his hands into fists. 'We all did.'

Sylvia turned to Hazel in mute, trembling appeal.

'I kept my word,' Hazel promised. 'Earl Ray didn't hear about it – not from me, anyway.'

Her words brought a shudder of relief and she rested her pleading gaze on Norman. 'Good. He mustn't. It was horrible. I can't bear ever to see him again.'

Another step brought Norman to her bedside. He knelt beside her and spoke gently. 'I'm sorry I ran away. It was the shock.'

She stared at him with trembling lips then took his hand. 'You're not the one who should be sorry. It's me. I am – I'm so, so sorry.'

'No, there's no need.' Slowly and gently, with his eyes fixed on Sylvia's face, he raised her hand to his lips.

She gave a sob. 'Can you ... will you...?' The plea for forgiveness lay half formed on her lips.

'I do and I will,' he said as he sat on the bed and drew her to him. 'Bring me the baby, Hazel. Let's have a proper look.'

Next day, Hazel's swollen ankle put paid to any thoughts of walking out to Dale Head Farm. Instead, she and John stayed in the car as they

410

revisited his favourite haunts – the stretch of river where he'd fished for trout as a boy, the larch copse where he and Fred had camped out under the stars.

'By the way, tell Norman and Sylvia not to worry about bumping into Earl Ray,' he said over a drink in the Red Lion. 'I doubt that our American friend will be back in our neck of the woods any time soon.'

Hazel bridled at the mention of the name.

'Reggie made sure of it.' Deliberately mysterious, John paused to take a sip of beer.

'How? Don't keep me in suspense,' she pleaded.

'Let's put it this way. Reggie happens to be a good pal of George Lockwood, the wool merchant who owns half of the buildings in the town centre, including the one where the jazz club is held. Once Reggie learned the facts about Earl Ray and the baby, he went early this morning to drop a word in Mr Lockwood's ear about the fight last night, making sure to lay the blame for the damage fair and square at Earl Ray's door and building up his reputation as a troublemaker – without going into details, of course.'

Hazel's eyes opened wide and she gave a short laugh. 'Oh dear – Miss Bennett will be disappointed to lose her lodger. So will Gladys. No – I take that back. Gladys is gunning for Ray now, just like the rest of us.' The Drummonds and the Prices – in fact, all the residents of Raglan Road and Nelson Yard – had joined forces in a chorus of condemnation.

'That's how it is if you have friends in high places. Mr Lockwood took Reggie's word for it.

411

From now on, Earl Ray's name will be mud.'

'Quite right and good riddance.' Hazel was glad that, despite the damage done to Sylvia, the band leader had in part got his comeuppance.

John wasn't so sure. 'You and I both know he got off lightly. He didn't get what he deserved.'

'He didn't,' she agreed. Hazel forced to one side the memory of Sylvia's haunted, fugitive face when she and Norman finally tracked her down on Bridge Lane. 'Then again, who does?'

'Us?' John queried as they finished their drinks and left the pub hand in hand. 'We did, didn't we?'

Light white clouds scudded across a blue sky, driven by a stiff breeze and she leaned in towards him. 'What did we get?'

'Each other.'

'Ah,' she said, low and soft, slipping her arm around his waist.

They went back to the car and set off for home, driving in sweet silence for most of the way.

'Sylvia wants to call her baby Joy,' Hazel reported as they came to Brimstone Rocks. From here they had a long-distance view of their valley – rows of houses lined up on the hillsides ready to topple like dominoes, the canal cutting straight through the middle of town, the snaking railway. 'Joy Bellamy. It's a good sign.'

'Yes. They've been through a lot. I hope they can put the past behind them and be happy – Norman, Sylvia and Joy.'

'I hope so too – now that it's all out in the open.' Hazel saw that the very thing that had threatened to pull them apart could after all be the making of them.

'Bring me the baby,' Norman had said. 'Let's have a proper look.'

Sylvia had covered her mouth with both hands and seemed to stop breathing as she watched him gently take her daughter into the crook of his arm.

'Well,' he'd murmured after an age of holding and looking before he'd passed her on to her mother. 'We'll have to see what we can do.'

Now John slowed the car and pulled into a lay-by. The wind shook the newly green buds on the hawthorn hedges and laid flat the long grass on the roadside verge.

'We've all been through a lot,' Hazel said as she took his hand and looked into his eyes.

'Yes.' He kissed her and breathed her in, his lips against her cheek.

What she loved about this moment – what she would always remember with joy – was the feel of John's warm hand in hers and the light in his clear brown eyes, his smile. She rested in its grace, looking neither forward nor back.

Acknowledgements

I'm grateful to Sylvia Vida for sharing with me her long experience as a practising midwife and for passing on her knowledge of midwifery in the 1930s. Her help proved invaluable.

The publishers hope that this book has given you enjoyable reading. Large Print Books are especially designed to be as easy to see and hold as possible. If you wish a complete list of our books please ask at your local library or write directly to:

Magna Large Print Books
Magna House, Long Preston,
Skipton, North Yorkshire.
BD23 4ND

This Large Print Book for the partially sighted, who cannot read normal print, is published under the auspices of

THE ULVERSCROFT FOUNDATION